W9-AFU-442

A Collection of Novels

LEVEL SEVEN,
JAMMIN',
THE COOL SHADE

BOB COLEMAN

Order this book online at www.trafford.com
or email orders@trafford.com

Most Trafford titles are also available at major online book retailers.

Print information available on the last page.

ISBN: 978-1-4907-9152-4 (sc)
ISBN: 978-1-4907-9151-7 (hc)
ISBN: 978-1-4907-9153-1 (e)

Library of Congress Control Number: 2018912261

Trafford rev. 10/30/2018

www.trafford.com

North America & international
toll-free: 1 888 232 4444 (USA & Canada)
fax: 812 355 4082

"With the greatest love and affection, this offering is dedicated to my friends, family, and especially my sister Patricia Lynn Coleman."

"Special thanks to Cara Selgas for assisting me in the editing, and the interior and exterior art and formatting. Also thanks to Jim Patten for his proof-reading and editing assistance."

Contents

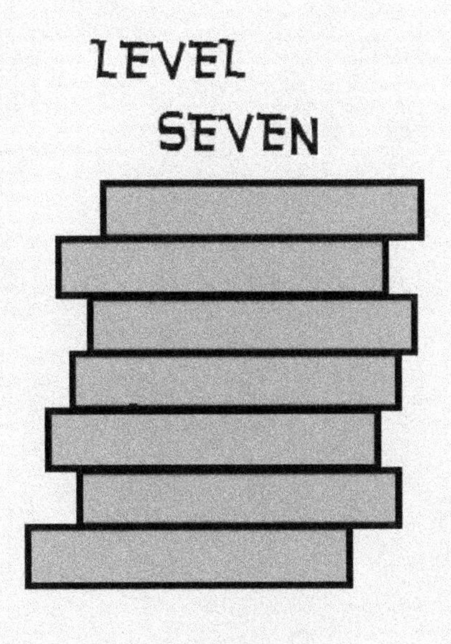

1990

1

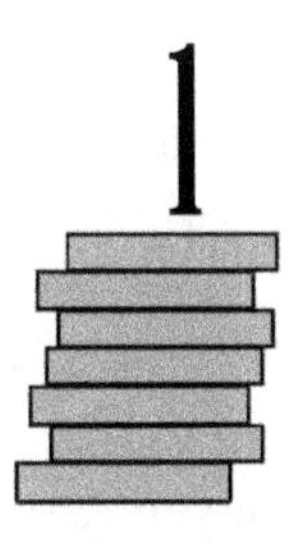

Rarely there were tall sea stories told among us, mostly, just the day-to-day dialog of our lives. The dark wooden booths, bar stools, walls and sideboards that surrounded us, were polished from spit and spilt beer. The captain's wheel, nailed to the wall, had long since guided a rudder, and the rotten rope nets had never snared a fish. This was a tavern-the Captain Benbow Lounge-'Bows' to us regulars, not overlooking a deep blue sea, but the heart of a great concrete world of a city. There was no ocean's roar, no smell of salt air, no tides to mark time and travel, only the steady, low murmur of the jukebox box and idle laughter. Thieves and liars, pimps, prostitutes and fools sat, consorted, imbibed with speculators, thinkers, gamblers and men of business, both fair and foul-the pirate and the prince drinking from the same well. But adventurers we were also. Though the days were spent sipping warm beer and joining in these seemingly trivial amusements, we ventured into uncharted waters-the hidden places unto each of us.

"It's Crazy Paul ... he's at it again!" said Luke.

I looked up from my notes. Through the dark shadows of the late afternoon and cigarette smoke, I could see him. He had taken a roll of toilet paper from the bathroom and was carefully tearing each square piece off neatly and placing each one on an empty bar stool. Luke and I didn't stop him. We just watched.

Ruth moved from table to table with her wet towel, wiping them clean. Then, she too looked up only to wipe the sweat from her brow and continue her chores. Luke spoke up again, this time loud enough for the 'Capt'n' to hear.

The 'Capt'n', John Lee Washington, short, bald and full-bodied, was a retired Army sergeant and owner of the Captain Benbow Lounge. But to all who knew him, he was simply-'the Capt'n'.

"Paul! What in the hell are ya' doin' now?" he bellowed. Crazy Paul just looked up and smiled through very dirty teeth. "Damn it!" the Capt'n exclaimed, coming out from behind the bar and picking each piece of tissue up off the stools. "Now you know I run a clean place and ya' don't need t' be doin' this!"

Still, Crazy Paul smiled. It was as though he didn't understand. No one ever really knew just what Crazy Paul was thinking.

"Now Capt'n, leave poor Paul alone," said Ruth. "He jus' saw me a' cleanin' over here and he wanted t' help." She came over and patted him gently on the shoulder. She cared for him in a very motherly way. "Come on Paul ... come on back t' the kitchen. Let me make ya' a nice egg sandwich. The kind ya' like," she said to him. She took him by the arm and led him away.

"You would think this is some kind'a fruit farm," said the Capt'n, getting up the remaining tissues.

"Crazy Paul is jus' ... 'Crazy Paul'," said Luke.

"Well some folks may wonder 'bout you too, the way you play with that set'a checkers all day. Maybe you ought'a go on out and get a job!"

"Now do I pay m'way or don't I?"

"And how do ya' pay? Asked the Capt'n, suddenly looking over at me. I picked up my warm draft and took a sip.

"And you think I'm jus' bein' some up'ty nigger huh?" he asked me.

"No," I replied, "I was just thinking ... that's all."

"And that's your problem 'Pilgrim'," that's what they called me at 'Bows'-'Pilgrim', "you always thinkin'. Always watchin'," he said pointing his finger to his head, insinuating that I was nuts.

I said nothing. He turned his attention back to Luke. "And how do ya' pay? Jus' tell me that!"

"Look here, there ain't nothin' wrong with a supplemented income," Luke told him.

"Supplemented? You ain't worked as long as I've known ya'! Welfare! That's what it is ... welfare checks!!"

"First off, it ain't none of your business jus' how I pay my way. Second of all, I'm .. sort of a ... philosopher, an' philosophers don't work. Shows how much you know!"

"Philosopher Huh? All I see you do is drink beer, smoke cigarettes, an' look at that checker board!"

The Capt'n looked at me again. "Do ya' think this man is really a philosopher? I mean really? Tell me."

I looked down at the residue of suds in my mug. "Well ... maybe everyone is a philosopher at heart," I said.

"Oh Great Mother Mary help us!" he exclaimed, "I got a thinker and a philosophizer! Heaven help us!"

"Go ahead an' laugh. Go ahead!" Luke replied.

"Look .. you jus' show me what starin' at that checker board all day does for ya'? A' movin' them pieces 'round by yourself?"

Luke looked at the faded, tattered game board on the bar, and shifted his weight on the bar stool, grinning. "I dunno ... I jus' been thinkin' ..."

"Hell! That ain't no answer!"

Luke took a red checker piece and placed it carefully on a middle black square. "It's .. it's like black 'n white, right 'r wrong, .. us 'n them ..."

"Oh Jesus help us!" the Capt'n lamented.

Luke looked at me for encouragement. "Go on," I replied.

He continued. "Us 'n them .. sort'a like you against the world. Ya' got'a make a move and ya' can't take it back. Ya' can't take it back. Life's such a gamble. Ya' take one piece and it's candy. Take another .. an' it's poison... "

"... life and death, yin and yang, happiness and ... sorrow ..." I reflected.

"What?" said the Capt'n.

"It's a fair analogy I suppose."

"Anala-what? There ya' go with them fi'dollar words again. What do ya' mean .. anala .. whatever you said?"

"'Analogy'," I pronounced the word carefully.

"Yeah ... a-n-a-l-o-g-y," he said with difficulty.

"It means .. well it means that the game of checkers is sort of like the game of life."

"Well, it's sounds like bullshit t'me," replied the Capt'n.

"It's like an analogy," parroted Luke. He fiddled with the old checker pieces. I watched him quietly from my corner table. His greasy hair flowed down past the collar of his torn Hawaiian shirt. And his pants, his dirty jeans, perhaps they were the only pair he owned, along with his shabby tennis shoes. No socks. He was a drunk, but a likable one, seemingly always on hand to help the Capt'n or Ruth with the daily chores of running a saloon.

I yawned and looked back at my notes. They had become a mess, just a series of words and phrases. It was late in the afternoon. I had been there all day, and I knew I should get home. I had to put these notes to use while they were still fresh in my mind. But then again, maybe I would just go home and to bed. No. I couldn't. I just couldn't, I thought, as I stared down at the crumpled papers on the table. Tonight I would write.

Suddenly, the figure of a stranger appeared in the light of the opened door. He stood there for a moment, looking around, at me, then Luke, and then the Capt'n. He sat down on a stool at the end of the bar and ordered a drink. He was not like any of us. He wore a fine suit and carried a brief case. He was older, his hair slightly graying at the temples. He was of average build. There was something about his manner that demanded respect.

With interest, I watched him, his clean hands and starched white shirt cuffs. His movements were diligent and precise. He drank slowly, but then put his hands to his face. Obviously, there was much on his mind. I could only imagine who he was, what great business was his.

Then, he turned around. Again, he scanned the room. It was then that I could see his eyes. They were warm dark eyes. They squinted as the edges of his lips formed a tight lipped smile. There was a quiet sense of acceptance in the way he fit into the room. Though probably accustomed to the finer things, he didn't seem bothered by the torn, beer stained carpet or the shabby surroundings which now confronted him.

Suddenly, his vision became focused and directed. I turned around to see what had caught his fancy. It was Crazy Paul, who was leaning against the kitchen door with a broom in his hand. He was smiling back at the man with such idiotic demeanor. To my surprise, the stranger broke a full smile and nodded back cordially.

2

The birds. Always those damn birds. I could hear them chirping from the window's ledge. I opened my eyes enough to see the weak strips of light through the blinds. Grey. I closed my eyes in a vain attempt to go back to sleep. It was useless. My mind was already working, weaving webs of thought. I rolled over and gazed at empty wall. I was tired, always tired, no matter how much I slept.

Wearily, I sat up on the mattress. There was no frame, no box spring, just a mattress on the floor. In fact, there were no dressers, no pictures. The room, an efficiency, was bare except a simple table and chairs and my computer. In the corner, was a pile of clothes. I searched and found the cleanest shirt and put it on. In the bathroom, I looked at my tortured face in the mirror, urinated, and washed out my coffee cup.

Out on the table, I turned on a hot plate to make coffee. There was a crumpled pack of cigarettes. I opened it to find only two left. Ruth lived next door. Maybe she had some. But, no. She had quit smoking. I would have to go to the store later and get more. Maybe later, at 'Bows.

Sitting down, I turned on the computer. As it booted and whirred to a stop, I looked out the window on another day. Just another day. Perhaps a day of joy, of creation, or maybe of sorrow and pain. The rewards reaped from past wrongs, guilt and self-denial. But I turned to my work and remembered another morning, in the distant past ...

... It was early in the morning, a summer morning in my Uncle Abner's house. He was still asleep as I wandered down stairs. There in the living room, I sat on the sofa, still rubbing the sleep from my eyes. I looked down at the coffee table and my Uncle's Bible. The old black leather was cracked from years of obsessive wear, and although it had an otherwise ordinary appearance, it was h-i-s Bible and I held the greatest reverence for it. It was a part of him and always within his reach.

There was also the old ceramic planter. It was an antique, ornate with three young girls looking down into the bowl which was fashioned as a well. Their feet dangled over the edge and they held each other close. In my mind, I could hear their girlish laughter. What fascination I found in these and all the other of my Uncle's furnishings. Old, strange, from a bye-gone era; the old wind-up Victrola; the high-backed chair and ashtray stand where he would sit at night smoking cigarettes and laughing at shows on the TV.

And those nights, hot summer nights, with the sound of the attic fan running and the faint sound of the TV down stairs. In the old squeaky bed, I would conjure up demons in the shadows and the dark outlines of the bed posts. There was an evil eye and low hideous laughter. Oh, how tormented I was of the dark in those days. Such a young boy among these old and musty surroundings. Only to wake up, as always, with the bright light of the morning sun coming from the window-streams of light like rays from heaven. Golden. Indeed, once again, to be very much young and alive.

There was a knock on the door. I pulled the curtain away. It was 'Mooch'. His real name was Billy, but we always called him Mooch. He was always bummin' dimes and nickels. I opened the door.

"Hey," he said, standing on the door step. I could see Kyle waiting behind him on the sidewalk.

"Hey."

“Ya gotta come out”

"Sure ... what's up?"

“Ya just gotta come out.”

“All right already. I'll be right out."

I tip-toed up the stairs and past the closed door. I knew my Uncle was still sleeping. In my room, I put on a striped, pull-over shirt and my old sneakers. The shoe strings had long since been knotted and I had resorted to pulling them on over my heel. I thought about my toothbrush that hung on the bathroom wall, but decided that running the water might make too much noise. I wouldn't wake Uncle Abner. No. Let him sleep I thought. I quietly went downstairs and I pulled the front door gently until it latched and turned to my friends who were waiting out by the curb.

"All right. What's up?" I said.

Mooch scuffed the ground with the sole of his torn sneaker and looked at Kyle before he spoke. "I got proof."

"Sure!" I exclaimed, "here we go again."

"No really! Right Kyle?"

"Honest Injun', said Kyle, looking at me in earnest.

"Look, I said, "there's no such thing as spacemen! We've been through this before. Anyways, we looked all over the woods. Three times!"

"Tell 'im," said Kyle, urging Mooch on.

Mooch leaned over closer. His eyes were wide and brimming with excitement. "Last night, when I was in the kitchen eatin' dinner, I saw a flashin' red light comin' from the woods, from my window out the back."

"So?" I replied.

"Let him finish!" Kyle exclaimed.

"Okay! Okay!"

Mooch continued. "Well, anyways, no sooner did I look out the window at the flashin' red lights, and I saw a face. Right there! looking back at me!"

"Oh g-e-e-z," I exclaimed.

"I'm tellin' ya'. Cross m'heart!"

"Tell 'em the rest," said Kyle.

"And the face had big red eyes that glowed in the dark!"

Both of them stood there looking at me, waiting for my reaction.

"So... you saw the spaceman? Maybe the red lights were from the ship, the space ship. A flying saucer maybe," I joked.

"Yeah right!" said Mooch.

"What time was it?"

"What d'ya' mean 'what time was it?'"

"What time was it when ya' saw 'em?"

"That doesn't matter!" he protested.

"Maybe it was a planet or ... stars in the sky or somethin'."

"I'm tellin' ya', I saw it!"

"All right. All right already!"

Quietly we stood there on the curb contemplating what could have happened. I was still skeptical. Mooch kicked a stone in my direction. I kicked it back to him and hit his shoe. "Maybe it was Tarese and the other kids from the apartments. Remember when we egged 'em a few weeks ago," I went on. Tarese was the neighborhood bully.

"Look smartaleck, this was real!" Mooch insisted.

"There's only one thing to do," I said, "We got'a go through the woods, along the path by the superhighway. You know, the place where we found the large area of burnt grass. Maybe we'll find some more clues."

"Yeah." said Mooch.

"What d'ya' think?" I asked Kyle. He nodded in agreement.

We approached the entrance to the woods, the thick forest that lined the end of our housing development. There were two huge trees, one on each side of a dirt road, like giant pillars in a cathedral, they marked the beginning of our domain. That road continued on into the dark foliage beyond. Then we turned left, down past a row of old oak trees, along paths of velvet moss, and bright lichen, plush green branches. Red, orange and brown leaves and twigs crackled beneath our feet. I could smell musk, and evergreen, and the honeysuckle in full bloom. All of which, this wondrous mixture, blended together into a potpourri for all the senses. There was no other place on earth like this, and it was a part of me, I thought, for I knew every road, every path, every broken limb and fallen tree trunk. We walked on, deeper and deeper into the heart of the forest.

Soon we entered into a plush meadow, and squinted and shielded our eyes from the bright sun that lit up in our faces. On the opposite side, we entered back into the dark shadow of another large, old oak tree, and scooted down a steep embankment. We steadied ourselves, holding onto thick vines that hung like snakes from the huge trees above. At the base of the hill, we stopped and breathed the moist air. I surveyed the surrounding terrain.

What a' ya' lookin for?" asked Kyle.

"Just clues...anything really," said Mooch.

"What d'ya' mean clues?" I asked.

"You know ... burned places on the ground, or ... pieces o'junk, like from a spaceship. That kind'a stuff."

I looked at Mooch, only he was looking the other way. He was my best friend. I liked Kyle okay, but with Mooch, there was something special between us. "Hey," I said to him. He turned his head to face me. "Yeah."

Changing the subject ..."Ya ever think about ... growin' up?" I asked him.

"Ya mean like what'cha gonna be when ya' grow up?"

"Yeah."

"Doctor ... Lawyer ... Indian Chief!" Kyle joked, laughing.

"Maybe," added Mooch, "even like President of the United States!"

They laughed, and suddenly I felt foolish. Why did I bring it up? What a stupid thing to talk about. I mean who cares about growing up, growing old anyway? It was a clunky thing to say.

But no, Mooch looked at me in earnest. "What are you gonna be?" he asked me.

"My Mom and Dad always ask me that," I said.

"Yeah," said Kyle, "my Dad wants me t' be a doctor ... Says that doctors make a lot'a money and stuff."

"Maybe we could just stay in the woods," I said kidding.

What?" Mooch responded.

"Live in the woods and never grow up?", asked Kyle.

"I dunno ..." I replied.

"Sounds neat," said Mooch.

"We could build a tree-fort near the old school," I said. "We could live in the woods forever."

"Like Tarzan!" Kyle joked.

"You Jane ... you boy … me Tarzan!" Mooch teased. He stood up and beat his chest wildly, screaming as if he were truly the 'king of the jungle'. His shrieking voice faded into the thick underbrush and died away. I grabbed his shoulder and we laughed together.

We continued walking, heading for the path along the superhighway. I could hear the sounds of cars, and birds, and of the wind blowing through the tall branches. At times, I heard strange sounds. Perhaps it was a bird screeching from a far-off hillside. I glanced at Mooch and Kyle. They too heard the sound, for their footsteps, like mine, increased in rhythm. The wind picked up again, and brought the huge tree branches into motion. Then I heard the sound again. It was shrill and sent chills to the marrow of my bones. I ran. I ran over the ridge and down into a gully, my sneakers hitting the shallows of a creek bed, splattering my face and legs with the cool water. Rumpty-rump went my heart, the blood raced in my veins, and I ran on.

Rumpty-rump!

Through the thicket of tall grass and into the sassafras roots. I ran. Wildly, with abandon.

Rumpty-rump!

Without knowing, feeling nothing but the power of my own strides. Without caring, about the others, about growing up, about Mom and Dad and their separation, having to stay with my Uncle Abner, and that insecurity and pain that lived inside me. Rumpty-rump went the beating of my heart!

Reaching the path, chest heaving, I fell to the earth in sweet resignation, feeling somehow cleansed, baptized. Mooch and Kyle also fell to the ground, breathing heavily.

When I regained my strength, I sat up, leaning on one arm. "Well .. I didn't see any thing that looked like a spaceship landed," I said.

"I told ya'," Mooch protested, "I saw it with my own eyes!"

"You didn't see anything but flashin' red lights."

"What about the face huh? The face with the red eyes?"

"I dunno ..."

We followed the path as it cut deeper into the forest near the superhighway. Impatiently, we quickened our pace, for around the next bend, we would reach our destination-the burned grass of the spaceship. As it came into sight, we stopped dead in our tracks. Scanning the terrain, we could see that nothing had changed since our last visit.

"I dunno Mooch," I said.

"I saw what I saw," he replied.

Suddenly, something had caught Mooch's attention. "Hey!. Hey Guys!" he exclaimed. "Come here!" Kyle and I looked to see a new patch of blackened earth. "Look, there was a fire here! See I told ya'! This could'a been from the spaceship!" he said excitedly.

I bent down and carefully combed through the ashes to pull out an old tin can. "Mooch," I said, "look, it's a can. A plain old can!"

Mooch warned us, "I wouldn't touch it if I was you. It might have space germs on it!"

"Space germs?" I exclaimed. "Some old bum was probably out here buildin' a fire that's all."

"Hey, you callin' me a liar?"

"I dunno. You're jus' mistaken."

"Well, maybe you're crazy, jus' like your Uncle Abner!"

I was angered and ran into him, knocking him to the ground. He knew me, he knew me only too well - the vulnerable places. "Look

Mooch, you keep my Uncle out of this!" I screamed, brandishing my fist in his face.

"Go ahead sissy, make me!"

"You leave my Uncle alone, you hear?" I cried.

"Wait!" shouted Kyle.

There was a sound. It was a sniffling sound, a sobbing sound. Someone was crying. All of a sudden, from the pathway, a girl appeared, a Negro girl. She was walking slowly towards us. Mooch and I jumped to our feet as she approached.

"Golly, are you okay?" Kyle asked her.

She said nothing. Kyle stepped in her way. She stopped walking and stood there weeping. She was older than us, probably fifteen or so.

"I said, are you okay?" Kyle asked her again.

She didn't speak. She just wiped her eyes with the back of her hands.

"Let her go Kyle," I said, "there's nothin' you can do anyways."

But Kyle just stood there in her way, just standing there looking at her. I walked over, in between the two of them to intervene.

"What are you doin' Kyle?" I asked him.

"Nothin' ... I jus' want to know what's wrong, that's all."

The girl started to cry again. I put my hand on her shoulder in consolation. "Look, we jus' want to help."

"... Nothin' you can do. Nothin' nobody can do," she said. Her voice was monotone-like and there was a vacant look in her eyes.

"Ya sure?"

She shook her head to mean yes, her eyes looking straight ahead, not at any one of us.

I turned and looked at Kyle. "Kyle ... let her go," I said.

"Yeah, what'cha gonna do?" Mooch said, teasing him, "Who are you? Robin Hood, or the Lone Ranger?"

"Screw you too!" he answered.

"Let her go," I said again.

"And who are you? The King of England?"

"Jus' let her go Kyle," I insisted.

He looked at Mooch and me, and then stepped aside.

The girl walked away. We watched her until she was out of sight...

3

"Well I tell ya', if I had a million dollars ..."

"Go on Luke, tell us what you'd do with a million dollars!" the Capt'n exclaimed.

It was Friday night at 'Bows'. There was loud music and laughter, the air heavy with cigarette smoke. We were all a little giddy from the noise and the booze. Luke and the Capt'n were having in a very lively conversation. I remained quiet, listening intently to what they were saying.

"Everybody always thinks about that at one time 'r another," Luke grinned.. "What about you?" He threw the ball back to Capt'n's side of the court.

"I'd fix up the place. Yeah! I would give the Captain Benbow Lounge a real face lift!"

"Hell, I'd put it in t' bank and never work a day in my life!" Luke proclaimed.

"You would? Hell, ya' don't work anyhow!"

"So?"

"I been alive on this earth fit'y three years and I can tell ya', John Lee Washington has worked since he was this high," the Capt'n bragged, holding his hand low to the ground.

"Jus' cause you did, does it make it so for everyone else? It's a free country ain't it?"

"See! That's where ya' got it all wrong Luke boy! Work ain't jus' for makin' money. Work is good for the soul!"

I smiled. The Capt'n noticed. "And what you smilin' about Pilgrim?" he asked me.

"Nothing. Nothing really."

"Now come on 'Mr. Thinker' and 'Mr. Watcher' of everything. Tell us what's so damned funny."

"Well," I replied, "you're quite a philosopher yourself!"

Luke laughed out loud and slapped his leg.

"Very funny," said the Capt'n, sarcastically. "Well I happen t' think that workin' is good for the soul. 'A man is as a man does' is what I always say!"

"I agree," I said.

He snorted. "Ya' do, do ya'? ... Well Pilgrim?"

"Well what?"

"What would ya' do?"

"What do you mean?"

"What would ya' do if you had a million dollars?"

I thought about it. Patiently, they waited for my answer. Perhaps I enjoyed keeping them in suspense. Finally, I spoke. "Maybe I would give it all to charity."

"Oh great Mother Mary!" the Capt'n proclaimed.

"No. Really, I could help some foster children or feed the homeless."

Luke just shook his head and sighed.

"Foster kids ... feedin' the homeless," said the Capt'n. "You know somethin' Pilgrim?"

"... What?"

"You know what you are?"

"No ... what am I?"

"You're a self-righteous bastard ain't ya'?"

I took a swig of beer, lit a cigarette, and looked back at him defiantly. "And how is that?"

"Give it all t' charity! Like you is some kind'a saint or somethin'."

"Maybe I would. So?"

He smiled and reached for my beer mug to refill it. "You know Pilgrim, sometimes I wonder about you. I mean ... why a-r-e you here anyway?"

"Yeah. That's true," added Luke, judgmental.

"I mean, you is a college boy ain't ya'?" the Capt'n continued.

"Yeah ..." I nodded.

"Some kind'a scientist ... or-"

"An electrical engineer. That's what I was .... an engineer."

"Well, let me ask you this ... what in the hell are ya' doin' here?"

"I dunno ...."

"Slummin'?" asked the Capt'n.

"That's not fair."

"Not fair! Hell! Why ain't you livin' in the nice neighborhoods with the rest of the rich folks?"

"It wasn't right for me," I said with a shrug.

"It wasn't right for me!" the Capt'n said, mimicking my words sarcastically.

"Look, I drink here, I eat here. I live in the city just like you."

"Yeah, but Pilgrim, you have a choice. We don't."

"Yeah," Luke parroted the Capt'n.

"... Maybe sometimes you don't have a choice," I said solemnly.

"Sometimes you don't have a choice," the Capt'n said playfully.

I lost it. I stood up, knocking my stool out from under me. It fell to the floor with a crash. "Look you! What makes you so goddamned special?" I said bitterly. "Are you the only ones who have problems? Do you have some monopoly on pain and suffering?!? Do you have to be poor or ... or a black man to sing the blues?!?"

I had stunned them into silence. With a slightly shaky hand, I lit another cigarette.

Hearing the commotion, Ruth came and sat down beside me. "Are y'all givin' the Pilgrim here a hard time?" she asked them. She put her hand on mine. "Don't let 'em rile ya' boy. They jus' jealous, that's all. What ya' do with your life is your business," she told me.

"Sorry," said the Capt'n, "didn't mean anything personal."

"We didn't mean to rile 'em," said Luke, "its jus', we can't figure out what he's a' doin' here with us ... bein' some high an' mighty engineer an' all."

"The Lord does his work in mysterious ways!" Ruth said.

"Oh great 'Mother Mary' help us!" said the Capt'n.

Having calmed down, I spoke up, "Maybe it's like you said, 'A man is as a man does', and maybe I just wasn't cut out to be an engineer."

"Everyday I see ya' a'sittin' and a'thinkin' and a'writin' in that pad you got," said the Capt'n, "What are ya' doin' anyway?"

"... Writing ..."

"Oh, a writer huh?"

"What's wrong with bein' a writer," Ruth said.

"I like that," Luke beamed, "yeah ... a writer! That's sounds excitin'!"

"Lord have Mercy ... Mercy me!" Ruth swelled up in her seat. She took her hands to her hair, primping it with care. I could see a trace of the beauty that once was there. "Yeah ... I was gonna be an actress once," she said dreamily.

"You? An actress!" Luke said with laughter,

"You, 'chicken woman', an actress!" He called her 'chicken woman'. Perhaps it was because she wore her hair, bleached and up in a beehive, a style that had long since gone out of fashion.

"Don't call me that," she said, slapping his arm playfully, "I tol' ya' not t'call me that Luke!"

"Yeah, but you? ... An actress?" he teased.

"I was a model way back when," she said, fanning herself with a paper napkin. "I was a very pretty model once. Modeled plenty a' pretty clothes ..." There was an awkward moment of silence. "Well I did!" she exclaimed.

"Great 'Mother Mary' help us!" lamented the Capt'n. "I got me a philosophizer, a writer ... and now an actress! Mercy!"

"Well what's wrong with that?" Luke protested.

"Y'all regular people t'me," said the Capt'n, "But sometimes, I ain't so sure 'bout you," he teased, singling out Luke.

We all laughed. It felt good to laugh. Perhaps in a way, we were all regular people, and, there was a humble bond between us. The Capt'n started back in with his playfulness.

"Well Ruth, we asked everyone but you. What would you do with a million dollars?"

"Oh Lord! I know jus' what I would do. I would get me a little house. A little white house. And I'd plant flowers and breathe that fresh air like a lot 'a happy folks do. Sit in the cool shade." We all moved closer and nodded as she continued. "And in the Spring time, I would a stand in the rain and let all that soothin', clean water run down m' face, that cold, cool rain."

"Ya sure make that sound good!" said Luke.

"Yeah it does that," the Capt'n agreed.

`"Jus' to sit down, easy among the flowers," she said, in a slow, longing way. I could see tears in her eyes as she looked down at her rough, red, weary hands.

"You deserve that little white house," said Luke. "If anyone deserves that house, you do."

"Amen!" added the Capt'n.

Suddenly, through the front door, Crazy Paul entered. We looked at him with utter amazement, for he was wearing a dress! It was stained and torn.

"Oh Jesus!" the Capt'n complained. "You'd think I was runnin' some kind'a circus or somethin'!"

"Paul, now what are ya' up to now?" Ruth asked him.

He just walked up and smiled at her. "I was enjoyin' the weather. The suns out today. Jus' enjoyin' the weather," he replied.

"Now darlin'," she said, "you shouldn't be wearin' a dress. Wearin' dresses is for women. You're a man and men ought'a be wearin' pants."

"Women wear pants too," he said.

Luke laughed out loud. Crazy Paul looked at him. "You wearin' pants," he continued.

"That's right ... I'm wearin' pants," Luke agreed.

"Then you must be a woman too!" Crazy Paul said and then laughed himself. We all laughed.

"Come on Paul," Ruth said to him, taking him by the arm, "let's go in the back an get ya' some manly clothes t' wear." She got up and started to lead him back to the kitchen.

"Hey Crazy Paul!" the Capt'n shouted to him. "Hey Crazy Paul!"

Crazy Paul stopped walking and turned around. "What would you do with a million dollars?" the Capt'n asked him.

Crazy Paul smiled and rubbed his matted, gray beard. "I'd give it back t' the Lord," he answered, "Back t' the Lord! ...Earth t' earth, ashes t' ashes an' dust t' dust ... an' all the money back t' the Lord!"

4

It was late in the afternoon. Outside my apartment window, I could see the children playing in the street, surrounded by trash and the broken glass. They were playing ball, and when cars passed by, they would move reluctantly and stare back defiantly. After all, the cars, most of them shiny and new, were only passing through, and those within would look on with horror and pity at the poverty they saw. But for these children, this was their world, in essence, perhaps their future. So much for growing up in the inner city, in the ghetto.

My childhood? Different? Maybe not. Sure, my childhood memories were filled with visions of warm, lazy summer days, of ice cream trucks, and of sunny backyard birthday parties. But there were other memories. There were terrible times, times I would just as soon forget. I wrote ...

... "I told you about those trash cans!" my Uncle Abner was yelling. I heard him in the kitchen. He was looking out the back door and had seen the trash cans that I had left in disarray. "Come here now young man!" he commanded.

Hesitantly, I went to him.

"I want you to come here," he told me. I could see him standing there in a stupor. I could tell from his voice that he was drunk, very drunk. "What is that?" he asked, pointing his finger out the doorway.

"I'm sorry sir," I said, lowering my head so as not to make eye contact.

"That's not what I asked you!"

"They're trash cans sir." One was laying on its side and the lid was hanging off the back porch.

"Yes, but they are a mess! How many times have I told you that anything worth doing, is worth doing right!" I flinched as he swung at me. He missed me but I fell to the floor. "How many times have I told you to put them away neatly?" he screamed as he stood over me. "Huh? Just how many times?"

"I'm sorry," I said with a whimper. Actually, I was okay. By faking injury, I might be spared further blows.

He drank from his glass, and I could smell liquor.

"I'm sorry sir ... I won't do it again..."

"Well .." he muttered. He wiped his face with the back of his hand and bent down over me. Again, I flinched, only to realize that he was helping me up. I sat down on one of the kitchen chairs and watched as he took another drink. I couldn't stand it when he was drunk. He was so unpredictable.

"You know son," he said, "I've always told you, anything that's worth doing is worth doing right."

"Yes sir."

"If I ever teach you anything in this world, it should be at least this one thing. Responsibility."

I looked down and noticed that my shirt was torn. It must have happened when he swung at me. He realized that I was looking at it and walked over. I was frozen with fear.

"What have we here?" he said, examining my shirt.

Suddenly, I could see a sadness in his eyes. It was as though he was sorry for trying to hit me, sorry for being drunk, again. For an instant, I could almost feel the utter torment that must have possessed his soul.

"Sorry about the shirt," he said.

".. It's ... it's nothin'"

"Oh Gawd!" he said, covering his face.

I was quiet. I didn't dare speak.

"Responsibility boy!" he cried. "That's what we've got to learn ... responsibility!"

"You mean the trash cans?" I replied meekly.

"No … more than the trash cans!" He started to cry, and it was deep rooted and visceral, from the recesses of a lonesome suffering that I, as a very young boy, could not even begin to fathom. It made me feel terribly uncomfortable. It was a part of him that I didn't want to share. It was his private place.

"I'm sorry Uncle Abner," I whispered.

"Never mind ... never mind ..." he whispered.

There was a knock at the front door. Quickly, he pulled himself together went to see who it was. I got up and stood in the hallway as he peeked out the window.

"Who is it?" I asked.

"Never you mind. You better let me do the talking," he said. He took his hands to his hair in an attempt to straighten his appearance. As he opened the door, I was surprised to see that it was the police.

"Yes officer, how may I help you?" my Uncle asked.

"Sorry to bother you sir, but I was wondering if I could ask you a few questions?"

"Well yes ... of course," he replied. He stepped back and swayed slightly in doing so. I was sure the policeman could tell that he was drunk, but he kept a blank expression and remained business-like.

"Did you happen to hear or see anything unusual a week ago, last Friday evening say ... eight thirty or nine?" He spoke quietly, so that I couldn't hear, but I heard every word he said clearly.

"Why no ... I don't believe I did. What seems to be the problem?"

"There was a ... molestation of a young girl ... It happened in the woods up at the top of the hill. We have been asking everyone in your neighborhood if they had seen anything suspicious."

Instantly, I thought about the flashing red lights that Mooch had seen in the woods. Sure! That had to be it! Mooch had seen the police cars, not a spaceship! Maybe an ambulance.

"That's terrible," my Uncle said. "Who was the victim?

"It was a young girl, a young Negro girl," the policeman replied.

My mind reeled. Could that be the young Negro girl that Mooch, Kyle and I had seen down on the highway path? It seemed too incredible to be true! I listened intently as the conversation continued.

"There are no Negro families around here. Where could she live?" My Uncle asked with concern.

"I'm sorry, we can't give out that information."

I wanted to speak. Words burned in my mind and I moved away from the doorway. The policeman looked at me. "What's wrong son?" he asked, "is there anything you want to say?"

I looked at my Uncle and saw his displeasure. "No ... no sir," I replied.

He looked at my Uncle and then back at me. "Well ... Very well," he said, "if anything does come to mind. Please let us know."

"Yes, we will do that," my Uncle said.

As policeman walked back to his squad car, Uncle Abner closed the door and slumped down into his high-backed chair. He closed his eyes, and I prayed he would go to sleep. Quietly, I turned to go out the back door. "And where are you going?" he asked.

"Nowhere."

"So, what were you going to say to the policeman?"

"Well ..." I was hesitant.

"Go on, tell me."

"Well, Mooch ... he said he saw flashin' lights out his kitchen window last week. 'Must have been the police cars that night."

"Hmmm ... yes." He sat up and studied me carefully. "Is that all?"

"Well ... the next day, me and Mooch and Kyle, we went along the highway trail and ... well ... we saw a Negro girl walking along the path. She was cryin'."

"Hmmm ... Did any of you talk to her?"

"Well ... Kyle, he asked her what was wrong."

"What did she say?"

"She said, '.... nothin' you can do, nothin' nobody can do ..'"

"Is that all she said?"

"She looked funny, like she was in a trance. It was kind'a spooky."

Uncle Abner looked away, at the wall. I could tell he was very tired ...

I stopped writing and looked up to the open window. It was starting to grow dark outside. Down below, the street was empty. The children had gone home or somewhere else.

Turning off the lights, I lay down. As my eyes adjusted to the darkness, I thought about my writing. But sleep, precious sleep was what I needed. But to sleep, if only I could. A deep, restful sleep. The type of sleep that would sooth the anguish within, the quilt, confusion, and this personal, inner obligation that drove me on; the purpose, unknown to me. I could only wonder if others shared this madness, this insane quest. It was as though there was something in the back of my mind, something I had forgotten, just beyond my grasp, my comprehension.

In the distance, out on the lonesome streets below, I could hear the sound of a car traveling in the night. I wondered, if it too was lost and hopelessly searching. I wondered, just where it was going.

5

I was awoken abruptly by the door bell. I wondered who it could be as I had few friends and seldom had company. Pulling on my jeans, I went to the window. Down below, I saw no one. The door bell rang again, only this time twice. Whoever it was, they were growing impatient. Looking out the peep hole of the door I saw Peter. We were best friends. I opened the door. At first we just looked at each other, neither of us could speak.

"Well?" he asked.

"Oh yeah, sure, come in," I said, still half asleep.

He entered the room and looked about with mild curiosity. "Looks like you're living like a high-roller," he said jokingly.

"It's not much," I agreed.

"That's an understatement!"

"Here, sit here," I said, pointing to one of the two chairs at the lone table. "Can I get you some coffee?"

"No thanks."

"Well you know me ... never was very coherent 'til I had my first cup in the morning." I grinned but Peter just watched me strangely. It made me feel uncomfortable. "Look ..." I said, searching for some way to start the conversation which I knew was inevitable. "It's nice you came ... really ..." Still, he said nothing. I put the coffee can down and turned around to address him head on. "All right Peter, I know why you're here."

"Do you?"

"I know you're a great friend, always have been. And I know you're worried about me ... but ..."

"What would anybody think?" he asked shaking his head.

"It's my life."

"What about Jill ... and Joey? You can't just walk out on your wife and son."

"Geez! ... Who do you think you are? Some Patron Saint? Is that why you're here, to judge me?"

"Shit! Man, you are fucking up royally!" he said with a raised voice.

"Goddamn it Peter! Get the hell out 'a here if you're just going to put me down!" There was an awkward silence. "... Sorry ..." I said quietly. "Are they okay? Jill and Joey?"

"... Yeah ... as well as can be expected. But what happens when your severance pay and savings finally run out? I dunno..."

I fixed a cup of coffee and took a few sips in the silence, knowing only too well there was more to be said. I would let him start this time. He looked at me and thought for a great while before he spoke. "Why?" he asked.

"...I dunno ..."

"I think you do."

"... There's just something missing ... missing in my life ..."

"What? Sex? Money? ... Excitement?"

"I really don't think you'd ever understand," I said.

"Try me..."

I took another sip of coffee, thinking.

"Do you remember ... in high school or college, did you ever take psychology? You know, 'Introduction to Psychology', something like that?"

"I don't think so."

"Well ... there was this guy ... Maslow. Have you ever heard of Maslow's self-actualization theory?"

"No, I've heard of Freud, but not Maslow."

"I don't remember exactly, but he said that there were levels of needs, such as ... physiological needs like food and shelter, safety needs, and those of love and esteem. And finally, after all these other needs are met ... the need for self-actualization."

"... So you mean if the lower needs are met, then a person tries to achieve higher levels of needs?"

"Something like that."

"So?" he asked, unimpressed.

"Maybe ... maybe I have needs that aren't being fulfilled."

"You sound like some crazed lunatic. Or maybe just some spoiled rotten yuppie kid!" His words burned in my ears. "Anyway," he added, looking around the empty room, "is this what you call meeting your needs? This looks like just plain poverty to me."

"I told you. There's no way you could understand," I said bitterly. I drank the last of the coffee.

More awkward silence.

"... How's work?" I asked, only to change the subject.

"Okay ... you know ... same as always ..."

"Yeah, the same bullshit."

"You know," he said, "they will take you back. All you have to do is say the word."

"Peter, you know I can't go back. I just ... couldn't stand it anymore."

"Shit! You're an engineer and a pretty damn good one too. You're not a ... some stupid writer or what ever the hell you think you're trying to be!"

"Hey. Do I tell you what to do with your life? Do I?"

"Well I never did anything as stupid as this either! You simply running away from everything ... from your wife and kid, your career, ...from responsibility!"

"I'm am not running away from anything". Responsibility. I thought about Uncle Abner. But I continued "... on the contrary ... I'm running toward something! What that is, I'm not sure just yet."

"... What's wrong with being what you are?" he continued.

"Nothing ... for some people."

"It's not good enough for you?"

"It's just ... I'm just not a company man."

"And I am? You know I hate that bullshit as much as you do."

"Do you?" I asked. "Do you know how much I hate having to be nice to some jerk every day, day in and day out, year after year, just so he might give me a raise! Can you imagine having to have that mind-set for a whole lifetime! I'm sorry, but I can't make a career out of that!"

Peter was suddenly quiet. Perhaps I had finally struck a blow to his impenetrable wall of reasoning. I kept talking. "I'm tired of the political bullshit, the ass-kissing and back-stabbing going on around me when I'm in that environment. I'm tired of hemorrhoids, heartburn and ulcers. It's not worth it. It's not healthy!"

"So ... you turn forty and you're not sitting in the corner office. You didn't make your first million. Maybe this is traumatic for you, but wake up! You're not the only one who couldn't live out his fantasies! This is real life. Not some dream with a happy ending. Just because life didn't turn out quite what you expected, you can't just give up ... drop out!"

"That's what I'm talking about."

"What?"

"The corner office, the million dollars before you're thirty. These things are fine for some. But for me, they're just some bullshit that someone else put up as goals, they're not my goals."

"I give up!" he conceded. "I just don't understand you!"

Through the window, I could see that the sun was up full. It was getting hot in the little room. "Sorry about the heat. I don't have air conditioning," I told him.

"That's okay. I wouldn't expect it from such a non-material, self-actualized person as you!"

"Christ Peter!" I was getting frustrated.

Again, a period of awkward silence.

"You know you can come back to the company if you want," he said, again.

"Even after what I did?"

"Yeah. I told them you were under stress."

"Huh. Under stress!" I had to chuckle.

"You caused quite a commotion," Peter said with a laugh.

I remembered the whole affair. How could I forget. It was at a meeting, a review of some kind. They were all there, all the corporate big wigs. The junior members sat quietly. They were all dressed the same. I had to laugh. They had on the same ties. It was as though they had been pressed from a mold. I was to give a design presentation. I don't know why but, suddenly, I lost it. Maybe it was nerves, I don't know. Something broke. The last thing I remembered was standing up on the conference table foaming and spitting like a wild dog, telling each and everyone of them just what I thought of them. It was a very ugly scene. "Not bad for a basket-case huh?" I said and we laughed. It was our old laugh that we had shared many times before. But then he became quiet again, serious.

"You know," he told me, "if you don't come to your senses ... there's no telling what could happen."

"That sounds like a threat."

"People have been committed for less."

"Right. I am going to be committed? To an insane asylum? For what?"

"People just don't pick up and leave their family for no reason. What you're doing just isn't sane, normal."

"Normal for you? Or me?"

"Look, I'm just trying to help. Jill .. Joey ... they're worried about you and I can't say I blame them."

"Peter, just tell me one thing ... are they okay?" He looked out the open window. A swift breeze blew in and it felt good against the intense heat. Somewhere, I could hear the buzzing of a fly a midst the silence. I waited for his answer. But he remained silent, only shaking his head.

6

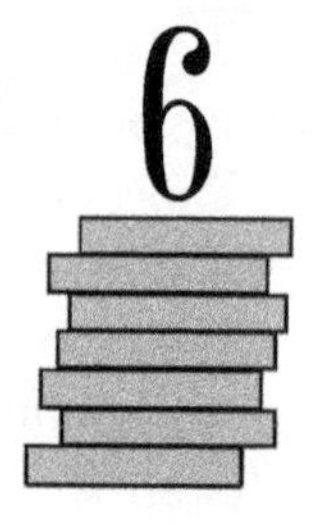

Luke and I were sitting at the bar, making small-talk with the Capt'n, when an older gentleman took a barstool next to mine. There were plenty of other bar stools available so I was surprised that he sat next to me. Trying not to seem obvious, I turned my head casually to get a better look at him. To my astonishment, I noticed that it was the same man I had seen come in for a drink several weeks before; the same fine suit, starched white cuffs, and brief case. The same dark eyes.

"Can I get ya' somethin'?" the Capt'n asked him.

"... A scotch, 'neat', please," he replied.

As the Capt'n turned around to get the bottle off the shelf, I turned to Luke. I could see he was, as I, curious about our guest. When the drink was placed on the bar, the gentleman immediately drank from it.

"Nothin' like a good shot t' wet the whistle hey?" said the Capt'n.

"Yes, it does hit the spot," he said. Again, he took a drink from his glass.

"You from 'round here?" the Capt'n asked him.

"No ... not really ... from Iowa ..." he said.

"What brings ya' t' town?"

The stranger just smiled and reached into is vest pocket to bring out a business card. He handed it to the Capt'n.

"Matthew L. Hartley ... Congressman ... House of Representatives ...." the Capt'n read out load. "Well ... Congressman, I'm very pleased t' meet ya'!" He reached over the bar to shake the his hand. The gesture was awkward and overenthusiastic. "'John Lee Washington', that's m' name," he continued, "I own the 'Captain Benbow Lounge', but you can jus' call me 'Capt'n'."

"Pleased to meet you," the gentleman replied.

"Hey ah ...," Luke said, butting in, "what would a congressman like you be doin' in here-the Captain Benbow's Lounge?"

"Look you!" the Capt'n said, scolding Luke for his lack of manners. "Don't pay him no mind," he said to Mr. Hartley, "I'm glad you decided to come into m' place."

"I didn't mean nothin' by it," Luke said.

"That's okay," Mr. Hartley replied, as he placed his empty glass back on the bar. The Capt'n filled it without having to be asked.

"Thank you," he said. He drank the scotch quickly.

"Iowa, sure is a nice place, Iowa is," said the Capt'n.

"We sure are gratified t' have a congressman come in here," Luke said.

"Why?" Mr. Hartley asked, amused.

"Well ... this ain't exactly the best 'waterin' hole' in town."

Mr. Hartley looked around, studying the surroundings. "Oh I don't know ... place looks okay to me!" he said cheerfully. Then, without cause, he turned to face me. "And you?" he asked. "You seem awfully quiet."

"He's always like that," said the Capt'n.

"He's our resident thinker. He's a writer!"

I was at a loss for words.

"Pleased to meet you," he said, holding his hand out.

"Pleased to meet you," I replied in return.

We shook hands. There was an understanding, a recognition of congeniality, of an educated mind. And, there were secrets hidden behind our faint smiles, hidden scars. Sitting in this little, shoddy bar, we were hiding from the world outside, away from our element, each with his own story, his own past. Perhaps, we were fugitives. He then looked away and finished his drink.

"Can I get ya' another?" the Capt'n asked him.

He brandished the glass in his hand, perhaps thinking about the drink. "Sure ... that would be fine," he said. "Make that drinks all around!"

"All right!" Luke blurted out. The Capt'n glared at him as he went about making the drinks.

Once again, Mr. Hartley turned his attention to me. "You are a writer?"

I was befuddled, "Well ... yes ..."

"You say that with reservation."

"... I've never been published."

"Oh. You do something else then?"

"No."

"Really?"

"He used t' be an engineer or somethin' like that," Luke told him.

"I see," said Mr. Hartley. His tone was somewhat sympathetic. Perhaps, like his apparent heavy drinking, my lack of stability was an open wound, a symptom of a discontented soul. I knew that if his mind was at all like mine, he would now continue our little conversation, probe, and ultimately put the pieces together.

"Soul searching?" he continued.

How astute I thought. "... Yeah ..."

He didn't respond, just nodded.

"What's it like bein' a congressman?" said Luke, oblivious to our conversation. He pulled his greasy hair from his dirty face.

"Now Luke, don't go on bein' so damned nosy!" the Capt'n said, chastising him.

"That's okay," Mr. Hartley said in his defense. "It's something ... I felt I had to do, ... public service I mean."

"Jus' one man's way 'a servin' his country," said the Capt'n. He poured more scotch into the glass. The pouring became so automatic, that he kept the bottle beside him on the bar.

"Thank you," said Mr. Hartley. He didn't drink, he held the glass up to the light, relishing it. He was becoming slightly drunk.

Luke finished his beer and placed the bottle in front of him. He too was feeling the effects of his drinking. "Well?" he asked the Capt'n.

"Well what?"

"Ain't ya' gonna get me another beer?"

"You got'a buck fifty?"

"A buck fifty?" Luke asked with amazement.

"That's right Luke, a buck fifty."

"Well how 'bout the Congressman here? Ya ain't chargin' him nothin'."

"Luke damn you! Ain't ya' got no respect for your country?" said the Capt'n. "We got a congressman come t' sit with us and you got'a be actin' this way?"

"I'm jus' sayin' it ain't fair, that's all!"

"Luke if you don't shut up, I swear by the Lord above!"

"Ha! What d'ya' gonna do old man? Smite me down like Abraham of old? You righteous old bastard!"

"That's it Luke! Get out'a here you drunken no good welfare case ... bum!"

"Get out? 'Cause I ain't got no money? I get it, he's rich and I'm poor huh? Is that it? You make me sick! You sittin' there jus' a' pouring that liquor and a' runnin' your mouth ... 'Yes Mr. Congressman!' ... 'Jus' servin' your country Mr. Congressman!' You're jus' a brown-nosin' son of a bitch if ya' ask me!"

"Enough!" Mr. Hartley loudly interjected. He pushed the glass of scotch away from him, tipping it over behind the bar. It whirled around and around on the floor, in the midst of a deadening silence, before it came to a stop. We were in awe of his sudden outburst.

With both hands he gripped the edges of the bar, the veins pumping in his temples. I pictured him as a hell-raising preacher at his pulpit, ready to cast out the demon among us. Then, his head dropped down and he sighed. "... Forgive me. I'm sorry ... very sorry," he said.

"... I'm sorry too ..." said Luke.

"... me too ..." said the Capt'n.

Mr. Hartley straightened himself. "You're right. You're right," he said. "You're right Luke. If you have to pay for your drink, so should I. It's not fair that I should drink for free. We should all pay equally."

"Well, I was jus' showin' some respect," said the Capt'n.

"You don't understand ..." said Mr. Hartley. "Oh God ... can't you see? I come in here and impress you with my credentials, and you give me free drinks. Forgive me," he said.

Silence.

"Well ... that's okay," said the Capt'n.

Silence again.

"...It's right here," Mr. Hartley said, looking around him, as if there was some invisible spirit surrounding us.

"What's here?" asked Luke.

"The great foe, that black side there is to each of us."

"It's everywhere," I said. "Perhaps it's in each of us."

"What in the hell are you guys talking about?" asked the Capt'n.

"... Greed ... hate," said Mr. Hartley, "... deceit, it takes many forms and has many faces. I see it every day. People like you and me are bought and sold just for that God-almighty dollar! From some billion dollar Wall Street scam to a person like me-coming in here and getting a freebie high."

"I never thought about it like that," said the Capt'n," I was jus'-."

"I know, you were just trying to show some respect for me because I was this big and important congressman. Well I can tell you, this is the very thing I loathe! And I have made it my cause - to fight against these injustices. This cause, this quest, it has followed me all my adult life..."

"The call of duty." I said, with empathy.

"... Kennedy, remember him? John F. Kennedy? His brother Robert? Martin Luther King? These were my heroes ... Like them, I was going to change the world ... once," he said slowly, sadly.

"An idealist," I whispered.

"Yes ... an idealist. I was going to help rid mankind of injustice, ignorance. What a grand task! And what a fool I was!" Hartley said quietly.

"What happened?" said Luke.

Hartley paused but then responded, "What happens to any idealist? The great campaign gets bogged down, turns into little battles. It all gets ... blurred ... faded ... lost ..."

"You can still try," I said.

"Oh yes! We should never give up! We must stand by our convictions!"

"We can't give up ..."

He looked at me solemnly. "No ... I don't believe we ever will ... will we?"

I was writing...

...A shiny new car turned the corner, down at the far end of the street. Its bright chrome glistened in the midday sun, and in the reflection of its mirror-like finish, were the well trimmed lawns as it passed them one by one, as it paraded past the buttercups and sunflowers, past the battalions of white fence pickets. From the bedroom window I watched its slow, grand procession up the street. I knew it well, for it was my father's car. As it slowed to a stop, I could see my mother, looking out in anticipation, looking for me.

I ran down the stairs to the front door and met them coming up the stoop. Uncle Abner stood in the kitchen doorway. I could feel his icy presence behind me. But I was so glad to see them, that my mind had a joyous multitude of feelings.

"Hi honey!" my mom said, kneeling down to kiss my cheek.

"Oh gosh Mom I miss you!"

"I miss you too sweetie!"

I looked up to my dad. "Hi son," he said.

"Dad oh dad!" I cried, holding him close to me.

"Is everything all right?" My mother asked Uncle Abner.

He stepped up, closer to us and our gushy reunion. "Why yes," he replied, "but I must say, he loves and misses you both very much indeed!"

"I guess so! And how have you been?" Mother asked him.

"Fine my dear, as always ... fine."

She made a kissy-motion to his cheek, which he accepted awkwardly.

"We have big news for you," said my father, pulling out several gift boxes. "But first, we have a few surprises too!"

"Wow!" I squealed.

"Why don't we have a look!"

I pulled the smaller package to me and began to rip away the wrapping. Underneath, I found a baseball glove, with a pre-made pocket! "Just what I wanted!", I said. "How did you know Dad?"

"Mmmm ... I knew," he said.

Then my smile faded.

"What's wrong honey?" asked Mom.

"Nothing ..." I shrugged.

"Uncle Abner, are you sure there isn't something we should know?" she asked him.

"...Its the excitement I would say, the excitement that's all."

"Here son, open this one," my dad said, offering me the other package. It was larger, wrapped with little hearts and Cupid's arrow.

Tearing the paper away, I found a cake. Written with red icing it read, 'We Love you and Miss you!'.

"Vanilla icing with chocolate cake, your favorite," said Mom. She held me in her arms.

Looking into her eyes, it was Dad she was looking at, not me. There was a look on her face, an adult look, that of anguish and deep concern, shared only between them, like when they spelled out their words to prevent me from understanding their meaning. These gestures gave no consolation, they only made me feel more confused and more afraid. I felt my father's hand upon me. "Son, we, your mother and I, have something to say."

Suddenly, there was a knock at the door. Uncle Abner went to answer it. Through the doorway, I could see it was the police again. Putting the door ajar, he turned to us. "Excuse me please," he said, "I'm going outside to talk to the policeman. I won't be but a few minutes."

"Is anything wrong?" My father asked.

"No, it is nothing." Uncle Abner answered, going outside, closing the door behind him.

My father continued, "We do have something to say." He looked at mom before he continued. Again, there was that look between. "Look son, I know this ... separation between your mother and I has not been easy on you, believe me, it hasn't been easy on us either."

"I guess ..." I was speechless.

"Maybe this isn't a good time," she cautioned him.

"Maybe not," he replied.

"I ... I just don't understand," I said, "What is wrong with you two?", my voice slightly breaking.

"Sometimes its hard for two people to love each other all the time. Perhaps it is even harder for two people to even like each other all the time."

"Do you love Mom?" I asked him.

He looked at her warmly. "Yes, I love your Mother," he said.

"Well, do you love him," I asked her.

Her eyes never left his. "I've never stopped loving him," she said.

"Then what's the problem? I mean, you both love each other don't 'cha?" I said. We all laughed.

"The problem is," Dad said, "sometimes we don't like each other very much, that's all."

"You mean ... you can love someone and not like 'em at the same time?" I asked.

"Yes, that's right."

"What does all this mean? When are we all gonna get back together?" I said, choking on the words.

"That's the good news," he said, "your mother and I are starting to see each other again. We have some problems to work out but I think everything will turn out okay. And .. we're looking into buying a new house!"

"A new house? A new house where?"

"Far away from here," said Mom, "out in the country. Lot's of woods. You'd like it!"

"Oh mom, I can't wait!" I exclaimed. "When?"

"Well son, not for a while," Dad said.

"Why?"

"... These things take time."

"So I have to stay here ... with Uncle Abner?"

"Just for a short while longer. I promise. Remember son, sometimes we have to do things we don't want to do. We have to learn to make these sacrifices at times."

"Is everything all right?" my mother asked me, sensing that something was wrong.

I paused. "... Yeah, sure ... Fine," I said with my chin on my chest.

The front door opened and Uncle Abner stepped into the room. His face was sullen.

"Are you okay?" my mother asked him.

"Yes, I need to sit down that's all, I just need to sit down," he said.

"What seems to be the problem?" asked Dad.

"Problem? What problem?" Uncle Abner asked. He was agitated.

"With the police."

Before my Uncle Abner could speak, I blurted out, "Dad! There was a rape in the woods ... with a young Negro girl, and..." I said excitedly, but then realizing that I had spoken out of turn.

"A rape?! How hideous!" Mom said.

"What's this all about?" my father asked.

"There was an unfortunate incident in the woods," said Uncle Abner.

"The police ... what did they want with you?"

"It is nothing really, nothing at all. They merely wanted to ask me some questions, that's all. Just some routine questions."

My father paced the middle of the room with a puzzled look on his face. He turned to me. "What do you know about this?"

I looked to Uncle Abner, and chose my words carefully. "Well ... me and Mooch and Kyle ... we went into the woods. It all started when Mooch saw some flashin' lights in the woods at night and he thought it was a spaceship. The next day we went into the woods, on the path down by the superhighway and we saw a young black girl cryin'."

"Well ...," said my mother, "maybe you shouldn't be going down on that path. It might not be safe."

"Awe mom. We always go down there," I protested.

"Perhaps your mother is right," said Dad.

Uncle Abner sighed and fell deeper into his chair.

"Are you sure you're okay Uncle Abner?" Mom asked him, "You don't look well."

"Oh yes, I'm just tired." he replied...

8

She was young, petite, with soft brown hair and the palest of blue eyes. Standing in the doorway at 'Bow's', suitcase in hand, she looked pensive, peering in, searching for something or someone in the hot, smoke filled bar. The room hushed to silence, until only the ever-present jukebox droned lazily in the background.

Ruth, cleaning a table top, looked up and dropped her towel to the floor in disbelief. "Oh praise God!" she exclaimed.

The young girl just stood there speechless.

"Is it you? Is it really you?" Ruth continued, as she slowly walked through the room toward the girl. Upon reaching her, she reached up ever so gently, and stroked her hair. "Oh how many times I have thought of you."

"Oh Mama," said the girl, holding back tears.

"Rachel," said Ruth, finally putting her arms around the girl. They embraced. "Oh Rachel, I missed you!" Pulling herself away and wiping her eyes, Ruth turned to face all of us.

"Listen up everybody!" she said, "Luke, that means you too!" Luke put down his beer mug and quickly tucked in his ragged shirt tail. "Listen up now! I want ya' t' meet m' daughter 'Rachel'. We haven't seen each other in a long time, so you'll have t' excuse all the carryin' on."

Luke spoke first. "Why Ruth, you didn't tell us ya' had such a good lookin' daughter!"

"Thanks, that's sweet," said Rachel.

"That's 'Luke'," said Ruth, "he's a real joker he is!"

Ruth turned to introduce me. "This here's ... well ... we jus' call 'em 'Pilgrim'."

"Hello," I replied.

"An' this here's the 'Capt'n', he owns the joint," said Ruth.

The Capt'n wiped his hands on a bar towel before offering a handshake. "John Lee Washington, that's m' name, but you can call me the 'Capt'n'," he said.

"Well ... its nice t' meet y'all," said Rachel. She turned around to get her suitcase only to be startled out of her wits. "Oh!" she exclaimed. Crazy Paul had walked up behind her carrying her things. He laughed wildly.

"Rachel dear, this is Paul," said Ruth.

"We jus' call 'em 'Crazy Paul'," joked Luke.

"No. 'Paul' will do jus' fine," Ruth corrected him.

Crazy Paul offered his dirty hand. Rachel looked at it with reservation, then offered hers. To everyone's surprise, he bent down and kissed it in a genteel way. "Very pleased t' meet ya'," he said.

"I'm pleased t' meet you too," she replied.

"... For this my son was dead, and is alive again; he was lost and now is found!" said Crazy Paul.

"What did he say?" said Luke.

"I think it's from the Bible," I said.

"What do ya' mean?"

"The prodigal son. You know, the story of the son who runs away, squanders everything and returns home."

"Great Mother Mary help us!" the Capt'n exclaimed, "Paul, you a-r-e crazy!" His remark drew laughter.

"Now Paul," said Ruth, "why don't 'cha make yourself useful and take Rachel's bag back t' the kitchen for me."

"Hey Rachel, pull up a bar stool," said Luke.

She sat down in the vacant stool and carefully pulled her skirt down to cover a shapely knee.

"Now what can I get ya'?" asked the Capt'n? "It's on the house!"

"Well I don't know," she said, surprised.

"Go on, get somethin'," urged Luke.

"I don't know if should."

"Now if she don't want to be 'a drinkin'," said Ruth.

"I'll have a glass of red wine," said Rachel, quickly, before her mother could intervene.

"A glass of red wine it'll be," said the Capt'n.

Rachel pulled out her make-up mirror, applied some powder to her nose and tucked it back into her purse. The Capt'n placed the wine on the bar and she took a small sip.

Luke leaned over into her face. "Where ya' from?" he asked her.

"... From New York." she replied, backing away from his advance.

"New York!"

"Yes."

"It must be somethin' ... livin' in New York!"

"Well ... New York is ... just New York. I guess once ya' see one big city, ya' seen 'em all."

"What did ya' do there?" Luke continued.

She took the glass of wine and drank most of it.

"Luke, do ya' have t' be so nosey?" Ruth scolded him, "the poor girl just got in town for heaven's sake!"

"Jus' wondered what she was a' doin' up there in New York City was all."

Rachel finished the wine. "I ... I was a dancer ... mainly," she said, almost with reluctance.

"A dancer!" Luke echoed.

"Holy Moses!" said the Capt'n.

"Where did ya' dance?" Luke asked her.

She didn't answer. She lit a cigarette and exhaled the smoke.

"Rachel dear," said Ruth, "I know you got'a be tired after your trip. Wouldn't ya' like to rest a little?"

"No Mama."

"A dancer!" Luke exclaimed.

"A bet 'cha she danced in some fine places too!" added the Capt'n.

"Where did ya' dance?" Luke asked again.

"... places ... different places ..." she replied.

"Damn you Luke!" said Ruth, "I tol' ya' she was tired. She must need a rest, that's all. She needs a rest."

"Could I have another?" Rachel asked the Capt'n, offering her empty glass.

"Yes you can!" he said, turning around to get the bottle.

Again, Rachel looked into her small make-up mirror. Casually, she looked with satisfaction at her own reflection; the way her hair covered the side of her face, hiding within its soft, opaque veil, the smooth curve of her cheekbone; the lips, full and sensuous, pouting; and the eyes, blue and dreamy. Within her beauty was the confidence she possessed, perhaps the power that was always there for her. The lips could be worrisome at times, and the cheeks, stained with tears, but there was always her beauty. Without reservation, she was a beautiful woman. Her dreamy eyes looked up and became alert. Those sensuous lips broke a pleasing smile, for it was not her own reflection she now looked upon, it was Mr. Hartley as he stood before her.

"I don't believe we've met," he said.

"No, we haven't. I'm Rachel," she replied, offering her hand.

"Matthew Hartley", he said, as he delicately took it within his grasp.

"He's a congressman," said Luke.

"Oh!" said Rachel, "Well I'm very glad t' meet 'cha Mr. ..."

"Hartley ... Matthew Hartley."

"Yes, Mr. Hartley. ... I am terrible with names."

"Aren't we all at times-and the pleasure is mine," he said. He placed his brief case on the bar and folded his overcoat neatly on top of it.

"Can I get ya' the regular?" asked the Capt'n.

"Ah, no," replied Mr. Hartley, "I'll have club soda with a twist."

"Rachel?" the Capt'n asked her.

"She won't be needin' any," said Ruth, breaking in.

"Oh Mama!" said Rachel, "This here's m' mama," she said to Mr. Hartley.

"We've met," he said.

"She's always watchin' out for me. She's afraid I might drink too much."

"Well ... what are mothers for?" He laughed a good-natured laugh.

Rachel turned to Ruth. "Mama, you just go off and don't worry 'bout me. I'll be all right. Okay?"

With that, Ruth wandered off to the back of the room. "Well ..." said Rachel, her attention back to Mr. Hartley.

"Yes?" he said.

"It must be somethin' to be a congressman."

"... It's a job ..."

"You're so modest."

"No. Not really."

"It must be hard on Mrs. Hartley. You bein' away all the time."

"... Mrs. Hartley and I don't see each other very much."

"Oh, that's too bad. She doesn't live here with you?"

"... Unfortunately we have been legally separated for quite some time."

"Oh I'm so sorry!"

"That's okay. Really," he assured her.

"I didn't mean t' be so nosey."

"It's okay. It's just the way it is," he replied.

She lit a cigarette. "You know, I was wondering," she asked, "Why do you come in here? I mean, Luke ... and Crazy Paul? This is jus' not your kind'a place."

"And how is that?" He seemed surprised.

"Well ... I mean, you bein' a congressman and all, shouldn't ya' be goin' t' the finer places in town? Maybe even a White House dinner-party or somethin'. Goodness knows! I mean bein' a congressman! Don't you do things like that," she asked.

He did not reply. It was as though he was temporarily lost in his thoughts.

"Mr. Hartley, didn't you hear anything I said?"

"I'm sorry. You know, I probably didn't hear a word you said," he joked, smiling.

"Why not?"

"Rachel, can I say ... you are a very, very beautiful girl."

"Oh now Mr. Hartley, go on!" she said with a laugh.

9

Ruth had promised her daughter that she would not wait up, not worry about her, and not inquire of her where-a-bouts. For the last few weeks, within the confines of the humble, three-room apartment, they had shared a coexistence. But it was strained, and tense. There had been times when Ruth wanted to talk to her, to lecture and console her-a mother's ceaseless meddling. But she had promised to mind her own business. But things had happened to so fast. Rachel had been seeing Mr. Hartley almost every day since they had met, and tonight they went out to dinner. And now it was getting very late. The clock on the wall chimed two o'clock. The TV had long signed off, and the newspaper had been re-read. In spite of the promise, Ruth waited for her daughter to return, listening for footsteps in the hallway. But there was only silence.

Looking at the wall she admired the wall paper; white with lilacs tied with little yellow bows. There was a large bouquet with two smaller bunches to each side, each connected by a little yellow ribbon. The pattern started in one corner and continued over and up to the ceiling; an endless sea of lilacs. Though it was now faded and dog-eared in places, she loved the pattern. Especially the little yellow ribbon. It was the kind of yellow ribbon she wore in her hair when she was a young girl, and when she was older too, to tie the long light brown locks of hair from her eyes. Or down, tied in the back into a pony-tail. Yellow was her favorite color.

And her clothes. She remembered sunny dresses for sunny days, carefree days. She could remember with such clarity certain things from her childhood. Many with delight. She could almost feel the cold water of the pond near her daddy's house, where she would dangle her feet from the small cart-wagon bridge. Pulling up her dress and petty-coat so as not the let the muddy water stain them.

And toys. There were dolls, and stuffed animal toys, and tea sets and little tea parties with her little tea party friends. All this, in her memories, were like some fairy tale she could recall as easily as opening a locket or hearing the tinkle on an old music box.

And Romance. She would smile as she reminisced those cool spring days and so many hot, lurid summer nights; a simple walk down a crimson path with that special boy of her dreams, and a kiss stolen under the harvest crescent moon; the feel of the tall cool grass against her skin while making love. These visions poured from somewhere deep within like so many words from a pocket diary. But, though faded from passing years, these passions still lived inside her, as she looked to the virtual sea of lilacs in the faded wall paper, laying among them, enraptured and perfumed, with only that of her solitary beating heart.

Downstairs, she heard the closing of the heavy lobby door. Quickly, she turned off the light on the side table and stood up in the darkness. She had promised that she wouldn't sit up waiting for them. She really wanted to keep that promise. Perhaps she could hide in the darkness, hide her betrayal. As she moved to the bedroom, she closed the door behind her just as they entered the living room.

They left the lights off. She could hear the sound of keys being placed on the table. A few minutes passed, and still there was no light from the bottom of the door. Ruth, her consciousness tormented, carefully turned the door knob, carefully, ever so carefully, until the door opened slightly. Holding her breath, she peered out with one eye, one shameless eye, looking into the darkness, spying on Rachel and her lover. As her eyes adjusted to the available light, she could see only their silhouettes.

Rachel had placed her back to the wall as Mr. Hartley pressed his body against hers. He was kissing her neck. Lost in the moment, Rachel kicked off one shoe, and then with her toes, she nudged off the other. His face remained buried in her bosom. In their passion, they were rolling, falling through the field of lilacs. Ruth closed her eyes. How shameful it was to watch them, to perhaps feel what Rachel was feeling, to perhaps pretend, fantasize and feed a burning desire deep within her own arid, withered soul.

But she couldn't help herself. Taking a deep breath, she looked again through the door. They were kissing. Tenderly, he kissed her nose, and brushed his hungry lips across her cheek, to her wanting mouth. The fervor increased with such intensity, with such lust, until the strength of their convictions could not hold them, could not stop them.

Down, against the wall they surrendered, to the floor where they became undressed, unashamed and committed. Swirling, down deeper into the cool tall grasses they fell. Lost within themselves, Lost in that wall-paper, their limbs flailing and turning, twisting, among the lilacs, knocking them down, cutting off the tender petals and sending them off to the sweet winds in random patterns, tearing away the little yellow ribbons and bows.

Ruth closed the door and breathed heavily. She sat down on the edge of the bed, her heart pounding in her ears, pounding so loudly, surely they could hear it in the other room! But within, there were only the sounds of rustling, and cooing. She could picture Rachel in his arms, close and as one. Then, for a while it was quiet.

Suddenly, the door opened and the room became bathed in brightness as Rachel turned on the light and stood in the doorway.

"Mama, what are ya' doin' sittin' there in the dark?" she said.

"Nothin', 'chile, nothin'."

Rachel was unconvinced.

"Where's Mr. Hartley?" Ruth asked.

"... Went home ..."

"Did ya' have a nice time?"

"Please don't make small talk. I know you were waitin' up for me, weren't ya'?"

"No Rachel ... I was ... jus' ..."

"Sittin' in the dark huh? Jus' sittin' in the dark."

"No."

"You were waitin' up for me weren't ya' ... listened through the door!"

"I ..."

"No. You were ..."

"Oh Rachel ... I didn't mean to ..."

"Oh my God! Were you watchin' through the door?"

"I ... well I ..."

"Great! mama!"

"Rachel honey," Ruth cried out, pleading, "I don't want ya' t' get hurt 'chile."

"Mama, I been with plenty of men and I can take care of myself. Besides, Mr. Hartley likes me. In fact, I think he's in love with me!"

"He don't love you. He can't!"

"What do ya' mean - can't?"

"That kind'a man only wants one thing from a girl like you. Jus' like that no good man that was your father!"

"I never even knew my daddy! He couldn't even stick around for me t'be born, the bastard!"

"Your Mr. Hartley will do you like that too if ya' let 'em."

"That's right Mama, and I'm gonna give it to 'im too. Is that what ya' want to hear? I guess your daughter is jus' like you were ... a two-bit whore!"

"Oh Rachel honey!" Ruth cried, choking on her tears.

Rachel turned off the light and walked over to the window. Ruth could see her shadow against the dim light.

"Oh Mama ... mama..." said Rachel, looking out the window at the street below.

"I only want what's best for ya'," said Ruth.

"What's best for me?!? Like what's best for you? Mama, I don't want to live like this. Look at this dump! All your life you scraped by and jus' made it month t' month. There's a whole big world out there and I'm gonna have it for myself. All for myself!"

"And ya' think your Mr. Hartley is gonna give it t'ya'?"

"He's rich ain't he? He could be my ticket out'a this hell-hole Mama!"

"So that's it ... you're jus' gonna ..."

"That's right. I'm gonna be his whore, his personal little whore!"

"... Do ya' love him?" Ruth asked her.

"What's love got'a do with it?"

"Oh Lord! Jus' listen to yourself. Did I bring ya' up to be like this?"

"Mama, you can learn t' love anyone with money."

"Can't buy love," Ruth said softly.

There was the sound of a car out on the deserted street. And it drove off into the distance, into the darkness.

10

"Row, row, row your boat, gently down the stream..." The little girls were singing, sitting in the alley and playing jacks. From my apartment window, I could hear them. I looked out into the alley. Their legs and bottoms were dirty from sitting on the dusty ground. "Merrily, merrily, life is but a dream..."

I sat down at my table listening to their voices which, though discordant, had a simple beauty and were almost hypnotic. It was that line, 'life is but a dream', that lingered in my mind. Maybe life was just a dream and all around us was just an illusion, a delicate, timely event that could be but a fraction of a second within the galactic eternity of the universe. This notion made me shutter, perhaps like some far-distant ancestor, who, pondered the world around him; like a full, orange moon, the multitude of stars above, the tremendous roar of lightning as it struck the earth, or just the delicate wings of a butterfly. Like me, he questioned his existence, and looked skyward, to the heavens for a reason, a creator, a God.

Placing my hands together as in prayer, I wondered ... God, a God, my God, that faceless deity that created this universe. It was rare that I called upon him. Yes, always in desperation, turning to him in time of need, to ask a favor, to ask for a miracle. No, we weren't close friends, as if we could be. Can a man be friends with God? Can a man come face to face, toe to toe, eye to eye with his maker? With God himself? I wondered. Can a man have the audacity to place himself on the same level as He? I thought not. Being the worthless sinner I was, our meeting were always awkward. I spoke, whispered in low meaningful tones, and only hoped that he heard me; that perhaps even my frail belief in Him would save me in times of peril.

I wrote ...

... "And if your eye makes you turn away, take it out and throw it away! It is better for you to enter life with only one eye than to keep both eyes and be thrown into the fires of hell!" Uncle

Abner proclaimed. In one hand he held the Bible, fully with the ribbon marker swaying wildly. With the other, he mad gestures, orchestrating each phrase as he spoke, "Jesus will forgive you my son!"

I was in a kneeling position and lifted my head to speak. "But I haven't sinned."

"We have all sinned in the eyes o' the Lord!" He shouted.

"But-"

"Be quiet!"

Obediently, I closed my eyes and raised my hands in prayer. He turned around and moved in such a way as to suggest he was adjusting his rosary, but I knew he was taking a drink. I could smell it on his person, his breath as he spoke. He continued, "All manner of sin and blasphemy against the Lord shall not be forgiven!"

Again, I could not be quieted. "But Uncle Abner, I am not a sinner!" I protested. "I haven't done anything wrong. I'm too young to have done anything wrong."

"Jesus died for our sins!"

"But Uncle ..."

"He died for our sins!" he cried out.

I cringed as he drew back, as if to strike me. "Please no", I screamed.

"Wait!" To our astonishment, a voice cried out. It was Mooch. He was standing in the doorway.

"And who said you could enter this house?" Uncle Abner demanded.

"Well ... the door was ajar," he replied.

"I don't remember the door ever being ajar in this house. The door is either opened, or it is closed, but it is never ajar."

"Yes, it was," I said quickly, "... I left it ajar."

Uncle Abner closed his Bible and looked to Mooch with a stern eye. "Well?" he asked.

"I was jus' going up to the woods," he said.

"Can I go?" I asked quickly.

"Well ... yes," he said, "Yes, you might as well go. Go on!" Uncle Abner exclaimed with resignation.

Outside, we ran down the stoop to the sidewalk and turned toward the entrance to the woods.

"It's gonna rain," said Mooch, "you can smell it in the air."

Yes, there was a storm coming with dark clouds above, but I knew Mooch was just making small-talk. "...You opened the door and came in didn't you?" I asked.

"Yeah ..."

"It wasn't really ajar."

"... No ..."

"... Thanks .."

"I had to," he said, "I jus' knew I had to."

"I know. I'm glad you did."

"I was coming up to the door and heard your voices arguing. I knew ... well I figured ..."

"That he would hit me," I said, completing the sentence.

"Well ... yeah ..."

As we approached the entrance to the woods, we stopped walking. I looked at Mooch. The wind was blowing now with the coming storm. "... You ever think about God?" I asked him.

"I guess ..."

"I do ..."

"You do?" he seemed surprised.

"Sometimes .."

"Like how?"

"He's always watchin' ya' when you're doin' secret things and thinking secret thoughts. There aren't any secrets with God."

"Yeah, it's like that for everyone," Mooch said.

"I dunno ... my God could not be the same as Uncle Abner's God."

"There's only one God," Mooch insisted, "everybody knows that."

"Maybe it's just the way people see him," I said. "For Uncle Abner ... God makes him sad."

"Hey, ya' know, if they call him 'Reverend Abner', how come he ain't head of a church or somethin' like that?"

"I dunno ... he used to be, but ... something happened I guess. I was too young to remember him when he had a church."

"Well he must'a done somethin'."

"You know, I always wondered ... maybe that's why he drinks."

There was an awkward Silence.

"Mooch ... I'm sorry ..."

"Sorry for what?"

"I dunno ... for ... you know ..."

"Look, it ain't your fault you got an uncle like Uncle Abner. It's not your fault."

"He says I'm a sinner. He says we're all sinners ... You think I'm a sinner?"

"... I dunno ... maybe we are all sinners."

"I don't mean like tellin' little white lies, I mean tellin' big bad lies, and hurtin' and stealin' ... killin' people ... things like that."

Mooch paused to think and then replied, "No ... We're not sinners, not if you look at it like that."

The wind blew harder, and the tree limbs shook with each gust and the wildflowers at my feet bowed to the earth on their stems. We stopped walking, became silent for a moment, hearing only the wind.

"... Hey Mooch."

"Yeah."

"Ya' think I'm crazy?"

"What'cha mean?"

"Talkin' 'bout God and growin' up and ... things like that?"

"Ya' mean crazy like your Uncle Abner? ... Nah."

"I don't think he's crazy," I said, "he's just ... lonely. Real lonely. Like bein' lonely even when there's a whole lot of people around."

In the distance, over in the north-western sky, it was pitch black and I could see the low clouds rolling, tumbling in. The wind sent a chill over me as I stood there watching the storm overtake us. Then, a bolt of lightning lit the far-off heavens. The thunder roared.

"We better get goin'," said Mooch.

I said nothing. I just closed my eyes and listened to the thunder and let the large rain drops start to caress and cleanse my face. Cleanse my soul.

11

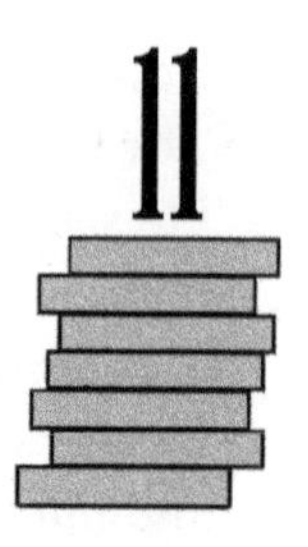

It was the night before Thanksgiving. With the lights turned down low, I sat in there in my apartment feeling somewhat empty. I wondered what Jill and Joey were doing, if they missed me. Tomorrow they would probably go to Nana's. There would be turkey and good cheer. Would they miss me as I missed them? But one thing I knew, they didn't understand, couldn't understand why I wasn't with them. But how could they? Besides, according to Peter I was crazy, deranged. In a way, perhaps he was right. It was wrong to abandon them this way.

On the table were the piles of books and papers that were recently a part of me, part of my writing, the ideas that haunted me the last several months. At times I marveled over them, these gems of wisdom and acute perception, raw slices of life to be observed, to be studied, to be savored. But sometimes a casual glance would expose the weaknesses and mediocrity within them. I would puzzle over the words, the phrases, the visions, until I was dazed senseless. Then I would turn away, shrug it off. After all, these things were a part of me, as much as the air that filled my lungs. I was a creator, even if only unto myself; the muse who sings into the empty forest only to hear his lone voice among the trees. And in this, only this, I would revel. But tonight? Not tonight. Tonight my mind was blank, numb, even wounded by loneliness.

Taking the wine bottle, I poured some into my coffee cup, and drank. I brushed my hair back and rubbed my tired face. Yeah, I was probably crazy all right. I remembered other Thanksgivings. Like Christmas, Easter, even Halloween, these special times were like place-markers in my life. Unlike other joyous celebrations, this one was an anomaly. At this sign-post in my life, I found myself, not sitting among family and friends, but alone in this little apartment drinking cheap wine and feeling sorry for myself; looking back at memories or puzzling over my future, but not really looking at the present. I was looking at my life, assessing, reporting, but not being an active player. Had life hurt me so badly that I was forced to drop out, to take this sabbatical? A wimp? Maybe not, I would have rather fancied myself as a courageous solder, striking out against the cruel unfair world that surrounded me. I would be decorated for bravery. How clever was my madness.

Suddenly, there was a frantic knocking at my door! It was Rachel. "You've got to help me!" she pleaded.

I opened the door. "What's wrong?"

"Mama won't answer her door. It's locked from the inside!"

We rushed into the hallway, to Ruth's apartment door. I grabbed the handle only to find it turn but the door unyielding. "Is there a deadbolt?" I asked.

"Yeah, and it's locked!" said Rachel.

I had seen it done in the movies, the hero breaking down the door. Moving to the far wall to make room, I ran and jammed my shoulder against the upper panel. The door groaned, cracked, but remained intact. Again, I lunged at it, only this time, a piece of the door broke away. I reached into the hole and freed the bolt. The door flew open. Inside the room, there was the nauseating smell of gas.

"Oh God!" Rachel screamed, "the stove!"

Taking a Kleenex from the nearby table, I handed it to her. "Here, put his over your mouth." Looking around the room, I saw Ruth's legs protruding from the kitchen door. She was lying on the floor. "Open the window!" I yelled.

Rachel rushed to the living-room window and pulled without success.

"Open the window!" I screamed.

"I can't. It's painted shut!"

I took a wooden chair and threw it through the window. Picking up Ruth under her arms, I drug her through the broken glass to the fresh air, as Rachel raced to the kitchen to turn off the gas in the oven. It all happened so quickly. We stood there breathing heavily amid the lingering gas.

"Is she okay?" Rachel asked, sick with grief.

It was then that Ruth came to, sat up with a start, coughing violently.

"Mama! Mama! Are you all right?" Rachel said, kneeling down at her side.

Ruth, still coughing, shook her head to mean yes.

"Help me get her into a chair," I said. With Rachel on one side, we lifted her into the old arm chair. She sank limply into an old pillow.

"Get me a glass 'a water," she wheezed.

I rushed to the kitchen sink to get it for her, when I noticed the dinner on the counter. It was burned, charred black. When I returned, Rachel was pacing the floor. I handed Ruth the glass.

"Are you okay," I asked her.

"Yes. Yes, I'm fine," she whispered.

"Oh Mama! How could you?" Rachel said.

"I'm sorry."

"Why?"

"Maybe because she burned the turkey," I said.

"She burned the turkey?"

"Yeah. She burned the turkey."

"So that's it? She burned the goddamned turkey!" Rachel exclaimed. She stopped pacing, and turned around briskly. "Mama, who cares about an old turkey anyway?"

"I don't know. I jus' got t' feelin' depressed I guess."

"Depressed about what Mama? What are ya' depressed about?"

"I don't know ...."

"It's more than jus' the turkey. It's more that jus' Thanksgivin' ain't it Mama?"

"I don't know what'cha mean 'chile."

"It's me ain't it? It's me and Mr. Hartley ain't it Mama?"

"Why no 'chile."

"Yes it is. Jus' like the other times. You're jealous ain't ya'?"

"No!" Ruth replied, becoming more animated.

"Jus' like the other times," Rachel said. "Ya jus' can't stand me bein' with a man can ya?"

"No! No!" Ruth said, crying.

Rachel looked at me and shook her head.

"Oh I'm sorry Rachel dear!" Ruth moaned, "It won't happen again. I promise! It won't happen again!"

Rachel resumed pacing. "Oh Mama," she said quietly, "Oh Mama, Mama ..."

"I jus' can't take it no more," said Ruth.

"What? My happiness?"

`"No honey. I want to see ya' happy an' all. It's jus' ..."

"What Mama? Talk t' me Goddamn it!"

"... Your Mr. Hartley an' you. Oh you got'a bed full 'a roses don't 'cha? Like a fairy-tale come true!"

"You a-r-e jealous!"

"No ... not jealous, I just know that's all ... just how empty a life can be. Ain't your fault though, ain't your fault," Ruth said through her tears.

It became quiet in the room. Just the sound of Ruth crying. She continued, "... The other night, when you tol' me 'bout havin' it all. Well .... maybe you were right. Sometimes ... well sometimes it seems like life jus' ain't worth livin'."

"... Oh Mama."

"Remember that red dress?" said Ruth, "you know, the one with the white lace around the neck, and the sleeves, all full and lovely?"

"Yes ... I know the one," said Rachel.

"That was the prettiest dress I ever saw. But it rotted right on it's hanger! I wouldn't wear that dress no matter what. I was savin' it for the right time, the right man. Only, he never came along! I'd wear rags before I'd wear that dress! I was going t' wear that dress like a princess. But my knight in shinin' armor never came and that pretty dress collected the dust, and moths, and rotted away jus' like the dreams, witherin' away 'til there's nothin' left. Is that a life worth livin'?"

Ruth looked to me with sadness. Looking into her eyes I could see the hopelessness, the shear magnitude of sorrow that gripped her, the broken dreams, all encapsulated in the person that I knew as Ruth, sometimes strong and caring. I thought about myself. I empathized with her.

"Is it my fault?" asked Rachel, "Did I do this to you?"

"Of course not darlin'," said Ruth, "It's nobody's fault. It's jus' life. I had big dreams once. Maybe that was the problem, I had way too many dreams. They were like shiny pennies I picked up off the ground, and collected in a silk purse. So many, that the silk linin' jus' plumb give out and it all fell apart."

"Mama, we all have them kind'a dreams."

"I guess I'm jus' an old fool," said Ruth.

"You ain't no fool," said Rachel, "we all need to dream ..."

"Maybe your Mr. Hartley can make your dreams come true."

"Yeah ... maybe ..."

"Jus' think ... Mrs. Rachel Hartley, wife of Congressman Mr. Matthew L. Hartley. You'll be givin' big parties and holdin' high tea with real, proper ladies, 'a wearin' those pretty party dresses. Wearin' that red party dress."

"Do ya' really think I could forget you Mama? Why you'll be right there with me, 'a sittin' there in the middle of everything, a' drinkin' and a' chattin' with gentlemen, an' a' wearin' that red dress! Jus' a' beamin' like a bright star!"

Ruth clasped her hands and her eyes closed, swooning. "But Rachel, Rachel ... it's jus' a dream. Jus' a silly dream."

"Oh no Mama, it's not jus' a dream."

"You think that man is really in love with you?"

"He will be," said Rachel. "... I'm carryin' his baby."

12

... Abner's eyes were heavy lidded as he beheld the young Negro girl who stood before him in his doorway. She was wearing a simple cotton dress and her hair pulled neatly back. It was her eyes that stood out from her plain appearance. They were alert, wide-open, starring back him. She was very nervous. "Could I ... talk to you?" she asked.

He sighed deeply. "... Of course child. Come in," he said.

She walked inside, carefully over to the table where lay his Bible and rosary.

"You came," he said.

"You knew I'd come, didn't you?" she said.

"... Yes ..."

"... I'm so confused," she whispered.

"We are all confused," he said, "... all lost souls ..."

"I must tell the truth," she said.

"... Yes ..."

"In the Bible, in the commandments, it says 'thou shall not lie' and I can't! I jus' can't!"

"Of course ..."

"I jus' can't!" she insisted.

"You musn't ..."

She looked away and bit her lip nervously. "I lost ..." she said, but then broke down as if to cry. Her voice was choked with tears. "I lost ... a God-given part of me ..."

"Oh Lord G-a-w-d-d-d! Have mercy!" the Abner cried, clasping his hands over his face, and then in prayer.

"... A part of me ... that I can't never get back! This thing that happened to me!" she continued.

"The Lord is a merciful God!" he cried.

"And I can't lie! No more!" she wept.

"We must kneel in prayer," he told her.

There on the polished wooden floor she knelt. He faced her, kneeling down on one knee. He opened his Bible and read quietly, teary-eyed, but then closed the book, using the rosary for a marker.

"Oh Lord ... please forgive me for my sins!" he cried. "For we will surely pay on earth as well as in the burning fires of hell and damnation!"

"You ... you should pay," she said.

"... Yes ..."

"Yes, you should pay for what you done to me!" she cried out.

"As there is a God in heaven ... we shall all will pay!"

They both wept.

"I must go tell the police ..." she said.

"O' dear merciful G-a-w-d-d-d!" he said, "Faith can be strong, but the flesh! Why so weak? Why would you give us such strong convictions with such weak wills? Must we be destined to be hypocrites in your eyes?"

He looked up to see the young girl standing now, standing over him. "You must go. You must go tell the police everything child," he said reluctantly.

"Yes ... I must go ..." she whispered.

He remained kneeling, his eyes downcast, not watching her walk to the door, hearing only the clasping of the door as she closed it behind her.

It was late in the afternoon when I came home.

The sun was low in the sky and I knew Uncle Abner would be wondering about my where-a-bouts.

Inside, in the living room, I noticed the Bible and rosary lying on the floor. Then there was a sound, a quiet sound, a very odd sound, one I had never heard before.

"Squeak-squeak ..."

What I strange sound! I looked to the kitchen door.

"Ding-dong! Ding-dong!" the wall clock chimed.

"Uncle Abner!" I yelled at the kitchen door.

Silence.

"I'm home!"

Silence.

"Uncle Abner ..." My voice trailed off into the silence.

"Squeak-squeak ..." Again the sound.

I ran to the kitchen door and peeked inside the room. Nothing.

"Clip-clop," went the sound of the water droplets from the faucet. I walked over and turned the handle. It was absolutely quiet. But then that sound!

"Squeak-squeak ..."

I went back to the living room. It was dark, filled with late afternoon shadows. My heart raced as I slowly turned around and scanned the room, the high-backed chair, the Victrola with the lid down, the TV with its blank, lifeless screen. A strange feeling of emptiness surrounded me.

"Squeak-squeak ..."

Placing my hand on the railing, I put one foot on the first step and taking a breath, I moved slowly upstairs. I could see the bathroom door fully open.

"Uncle Abner! Are you there?"

Silence.

"Squeak-squeak ..." went the sound, only louder.

He was in his room. He must be in his room.

Climbing the remaining steps, I stood at the top of the stairway. Uncle Abner's door was closed shut.

"Squeak-squeak ..." The sound was coming from his room!

My heart was pounding in my ears as I slowly approached the door.

"Squeak-squeak ..."

I could hear the sound clearly now.

From the bathroom window, far down the hall, there was only a faint light from the afternoon sun. I was standing in the shadows.

"Squeak-squeak ..."

I took hold of the door knob and started to turn it slowly, slowly, to find it unlocked. But I didn't open it.

"Squeak-squeak ..."

"Uncle Abner!" I screamed, my voice quivering from the fear that engulfed me.

Silence.

Then, with courage, I pushed to door open wide.

"Squeak-squeak ..."

My mouth opened to scream but I was frozen, mortified, and mute. My small body trembled and shook from the depths of my soul. For in the dim light from the window's edge, I could see Uncle

Abner's lifeless body, hanging high from the light fixture above, humped-over, and his face twisted and grotesque!

That sound was the sound of the leather noose around the brass arm of the old light fixture.

"Squeak-squeak ..."

13

It was inevitable I thought, as I watched from my apartment window. Peter walked around to the other side of the car to help Jill get out. As she popped her head out of the passenger side, I could see her face. She looked tired and grief stricken, and I knew, it was all because of me. I felt wrecked with guilt and in no way prepared for the confrontation which was to follow.

I didn't run to the mirror to straighten my hair, or to change my dirty clothes. I simply stood there and waited as I heard their footsteps approaching the door, like a schoolboy who was facing a reprimand, and it made me sick to my stomach. But there was no escape. More steps, and then, a knock at the door. I hesitated. I knew I must greet them, and get it over with.

"Hi," I said with a cheerful facade, as I opened the door, as if I was expecting them with a devil-may-care attitude. They didn't speak at first. They just stood there in the doorway. It was then that I looked into Jill's eyes, that dreadful moment that I had anticipated for so long. In her sad eyes, I could see the hurt that I had placed upon her. Those eyes that were once happy and filled with joy, hope for our future, like when we were both young people in love with a thousand-and-one dreams, those eyes that captured my heart so many years ago, those eyes that looked into my mine now were care-worn.

"Hi Jill," I said. The tone of my voice sounded empty.

"Hello," she said, trying to break a smile. I went to hold her but she backed away. It was a clumsy gesture on my part.

"Come in, come in," I said. "You ... wanna sit down."

They slowly entered but only looked at the simple, hard-backed chairs in the middle of the room.

"It's ... not much. … I know ... can I get you some coffee," I said.

"You look awful," she said.

I looked at Peter. "You do look bad," he agreed.

"Well …, I've been busy," I said.

"Yes, so we see," he said, studying the paper-strewn table.

"How's Joey?" I asked, turning to Jill.

"Not good, not bad. How would you expect a young boy to feel when his father has deserted him?"

"Well ... that's not fair," I said.

"That's not fair? Well excuse me!" She responded quickly.

"... I am sorry. Really. It's ... been hard for me, hard to explain", I said.

"Hard for you? I can't believe you! Hard for you?" she exclaimed, shaking her head.

"Have you thought it over?" asked Peter.

"Thought what over?" I asked.

"About coming back to work .... taking the job offer. All you have to do is say the word."

"... It's hard for you both to understand. It's hard for me to understand," I said.

"We can't go on like this," said Jill.

"... I ... don't know ..."

"What is wrong with you?" she pleaded. "I just can't understand. You, a full grown man. You can't just quit your job and leave your family. Why are you doing this? Is it something I've done? If so, then I'm sorry, but please, please tell me what is wrong?" She was now close to tears.

"You wouldn't understand," I said.

"I'll try ..."

"I need something ... I'm just trying to find myself ... I need ... to find something ... I don't know ..."

"This so-called 'Self-actualization'?" asked Peter.

"Yes, perhaps."

"Maslow's levels of attainment huh?"

"Maybe ..."

"Let's see if I remember correctly. There were physiological needs such as food and shelter, safety needs, a feeling of belonging, love needs, esteem needs, and that almighty need for self-actualization!"

"I see you've done your homework."

"Now ... do you take these like vitamins. Let's see ... I'm feeling a little lonely today, maybe I should make new friends on level five, or better yet ..."

"Shit Peter! Is that what you came here for today? To make fun of me?"

"Of course not, but can't you see? You need to get a hold of yourself".

"We just want you to come to your senses," said Jill.

"That's what I'm trying to do," I said, "... like I said, it's just too hard for you to understand."

"Have you reached that final level yet?" asked Peter.

I couldn't tell whether or not he was kidding. "I don't know ..."

"It all sounds so ridiculous," said Jill.

"Maybe not," I said, "in a way, maybe there are seven levels."

"A seventh level? And what on earth would that be? To be God himself?" said Peter.

"No. Perhaps it is 'self-fulfillment', to find the ultimate meaning of life," I said.

"Oh Christ! Now it's not good enough to be self-actualized, now we need to go around building monuments to commemorate ourselves!"

"... I knew you wouldn't understand!"

"Do you know just how crazy this sounds? Maybe you need help?" said Jill.

"Professional help," Peter added.

"So you still think I'm crazy huh? A loon? Just another insane man the world can't understand!"

"I want to understand," said Jill. "If only I could."

I looked at the window. Then the wall. I paced the floor. I was searching for a way to tell them, to show them the way I felt. I saw the coffee cup on the table.

"See the coffee cup on the table?" I asked them. That coffee cup may be here, if it isn't broken, many years after we're dead and gone, perhaps millions of years."

"That's it! You want immortality?" said Peter.

"No, not really, maybe just ... a purpose ..."

"You're right," said Jill, "I don't understand."

I reached for the coffee cup and relished it in my hand. "It's just a plain coffee cup, a molded lump of clay, fired in the kiln and painted. It is so pure, simple, it has but one purpose-to hold a liquid so that someone may drink from it. And when it is empty, it is filled up again. Now, look at ourselves. How so much more complex we are. God gave us a brain that could reason, remember, and relate to others. Yet because we are so complex, with so much potential, we fill our lives with so much abstraction. So, I am born, to go to school, to go to work, spending my whole life working a job, paying my bills, falling in love and having children, and then put them through school so they can join this endless chain of life. In the end, I move to some paradise-like place to die. All this for what? There's got to be something more. God couldn't have put us on this earth just to live an seemingly, empty life. If only just to find a purpose, this thing which is lost, which is hidden from view, and when found, to rejoice in it, to find wonder in it, that clear sense of being, of worth, that purity, even if only as simple as this coffee cup. Perhaps only then could we be right with the world, as one with God ..."

"And that purpose is self-glorification?" said Peter satirically.

"No, but there must be a purpose, something. A reason."

"It sounds like a middle-aged crisis to me," said Jill.

"I need a reason for living!" I blurted out loudly. Perhaps I was insane. I shuttered as I thought of my own instability.

"... So you want notoriety, to be famous," Peter continued.

"No, I just need to make some mark upon the face of the world, some indelible footprint in the sands of time ... I know it all sounds crazy."

Peter looked at the pile of papers on the table. "And this is why you are writing?" he asked.

"Maybe ..."

He picked up several of the papers. "Can I read them?"

"It's not finished yet. It's just ... notes and ... ideas really."

He thumbed through the manuscript, only stopping to read bits and pieces of the material. Then, shaking his head in disgust, he threw them back down on the table. "It's a story about a young boy," he said, "it's about you? Is this story about you?"

"Maybe ... some ..."

"An autobiography?"

"No, goddamn it!" I stammered.

"It all seems so senseless," said Jill.

"Look, you're an engineer, not a writer. Why can't you make your contribution as an engineer?" Peter asked.

"... I knew you wouldn't understand," I said.

Peter threw up his hands in resignation and sat down in one of the two chairs.

"I've been talking to a lawyer," said Jill.

"You want a divorce," I said.

"No, actually ... I have almost enough evidence ..."

"For what?"

"... to have you committed ... you need help," she said with amazing tenderness.

"To have me committed?" I said. I looked at both of them with utter amazement. "To have me committed?"

"It's for your own good," said Peter.

"It's only because we care about you honey," she said close to tears. "And, while you are committed, then the insurance and disability pay would take care of Joey and me until you are well again. We love you."

"Great! That's just great! You know I'm not crazy!" I screamed.

"Fine, so we'll just let you alone to search for this ... 'level seven' and write your memoirs," said Peter.

"If you could just give me some more time. There is something I need to do," I said, "I just don't know what it is yet!"

"So the rest of us just put our lives on hold while you pursue some half-baked scheme?" said Jill.

"Fine. I was right. There is no way either of you will ever understand."

"You must come to your senses," said Peter.

"Or else?"

"It's up to you," said Jill, "I tried my best. The final decision must be up to you."

14

Outside, the snow fell in large flakes, wet, clinging to the windows and the door, allowing only the faintest light and warmth to glow from inside our Captain Benbow Lounge. But within, the dark mahogany walls were decked with fresh pine garland and holly berries. Poinsettias adorned the tables, and in the center of the great oak bar, a large basket of fruits. There were nuts and chips, and chocolates, port wine and even clam chowder. 'Twas Christmas, a special night and for the Capt'n nothing was spared for us, his patrons, and his friends. "Come on Ruth!" bellowed the Capt'n, "there'll be no work done tonight. Come and join us!"

She put aside her broom and sat down at the end of the bar, close to Rachel, who sat next to Luke, who was sitting next to me. The lights burned dimly, and though the door was unlocked to the public, but there was no one else among us. For one reason or another, without families of our own, tonight, for better or worse, we would be each other's family.

"Where's Crazy Paul?" said Luke.

"He's around here somewheres'," said the Capt'n. "And Mr. Hartley, I wonder where the hell he is?"

Rachel turned around on her stool. "He'll be along soon. Tol' me so," she said.

"Bet'cha he ain't comin'," said Luke.

"Of course he's comin'," she replied.

Ruth was quiet, looked at her fingernails and then looked at the wall.

Rachel straightened the stocking on her leg. Then lit a cigarette. "He's probably late 'cause he's bringin' all those presents. He's probably loaded down with an armful of presents," she said.

"The bearer of precious gifts," I mused, and then buried my face in my beer.

"Yes, the bearer of precious gifts!" Rachel continued.

"Rachel you should be ashamed of yourself," said Ruth, "'a talkin' like that."

"Go for it," said Luke, "hey, the man has money."

"Don't worry, Mr. Hartley an' I will do fine, jus' fine," said Rachel.

"Ya' really think he'd dump his wife for you?" said Luke.

"Sure he will. I tol' ya' he will!"

Capt'n walked over and wiped off the bar where I sat. "Hey Pilgrim," he said, "you really ought'a go home. Jus' go on home."

"I'm not really sure just where that is," I said.

"It's with you wife and 'chile man."

"... Maybe ..."

"It's Christmas Eve."

"So it is."

"Can I get ya' another?"

"Sure."

"Hey man ... ya' think they really gonna ..."

"What? Send me to the 'funny farm'? ... I dunno ..." I pushed my empty mug to him. "Fill'er up please," I said.

Mr. Hartley appeared from the doorway. "Oh Matthew, I didn't think you'd ever get here!" said Rachel, getting up to help him with his coat. There were no presents and she pretended not to notice.

"The subway was running late tonight," he said.

"What'll ya' have?" asked the Capt'n.

"The usual," he replied.

The Capt'n poured the scotch into a small glass and then a glass of water behind it. Mr. Hartley drank the scotch, savoring it.

"Well honey," said Rachel, taking his hands into hers. "And how was your day?"

"Oh ... busy ... you know ... busy ..."

"Of course, a congressman's always busy," said Luke, "everybody knows that."

Rachael grabbed Mr. Hartley by the arm. "Well?" she asked him.

".... Yes?" he inquired.

"Remember? Remember what we decided?"

"... Oh yes ..."

"Don't 'cha think we should tell 'em?" she said, prodding him.

"Well ...."

Rachel grabbed a spoon and tapped her glass rim to make a pinging sound. "Hush-up y'all!" she exclaimed. "Matthew is goin' to make an announcement!" She turned to him, eyes wide open, full of enthusiasm. But her lover seemed befuddled. "Well?" she said, "go on ... tell 'em."

He seemed troubled. "... Well ... Rachel ... we need to talk ... alone ..."

"Oh come on. Don't," she said, "No ... don't do this to me."

"Rachel ... I have been thinking ... perhaps we need more time," he said.

"No. You bastard!" she screamed.

"Rachel, not here ... not like this," he begged.

Ruth stood up.

"Go on," Rachel said to him. "Tell 'em 'bout the wedding plans. Jus' like we talked about. Remember?"

"Rachel ... look ... I'm sorry … You're putting me on the spot."

There was a sad moment of silence. Rachel hung her head. "Fine. So you're not gonna marry me after all ... are ya'?" she whispered.

"Rachel, I didn't want to have to tell you this way, not tonight." Silence. "... Look ... my wife wouldn't allow an easy divorce. And anyway ... it might not have worked in the end. Perhaps later on..."

"It wouldn't work out with someone like me. That's what you mean don't 'cha?" she said.

"No, I mean, perhaps we need more time ... I have been busy."

"Of course, we mustn't forget your big glorious career," she said, facetiously.

Mr. Hartley was embarrassed and at a loss for words but then told her, "... But I want you to know that the child will be taken care of. You have my word on it," he assured her.

"Oh yes! The love child!" said Rachel.

Yes ... the baby," he said.

Rachel took a long drink and then turned to face him. There was a slight trace of tears in her eyes. But it was only momentarily. "Maybe it's just as well ..."

"What do you mean?" he said.

She laughed sarcastically in his face. "There ain't gonna be no 'chile."

"No child? There is no baby?" he asked, astonished.

"Oh you big, beautiful, stupid man."

"I'm ... sorry," said Mr. Hartley, suddenly shaken and confused. Apparently it had all been a ruse. There was a quiet sadness in the room.

Suddenly, Crazy Paul appeared. He wore a Santa's cap of red with a dingy white band. With his gray beard, he almost resembled Santa, with the exception of his thin, wiry frame. "Tol' ya' he was 'round here somewhere," said the Capt'n.

As he approached us from the far end of the room, I noticed the small sack he carried which looked like an old pillow case. It appeared to be empty and hung limp from his shoulder.

"What's in the sack," Luke asked him, being amused.

"Christmas presents of course!" he said, "It's Christmas time isn't it?"

"I don't see nothin' in there, that bag looks empty t' me."

"It's only empty to those who can't see," said Crazy Paul.

"Oh go on!" said Luke.

"True!" Crazy Paul replied.

"You ain't got nothin' in that bag I want," said Rachel. She lit another cigarette.

"I wouldn't be too sure of that missy!" he replied and laughed.

"Oh you're jus' a crazy ol' man. Wouldn't have nothin' if these here didn't take ya' in, feel sorry for ya'," she replied sarcastically.

"... Seems funny," I mused.

"What seems funny Pilgrim?" asked the Capt'n.

"Maybe Paul is the only one who is really sane among us," I said.

"Oh don't go on with those silly ideas of yours!"

"Can we say that for ourselves? In his own way, maybe Crazy Paul is better adjusted than any of us,"

"Crazy Paul?" said Luke, "he's as crazy as a loon!"

"Haven't you ever noticed that he's always smiling, always happy?" I went on.

"He don't know no better," said Rachel.

"He's a man of God," said Ruth, "he may be touched, but he's a man of God."

"And with the star of Bethlehem, came three wise men," said Crazy Paul, "and they brought gifts to the Christ Child."

"What did ya' bring us?" asked Luke. "Show us what's in that old sack?"

Crazy Paul smiled at him. "Soon. But first. I would like brandy," he said.

"Get him a brandy," said Luke.

"Yes. I would like to buy Paul a brandy," said Mr. Hartley.

"Thank you sir," said Crazy Paul.

"My pleasure," said Mr. Hartley.

Crazy Paul then winked his eye and downed the drink.

"Now, what's in the bag old man," said Luke.

Taking the sack from his shoulder, Crazy Paul laid it across the bar. It made a clinking sound like metal-against-metal, as if there were coins in the sack.

"How nice!" said Rachel, "he brought us some pennies! Maybe they're pennies from heaven huh?" She laughed.

"Leave him alone," said Mr. Hartley, "Obviously he has something planned we should let him finish."

"Well ... go on!" said Capt'n to Crazy Paul, "go on. What 'cha got in that bag?"

Crazy Paul pulled up his sleeve and then reached down deep into the old sack. He pulled out what looked like old coins and proceeded to hand one out to each of us.

"It's an old key!" said Rachel.

"Mine too!" Luke exclaimed. "It's jus' some old key!"

I looked down at mine. I was indeed and old door key, slightly rusted. I imagined it hadn't been used for years.

"Oh Paul," said Ruth, "what on earth would we do with these?" she asked him.

"Open doors," Crazy Paul replied.

"What doors?" said the Capt'n.

"Any door."

"You mean this key will open any door?"

"Anything that's locked," he said.

Oh Lord. He i-s-s Crazy!" said Rachel.

"Where did you get these?" asked the Capt'n, "you didn't get yourself in no trouble did ya'?"

"No, I found them, or I should say ... they came to me," said Crazy Paul.

"Well ... I don't need no damn key to some old door somewhere," said Rachel.

Suddenly it became clear to me, "Wait," I said, "I think I understand." I looked at Mr. Hartley. He nodded back. "Paul is speaking symbolically," I said.

"What?" said Luke.

"When he says that the keys will unlock any door, anything that's locked, he's speaking symbolically."

"What do you mean?" Luke asked.

Crazy Paul walked up to him and placed his hand on his shoulder. "You Luke, you could use this key to unlock the world around you, to unlock your ambition, your determination, maybe your imagination. You've been a talker and not a doer."

Then he turned to Rachel. "And you Rachel," he said to her, "you could unlock your heart. Don't you know girl, that love, real love, is the greatest possession one person can have, greater than all the riches in the world!"

"And you Mr. Hartley. You need to unlock your guilt. Brooding over your failures and drinking scotch whiskey will not help you to save the world from its problems. You need a clear head not a guilty conscious."

"And you Capt'n, you could unlock your mind! There's a lot things to learn in the world, but you'll never do it by bein' narrow-minded, stubborn old fool!"

"And Ruth ... poor Ruth. You're a good soul who doubts your own strengths. If you could only unlock your courage, you could turn your fear into devotion, and you loneliness into wisdom to share with others. Perhaps you would find happiness knocking at your door and singin' in your heart!"

Then, Crazy Paul stopped talking, and slowly, turned to me. "And you?" he said, "How would you use your key? You are the only one here who has really thought this thing through haven't you? You've sat up nights wondering about your existence, left your family in search of an answer. All these months you have sat and watched us, judged us, thought about these things. And what have you learned?"

I was stunned at his sudden insight, his clear line of reasoning. "... I don't know ... it seems the harder and longer I look, the more it escapes me."

"The meaning of life!" he said playfully. "Yes! That age old question, handed down from Moses, and from the great Pharaohs of Egypt, the Buddhists, Hindus and the great thinkers of Greece, Rome, and men of the Age of Reason. The Enlightenment. 'The meaning of life'! To reach into the heavens, up to and beyond the stars and caress the very hand of God! Hey?!?"

"And this key will unlock that answer?" I said, incredulous.

"... No ..." he said. "This will be hard for you. You are a deep thinker."

"Then ... why the key?"

"The key will not unlock that answer, but it may start you on your journey. Perhaps first you need to unlock faith!"

"Faith? Faith in myself? Or faith in the future?"

"Faith should not stand in the wisdom of men, but in the power of God!"

"I can't," I said, "I've tried. I have never been able to have faith in anything beyond the things I can see, hear, or touch."

"That is why the key will only open a door, but finding and keeping the Faith is a long and perilous journey. To believe in things intangible is the building block toward having great faith in the face of doubt and despair."

"But a faith in God? Whose God? Your God or mine?" I asked.

"It must be your God," he said, "although mine and yours are all one and the same."

"I don't know, it all seems so impossible. I've tried finding God, but I always end here ... confused and lost."

"You say your life has no purpose?"

"There must be a purpose for all of us, but what it is-I just don't know."

"There can be no purpose, no reason, no real understanding of life without a belief in God! It has been the foundation of mankind since he crawled out from his cave to gaze with wonder upon the starry heavens above. The Universe did not come from nothing."

"I've only to believe," I said.

"Faith!" said Crazy Paul.

"Yes ... if only to have faith! If only I could."

"It is easier than you think."

"Not for me. I've tried. I can't just ... just say the words."

"Of course not! You must feel it in your heart not in your mind!"

"How can I do that? How does man come to have faith in his God? How does he gain that faith for himself?" I was tormented.

"It does not happen suddenly. But starting with just a little hope and much determination, this small seed can grow into a great, enormous faith. And not just for great men, but perhaps even more for small men. Just as a farmer sews his crops, a man spreads this seed of faith; doing good deeds, raising children, caring for his family and maintaining friendships. With hard work, love and understanding, he nurtures them and watches them grow. And behold! The laughter of his children, and the accomplishments of the young men and women, the warmth of family, and the firm handshake of an old friend. And walking out from his garden of life, all these things a man sees, and in it, many of his prayers answered, his commitments, justified, confirmed and complete. No, having faith is not just a few simple words spoken, but a lifetime commitment, the slow and steady building of faith over a lifetime.

15

... Up in the sky, the geese were flying south. It was an autumn day and a fragrant breeze blew as I stood there on the patio of our new home, admiring the view. The air smelled of dried harvested corn, and pumpkins ripe on the vine.

It was Sunday, and inside the family room, I could hear my father watching the football game on TV. And in the kitchen, mother was preparing dinner. But I was bored. Since we had moved, I was slow to make new friends and was forced to spend time alone, alone with only my thoughts. I decided to take a walk.

In the backyard, on my way to the pond, I looked over the tall grass to see a group of black-eyed-Susan's growing on the near ridge. They stood tall, proudly in the noonday sun. And at their feet, grew a smattering of violets, strewn here and there, as if nature's hand had cast their seeds recklessly about. There was the buzzing of the bumble bee and the sound of crickets underneath my feet as I walked along. At the pond's edge, grew a tender green grass, pussy-willows, and a tall weeping willow tree. I sat down in the shade.

Looking down into the clear pool, I could see, in my reflection, the water bugs jumping as they became aware of my presence. And just below the water, there were tadpoles darting every which way. I heard the croaking of a frog. It was on the other side of the pond. It croaked again, and I scanned the water's edge for it in vain. But then, I saw it perched on top of a lilly pad. It's eyes were bugged-out, motionless.

Taking off my shoes and socks, I lowered my feet into the cool water, pulling my pant-legs up so as not to get them dirty. I giggled as I felt what had to be the tickling of the tadpoles on my toes. I thought about the three girls looking down into the ceramic planter bowl, on the coffee table, the one in Uncle Abner's home. His tormented life and eventual suicide was a horrible memory. It would probably take me years, or perhaps a lifetime to get over it, yet even to understand. Maybe I would never get over it and that memory would probably always be there to haunt me in my dreams or my private thoughts; like now, as I sat among the tall reeds, thinking about the three girls in the planter.

I looked back at the black-eyed-Susans on the ridge. How perfect they looked standing there. It was a glorious day. And somehow, in someway, I thought that things would be alright. I would be okay. Life would go on. Life would be good.

That night, Mom tucked me in. She kissed my forehead. Her kiss was soft and reassuring. How could she know how desperately I needed that show of love? I was convinced of her uncanny ability to know what I felt, what was on my mind, and how to sooth my pain, doubts and fears. She turned out the light and left me there in the darkness. I clutched my pillow and closed my eyes.

In the distance, out on the lonesome highway, I could hear the sound of a car traveling in the night, that quiet night. I wondered, just where it was going, perhaps being guided by the loving hand of God.

1985

... It was getting hard to breath. I started to loose feeling in my hands and I was hyperventilating badly. I thought I was going to pass out. Perhaps it was the lack of food and sleep. I walked to the bathroom on shaky legs and closed the door behind me. I rubbed my hands together to try to regain the feeling in them and strained for another breath. I turned on the water from the tap and let it run over my hands. I drew a breath. I looked into the mirror and saw my tortured face among the elegant fixtures in the room. What a strange person I had become. Drugs were destroying me and I couldn't stop.

Poets and Dreamers

1

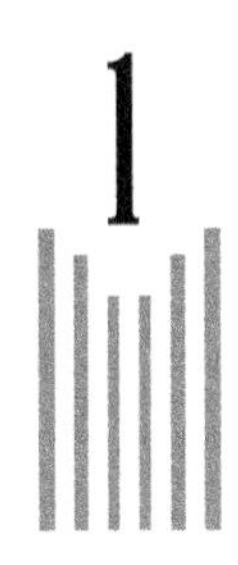

From high atop a hill, from the front porch of my house, these eyes of a sixteen year old took in the world around him. I could see houses in the distance, with their long white fences. On the farthest hill was an old barn that had turned to ruin; tattered and faded from years of neglect. Behind that barn was the great superhighway. In my mind that was the pathway to my future, and far from the anonymity of this small town community. Surely, I thought, that road led to success for those who were pure of spirit and purpose. For me, perhaps this was the world, the world as I knew it; simple, unassuming and fair - there for the taking. It was from this vantage point, that I would invent in my mind the great things I could accomplish in my life. As if from this hilltop throne, I could flex and test my imagination, my determination, my sheer will, as easily as one might survey the distant horizon. And as with any youth with his head in the clouds, any words to the contrary would be ill-spent in my shallow ears, for my proof was in the doing and in this, I was ready and willing to face the task at hand, the molding of my dreams into realities.

I was a young poet, smitten with the visions and emotions of youth, especially with those of young love. My objects of affection were tender, fair-haired girls for whom I would pen those perfect verses. I would sing to them my songs as any other young man might show his prowess by tight-rope-walking a fence rail. And in the act of committing these thoughts to words, I would daydream. Even now, the words to a song were running in my mind ...

"Short steps slowly down a hill
From my window sill
Her hair blowing in the breeze
Flowing as it please ...

Green eyes watching flowers sway
On a windy day
Deep sighs, signs of deep content
Lavishly they're spent ...

The moon and stars are there
As diamonds in her hair
Her heart pours love, and her beauty
Everywhere ..."

Someone was behind me. I turned around. John was standing there. We called him 'Fuzzy'. He was the bass-player in the band.

"I was just thinking about some lyrics," I said.

"Another song huh?"

"Yeah ..."

"... Wanna smoke?"

"Nah ..."

"What's on for tonight?" he asked. "It i-s-s Friday night."

"I've got a date. Man, you wouldn't believe this chick I met at the teen club last weekend ... Joanne. Her name is Joanne, and she's got the dreamiest green eyes."

"Where 'ya gonna take her?"

"I dunno ... just going over to her house."

"Gonna do the dirty deed huh?" Smoking his cigarette, trying to blow smoke rings .

"She's special," I rambled on.

"That's what you always say."

"It's different this time."

"Look, let's face it ... you're a dreamer."

"And what's wrong with that?" I asked.

We descended into the basement, into a room full of microphone cables and humming amplifiers. Mickey was bending over his guitar trying to copy the weak strains of music coming from the record player at his feet.

"Where's Duane?" I asked.

Mickey looked up puzzled. "I dunno ... upstairs."

"Duane!" I yelled at the ceiling.

Duane came running down the stairs. His boots, high-heeled boots, the kind the Beatles wore, made a clip-clop sound on the steps.

"Hey ... where you guy's been?" he asked, as he plopped down behind the drums. His long Beatle-bangs flopped down into his eyes.

"Romeo here's been writing more love sonnets for his new girl friend," teased Fuzzy.

"Stranger's in the night ..." Duane crooned in mockery. With the drum sticks in his hands, we revved up the plinks and plunks of our guitars into the hypnotic beat of a song. We were young men straining, bucking, searching to find the place where the music could take us, and chasing the dreams of stardom in that dusty old basement.

Mickey and I were sitting with Roy Buchman in his old 'Buick Eight'. Roy Buchman - probably the best guitar player in the city. He was a local legend. We were sprawled out on the back seat, waiting to go into the recording studio with him. Imagine ... recording a song with Roy Buchman!

"Man I'm hungry," Roy said, fondling the guitar that lay beside him on the front seat. There was no guitar case, only the guitar itself, perched up next to him in the passenger seat.

"Well, why don't you get something to eat?" I asked.

He looked at me in the rear view mirror and frowned. "I think I'll eat later ..." He plucked a string on the guitar and took a long drag on his cigarette. I was amazed that someone with his level of celebrity status would be driving an old car. And be hungry. How curious I thought. "Tell me again ... how you know Steve Winter?" he asked me.

"Well you see," I replied, "our band won a contest on WFAB and the prize was to record a record. Mr. Winter, he was the one who arranged it all."

"He's the money man," said Mickey.

"The 'money man'," said Roy to himself, savoring the words. He laughed, and then took another drag off his cigarette.

A car pulled up beside us. It was a big brand new car. Steve Winter got out and stood up. He was tall, a big powerful man. He was smoking a cigar. Duane and Fuzzy jumped out the other side.

"Okay ... you guys ready to go?" Roy asked us.

"Sure! Where's the studio?" I asked. We were all expecting a big new building. We were standing in front of a small grocery store. It turned out it was back in the alley. Halfway down, past the trash and garbage cans, we entered a door which led upstairs. The studio was over top of the store.

Inside, it was not what we had expected. It was a dingy little room with old rugs over the floor and walls. Over in the corner was the tape deck.

"Just put your guitars down here boys and tune up," said Roy.

"Now what's the name of that song you wanna do?" asked Steve Winter.

"'She's Just a Girl," Mickey said.

"That's right," he said, "'She's Just a Girl ... I like that song ... yeah I like that one ... do that one."

He and Roy walked over to the other side of the room where a technician was checking the tape recording equipment.

"Well, what do you think?" Mickey asked me.

"Hey, let's just go along with the whole thing and see what happens," I said.

One of Duane's cymbals crashed to the floor. He had accidentally knocked it over. The technician looked up in disgust. "Be careful there boy! Those microphones are expensive!" he yelled.

"Are you sure this drummer can play?" I over heard Steve Winter ask Roy. He just mumbled something.

Meanwhile, I turned to the others. "There's no need to be nervous. Just play the song the way we rehearsed it," I said.

"No problem," said Duane.

We each plunked on our instrument to get the levels. Roy setup his guitar to play along with us. I was excited at the prospect of playing with him. We went over the chords several times so he could learn the song. Then when the engineer was ready, we started to play. Roy played the intro. Then Mickey sang ...

"She's just a girl who loves me
And I love her ....
There's nothing fancy about her ...
She's my kind of girl ...

You know I'm glad to have her
And I tell her so ...
I'd do anything for her
Yes anything at all ...

She's just a girl ...

And I love her ...
She's just a girl ..."

When we finished, the last chord trailed off to silence as we waited for the tape machine to stop.

"Not bad! Not bad!" Steve said. "What do you think?" he asked Roy, who looked at Mickey and then smiled. "Whose it about? You?"

"Well ... it's about my girl friend," Mickey said.

"Your girl friend!" Roy laughed. Steve laughed too.

Mickey felt embarrassed and angry. "Hey, if you don't like the song-"

"Whoa! Hey! It's fine ... its okay ... " said Steve as he chewed on the end of his stubby cigar. "What's the other song? We need another song..."

"She's a Funny Girl", I said.

Steve was amused. "So we have 'She's Just a Girl'", and now "She's a Funny Girl!" Steve exclaimed. " Which is it?!" He chuckled. "I guess this is about y-o-u-r girlfriend?"

"... No ... Not really," I replied.

We readied ourselves and then started to play. For some reason, Roy did not play this time. It was just us. I sang ...

"Though she said to ... call her
...I know I will ...
Even though she won't be there ...
... I'll call her still ...
... Yeah ...

'Cause she's a funny girl ...
... she'll leave you hurt and then she'll never care ...

You all think I'm ... some fool
... To care for her ...
Even though she may seem cruel ...
... I still need her ...
.... Yeah ..."

Duane played a slight drum roll before I sang the bridge.

"I give her my love but she don't care ...
I give her my love but she just laughs when I'm not there ...

"Though she said to ... call her
...I know I will ...
Even though she won't be there ...
... I'll call her still ...
... Yeah ...

'Cause she's a funny girl ...
... She's a funny girl ...
... Yeah she's a funny girl ..."

Again, we were quiet and waited for the tape to stop. I noticed that Steve and Roy both looked unimpressed.

Then Steve spoke up, "Not bad, not bad ... I tell you what ... here's some money." He handed me a five. "You boys go on down to the store and get some candy and sodas. Come back in a while. We've got some work to do."

We went downstairs, back out into the alley. "I hope there's no rats out here," I said, teasing.

"Hey, I ain't afraid of no rats," said Mickey, as we walked out to the street. We turned the corner and suddenly Fuzzy ran into two roughnecks. One was taller. "Hey, dude! Watch where you goin'!" he said.

"Sorry," Fuzzy said.

The two strangers looked us over. "Sorry huh? I don't think so," the shorter one said. He pushed Fuzzy back and he fell to the sidewalk.

"Hey. You didn't have to do that," said Mickey.

"Oh yeah?" the tall one said walking up to him.

"I mean .... what's the hassle man?" Mickey tried to reason with him.

"I don't like runnin' into hippie punks like you. That's what!"

"Look man ... we don't want any trouble. Ok?" said Duane.

"Was I talkin' to you?"

Duane looked down and remained motionless. "... No ..." he finally said in a low voice.

"What did you say punk?" The tall one sneered, "I didn't hear ya."

Duane shifted his feet but still looked down. "... Nothin' ..."

"Move back in there!" the tall one told us, pointing to the alley. We turned around and walked back into the alleyway. The short one remained behind to keep lookout. "Now what'cha got?" He asked us.

"What do you mean?" asked Mickey.

"Don't play dumb ... 'gib me that watch."

Mickey looked down at his watch.

"Come on punk!" he sneered.

He unfastened the watch and held it out to him. He pulled it out of his hand and examined it. "Shit! This is a 'Mickey Mouse' watch!" he said laughing and threw it on the ground. ""Gib me some money. Now!" he yelled. No one said a word. Suddenly he pushed Fuzzy down into some garbage cans. The lid went rolling away in the clatter. He grabbed me by the shirt and threw me up against the wall. My heart was pounding.

"Hey! A real punk! You got any money?" he hissed in my face. I felt the five dollar bill in my pocket. I looked over at the others in horror, speechless. I pulled out the crumpled bill and handed it over.

"A five! Is that all you got?" He punched me in the face and I toppled over into the boxes and trash. I could hear his foot steps as he ran out to the street.

"Hey. Are you all right?" Mickey asked, bending down over me. I felt warm blood as it trickled from my nose. I looked out at the street. They were gone. "Are you sure you're ok?" he asked again.

"Yeah ... I'm ok." I said with resignation.

He helped me up onto shaky knees as we all stood there, leaning against the wall trying to catch our breath.

"Why didn't we do something?" said Mickey, angrily, "There were four of us."

"Let's just be glad we didn't get hurt," I said.

"Not hurt?" Mickey scoffed incredulously.

"Well, it could have been worse ... I think my nose has almost stopped bleeding."

Upstairs, in the studio, we could hear Mickey's song playing. As we entered the room, other musicians had shown up. One playing the drums and the other was playing the bass along with our song. We were surprised and a little insulted.

"What's this?" asked Fuzzy.

"What's going on?" added Duane.

"Now boys ... don't get excited. We're just trying something," Steve told us.

"Hey! You're replacing our parts on the tape!" said Mickey.

"Just the drums and bass," said Roy. "It needs to be stronger".

Steve noticed the blood on my shirt. "What's this?" The attention turned to my bloody nose.

"Some guys robbed us in the alley. They took the five dollars you gave me and punched me in the face."

"Are you sure you're ok?"

"Yeah ... I'm all right."

"Should I call the police?"

"No, there's nothing we can do ... But wait! What about our tape? You never said that we wouldn't play our own instruments."

He grabbed me by the arm and pulled me aside. "Look, I don't want you to get the wrong idea. I like the songs. I just want it to sound right. That's all."

"But we want to play the music ourselves. Isn't that the deal?"

He took a long drag on his cigar and blew the smoke out. "No. The deal is ... I'm paying the money and it's going to be the way I want ... understand?"

We stepped onto the curb in front of the '007 Club'. My old childhood friend Andy was among us, but he wasn't up to this task-he was going to assume the role of our 'manager'. "Look, I'm not sure about this ... I've never been the manager of a rock band before," he said.

"You can do it," I said. He looked into the doorway of the club. He was nervous. I continued the pep-talk. "All you have to do is talk to the bar manager. Tell him-"

Andy interrupted me, "I know what to tell him. We've been over and over it." He took a deep breath and looked into the doorway again.

"Go on in ... we'll wait out here."

"Ah, why don't you guys come in with me. I mean, what's the big deal?"

"Look you're supposed to be our manager."

"All right! Let's all go in!" said Mickey. We followed him in the front door.

Inside, there was the smell of stale beer and cigarette smoke. There were only a few customers scattered around the room. A waitress came to greet us. She was good looking, wearing a short skirt and fishnet stockings with a hole up on one thigh. This was a sleazy nightclub. "Can I help you boys?" she asked us.

"Ah ... Yes," said Andy, "I ... I mean, these guys are in a band and I would like to talk to the manager about an audition."

"How old are you guys?"

"We're eighteen," said Fuzzy.

"Eighteen hey?," she said with a laugh. I thought she was going to ask us for an ID. "Well ... all right, wait here."

"I'll go with you," Andy asserted himself suddenly.

"The rest of you wait here," she told us. We watched them walk to the back of the club. Andy talked with an older looking guy who kept looking our way.

After a few minutes, he rejoined us.

"Well?" I asked impatiently.

"Okay. Go out and get you're stuff-you got an audition!" he said.

"Way t'go!" Mickey exclaimed, mussing his hair.

We started setting up our equipment. Some customers were coming in. They sat down right across from the bandstand; two couples. They watched us with interest as we struggled with our amplifiers. We were feeling a little nervous.

One of the girls at the table singled-out Fuzzy. "When do you guys start?" She asked.

"In just a few minutes," he replied.

"We'd better leave soon," her date joked, as the rest of them laughed.

The bandstand was a raised a few feet off the floor. Although it made us the center of attention, no one in the room looked our way. We were largely being ignored. "What'cha wanna do?" I asked the others.

"Let's do 'Misery' by the Beatles," said Duane. The moment had come. He started the count. One... two... three... four ...

"... The world is treating me bad ... Misery ..."

To my horror, I sang totally out of key! I had started to play my guitar in the wrong key! Especially since the word 'misery' was being sung totally out of tune, it was actually hilarious. The front table was rolling on the floor with laughter. I was humiliated.

"Damn it! Let's start again!" I shouted to the others. We started the song again. This time, I was on key, but things still didn't sound right.

When we finished, there was no applause. Some at the bar went on drinking and flirting with the waitress, while the table in front continued to make rude remarks. The audition was turning out to be a disaster.

When the set was over, we simply packed up our equipment and headed out the door. We knew it wasn't good, and didn't even have the nerve to talk the manager. We just left.

We piled into Fuzzy's old Chevy. No one said a word for a few minutes. The only sound you could hear was the faint music from the jukebox that was now playing from within the club.

"Man ... it was all so weird," Mickey said.

"What happened?" said Duane, "We sounded like shit!"

"Y-o-u sounded like shit!" said Fuzzy.

"Oh fuck you man!"

"Come on guys!" I said, "It was just an off-night. That's all ... just an off-night."

I looked at Andy to get his reaction. "Fuck it Man!" Andy exclaimed. "This ain't the only gin-mill in town!"

"Fuckin'a man!" Fuzzy replied "I didn't dig this sleazy joint anyway!"

4

Time passed. We continued the struggle for success, learning how to play music and perform as a band. But there were also changes. We added a piano player named Mike. Sometimes we called him 'Magic Fingers'. Fuzzy left the band and we had tried several bass players without success, so I gave up the guitar and took up the bass guitar. But the major change was that Mickey was replaced with Freddie on guitar. Sometimes we called him 'Fast Freddie'.

And, we finally got a steady gig. It was at a bar called 'Sal's Place' - a small, out-of-the-way, uptown bar and not one of the regular hot-spots. But it was a steady gig. The air was hot and cigarette smoke streamed up through the lone spot light that hung from the ceiling.

From the dingy little platform of a stage, we played our music with determined looks and sweaty brows. After each song, the audience, mainly college kids, would cheer and shout for more. They were loud, boisterous and drunk. It was a Friday night and everyone wanted to party. At the end of set, we headed for the cooler end of the room. As I walked past a nearby table, a girl grabbed my hand.

"Excuse me ... what's your guitar player's name?"

"Freddie, 'Fast Freddie'," I replied smiling, looking at her and then her friends sitting round their bottle-strewn table.

"Would you guys like to join us?" she asked.

"Sure! Let me get a beer and we'll be right back."

The rest of the boys saw my encounter and were grinning ear to ear as I approached them at the bar.

"Who are they?" asked Freddie, looking past me, back at their table.

"I don't know ... but one of them wanted to know your name. They invited us to join them."

We swaggered up to the girl's table. "Are you Freddie?" one of them asked.

"Yeah ... I'm Freddie," he said as he pulled up a chair.

"My name is Brenda. We're from Dunbar up the street." Dunbar was an all girl's Catholic school.

The girl who had grabbed my hand, pulled me down to a chair next to hers. "I'm Carol," she said.

"Is this your first time here?" I asked.

"Oh no, we come here a lot. You guys are great!" She said. "How long have you been playing together?"

"About two years."

"We have a surprise for you!" Brenda squealed, turning to Freddie. "We had a contest and you won! We have elected you to be 'Mr. Bubbles'!"

"Well great! ... What does that mean?" he asked.

"You have been selected to take a bubble bath with the girl of your choice!"

"Really?" Freddie exclaimed, astonished.

"Really!"

"You can come too," Carol said, squeezing my hand.

"When?" I asked.

"Well ... how about tonight?" Carol asked, looking at Brenda for encouragement. "We'll sneak you into the dormitory through a side door."

So, later after the gig, Brenda, Carol, Freddie and I pulled his car slowly into the campus driveway. The old brown building stood high among the tall trees that dotted the courtyard.

Brenda briefed us. "Now, wait over by the side door of the cafeteria, by those garbage cans, and we'll let you in. Just remember ... be quiet."

The girls entered the front door of the building. Freddie and I walked cautiously over to the side door and waited. Freddie lit a cigarette and took a drag. "Put it out!" I hissed, "Someone will see us!"

"Okay man, don't worry ... it'll be cool," He said, crushing out the orange glow of the cigarette with the sole of his shoe.

The wind was blowing through the trees. It was late October and dead leaves swirled around the corner of the old building. I pulled my collar up to fend off the chill.

Then, the door started to open. First with a jerk, and then carefully, so as not to make a sound. It wasn't Carol or Brenda. It was someone else. We could barely make her out in the darkness. " ... Be quiet and follow me ..." she whispered.

Inside, the tables and chairs were lined-up in neat rows in the cafeteria. The light from the hallway was gleaming on the linoleum floor, and you could hear the sound of a TV from the far end of the hall. We followed her into the hallway when she motioned for us to enter a doorway into a stairwell.

"Who is that out there?" Freddie whispered. "It's just Mrs. Mable. She's the 'house mother'. She's watching her late night movies ... It's okay, she never hears a thing."

We followed her up the stairs, knowing that any minute, we might be caught in this folly. As we reached the next floor, we entered the hallway looking both ways for anyone who might be walking by. It was deserted. "You go in there," the girl told me. I opened the door and quickly entered, closing it carefully behind me. The room was dark except for a light that shown from the far corner. A stereo played quietly. I walked over and sat on the edge of the clean, neatly made bed.

Suddenly, a figure appeared in the light from a doorway. I could see it was Carol. She had changed her clothes. She wore an old pair of cutoffs and a tee shirt. "Hi," she said, trying to cover up a little nervousness.

"Hi ... I can't believe I'm here."

"Don't worry. You won't get caught." She moved closer. In the shadows I could see the contour of her body in the light.

She removed her tee-shirt. Her breasts were firm and white, contrasted by a late summer tan. We made love. The bed rocked wildly. I was sure someone would hear us.

Afterwards, we lay in the silence with only the soft sound of the stereo and the occasional sound of wind outside.

Finally, she spoke. "Wanna smoke?"

"Sure." We both lit a cigarette.

"Well ... what are your plans? ... I mean ... are you in college?" she asked me.

"No ... I dropped out of college ... I have plans with my music."

"Hey, you guys are pretty good, but do you think you can really make it big in show business?"

Suddenly, the image of myself as the rising rock star seemed silly. After all, she was probably a rich girl. And I? Perhaps I was just a past time; an adventure, something to joke about after class, or a topic of light conversation in the cafeteria. She would marry some rich guy. Hers was a bright future and maybe ... just maybe, I would get to be on the cover of the Rolling Stone magazine.

"Here, play me a song," she said as she handed me her guitar. It was an inexpensive classical guitar, the kind that was stylish for young girls to take to college. I placed it on my knee and plucked the strings one by one to check the tuning. I sang to her...

"... The leaves that fall help me recall the summer's end ...
Now that the fall is here to call I'll tell you friend ...
It's a long hard winter they say ...
So don't throw your love away ...

... Now people here and people there will say your wrong ...
But without her love there's not enough to keep you strong ...
It's a long hard winter they say ...
So don't throw your love away ...

... It's a long hard winter they say ...
So don't throw your love away ..."

Suddenly, there was an abrupt knock on the door! "Carol! Open this door! There's someone in there. I can hear them!"

"It's Mrs. Mable!" whispered Carol, as she jumped up to find her clothes.

"How can I get out!" I said in desperation. I looked over to the window.

"Open this door immediately!" Mrs. Mable demanded.

"You must get out of here right now!" Carol told me. She shoved me toward the window. "I don't care how. Just do it! Please!"

I opened the window. There was a nearby tree which made the ten-foot drop seem almost possible. I climbed out the window with my shirt in hand, clutching a tree limb. I felt a sharp pain in my ankle as I hit the leaf covered ground. With my heart pumping wildly, I limped over to a clump of bushes. I laid there out of breath, watching for head lights or the sound of a siren, but there was nothing. The wind rustled the leaves over my body as I gazed at the stars above. I wondered where 'Fast Freddie' was.

I showed up early the next night. I hadn't heard from Freddie at all. Duane was looking down into his beer, smiling slightly, as I told him about what had happened the night before.

Mike appeared at the doorway of the club and walked over to our table. "We'll how'd it go stud?" he asked me, mockingly.

"Man! I almost got caught right there in her room!"

"Really? Kiss and tell!" He teased. Suddenly, he realized that I wasn't kidding. "... Well, before you tell me about it ... I have some good news!" he beamed.

Freddie came in the door grinning in his casual way. "Hey man! ... I heard ol' lady Mable almost caught you and Carol. I heard that Carol was put on suspension or something like that."

"Wait a minute!" Mike interrupted. "Let me tell ya what happened last night after you guys left." He got our attention. "Last night, out in the parking lot, this guy came up to me. He said he was an agent. He heard us play and he thought we were pretty good. He wants to talk to us. Here's his card."

Freddie grabbed it from Mike's hand. He read it aloud, "... Bryan Elliot, Mystic Records."

"Let me see that," I said, grabbing the card from his hands. "Far out!"

"Yeah ... and he wants us to come over to his office. Tonight!"

"Hey! But what about Andy?" I said, "he's our manager!" I insisted.

"Look ... Andy's our pal but he can't do anything for us now. This is the big time man," said Mike.

"He's right," said Freddie. "I'm sure he'd understand."

"Hey, let's go see what he has to offer. I mean ... what have we got to lose?"

We all agreed. We decided to hail a cab. The address was just an old apartment building. Upstairs we found the office door labeled 'Mystic Records'. We knocked and the door opened. There stood a man in his early thirties, with horned-rim glasses, short and rather normal looking.

"Make yourselves at home," he said. "I've got a phone call ... I'll be right with you."

On the table next to his desk were a pile of magazines - Billboard, Variety. On the wall adjacent was a map of world with stick-pins placed randomly. Bryan looked us over casually, as he spoke quietly on the phone. Then he placed the phone on the hook and turned to face us.

"I'm pleased to meet you guys. I must say, I've been down at Sal's Place and I thought you were sensational!"

"Thanks ..." we said in unison.

"I'm a talent agent. I also own a small record label ... I think we could have a mutually beneficial relationship."

There was a pause as his words ringed in our ears.

"What are all these pins in the map for?" I asked, pointing to the wall map.

"These are places where my records are being played. We're getting some air-play in Japan right now."

"Do you sell many records?" Mike asked.

"I've never even heard of Mystic Records," Freddie added.

"Well ... it's a small operation, but we're beginning to make some substantial sales." He cleared his throat and readjusted himself in his chair.

"Why did you ask us up?" I asked. I was being a little impatient. It was time to get to the point. We had to play that night and didn't have much time.

"I would like to manage you guys. Maybe make a record."

We looked at each other. Those were magic words.

"Of course I want twenty percent, an even five way split. What do you think?"

"Oh yeah. Sure." I spoke up, and then looked around for approval. Everyone nodded.

"Good! Then you would sign a contract? How old are you boys anyway?"

"Almost nineteen," said Freddie.

"Is that like eighteen and a half?" Bryan said, amused.

"No ... like nineteen," said Mike, a little annoyed.

"Good!" said Bryan. He looked at his watch,

"I guess you boys have to get back to the club. Let me see ... I seem to be a little short on cash," he said, as he searched through his baggy pants pockets for our cab fare. I noticed the white socks he wore with his black loafers. Seriously out of vogue.

We finally we got a break. Maybe this would be our ticket to stardom.

The Stairway to Heaven

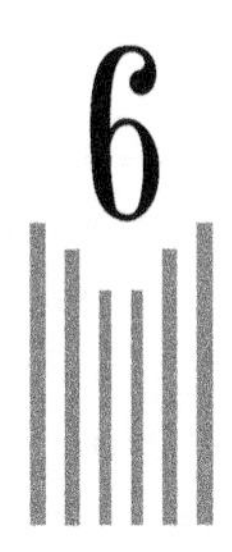

Stylish. We were stylish. We wore bell-bottom pants with freshly starched flowered shirts and new boots. Gone were the dusty floors and dirty ceilings of Sal's Place. They were replaced with clean carpets, fancy lamp fixtures and a long oak bar. And there were young men-the cream of the college campuses, holding imported beer bottles and glasses of sparkling wine. This was the scene at Sedgewick's, a well-to-do bar on the fringes of Georgetown. It was our first night. In essence, another audition.

No sooner had we set up and Bryan arrived. "I know you boys are going to do fine tonight. I can feel it!" he exclaimed. He was excited and nearly out of breath, excited. "By the way, here's a list of radio stations that are playing your record 'Why is the Sky?'... I've got it here somewhere." He shuffled through his papers in earnest. "Ah ... here it is ... only four stations but we're gaining momentum ... I can feel it!. I can just feel it in my bones!"

"You always say that," said Freddie. We all laughed and all gathered around looking down at the small list.

"We got eleven calls from the listeners on WGTR and all but two really liked it!" Bryan beamed.

"What did they have to say about it?" I asked, "the ones who didn't like it."

"I don't know. Does it really matter? ... most of them liked you and, after all ... you're on the air!"

"I was just wondering what someone wouldn't like about it ... a little feedback?"

"Okay. Both people who didn't like it said that they thought it was 'childish bubblegum pop music'."

"Great!" I said disappointed.

"Well ... it i-s-s sort'a childish," teased Freddie.

"It's supposed to be about innocent youth!" I protested.

"Tell that to the public okay. They don't know that."

"Look boys," said Bryan, "remember ... you're never going to please everyone and you might as well accept that now. You will have to get used to criticism as well as praise."

It was getting close to starting time as we drained the last of our beers. The place was crowded with many young couples talking, listening to the jukebox, drinking beer and smoking cigarettes. We took the stage and tuned our guitars. I looked up to see Bryan frowning but he looked nervous.

We started to play. Our music filled the room with such power; not weak and strained as before. We were a better band, stronger, and much more polished. And the song was gritty, soulful. After that song, we played another with such confidence, that soon, the dance floor was full. At the end of that set, there was thunderous applause. Bryan was leaning on the bar. His frown had turned to a smile. He wouldn't have to tell us that we passed the audition, we knew this job was ours.

Later, at the end of the night, after many beers and much congratulations, we packed up the car. The others left but Andy and I stayed behind.

We were the last ones at the bar, except one older gentleman who sat a few bar stools down. "And how are you boys tonight?" he asked us. He was very drunk.

"... Fine," I replied.

"I thought your music was terrific!"

"Thanks ..."

"I'm interested in guys like you. I'm sort of ... a talent scout."

"Who do you work for?" asked Andy.

"Nobody! I work for myself. Oh screw 'em all! I work alone," he mumbled.

I turned away and finished my drink. It was closing time and we had to go.

"I tell ya what," said the man, "Let's go get another drink and talk it over."

"Sure," said Andy, without hesitating.

But it was late and all the bars were closing. "Where are we going?" I wondered.

"Oh hell ... let's go to my place!"

What an odd situation I thought. A perfect stranger asking us home for a drink. Maybe he was a talent scout. Maybe he could help us. But then we already had a management contract. I was a little drunk and not really thinking clearly.

He lived in Georgetown. When we got to his townhouse, he loosened his tie and took off his jacket. "Can I get you a drink? ... What'll it be?" he asked us.

"Anything will be fine," we said in unison.

He reached into the cabinet for a bottle of booze. "You know ... I was at the Officer's Club at Quantico earlier tonight, a fine group of young men. Do you know what I mean? You two look like fine young men too."

What an odd comparison, I thought! Neither Andy nor myself were military types. "What's your name?... Andy ... that's right ... Andy! Would you get that bottle from the bottom shelf?"

As Andy bent down, the man caressed him on the ass! Andy jumped up with a start and backed up a few steps. The man continued as though nothing had happened.

"Here ... let's make rum and cokes. Everyone likes rum and cokes!"

When he handed us our drinks, we stepped into the living room. The strange man sprawled out on the couch and inserted a cigarette into a strange-looking cigarette holder. But oddly, he didn't light the cigarette. He used it to make gestures as he spoke. "Yes, you do appear to be some fine young men," he continued.

I felt uncomfortable. "You know ... it is a little late. Maybe we should leave now," I said. Andy and I glanced at the front door but did not dare move. "Hey, really ... maybe some other time."

"Nonsense were just getting started!" the man exclaimed as he finally lit his cigarette. Then, he leaned over as if he was going to whisper to me. Instead, he kissed my ear. I felt his wet tongue and I pulled away.

I was surprised, repulsed. "I really think we should be going," I stammered.

"Oh no," he said, "I hope I'm not making you nervous. I know. How about some fresh drinks. I'll get them. Wait right here!" He went into the kitchen.

We became desperate and rushed out the front door. I ran across the street to the corner and down the sidewalk. Looking back over my shoulder, I could see the shadow of the man in the doorway now watching us. There were headlights approaching in the cool night mist as I raced between two parked cars. The on coming car screeched it's brakes, almost hitting me. On the other side of the street, I ran down the sidewalk, dodging low tree branches. I could hear Andy's footsteps behind me. At the next corner, I climbed a small terrace and fell to the ground exhausted. Andy fell to his knees beside me. We sat in silence for a brief time.

"... Man," I said, "the band has one of it's biggest nights yet, a big success, and what do we do? We go home with a screaming gay guy!"

"How in the hell did you meet him anyway?" said Andy.

"It was your idea! You were the one to agree to another drink! He said he was a talent scout."

Andy laughed.

"You would think it's funny!" I said, not amused.

"Who gives a shit."

"I do. I mean ... hey, I'm trying to make it in this town. I can't afford to look like some naive jerk."

"It was just some dumb old gay guy," he said and then laughed again.

"Andy ... you have to promise me one thing. You can't let anyone know about this. I mean no one!"

"Hey, nothing happened!"

"I know, but ... you gotta promise," I insisted.

He looked at me in earnest. "Yeah, okay. I promise. Not a word." He turned his face skyward. He laughed again.

We woke up on the floor of Bryan's apartment early in the morning. We were to be professionally photographed and our hair had to be squeaky clean and our eyes clear and bright. Wearily, we drug ourselves one at a time into the tiny bathroom to shave and shower.

On the way to the session, we stopped by a small corner five-and-dime for a quick cup of coffee and cigarettes. Then, onto the studio which was atop an old brownstone only a few blocks away. It was being renovated into a night club.

As we entered the first floor, we were introduced to a distinguished looking gentleman. He was looking over the blue prints and we assumed he was an architect. We proceeded to the second floor.

The photographer greeted us at the stairwell that led upward to the third floor which was dirty and strewn with building supplies. Only one corner was cleaned up with large rolls of backdrops and a few towering lights. "Relax. I want you guys to be yourselves," he told us. "Is this your first professional photography session?"

"Well ... I guess," I said. We had never had a professional take our pictures before.

"We will just start by sitting on the floor. That's it! Now move closer. Now we're rolling!" He said cheerfully. He arranged the lights and then took a few shots. Then, many at a time. I smiled. Freddie smiled at Duane. Mike frowned. Freddie frowned back, all the time, the camera clicked and whizzed. Then, the clicking stopped.

"We need something different," said the photographer.

"What do you mean?" asked Bryan.

"I need something ... something different. These guys are just too normal."

"I don't know ... I'm not too sure I agree with you," Bryan said wearily.

"I've got it!" said the photographer. "Who wants to take off his clothes?"

"What do you mean take off his clothes?" Bryan asked, surprised.

"Just down to his underwear ... I mean it's worth a try ... huh?"

We looked at each other. "To hell with it. I'll do it!" said Freddie. Over in the doorway, I was surprised to see the gentleman from downstairs. He was watching intently as Freddie turned around and pealed off his jeans.

The next series of shots were of Freddie hiding behind the rest of us or running around behind us. It felt awkward, but we hung in there like real troopers. After all, maybe this was what show business was all about.

"Okay! Now we've got something," said the photographer. "How about some more of you guys taking your clothes off?"

I remembered the gay stranger from the other night, and turned to the others in horror. "Look! We don't have to do this!" I exclaimed. "We came here for publicity pictures not for ... for this!" I exclaimed. I was becoming visibly shaken.

"He's right," said Bryan, " ... let's call it a day. We've got enough to work with."

"Okay ... sure ..." the photographer replied, "Hey, I didn't mean anything weird. I just wanted something different that's all."

As we left the building, Bryan stopped us on the front steps to give us some encouragement. "I'm sorry if things got out of hand. But ... this guy has a good reputation as a photographer."

"Yeah ... and that ain't all," said Mike laughing.

"I dunno Bryan," I said shaking my head.

"What do you mean?" he asked.

"We're losing control." I replied.

"Control of what?"

"I think from now on we should have more control over things. I mean, we're creative with ideas of our own," I said.

"You don't think I'm doing a good job?"

"No. It's not that. People are going to make some decisions for us. I know that. But we have to have a say in what we do. Even though we may make a lot of mistakes along the way, it's important to us."

After all, it seemed like we had to make our own dreams come true. Me and Duane. Mike and Fast Freddie. We were the boys in the band. And, in our own way, it was us against the world. It seemed as though at times we were holding a candle, that faint glimmer of hope, against a hurricane, trying desperately to keep it lit.

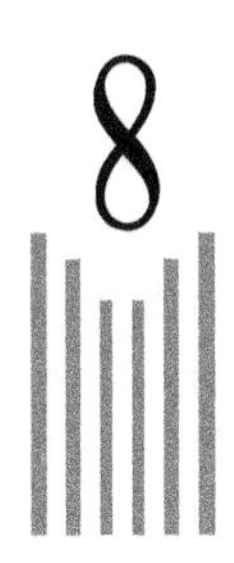

These were troubled times and Washington DC was a focal point. There was a 'Moratorium', which brought thousands of peace marchers from all over the country, the city was under siege. Demonstrators against the war in Vietnam. With many protestors lacking food and shelter, local restaurants and nightclubs that were sympathetic to their cause, opened their doors, offering the marchers floor space to sleep. A curfew had been enforced to restrict traffic after mid-night. National Guard tanks and jeeps were a common sight on the outskirts of the city. It was as if the war had come home.

One day I was driving up Embassy Row when I saw a mob of angry protestors ahead. They were heaving bricks and bottles into the front windshield of a police car which was desperately backing-up, coming directly at me! I pulled over onto the sidewalk and continued driving, just missing the broken glass and flying debris. When I got to the end of the street I pulled off the sidewalk, back onto the road.

When I reached the TV studio I saw Fast Freddie and Mike leaning against a car in the parking lot. I pulled into an adjacent slot.

"Hey! Where you been?" asked Freddie.

"Man! You wouldn't believe what just happened! I was in the middle of a demonstration! I mean they trashed a police car and I was right there!"

"Relax!" said Mike with a giggle. "Glad you're okay! ... Wanna a hit?" He held out a joint.

"Yeah sure" I said as I reached for the small, sticky thing. I took a long toke and then coughed violently.

"Too much for ya huh?" Mike teased.

"It's harsh!"

"Come on, we gotta find out what's goin' on inside," said Freddie.

We entered the back door of the studio. Duane was just finishing setting up his drums. I could see Bryan talking to some people over by one of the two huge TV cameras.

He turned and saw us step onto the stage. "There you are!" he exclaimed, rushing over. "Now look, here's the plan. You guys play 'Why is the Sky' at the beginning of the show and then come up and sit down on stage with the host. You will be asked a few questions and after a commercial break you will get up and play 'Love is'. Got it? Simple!"

We were all a little nervous because, other than a simple teen-dance show, we had never been on TV like this before. This time, there were no young kids and dancers, it was a studio audience and we were there to render a performance.

The audience was starting to file in and it was becoming noisy and disorganized. A makeup girl came by, looked us over and brushed a little powder on our faces. She was friendly and tried to cheer us up, but I felt light-headed from the pot I had smoked out in the parking lot.

Within moments, this was a scene of utter confusion. Suddenly we were on. We started playing. The two huge cameras wheeled in close. As I looked into one lens, I knew it could see every move I made. I tried to ignore it. I smiled. I was singing live on TV! ...

... "Why ... is the sky?
I've got to ask you why
Cause you look very special there
With the wind in your hair ...

You ... with the clouds in your eyes
You know they're twice their size
And the world is something more
Than I had ever thought before ...

Come on girl cause I want to take you!
Come on girl cause I want to wake you!
Come on girl cause I want to make you!
You know I want to take you,
You know I've got to take you there ..."

As we struck the last chord, a stagehand held up an 'APPLAUSE' sign behind the camera. The crowd clapped moderately, but I heard a few boos and rude remakes from the back of the room.

We put down our instruments and made our way up to the host stage. My heart was racing and my knees were weak. I took a seat right next to the host, in a setup similar to the Johnny Carson Tonight Show. The camera focused in for a close-up.

"That was fabulous!" the host exclaimed. "We'll be right back after this message!"

As we switched to a commercial break, the room once again turned to pandemonium. The camera men moving cameras. The makeup girl came up and made over the host as the a sound man adjusted the overhead microphones. "Get ready everyone!" said a voice from somewhere.

Suddenly, again we were back on the air. A camera came near. The heat from the lighting was intense and I began to perspire as the host continued. "Okay! You guys really sound great. Where are you currently appearing in town?" he asked.

He was asking me! The camera was pulling in close. My throat was becoming dry; my head still numb from the pot. It was hard to start talking but my lips moved, "Well ... we have been appearing at Sedgewick's in Georgetown every Sunday night."

"I see ... great place ... Sedgewick's. I also understand that the song you guys just played is out on a single. 'Why is the Sky'!" He held up a copy of the record. "This is the Mystic label? Is that right? Mystic Records?"

"Yeah ... Mystic ... it's a local label," I replied.

The host continued, "Your sound reminds me of ... well ... of psychedelic rock. Can you explain this sound for us?"

Again, I was on the spot and I was horrified. I had never thought about what style of music we played. My mind was racing, searching for an answer, something to say. I looked at the host. He too was sweating, nervous but smiling, and waiting for me to respond. The camera was moving in even closer. "Well ... " This is where I blow it I thought. "It's ... kind of a ... Washington DC sound. A sort of mixture of soft rock and well ... sort of psychedelic ... I guess," The sweat was streaming down my face.

"I see ... very interesting," the host replied, somewhat relieved as he knew I was nervous.

"Well ... would you play another song for us?"

"... Yeah ... sure."

"Groovy! We'll hear that in just a minute. "After this brief message!" Another commercial break.

Once again, the room was filled with confusion. We got up to play another song. The audience was growing restless. After all, who were we anyway? Just a local band with a record out on a small, unknown label. I felt vulnerable. We were on again. I sang ...

"... Good looks, fast cars
Oh we're so cool ...
One drink, one kiss
Oh we're such fools ...

... Love is ...
Something that I'm not sure of ...
But I know that with your love
There's nothing but happiness ...
Nothing but happiness ..."

... Peace march, cold war
All through my head ...
The world is better
When your not dead ...

... Love is ...
Something that I'm not sure of ...
But I know that with your love
There's nothing but happiness ...
Nothing but happiness ..."

The audience didn't seem as impressed with us this time. There was less applause and there were more boos from the back of the room. Louder this time. I wondered if they could be heard in the studio microphones. Luckily they started fading for yet another commercial break as we ended the song.

Bryan came running over. "Hey! I thought you guys were great! Really!"

"Right! If you say so," Mike said bitterly.

Freddie jump in, "Maybe we shouldn't have done this show. Something didn't feel right."

"Calm down," said Bryan.

"Man, you didn't have to get up in front of those cameras." said Mike

Yeah. Maybe this whole thing was a mistake," said Freddie

"Wait a minute," I said, trying to prevent an argument.

"No ... you wait a minute!" Fast Freddie exclaimed.

"Hey! Now hold up a minute ... Hold on goddamn it!" Bryan yelled, coming between us. "I'm trying to tell you guys!

... I just got off the phone with a concert promoter and I think I've got you guys on a show with 'The Brooklyn Bridge'!"

Suddenly we became calmer and quiet.

"Really?" I asked.

"Really .. Now pull yourselves together. It wasn't so bad. I've told you before ... you'll have to get used to a little ridicule." He put his hand on Freddie's shoulder. "Ok?"

"Yeah ... Thanks Bryan," Freddie said quietly.

We stood there in silence, realizing the power that we shared, the future that was ours. I couldn't help but wonder just how fragile our egos were - teetering on the razor's edge between failure and success. On the floor, at our feet was the card board sign, dusty now with foot prints which read 'APPLAUSE'.

Wedding bells. Joanne, 'Ol' Green Eyes', and I were married just two days before Mike and Jackie. Ours was a simple civil ceremony. But for Mike and Jackie, their wedding was to take place in a Catholic church.

And the guests. What a strange group of people. There were musicians, artists, and actors - our new-found-friends of the music world, dressed in bell-bottoms with bright colors, platform shoes, huge hats, feathers, and jewelry.

Mike and I made our way to the front door of the church. His mother had yet to arrive and it was almost time to begin the ceremony. "She should be here soon," I said putting my hand on his shoulder, trying to console him.

"She's not coming. You know how she feels about me and Jackie," he said sadly. She did not approve of the marriage.

The Priest walked up to us. He and Mike talked in low muffled tones. It was a private matter and I left them and walked outside. I lit a cigarette and exhaled the smoke into the cold November air. It was twilight over suburbia.

Nightfall always made me feel melancholy. I thought about Mike and Jackie, and how Mike's mother might have felt about them. But it was more than that. It was about us, our ideas, our big, brand new, radically different ideas were taking us far from our parents ways, as if some invisible hand was guiding us into the new world, a world that our parents couldn't understand. Our politics, the music. It all seemed so natural for us, right or wrong, it was the only way it could be. It was the only way that we could see it. But for them, our parents, would they ever understand? Would it ever be reconciled?

Mike opened the door and joined me outside. He too lit a cigarette. We didn't talk. Two dim headlights of a taxi pulled onto the street a few blocks away and slowly rolled along and stopped there in front. Mike's mom got out and paid the driver. As she walked up the stairs toward us, we could see the disgust and worry in her face.

"I'm glad you came," Mike said. He reached out to hold her, but she was reluctant to accept the embrace.

"I couldn't miss your wedding," she said, "no matter how I felt about it. I only hope you've made the right choice ... I only hope you'll be happy."

Inside, as she reached the archway to the alter, she gasped at what she saw. "Hippies! Drug addicts!" she exclaimed. "This isn't a wedding. It's a circus!" She tried to leave but Mike caught her by the arm and tried to hold her back. There were tears in his eyes. "Wait! You can't leave! Mom ... these are our friends," he pleaded.

"If you think I'm going to be part of this you're sadly mistaken!" The congregation noticed her displeasure. The stone figures of Jesus and the Virgin Mary looked over us with fixed granite expression. Silently, perhaps in our own minds, they judged us.

Reluctantly, Mike's mom walked quickly up to the front of the church and sat down in a vacant pew. Jackie and her Dad walked down the isle, Jackie was showing a slight 'baby bump' in her wedding dress.

The reception was at Jackie's parent's house just a few blocks away. With a Jimi Hendrix record blaring in the background, Mike's mom, now subdued, resigned, sat in the living room with a glass of wine. Jackie's mom soon joined her. They seemed to stay ... distant. Perhaps pretending maybe this wasn't really happening. We were their children. We were the ones that they had toiled so hard to raise. Perhaps the dreams of a lifetime lost. Or better yet, out of control. They were quietly losing control of the world. They stood helplessly by, trying hard to understand everything in the wake of it all.

Later, as we gathered for a picture with the wedding cake, with our glasses raised high, wishing each other the best the future could bring, the camera flashed and saved that moment for posterity. Mike, Jackie, Joanne and I, we were each only twenty years of age. Over in the corner, out of the picture, the Bride's father stood by. He was weeping.

10

A year had passed. We seemed to have hit a dead-end. Duane was leaving the band for college. That left only me, 'Magic Fingers' Mike and 'Fast' Freddie. We needed a drummer and replacing him was tough. We went through countless people, but finally found a talented guy named Johnny Lodz. He was a great musician. We jokingly called him 'The Polack'.

I arrived at the club a little early one evening. As I took a seat at the bar, the 'Polack' had arrived. I watched him as he approached me. There was a seriousness about him, different from the rest of us. Take Fast Freddie, he was carefree. He had charisma. It was as if he were being pulled through life by a kind hand of fate. He was a natural winner. No matter what, you had to like him. On the other hand, Mike, impulsive and high-strung, played a good lick on the piano. He was all business. And me? I was the dreamer. Perhaps more than any of us. No plan was too big and no idea was too outrageous. I was determined to make it in the music business and that was that. Freddie, Mike and I, we were on the road to stardom, and nothing would get in our way. Nothing. But the Polack? He was skeptical of our starry-eyed dreams and trendy ways. Instead, he looked for the quality in the music. There was no cutting corners. He wouldn't stand for shallow tinsel and glitter. The music had to be right. In spite of the differences, I thought he complemented us well.

"How's it goin?," I asked him. He didn't answer. It was as though he didn't hear me. There was a sense of separateness. "I think things are going pretty good since you joined the band," I continued.

"I haven't actually joined yet," he replied antagonistically.

"Well ... I think it'll work out."

"We'll see ... We'll see ..."

Then, Bryan entered the club. I knew he was coming to collect his pay. "Good evening!" he said.

"Hey Bryan ... Ah ... we need to talk," I said. "Maybe you should let Bryan and I talk alone," I said to the Polack, who nodded and moved farther down the bar.

"What's the problem?" Bryan asked."

"Well ... I ..."

"What's up?" he asked again, anxious. He took a seat next to me. I felt awkward, but decided instead of leading up to it with small talk, I would get straight to the point. "Bryan ... There are new people who want to handle us. I think it would be better if ... well maybe if we parted company." Without really trying, my words were cold and vicious. He was dumbstruck. I couldn't really look into his eyes.

"Why?" he stammered. "We've made a lot of progress together ... wouldn't you agree?"

I disagreed, "Well ... you've been busy lately. We haven't released a new record. You've signed a new group. You have done almost nothing with us in a long time., and you only stop by the club once a week just to collect your pay."

"Look! I've done a lot for you guys. You know that!"

"We've done a lot for you too,"

"Shit! When I found you guys you were playing in a two-bit bar, Sal's Place for a bunch of college girls!"

"So what are we doing now?" I asked.

"... These things take time ..." he replied.

"We don't have time Bryan. I'm almost twenty-two years old!"

"What about our contract? We have an option year."

"Bryan, you know we don't have to accept that option. You know that," I reminded him.

"Fine!" He looked at me. He was searching for words to say. "... I've got about five hundred copies of 'Why is the Sky'. And even a few hundred of 'Love Is'. What do I do with them?"

"Look ... Bryan ... I don't know ... we just want out."

I was looking at the floor. I felt like I was betraying him. The jukebox started playing a song and it was getting hard to talk over the music.

"Who are these new guys that you want for managers?"

"Lawyers. They think that they can sell us."

"Lawyers!? What can they do for you?"

I was resolute, "I'm sorry Bryan. That's what we want to do."

It was quiet between us as the jukebox stopped playing. He looked away. "How about my ninety dollars for this week?"

"Here." I reached in my jeans for a wad of bills and handed it to him.

He took the money and looked into the mirror, past the bottles lined up behind the back of the bar, at some far-off place. Then, quietly, without saying a word, he stood up and walked to the door. As I watched him leave, it was over with him. I felt sad. Ambition had driven us to this, where friends and associates would come and go and schemes and big deals would dance through our lives like dead leaves on a windy sidewalk. Bryan was gone. It was done.

11

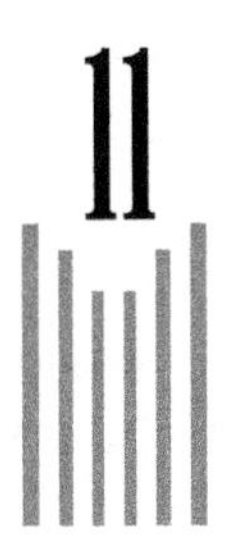

I could smell the steaks that sizzled on the hibachi next to me on the balcony. I was atop a high-rise where Greg and his friend James, our new lawyer friends and new managers, lived. The band was there to celebrate our new partnership.

"We're ready!" someone shouted to me from within the apartment. I entered the living room to find champagne.

"Grab a glass," said Mike as he handed me some. "A toast!"

We clinked our glasses and raised them high in a toast to success.

"All right. Let's get down to business," said Greg, with his wire-rimmed glasses he looked like John Denver, the folk singer. Both he and James were fresh out of law school. By day they held prime jobs in the straight world but at night they would become rock entrepreneurs, king-pins of the music business. With their high-rise apartment, expense accounts, and fancy cars, they were worlds apart from us.

"We've landed a deal for you guys with a record company!" Greg exclaimed.

"All right!" shouted Mike with glee.

We were all excited, all except the Polack. He was skeptical. "Which record company?" he asked.

'Karma Records'-that's who!" James exclaimed. "They have agreed to re-record 'Love Is' but there are some stipulations," he said, looking through the papers that were on his lap.

"Stipulations?" asked Freddie.

"You will have to play a tour of state fairs in the Midwest. They also have some songs that they would like you to consider recording."

"What!" I protested, "What about our own songs? I mean ... that's what we want to do. You know that!"

"Forget it!" said Mike, "Shit man. Forget it! Tell 'em to forget it!"

"Now wait a minute guys," said Greg.

"You have got to be kidding!" cried the Polack.

"Hey ... this isn't what we agreed on Greg," Freddie broke in.

"Okay! Okay! Settle down a minute," said Greg, trying to regain control of the conversation. He looked at James who appeared to be put off, "... Okay ... Maybe it's not such a great deal. We don't have to jump right at the first offer." He looked at James again before he continued. "We have some other things ... a concert at the University of Maryland with Ike and Tina Turner. It's not final but I think it is possible."

"That's more like it," said Freddie.

"It's a big show, probably fifteen, sixteen thousand people."

"Wow!" exclaimed Mike.

"When will we know?" I asked.

"I don't know ... soon."

"This calls for another drink," said Freddie. He anxiously poured the rest of the champagne.

"There is another point that we haven't considered," said James looking at Greg. "We need a binding agreement between us. As of yet, we have none."

"I suppose you will want a contract between us?" asked Mike. "I mean it is only customary."

"Well ... actually what we had in mind was to form a corporation," said Greg, "I would be the president and James would be the vice-president. You would each be stock holders."

"Ah ... Well ... that sounds fair ... What do you think?" I asked Mike.

"Yeah ... sure ... I think this is a good idea ... sure ..."

Greg continued, "James and I will buy you new equipment. That will our contribution. You will contribute your songs and talent."

We all nodded in agreement.

"Good! I'll check on the steaks."

"And I'll light the joint," said Mike, "Want some?" he asked Greg.

"No ... no thanks. None for me."

"James?"

"No, I'm good."

The band took turns taking a toke on a joint, and the room filled with pot smoke. Each of us drifted off into a lazy abyss. Outside, the sky had turned orange from the city lights below. I was watching the shadows as they clung to the far corners of the room.

Walking up to the back door of the coliseum, Joanne and I could hear the crowd within. They were waiting for the moment that Ike and Tina Turner would take the stage. But first we would open the show.

Inside, Greg was pacing the hallway. "Good! I'm glad you're here," he said, "the rest of the band is down the hall in the dressing room."

Reaching the door, I could hear laughter from within. "Well the superstar has arrived!" teased the Polack.

"All right knock it off," I said coolly.

"The equipment is ready," said Mike. "Have a seat and relax." We had done the sound check earlier that day.

"How long have we got?"

"About a half hour," said Greg as he entered the room. "Now don't run off. I'll come for you when they're ready for you to go on."

"You wanna try some 'angel dust'?" Freddie asked me.

"What is it?" I asked.

"I dunno ... try it you'll like it," Mike said.

I raised the joint to my lips. It had a medicine-type of smell. I took a puff. "This stuff tastes really weird," I said choking. After a few minutes I tried to stand up and felt weak in my knees. I knew this wasn't regular pot. I felt slightly sick and sat down again.

Joanne took a toke too. Soon we were both high. I held her in my arms and we became aroused. I stood up unsteadily and we walked out the door, and into the hallway. "I can't believe that you guys are actually playing in a concert with Ike and Tina Turner!" she said. I can't believe I'm here!" She kissed me tenderly. She took my hand and pulled me down the hallway. We ducked into a dark stairwell and shut the large door behind us. Before I could say a word she kissed me again,

Meanwhile, I could hear the massive audience out in the coliseum. They were restless.

She dropped her purse on the floor and kissed me passionately. "Kiss me ... kiss me now," she whispered.

In a reflex action, I ran my hand over her body. My head was throbbing. I must be crazy to be doing this, I thought but did not stop. I threw her up against the wall and forced my leg between her thighs. I could hear her sigh deeply, wantonly over the sound of the audience that was in the coliseum only a few feet away. "It's all right," she said softly. We quickly made love there in the dark stairwell. The sound of the crowd was getting louder and louder as we moved harder and harder. It was magic. We climaxed together. I fell in a heap on a stair step. My head was numb.

I heard a voice. Greg was calling for me. Joanne ran to the bottom of the stairs with her clothes clutched to her bosom as he came running in. He tried not to notice.

"Shit man! What are you doing? You're going on!" he screamed.

I ran out into the hallway. Down at the end I could see the rest of the band waiting by the large door that led to the stage. As I approached them, Freddie handed me my bass.

Inside the coliseum, it was another world. We walked onto the stage and when a huge spot light had caught one of us the crowd went wild. I picked a note and it resounded from the mountains of speakers that made up the sound system. The spot light shown in my face and my knees almost gave way. I could see the back of the enormous room. There were thousands of people there. I had never felt this kind of excitement before. It was overwhelming. It was magic!

"HELLO!"I yelled into the microphone. My head was still numb from the drug I had taken, the sex I had just shared with 'Ol' Green Eyes'.

The audience responded with a roar. We went into a song. It sounded loud and strong. My bass was rumbling the floor of the stage and the drums could be heard like gun-shots through the air as I sang ...

"... Hard hat, dirty hippie, university man ...
Everybody is a wonderin' just who they are ...
Ya got'a drop out to get into the runnin'...
Everybody's got to be a superstar ...
... Nightlife's just a social identification ...
But it gets blurry through a bottle of beer ...

Got'a let 'em know you're alive, well and kickn'...
Cause anyone whose anyone is here ...
... This is a singin' song ...
It ain't hard and it ain't long ...
But just his voice ...
Ain't gonna get it on ...
... Believe me when I tell ya that a band is a band ...
It depends on whose your friends ...
and who you are ...
Ya know he's doin' the best he can ...
He gets so tired and weary ...
ridin' home in the backseat of his car ...
... This is a singin' song ...
It ain't hard and it ain't long ...
But just his voice ...
Ain't gonna get it on ..."

The spot lights moved back and forth as flashes from cameras could be seen like tiny diamonds of light in the darkness. As we finished the song, the crowd roared even louder. They were cheering for our song the way we played it. They were cheering for u-s-s! All of a sudden the bad nights and the countless disappointments were all worth it. It all made sense. This was where the music could take us. We played another song and then another. In a way, this was our night. This was our time. Yes, perhaps we were on our way to stardom!

13

Cigarette smoke hung heavily in the room. We were at Gotham Studios in New York City. Greg had lined up a huge record company audition opportunity. The room was filled with people, representatives from several record companies. They talked freely as they passed around a joint and a big bottle of wine.

I was talking with one couple. "Which record company are you with?" I asked.

"'Action Records'," he replied.

"Really? What are you? I mean ... what do you do?"

"I'm A and R."

"What?"

"A and R," he repeated.

"What does that mean?" I asked.

He looked at his mate and smiled.

"How long have you guys been together anyway?" his girlfriend teased.

"It means 'artist and repertoire'," he said.

"Oh ... " I said with naiveté

"It means he can make or break you," she added.

In the control booth, Greg was talking to the engineer. He was a big man with a cigar. His hair seemed oily and was slicked back. The room itself was littered with old beer cans and cigarette butts. Greg introduced me, "I would like you to meet Ralph."

The big man shook my hand. He didn't smile. "I understand you boys have got some original songs. We'd like to hear 'em."

"Hey. We're ready! Whenever you say the word."

"Look ... just play 'em live. Any mistakes and we can punch in. Okay?"

"We can what?" I asked, confused.

"'Punch in'. If you make a mistake, we might be able to overdub just that part of the song. Dig?"

I was still a little confused but tried to seem confident. "Yeah ... okay."

"Can we do a sound check?" he asked, as he started fiddling with the vast array of knobs on the control board.

Fast Freddie was tuning his guitar while Mike was lighting another joint. The Polack was making the final adjustments to his drum kit. The group of record people, about twenty of them, were squeezed into the corner of the room nearest the door. They loosely resembled an audience.

"Are we ready?" came Ralph's voice over the studio monitor which was a large speaker that hung over the control booth window. I looked at Freddie and the rest of the band.

We started playing and I sang one of my songs ...

"Night wind is blowing ...
I'm riding faster on a windy sky ...
My hair is flowing ...
My mind is going back to you at will ...
I think of you ... I love you still ...

... I've got to show you that I know that I'm wrong ...
But what can I do with my words and my songs ...

"STOP! STOP!" Came Ralph's voice from the control room over the monitor speaker. "Okay ... Ah ... try another song."

There was a murmur in the crowd. They grew restless. We were confused and slightly put off.

Carefully, we started another one of our songs ...

"... Oh Please ... Don't wait ... too long ... for what you want ...
I've let ... you down ... so much ... I've lost the count ...

You find it hard ... to hide ... your own despair ...
It makes ... me sad ... to see ... you really care ...

We've got a long way to go ...
And where that is ... I don't know ...

You've sighed ... You've cried ... You've tried ... to lend a hand ...
You've failed so desperately to understand ..."

Again, Ralph interrupted us. "STOP! WAIT! I'm sorry can we try another song. Something 'heavier'. More like hard rock." The voice had an ominous, impersonal tone. It seemed Ralph was insinuating that our songs were not the style of music they were looking for. Our audience was beginning to lose interest.

We started another song when suddenly, "THAT WILL BE ENOUGH FOR NOW...," said the speaker on the wall.

Quietly, we put down our instruments. The crowd was quietly leaving. It seemed like in mere moments, that amazing opportunity at getting a record contract had disappeared. It had all vanished. Disheartened, we walked into the control booth. Ralph was rewinding the huge reel of tape and lighting another cigar. Greg was looking down at the trash littered floor. Over in the corner, there was a straight-looking businessman in a suit and tie. It was quiet in the room.

Finally, "Want to hear the tape?" asked Ralph.

"Sure," Greg said disheartened.

The huge reel of tape whirred to a stop and then started to play. The song started. We were horrified. Freddie's guitar was slightly out of tune and our voices seemed weak and strained. As each song was played, the room became more and more cloaked in doom. I looked up and the businessman, perhaps a final interested party, had too left.

"Would you like a copy of the tape?" asked Ralph as he drew heavy breath.

"Yeah ... that would be fine," Greg said. "Let's pack up boys."

We trudged out into the studio to collect our equipment. No one said a word. We had failed the audition. But not only did we just strike out with one record company, we struck out with a half a dozen all at once!

Out in the street, the night air was thick and humid and everywhere was the sound of heavy traffic. Greg drove us to Queens where we would spend the night. No one was up to conversation as we peered out into the lights of the city.

When we reached the house, we were surprised to see that there was a party going on. Inside, there was loud music playing. A black light hung in the living room and illuminated a wall full of posters, graffiti; the air, stagnant with the smell of beer and pot. On the floor were sprawled odd assortments of people, couples making love in the dark corners.

We mingled with the crowd, drinking from the numerous bottles and smoking from the joints that were passed around. I wandered down into the basement. There was another black light which made all the light colored clothes stand out luminescent against the shadows. Hanging on one wall was a hammock where a couple were necking feverishly. Others were scattered about the floor smoking wooden pipes of pot and hashish. I found it hard to breath.

"How's it goin'?" someone asked from the floor. I looked down to see a guy sitting there with a large bamboo pipe. He had a long beard and even longer hair. "Ya wanna hit?" he asked.

"Yeah ... sure ... why not," I agreed.

"This stuff is primo ... I mean primo!" I took the pipe into my hands as he placed a small portion of the green leaves into the bowl. He lit a match and held it to the pipe and I inhaled the smoke. I started to choke and cough.

He smiled. His eyes were squinted and glassed over. "Pretty good shit huh?"

"It's ok," I said. My throat was on fire and I could barely talk.

He looked away for an instant. He seemed distracted. Then he turned his attention back to me. "Are you new here?" he asked.

"... Yeah ... I'm from DC ... my band had an audition tonight for some record companies."

"Well ... how'd ya do?" His words were slurred and distorted. Communication was getting rough.

"Huh? ... Oh ... not too well. Not good ..."

There was a pause while he took another hit off the pipe. "That's too bad," he said as he started to laugh. "Want another hit?"

I took the pipe and this time it was easier to take the harsh smoke. I noticed that the room seemed different - things that had escaped my attention before, were now vivid, magnified somehow. There was a small crack in the concrete on the floor where I sat. I ran my finger along it. The floor was cool and the crack had a slight sharpness to one of its edges. I found myself totally engrossed in the crack on the floor. The music was playing upstairs and somehow I felt like I was lost in another world. It was different. I was stoned.

I mumbled, "Yeah ... It was a drag ... The audition I mean ..." It was hard to talk. Thoughts were racing through my mind but putting them into words was difficult.

"Hey! Fuck it man! Fuck everything man!" he exclaimed.

"Well ... Yeah," I said. I was getting weak. I could feel my face getting flushed and it was harder than ever to breath.

My companion seemed to quiet again but then blurted out, "Fuck everything man!"

It was apparent that he was really out of it now. I wanted to get away. It was an ugly scene. I was sad. Then afraid. Then sad again. The drugs had taken me too far this time. Maybe it was the pot, maybe the dense air around me. Perhaps I had overdosed! I had to get a hold of myself, I thought. It will be over soon. The blood was racing to my head. I was hot. I couldn't breath! I thought I would never get my breath. I fell back and the room vibrated with energy. The loud music and the smoke was too much. I needed another breath! Hold on, I thought to myself. I closed my eyes and visions of lights went through my head. I took a breath. And then another.

Finally, I was coming down. I knew I would be all right. I sat up and noticed that my companion was lying on his side, apparently asleep.

I stood up. My stomach felt queasy and my legs were weak. I walked upstairs and went to the kitchen to look for a beer. There were none. In the living room, the party crowd had thinned out except for the hardy few. I sat down and sunk into to the couch. Where was Greg? The others?

I was tired. It had been a long day and night. I remembered the audition. This utter failure could mean only one thing - Greg and especially James would perhaps lose interest in us. And, as with Bryan, this business venture would prove unsuccessful. Again, defeat; that brick wall that was seemingly always in our path.

Somehow during the drug-induced stupor and depression, I fell asleep.

14

It was a soft spring day when I first stepped into the house on Pine Avenue. Freddie and Jackie had moved in together. Amazingly, Jackie was married to Mike, but had left him for Freddie. She and the baby lived there with Freddie now. But, somehow, inexplicitly, the band stayed together. Maybe it was the new hippie culture. Maybe it was because the band and our effort to attain stardom was more important. It was a curious situation.

Freddie and Jackie shared the house with a girl named Cathy and an older woman named Terry from California which I suppose made her the 'guru' of the house. In the kitchen there was a long narrow table with many chairs and it was the 'hub' of the house. There were several people seated there. Terry with graying hair tied back with Indian beads and dressed in jeans sat at the head of the table. Her face was worn, but her eyes were soft. I pulled up a chair and joined the others - Jackie, Freddie, Cathy and Howie. Howie was Cathy's live-in lover. He took a sudden interest in me. "So you're in the band?"

"That's right," I replied.

"Wanna bong hit?" Cathy asked me.

"I dunno ... sure." She handed me the bamboo pipe from the table and I took a puff of pot.

Freddie strummed lightly on a guitar.

"What kind of music do you guys play?" Howie continued.

"Well ... a little blues ... some Zappa. Some popular music ... and of course our originals."

"Do you write?" asked Cathy.

"Yeah."

"What kind of stuff?"

"Well ... I dunno. Just stuff in my mind. I like the Beatles." I said.

"Don't you think music should have more than just a message?" said Howie, "There should be some artistic quality to it. I mean don't you get sick of the trash they play on the radio?"

"Yeah. Well ... I think popular music can have a message and be artistic too."

"Name one song. One that even approaches art," he said defiantly.

"'Eleanor Rigby' by the Beatles," Terry said, breaking into the conversation quietly. I wasn't aware that she was even listening.

"Yeah, but is that really artistic?" Howie countered quickly. "Like Beethoven's Fifth?"

"Sure," I said. "I admit that some of it is mere pop music. 'Art' has a more classic, timeless quality about it."

"I like it anyway whatever it is," said Cathy, yawning.

"Hey ... what about 'classic rock 'n' roll'?" said Freddie jokingly.

"I still think most of it is trash!" said Howie.

"Let's lighten up fellas!" said Terry, trying to maintain a peaceful setting.

Jackie got up and went to the stove. I watched her. Actually, I always had a crush on her. Sometimes, in spite of the breakup with Mike, and her relationship with Freddie, I would fantasize about being with her. It was a crazy idea.

"I gotta split," Howie said. He put the baggie of pot into a leather pouch which hung on his belt, and walked out the kitchen door into the late afternoon, slamming the battered screen door behind him. Jackie sat down in the chair next to mine.

"I guess we should get ready to go down town," said Freddie.

"You guys have a gig tonight huh?" asked Terry.

"Yeah ..."

"Would you like to eat before you go?" Terry asked.

"Nah ... That's ok," said Freddie putting down his guitar. "You 'bout ready to go?" asked Freddie.

"Yeah, let's do it," I replied.

Urban Blues

15

'Wild Bill' Wilder was probably the most complex person you could ever meet. To some, he was a local legend and just how much his reputation preceded him was anyone's guess. Some say he was a paratrooper from the Korean War. Others say he was a stock car racer from El Paso, Texas who ran into a fortune. Still, others say he was a rich kid, turned black sheep, from a wealthy family. He was any one of these or none of these, but whatever, he was an original. Local stories were numerous. One claims that he was thrown out of a posh Georgetown nightclub for urinating at the bar, and then brawling with the bartender. Another tells of him wiping away tears after watching a black blues songstress, perform. He could hobnob with the rich, but was as street wise as any urban punk. 'Wild Bill' Wilder. He owned a mansion in the hills of Virginia, a townhouse in Georgetown and a DC nightclub.

He had heard some of our music and wanted to meet us, and in this, I was one of the uninitiated. His nightclub The Pilgrimage was a tall brownstone off DuPont Circle. It was an amazing coincidence, but it was the same building where we had our professional pictures taken a few years earlier, back when Bryan was our manager.

Standing at the front door, I could hear the faint sounds of music within. It was Beth Williams, a local singer - songwriter who was well known as an activist for her female lesbian rights stand. Musically, she was great.

We were all a little nervous as we entered the club for this strange encounter. The room was packed with people who sat at elegant tables bathed in soft candlelight. We walked to the back of the club and it was at the end of a long oak bar that I saw a tall figure in the shadows. It had to be Wild Bill Wilder.

Unsure, I asked the bartender, "Could you tell Bill Wilder that we would like to see him," Before he could utter a word, the tall figure of a man turned to face us.

"I'm Bill Wilder. What can I do for you?" His voice was loud and gruff. He was a big man, barrel-chested and muscular, but there was a sense of refinement. He had a long handlebar mustache which was neat and well kept, his eyes were of a cold, steel gray color.

"We're the band on the tape. Freddie called you-" I started talking but he interrupted me.

"Right! I remember," he said quickly, "I liked that. It was very good."

"Well ... We-"

Again he cut me off, "Hey let's cut the bullshit. Hey barkeep! Let's have a round for these fellas!" He shouted. People watching the show looked up with disgust. They were trying to hear Beth Williams sing. "Whatever you guys want. Tell 'em! Whatever you want!" he exclaimed.

"Well ... we'll all have drafts," Freddie said.

"Hey barkeep! Four drafts! Now!" he bellowed.

Beth Williams ended her song. The audience applauded but she was annoyed by Wild Bill's loud, brash demeanor.

"I've heard great things about you guys. I would like you to play here," Wild Bill said as he lit a cigarette. "What do you think of the place?" The smoke curled past his piercing eyes.

"It's incredibility furnished," Mike said. "Who did all the work?"

He laughed, "Oh I dunno, some gay bastard! ... Hey some more 'ballerina piss'!" He motioned to the bartender and again he had to stop in his tracks to get the bottle of Galliano off the shelf.

The people near us were all wondering just who this big obnoxious man was. There was a beautiful girl near us at the bar. He backed up, cleared his throat, and spit onto the floor. "Baby ... I'd eat a mile of your shit just to see where it came from!" he told her jokingly.

Beth Williams finally finished her set to thunderous applause. She quickly put down her guitar and stormed her way to the back of the room. You could see anger in her face as she came nearer. She walked up to Wild Bill, obviously unaware of his credentials. "Listen, whoever you are, you are obnoxious! Can't you keep your voice down when I'm on stage?" she exclaimed. She was trembling she was so filled will disgust and anger.

"Well ... I'm sorry if I bothered you dear lady!" He replied. He spit on the floor again and then went for his glass of Galliano.

"That's it!" she exclaimed, "I'll have you thrown out of here! Where's the manager?"

Wild Bill stood back and took a drag on his cigarette. His fingers were tanned and his nails were elegant for such a big seemingly uncouth man. He spoke to her. "For one thing, my name is Bill Wilder and I own this place ... besides ... I don't know why you're so uptight ... I like to eat pussy just as much as you do!"

Poor Beth Williams was mortified. She walked away. Wild Bill reached for his Galliano, " ... so much for gay rights hey?", he joked.

"I think she's really talented," said the Polack.

Everything stopped. Wild Bill turned to see who dared to speak out. It was quiet all the way down the bar. The Polack looked him straight in the eye. Neither of them barely flinched. The next few seconds seemed like an eternity. Then, Wild Bill smiled and took another drag on his cigarette. " ... Hey ... She plays good music. After all... I'm just another drunken asshole in this bar. What do I know?" he said playfully. Everyone laughed. "Hey barkeep! Another round!" He yelled. Conversations resumed.

A well-dressed gentleman walked up to him. They stepped slightly away and began to talk. The jukebox started droning in the background and I couldn't hear what they were saying. I could tell by his hand gestures and demeanor that he was acting more civil. They were on a different level. I watched them.

"What do you think?" Freddie was asked me.

"You mean 'Wild Bill'?"

"Who else?"

"He's a strange dude," Mike said.

"He's ok. He's just rich, that's all. Rich people can do what they want," said Freddie.

The gentleman and Wild Bill continued their conversation. Then they shook hands and parted. Wild Bill walked over to the kitchen door at the end of the bar. Three of the kitchen help were standing there, sweaty and dirty from their work. Wild Bill talked to them and patted one on the shoulder. Then he motioned to the bartender who brought three beers. Wild Bill crushed out a cigarette on the floor and then disappeared through the kitchen door.

"Let's grab a table," Freddie said.

"Yeah ... Let's get another round!" said Mike.

"Well, I've got to make a phone call ... be back in a few minutes," I said.

"I'll keep your seat warm and the beer cold!"

Freddie, Mike and the Polack were talking music when a newspaper landed on the table top. They looked up in surprise to see Bryan. "Well boys ... I see you're all looking well. Where's the up and coming songwriter?" he asked.

"He went to make a phone call," said Freddie.

"How in the hell have you been?"

"Just fine! Just fine! By the way, this is my new newspaper," he said, pointing down to the paper on the table.

All reached for it but Mike grabbed it first. "We must have patience," Mike teased. He read the title aloud. "The Old Mystic Review. What is this?"

"It's my new venture. It's a music trade paper for local music, theater and arts. What do you think?"

"How about your record company?" asked Freddie.

"I decided to scrap that for a while. I think this paper will be a success. There's nothing like it in the city!"

"Hey, how about doing a story on us?" Mike asked.

Bryan grinned and didn't answer. Suddenly there were implications. It was obvious that he didn't owe us any favors since we had fired him as our manager way back when. Fate. Another brick in that brick wall blocking our way to success.

"How about a beer?" asked Freddie.

"No. I've got to be off. As you can see, I'm a very busy man!"

"Well, It's good to see ya. Keep in touch," said Mike.

"Oh I will. Don't worry about that. By the way have you seen Bill Wilder?"

"Yeah ... he took off somewhere. He'll probably be back soon."

"Okay ... See you boys later. Oh! Can I have the paper back? I've only got a few copies with me."

Mike looked down at the paper in his hands and then handed it to Bryan. "Take it slow ..."

"And you the same." He turned and disappeared.

"Shit! Wouldn't ya know it," Mike exclaimed. "We got rid of him, pissed him off, and now he's running the only music trade paper in town! What luck!"

Meanwhile, I walked slowly back to the table and sat down in silence.

"Christ! What's wrong with you?" Freddie asked, "Guess who we just saw?"

I didn't feel like talking.

"Bryan was just here. He's starting to publish a local music trade paper called The Old Mystic Review. Can you believe it?"

"What a stupid name for a paper," Mike added. "... Who did you call anyway?"

"It was Ol' Green Eyes, Joanne. She wants a divorce," I said sadly. I couldn't blame her. I had left her and the baby months before. I was realizing that my world was falling apart. And all for music? For a band? Sad.

"Shit man!" said Freddie.

It was quiet among us.

"Can I get ya another beer?" he asked.

"No ..."

"Hey maybe it will work out. You never know ..."

"It's over. You really can't blame her. I've been away too much with the band," I said. "Maybe I will have another beer."

"I'll get it." He jumped up and headed for the bar.

Music ... so far, it had cost me a friendship, and now a marriage. Music. Music would be my lady I thought. Fast Freddie, Magic Mike and the Polack. Andy. They were my friends. They would be my family. They would fill my lonely days.

We stayed until closing and we were just about to leave when suddenly Wild Bill returned. "Still here you pussies!" he exclaimed. "Close the doors and lock 'em. Now we're gonna have a party!"

The front doors were locked and the lights were dimmed. It was after hours at the Pilgrimage.

Me, Mike, Fast Freddie, the Polack and Wild Bill were the only ones left amid the empty tables, chairs, and the darkness.

"Get whatever you want from behind the bar," Wild Bill told us.

"Are you sure?" I said timidly.

"Get it! Whatever you want!"

Freddie went behind the bar and surveyed the shelves bringing down a bottle of Jack Daniels Black Label.

"Great! 'Jack Black'! Line up the glasses. Well drink to all the beautiful pussy in the world!" Wild Bill exclaimed.

I looked down. "What's wrong with you?" He was looking at me. He could tell that I wasn't in the best of spirits.

"Ah ... well .. His ol' lady wants a divorce," Freddie said in my defense.

"She d-o-e-s does she? Well fuck it! ... The world's full of used pussy!"

"It's not her fault," I said solemnly.

"Feeling sorry for yourself huh? Well 'doctor Bill' has just the medicine. Come here boy ... I'm gonna make you a star!"

He pulled a baggie from his pocket and emptied the white powder contents on the bar. It was more cocaine than I had ever seen before. It gleamed in the available light. He removed a knife from his pants and cleaned the blade with a few wipes against his pant leg. He cut out some of the powder and made six long lines on the bar as we watched with great interest. Then, he rolled up a twenty and handed it to me. "You first wimp!"

I took the rolled up bill in my hands. "Thank you."

"Thank you 'doctor Bill' you mean," he teased.

"Thank you 'doctor Bill'," I replied obediently.

He smiled as I inhaled the long line of coke. My head felt warm and I was getting high. We, each in our turn, did a long line of the cocaine.

"Now about your band ..." he was saying. Suddenly, there was a loud rap at the door. "Shit! Whose that? Stay here and hide that coke!" He went to the front door and laid his head against it. "Who's there?" He asked.

"Steve Hientz..." a faint voice replied.

"Shit! Its the Jewboy!" He opened the door and the man came in quickly. The door was relocked. "Boys ... I want you to meet Steve Hientz... I'm glad you showed up 'Hienie'!" He was short and slightly balding with glasses. He was trying hard to ignore Wild Bill's remarks. "Steve is a promoter. He's going to bring 'Bighouse Johnson', the blues singer, to perform at the Pilgrimage next week ... You have heard of 'Bighouse Johnson' haven't you?"

"Sure," said the Polack. "He's one of the greatest blues singers!"

"Hey 'Hienie', this is the band that I want to back him up," said Wild Bill.

Steve looked us over. "Frankly, aren't they a little too young and 'white' to be his back-up band?"

"Fuck you Hienie boy! This is my back-up band," insisted Wild Bill.

"Forget it Bill. I don't need this bullshit! 'Bighouse' is my act and I'll decide who will play with him."

"Whoa! ... Ok Hienie. Let's talk it over. Come on over here and let me make you a star ... do a line."

Steve did some of the coke. We all grabbed a bar stool and gathered around.

"So you guys play the blues huh?" Steve asked us.

"That's right," said the Polack. "The r-e-a-l blues."

"The r-e-a-l blues huh?" he replied, mockingly, a little amused by his boasting.

"We've heard 'Bighouse'," said Fast Freddie.

"I see," said Steve. He was grinning.

Meanwhile, I could feel my heart racing in my chest from the coke and I was breathing heavily.

"Look Jewboy ... I said these boys are going to back him up. See?" said Wild Bill. I wondered if it was just the liquor and coke talking.

"Isn't that up to me. I'm his promoter!" said Steve.

"Look ... you'll get your percentage. Isn't that all that matters?" Wild Bill quipped.

"Now you look Bill ... you're not going to dictate the terms of this deal!"

"I've had enough of you assholes!" Wild Bill screamed. His eyes were on fire, his massive chest heaving. "Okay Hienie! Let's have it your way. Let's fight for it! You against the band!"

"Now wait..." Steve responded.

"No! You against one of my boys here!"

We were all shocked. This was insane! "Are you serious?" I asked.

"You're god-damned right I'm serious!" Wild Bill screamed in the shadows. He picked up a bar stool and threw it against the wall. We were all speechless. The muscles tightened in my chest and I was sure I was going to fall down.

"Now fight for it!" He screamed at Steve. "You against one of them!"

We were all quiet, not sure if he was really serious and trying to hang on to some shred of sanity. No one moved. Steve stood partially in the darkness, all our faces partially hidden in the shadows.

Finally, reluctantly, Steve said, "All right ... As you wish. Your band can have the gig ... but I hope they are good enough to do the job."

"Good! How can I say I love you when you're sitting on my face!" Wild Bill sang playfully. "Maybe I'll be a blues singer." He laughed.

The tension had ceased and we all laughed nervously. Wild Bill cut out more lines of coke on the bar.

"This calls for a toast. How about some Jack Black!" He brought out the bottle from behind the bar. "To the blues!" said Wild Bill, raising his glass.

We partied into the night. Between the coke and the booze, we were all really getting high. In a while, over in the direction of the front door I could see the first strains of daylight coming through the window.

16

The embers glowed dimly in the fireplace, but the heat cut the drafty cold air of a December night. The living room at Pine Avenue was a tranquil scene, each person in their own world, Fast Freddie and Howie playing chess in the corner, Jackie cleaning her camera, and I, playing with the idea to a song.

With a guitar on my lap and a note pad in my hands, I was trying to put down the tune I heard in my head. Songs were like people who came to visit me from time to time, dropping by occasionally to remind me of their message, to tease me with their melody and haunting chords. 'Play me' they would say. 'Try this line', 'I need an ending' they would plead. I had an intimacy with each, an intimacy that only I knew. Sometimes songs were the only things you could know deep in the core of your soul. I was writing ...

"Think of all the songs that have been written ...
On wasted tears and bottled beer ...
A song's a singer's heart ... that's open wide....
To a full house ... but no one's there ...

He ... He gets so weary of his role
Of playing the hero ...
Who is really the fool ...."

"Oh ... what time is it, anyway?" Jackie yawned.

"I don't know," said Freddie.

"Who cares," said Howie.

"Well, I don't know about you guys, but I'm bored," she insisted.

"It's not even dark outside. The night's young," said Freddie. The clock on the wall chimed five o'clock.

"See ... it's only five," said Howie. He too yawned.

"Whose playing downtown tonight? Maybe we could go out," said Jackie.

"I dunno. Is there a paper?" Freddie asked half heartedly. He was contemplating his next chess move.

"Hey! Let's go to a movie!" she exclaimed.

"Shit! You really got a wild hair up your ass Jackie," teased Howie.

"I told you ... I'm really bored!"

"Ok mama! Ok! We'll do somethin'," Freddie said. "Just let me finish this game."

"We gotta finish this game!" said Howie.

Meanwhile, my song was weaving it's spell on me. I shuttered. Perhaps, I was writing about myself ...

"Think of all the singers who have been wasted ...
On dusty dreams ... and fading rainbows ...
His voice is getting weak his face looks weary ...
His song is almost over ... they come and go ...

We ... We are the children of rock'n'roll ...
Our dreams take us everywhere ...
Trying to find our very souls ...

Singers ... and Songs ..."

"What are you doing?" Jackie asked me.

I looked up. I was surprised to see her standing over me. "Oh ... I was working on an idea for a song."

"What's it called?"

"Oh ... I don't know ..."

"'I love you so much I could shit!'" Fast Freddie sang mockingly.

We all laughed.

"Well ... what's it about? I mean you must know what it's about," she said.

"Nothing really. I dunno. It's not finished yet."

"The 'nothing song'. That's what it's called, the 'nothing song'!" she teased. She was smiling. "Well I think we should do s-o-m-e-t-h-i-n-g!"

"Let's get stoned," Freddie said.

"I've got a better idea," said Howie. He pulled out a baggie from his leather pouch and carefully unraveled it on the table. A piece of paper with little orange dots fell out.

"What is it?" asked Jackie.

"It's acid. Real smooth stuff," Howie assured us. It was LSD.

"How much should you do?" Freddie asked.

"That's up to you. What ever you can handle."

"Oh Let's do it!" exclaimed Jackie, willing to do anything for excitement at this point.

"How about you?" Howie asked me.

"Well ... ok. Sure," I replied.

He tore off a dot and handed one to each of us in turn. I took mine and put it in my mouth. It had no taste. "How soon before we get off?" I asked.

"I dunno ... but you'll know when you do!"

An ember in the fireplace popped in the silence as we all waited for the drug to take effect. Freddie went over to stoke the fire. He added another log. In about fifteen minutes, I could feel my stomach start to churn. I had to vomit. I ran through the kitchen into the bathroom and fell to my knees in front of the toilet. I heaved into the bowl several times in misery. I was trembling. Soon it ceased.

I looked into the toilet. The contents seemed to be like a small pool of brown glass. I flushed. The water swirled and I watched the swirl go round and round, picking up momentum, and finally disappearing into the dark tunnel of the toilet.

I stood there for a few minutes and watched the clear water refill the toilet bowl. The sound of the rushing water stopped. I looked up into the mirror and saw a person, sweating and worried. The eyes looked into themselves. How curious.

I walked out into the living room and sat down in the chair. My stomach was still upset but somehow I didn't mind. Fast Freddie, Howie and Jackie, were singing along to a record they were playing, occasionally laughing for no apparent reason.

Then, Freddie ran to the bathroom, he too was sick. He seemed to be gone forever but came back and plopped down on the couch.

"W-o-o-w! ... look at the walls," said Jackie. She was excited.

"Yeah ... " said Howie.

"What ... what do you mean?" I asked or someone asked. I wasn't sure.

"The walls ... the walls," Howie said. "Can't you see?"

On the wall, opposite the fireplace, a shadow danced to and fro. It moved softly over the tapestry that hung there, covering each fold effortlessly. Like a boxer in the ring, it moved in and out. In and out. Farther in and still farther. It danced in the firelight. The pops and crackles of the fire accented each ebb and flow of movement. We all looked intensely at the wall.

"I'm really sweating ... It's really getting hot," said Jackie.

"Yeah ..." said Freddie mindlessly.

"Open the window," said Howie. "Just open the window!"

"I can't get up," Jackie said. Then she laughed in a silly way.

"Open the window," said Howie again in earnest. "You must open the window!"

"I ... I really can't go over there. You know ..." said Jackie. We all laughed. It seemed funny for some reason. "I'm really getting hot!" she said again.

"Open the window, now!" Howie was becoming anxious.

"I'll open the window," said Freddie. He got up slowly and walked over to the window. It was slow, the way he walked, like a movie in slow motion.

"It's really hot in here," said Jackie. She was becoming obsessive.

"Open the window Freddie! Open the window Freddie!" we all yelled.

"Man it's hot in here," said Howie. His face was red.

We had to get the window open. Nothing else mattered. We had to open that window. Freddie was still walking across the room to the window. All we knew was that Freddie had to open the window!

"Can't you open the window, Freddie?" asked Howie.

"We must open the window," said Jackie in earnest.

Freddie was at the window.

"Now he'll open the window. You'll see," I said.

"Open the window Freddie!" we all yelled.

Freddie opened the window and a cold wind blew hard against our faces.

"It's cold Freddie," Jackie said. "It's freezing cold!"

The clock chimed eight times as the room reeled before our eyes. It was eight o'clock! Time was racing by. For me, the bathroom, the mirror, the song, the shadows, ... opening window, all these events seemed to fill a long period of time. It was frightening.

"Hey!" Freddie shouted. He ran quickly over to the fireplace. The wind from the open window had set the rug on fire! We jumped up stamped it out with a nearby coat. The smoke had filled the room and we were all choking. It had been on fire for a while, but none of us in our drug stupor had even noticed it!

"Wow ... " said Howie.

"Big time!" said Freddie.

"Let's watch that rug," I said. "Really, we better watch that rug!" We all laughed. I stood over the rug as if it were a wild animal. "We better watch the rug. Do you hear me? Watch the rug!" I said.

"Yeah ... the rug," said Freddie.

We all watched the rug in a stupor.

"I've got to get out of here. I've got to get out," said Jackie nervously.

"Let's get out of here," said Howie.

"But ... we need to watch that rug, the fire!" I exclaimed.

We had to get away from the rug. It was imperative that we got away from the rug! We all got up slowly and tried to make our way to the kitchen. Jackie held onto Freddie's shirt as we walked through the dark hallway. The light from the kitchen was like a beacon. It pulsated with intensity. The walls of the kitchen were literally throbbing with energy. It was a different place. We all took a seat around the long table.

"It's smooth," said Howie.

"What?" I asked.

"It's smooth stuff," he said again.

"What do you mean?"

"It's smooth!" everyone yelled in unison and laughed. We were rocking back and forth uncontrollably.

“Got a smoke?” Freddie asked me.

"What?" I asked. Communication was tough.

“Got a smoke?” His lips moved again.

I watched as my hand reached out to give him a cigarette.

“Got a match?”

“Got a match? Got a match?” Everyone said in unison, then breaking out into laughter. The sound was reverberating.

"A match!" I could hear my words as they echoed off the wall.

Freddie struck the match and it lit up the room in a blaze! Everyone moved away as if it were a huge torch. Freddie lit his cigarette and we all watched the smoke twirl up to the ceiling. It carried you up and around and around, carefully, neatly, until it dispersed into a cloud.

I felt something on my leg and looked down to see Jackie's bare foot touching me playfully under the table. I thought for sure Freddie would see what she was doing but everyone was watching the smoke. They were lost in the smoke.

"I ... " said Freddie. He looked confused.

"What's happenin'?" asked Howie.

"I ... I ... No!" Freddie screamed! I thought for sure Freddie had caught on to the little game of footsie that Jackie and I were playing. Then Freddie jumped up and threw the cigarette on the floor and backed away. "The smoke! Fire!" Freddie yelled.

"Cool out man. Cool out!" Howie said.

"The smoke ... No! ... It's going up. Up past me. The fireplace!!" Freddie screamed louder.

Howie and Jackie jumped up and put their arms around Freddie who was looking at the cigarette, still burning on the floor, in utter horror. "Get it out of here. Just get rid of it man!" He cried.

"It's ok, man. It's ok," Howie said.

"Get it out!" pleaded Jackie. "We must put the cigarette out!"

Everyone backed up as I picked up the cigarette and put it out in the sink.

"I'm sorry man," Freddie said.

"It's ok man. You're having a bad trip man. That's all," said Howie.

"No! I'm sorry man!" Freddie, he was almost crying.

"Hey man, forget it," Howie assured him.

The LSD had taken us into another world. The room reeled wildly like a roller coaster and the walls vibrated in the light. I could actually feel the energy pulsating in my ears. It was insane. The serene evening that we had shared earlier had now turned into a nightmare! Everything had a tremendous glow of light around it and I could only see in a tunnel vision.

There was a chocolate cake on the table in front of me. I tried to focus my attention on it. It had a perfection, a symmetry. The icing, smooth and shiny, was like plastic. "A cake ..." I said stupidly.

"Yeah ..." Howie echoed mindlessly.

I watched my hand reach out to touch the cake. Like a Neanderthal creature, I scooped some of the cake into my hand and examined it with fascination as it slid down my fingers onto the table.

I was really into the cake. I was the cake and the cake was me. We were as one. I raised it to my lips. It had no taste. I had to vomit. It splat violently onto the table, spilling onto my jeans and to the floor. Everyone moved away as if I were a hideous monster.

"Shit man," I said in a dumb monotone. "I've got to get it off." I could feel the slime as it oozed down my legs.

"Wash it off," said Jackie

"Really," said Howie.

"Wash it off!" I could hear voices rebounding in my ears.

I walked slowly over to the bathroom. I felt as if I were drunk but it was a different kind of drunk feeling. I shut the bathroom door and heard a loud resounding click as I turned the lock. I turned on the water and it came gushing out clear and crystalline, like diamonds bouncing off the sink. The water was everywhere. I was swimming in the water. I got the cake and vomit off my jeans the best I could and started playing with the water.

I had lost my perspective, or I should say I had a new perspective. Everything was strange and frightening. The common everyday things around me, the water, the floor, I examined each with such interest. Time had lost it meaning. Seconds seemed like minutes and minutes like hours. I looked into the mirror and saw the person again. The eyes were different now. They were beast-like. I got lost in the eyes. I couldn't stop looking at the eyes. I was looking into the eyes that looked into the eyes. It took all my strength to pull myself away from the mirror and those eyes! I fell against the door and breathed heavily.

I opened the door. There was no one in the kitchen. I had no idea how long I had been in the bathroom. The clock on the wall read almost one o'clock in the morning now. I walked out into the living room. The fire had nearly died out and cast a dim light into the surrounding darkness. I thought I was alone.

"Hey," I heard a voice come softly from the shadows. It was Jackie.

"Wh ... Where's Freddie ... and Howie?"

"I dunno .... somewhere ..."

She moved closer. She was wearing a bathrobe. "Are you ok?" she asked. Her voice was soothing.

"Yeah ... I think I'm finally coming down."

She moved a little closer. "I think we're alone ..." She pulled the belt of her robe slowly and it fell aside exposing her breasts.

They were perfect and beautiful in the dim firelight. This was the moment I had fantasized about, being alone with her like this. I was consumed with emotion.

"Are you sure?"

"Come here," she said quietly.

I moved closer and reached to touch her. The robe fell completely away and she was naked. I fell into her lips with a soft kiss. I could smell her essence and I wanted her more than I had ever wanted anyone.

There were footsteps coming down the stairs! I jumped back as Jackie quickly put on her bathrobe and tied the belt. I fell to my knees in front of the fire and pretended to stoke the ashes.

“Hey... “ Freddie said.

I could hardly breath and said nothing.

"Oh .... we're just fine ..." Jackie said.

I turned around. I could tell from Freddie's demeanor that he had seen nothing. I looked at Jackie and she looked back smiling slightly. Her face was flushed.

"It's getting late. Maybe we should go up stairs," Freddie said to her.

"Yeah ... you guys go ahead. I'll just crash here on the couch," I said.

"Okay," said Jackie as she turned and walked to the stairs. Freddie followed her, as she turned to look at me. I could see in her eyes the desire which I too felt.

They ascended the stairs. I fell back on the couch and sighed. I undid my jeans. I was tired. The fire was almost completely out but I could still feel the warmth.

I thought about Jackie. I wondered how long this feeling would go on between us. It was intimate and special. We were friends, friends and so much more. It was like we knew each other in way that no others could. Where would it lead? Me, Mike, Fast Freddie ... Jackie? What a crazy situation we found ourselves in.

I closed my eyes and felt the coming of sleep. Again, I felt a tugging in my mind which was forming the words to a song. That's how it was, ideas would come to me at any time, day or night. I thought about the band, Wild Bill, Bryan, Greg, my quest for stardom. I heard a song in my mind ...

"I've been here before ...
With the cover on the door
And the lights on the wall ...

... I look at ourselves
Seeing nothing but shells
Feeling nothing at all ...

... You know I've been here
You know I've been here
Yes I've been here ...

I've seen you someplace
With that smile on your face
While you're shaking my hand ...

... You think I'm losing my head
And I ain't got no bread
Hope to see you again ...

... You know I've seen you
You know I've seen you
Yes I've seen you ...

... Well it's a long road
when you don't know where you're going to ...
... It's a long night
when you don't know what you're gonna do ...."

The LSD was finally wearing off.

17

It was a big night at the Pilgrimage - we would back up 'Lemon Bighouse Johnson'. There were many musicians in the city who would give anything to play on the same stage with him. But through our new, curious relationship with 'Wild Bill' Wilder, perhaps we had found a new path to success. It was another opportunity, another chance to be seen in the magical, silver sheen of the spotlight.

But, there were other things on my mind - Ol' Green Eyes. Perhaps by losing her, I was losing a piece of myself, a precious part of my life. She was my first true love and my wife, and I had left her and the baby. Was it the music, that and my immature selfishness that had destroyed our relationship?

Here, standing in front of the pay phone with a dime in my hand, feeling lost and confused - one of the countless highlights in my whirlwind career What a dear price to pay indeed! And now? Now I feared that I had lost her for good. Words. They always came to me in my thoughts. Words with music. How easily they came to me, rolled off my tongue, but now, I was at a loss. Words. I needed words to say. To say, not to sing. This was no song and dance routine, this was my life. What could I say to her? Something that would make sense. I dropped the coin into the slot and dialed the numbers as I tried to form the words in my mind, as if it could be as easy as pushing the buttons.

"Hello ..." I heard her say.

"... Hi ..."

"... Hey ..."

Silence ...

"Well .... How are you? ...." she said.

"Oh ... I'm ok ... I guess ..."

Silence ...

"Well ... what's on your mind?"

"I just called to see how you were."

".... I'm fine ..."

More silence ...

"... I've missed you ..." I said.

"Oh I'm sure you have ..." she said, mockingly.

"Really I have."

"I'm sorry but I have made up my mind. It's over. Really. Over!" She was distant, unreachable.

"But I love you!"

"You don't really love me. You're just feeling insecure," she said.

"I know how I feel .... Look ... maybe we could get together ..."

"... I don't know ... We will always be friends."

"I've already got enough friends. I need you ..."

"Oh yes ... you and your glorious friends!"

Fast Freddie walked up beside me. "Hey, it's time to go on," he said trying to get my attention.

I tried to cup my hand over the phone. "Not now Freddie! Wait a minute."

"But it's time," he insisted.

"Whose that?" Joanne asked.

"It's Freddie. It's time for us to go on."

"Look ... go away damnit!" I said to Freddie, "Can't you see this is important!"

"Okay. Okay man," he said. "Five minutes. All right?" He walked away.

I resumed the phone conversation, "Look ... can't we get together and talk about this?"

"... Maybe ..." she said half-heartedly.

"I do love you. I do ..."

"Well .... your great band and music is calling you ... You must not keep them waiting.... Heaven forbid!" Her facetious words stung.

Silence...

"Take care of yourself ... I love you ..." I said softly.

There was a click. She was gone.

With sadness, I slowly entered the barroom. The air was thick with smoke, and everyone was drinking, laughing wildly. On stage, Andy was helping to get the equipment ready.

Wild Bill came over to us. "What's the problem white boy?"

"Nothing ... we're ready," I replied, solemnly.

"Well get your white ass up there and start playin'!" he joked.

We took the stage and readied ourselves. 'Bighouse' lumbered up to the stage. He seemed out-of-place, more like an old black farmhand coming in from the fields, than a musician. He sat down on a chair and made an attempt to tune his battered old guitar. The waitress brought him a large glass of gin - straight gin!

A voice came over the speakers and the lights came up. "Now will you welcome to the Pilgrimage stage ... BIGHOUSE JOHNSON!" The audience roared and the excitement was at a fever pitch. Bighouse simply started playing his guitar. There was no count. He just started playing. We had to do the rest. The guitar was like a small toy in his large gritty hands as he chugged into a funky, sweaty rendition of a song ...

"If the river was whiskey!
And I was a divin' ... I was a divin' ...
I was a divin' duck ...

If the river was whiskey and I was a divin' duck!
I dive to the bottom ...
and I'd never come up ..."

His voice was hard edged and hypnotizing. There was no doubt that he had taken command of the room. Without pretension, slick arrangements and clever phrasing, the music was real and rugged. There was only feeling, that feeling known as soul, and Bighouse had it.

And us white boys? We played along, watching, perhaps as much a part of the audience itself, hoping to capture that feeling for ourselves, trying to learn this idiom called the 'blues' from the guru himself.

As we finished the first song, the crowd cheered. How strange, to see the young people in the audience, many of them professional people, rich and well-off, not your general run-of-the-mill crowd. And they were straining, trying desperately to see and hear this blues legend. The room literally rocked. We played for nearly two hours without stopping and the audience loved every minute of it. All the time, Bighouse was drinking glass after glass of gin. It was unbelievable his constitution. I leaned over to talk to him. "Bighouse, we don't have to play so long you know. We can take a break if you want to."

"Is tha' right?" he drawled.

"You only have to play a forty minute set."

"Ok. Sounds good t' me!"

He simply stood up which signaled the end of that long set. The crowd needed no fanfare. They applauded loudly. He had won them over with his song and they crowded to congratulate him as he left the stage.

There to greet him was his manager, Steve Hientz. "Sounded great Bighouse baby! Make way! Let us through!" he shouted as he and Bighouse made their way to the back of the club.

Wild Bill greeted us as we too made our way through the crowd. "You guys did ok for a bunch of wimpy white boys!"

"Thanks Bill," I said.

"Don't get any ideas ... you're still white, wimpy and forgettable!" he teased. "Hey Bighouse ... you just sit right down. Hey barkeep! You give Mr. Bighouse anything he wants. Understand. Anything!" Wild Bill ordered and then headed for the door that led upstairs to the office. I took a seat beside Bighouse, making sure that Steve Hientz wasn't near.

"Hey Bighouse ... you don't have to work this hard you know," I said. "Mr. Hientz tol' me to play so I play," he replied.

"But you only have to play for forty minutes at a time," I insisted. "Forty on ... twenty off. Get it?"

"Hell, where I come from, you play all night or 'til the drink run out!" he said laughing. "Mr. Hientz, he good to me. I do wha' he say do."

Steve Hientz noticed us talking and rushed over to hear the tail end of our conversation. "What are you telling Bighouse?" he asked.

"We ... we were just talking about his music. That's all." I replied.

"Look, don't go meddling in our affairs!"

"I wasn't meddling."

"Bighouse is my main man! I take care of Bighouse. You just play the music. Okay white boy?"

Rather than argue with him, I decided to go up stairs to see what Wild Bill was up to. Andy came with me. The stairs leading up to the office were bare wood. A sharp contrast to the posh decor of the club. Graffiti of other bands were scrawled on the plain unpainted walls. The office door was locked. I knocked loudly. "Whose there!?" I heard Wild Bill ask with his thunderous voice.

"It's Andy and me!"

I could hear the sound of metal clinking against glass. I knew he was doing cocaine. The door opened and we were allowed in. Freddie, Mike and the Polack were there along with Wild Bill who sat at his desk. In front of him was a dish with a huge mound of cocaine on it.

"You white boys are pretty good," he said, as he proceeded to cut out lines of the coke. "But I know what you want ... You want the 'white lady'!"

"Yeah ..." said Mike, watching the white lines of cocaine on the dish, hypnotized.

"Yes ... I've got the 'white lady' and you assholes would like to do some of it .... Cocaine and Camels for breakfast!" Wild Bill sang out jokingly. "You guys are a bunch of assholes aren't you?" he said playfully. Jus' waitin' around to do some coke, huh?" He bent over and snorted two of huge lines. We watched eagerly. "Are you an asshole?" he asked, joking, looking at me.

"Whatever ... sure," I said. He knew I would do anything to do some cocaine, even take his insults.

"This is bullshit!" said the Polack. "I'll see you guys down stairs." He got up to leave the room.

"Hey ... wait a minute! My apologies ... I'm just having some fun," said Wild Bill. "Stay Polack. I like you."

He turned his back attention to me. "Okay ... 'Mr. Superstar' ... go for it!"

I took the rolled up bill and snorted a line and could feel the potent warm buzz in my head.

"Even though you are white and wimpy ... I like your songs." He finished his Galliano and threw his glass into the corner, smashing it to pieces.

I took a good hard look at him. Who was this man who drank, snorted and swore? True, he loved music and musicians. In some ways, he had a heart of gold, but there was a dark side to his nature, a deep dark past that drove him on. Maybe he too had dreams like the rest of us, but, his were lost, blurred from vision. Maybe he tried to live the lives of the ones around him, trying to lose the past or prevent the future. But life was always a game to him and you had to play by his rules. I was a player in that game. At times, I felt like my soul had been laid bare for his appraisal. It was this way for most of us who withstood his arrogance. And I wondered why he liked us. Maybe it was because we were the only ones who could put up with him, who cared to play this game?

"What's that on your hand?" Freddie asked.

I looked down. A sliver of the broken glass was sticking in my hand. It must have come from Bill throwing and breaking his liquor glass. I pulled it out and wiped away the blood. "It's nothing ... Really ... it's ok," I said.

"Shit! Did I cut your playing hand?" asked Wild Bill. "Hey, I'm sorry ... Really ... Is it bad?" He was looking at my hand with the greatest concern.

I looked up to see Wild Bill's eyes looking into mine. For a minute he really cared and I could see it in those steel grey eyes. In that fleeting instant, I saw another side of him. Was it the real 'Wild Bill'?

In a dream, I suppose, it all happened in a dream. ... I was singing at the Pilgrimage. I could see Wild Bill in the back carousing with my Father! What would he think of all this? Looking around the room, I could see everyone - Andy, Bryan, Greg, Howie, Jackie, Steve Hientz, the Polack were there. Even Joanne, 'Ol Green Eyes! They were all there. My Mother. It was as if this was a testimonial and I was performing for them. The greatest performance of my life! This was my chance, a chance to show everyone what my life was about. What would anyone do given this situation? One chance, not a lifetime, not a year, not even a day, but one performance. How I could show them? What would you do? Like in an old movie, the happy ending, the final scene where everything fits neatly before the curtain falls.

I took the guitar in my hands. A string was broken. Oh well, I would play anyway. I was invincible. This was my time. I looked out over the crowd. I thought. Closing my eyes, I formed the words in my mind. I would sing the blues, not the rural country blues, but the blues as sung by this white boy, this suburban knight in shining armor. Oh ... I had come, had seen, put it all into words for this crowd to consume. Words of seeming wisdom, all cut and arranged by a cunning mind. But how cunning? How invincible? With shabby clothes and ragged guitar, I seemed more like the great underdog. Perhaps ... a charlatan enshrouded in the facade of greatness, the rock 'n' roll prophet singing of self inflicted blues. The joint was packed, the people eager with anticipation, the lights, lowered, and, the show begins. I sang to them ...

"... Feel the pain ...
Do you think you can feel mine? ...
The watchman comes
To tell me that it is time ...

To boogie man! ...
And do handstands until the morning light ...
I makes the blues
Seem darker than the black of night ...

But the times they are changing ...
and they changing fast ...
When the dreams of the dreamer ...
will come to pass ..."

The ending chord, and I swoop down my guitar neck with such savvy, befitting the greatest rock star and show business legend. All to thunderous, overenthusiastic, but well earned and humbly accepted, applause! The very heavens open to bestow rays of blinding light and pastoral glorification! The wonder boy has triumphed in this magnificent dream!

But, suddenly, it was quiet. I look up, and, there is only silence, solitude. In the back of the empty, dimly lit room, the bartender is putting away the bottles, cans and glasses. It is quiet as I step down to put the guitar away, close the lid, and turn the clasp on what seemed like another of a countless stream of uneventful nights. To once again put away the broken, battered dreams until the next time, when I would pull them out and test their mettle.

And the song, the words, the melody, the feeling, the great offering? The words are not heard. And the melody dies among the sparse sounds of too few hands clapping, into the dead wood of the table, chairs, and the dull scuffed floor below. The feeling, but a fleeting instant of tears and joy. All this. All this lost, gone, dissipated, mixed with the immense void of hopelessness and despair. Perhaps such is the end of one too many dreams of youth and of glory ...

I woke up to the smell of bacon sizzling and coffee brewing. Rolling off the couch, which, being essentially homeless, I had inherited at Pine Avenue, I rubbed the sleep out of eyes and walked unsteadily to the kitchen. Terry was at the head of the table reading the 'I Ching' and Jackie was working over the stove. "Well ... good morning ... rock star," she teased.

Terry remained silent.

"Yeah ... right," I said, still yawning.

"Well, I guess you haven't read the papers yet?"

"What papers?"

"Today's paper silly. There's a review on the band," she said beaming.

"Where!" I reached for the paper which was spread out on the table. I read it aloud. "The band that backed up 'Big House' Johnson at the Pilgrimage last night could possibly be one of the best white blues bands in the city, especially Johnny 'The Polack' Lodz on the drums. With this kind of soulful performance, it makes one anxious to hear the original songs the band has reportedly written. Notably by the singer-songwriter ... why that's me!"

"That's right. You're a singer-songwriter aren't you?" She came over and put her arms around my neck.

"I can't believe it .... some recognition!" I exclaimed.

Terry looked up unimpressed, and then went back to her book. "What's wrong?" I asked.

"I dunno ... she's been like that all morning," Jackie said, looking at Terry to see if there was some reaction. There was none.

"Where's Freddie? Has he seen this?" I asked.

"Oh yeah ... he saw it. He's on cloud nine. He went to store to get me some milk ... should be back soon."

I read the paper over and over. Turning the words over in my mind. It was such a sweet feeling of success! After struggling night after night, this was the reward ... a few lines of ink on a crumbled piece of paper. But it was so much more than that. It was a reason for believing, keeping the faith, keeping the candle lit in the hurricane.

The screen door slammed and I looked up to see Freddie. "Hey man! Did you see it!" I said excitedly.

"Yeah! Great isn't it?"

Jackie gave him a big hug. "Well this deserves a big celebration breakfast!" she exclaimed.

Freddie sat down and Jackie served the bacon and eggs and hot coffee. We ate heartily. Terry was still quietly reading her book.

"Well ... I have some better news. I thought I might save it for last," Freddie said.

"Oh yeah? What could top this?" I asked.

Freddie looked at Jackie and smiled. "I just talked to Steve Hientz."

"Well ... what did he say?"

"He said that there was a chance for us to go to New York."

"To record a record?"

"Well ... no ... not directly. There's an off-Broadway rock musical that needs musicians. I told him that we might be interested."

"A Musical ... would we write some of the music?"

"Well ... no. We would just play their music."

"I ... dunno ..." I was a little disappointed.

"Hey, it could lead to another break ... I think we should do it," he reasoned.

"Well ... how long would it last?"

"About six weeks ... that's all."

Again the screen door slammed and Cathy walked in.

"Hey 'Cath' ... How's it goin'?" Freddie asked her.

"Better after I've had a joint. Anyone got some papers?" She whipped out her baggie of pot and threw it on the table. "Hi Terry," she said. Terry looked at her but then continued reading. "Well ... be that way! What's wrong with her?" she asked Jackie.

"I dunno ... she's been quiet all morning." She went over to Terry and rubbed her arm tenderly. "What's wrong Terry? ... Are you ok?"

Terry dropped her book and bit her lip. Tears welled up in her eyes.

"Hey ... you can tell us. I mean we're all family here."

"I know that," Terry said softly.

"Do you want to talk about it?"

"I got some tests back yesterday ... I have a lump on my breast ... it is malignant."

"Are you sure? I asked. "I mean even if it's true, there are things that you can do."

"I'm sure," she said in between sobs.

It became silent among us. The food was getting cold. Words were needed but the silence endured. I prayed that someone would speak. Jackie rose to the occasion. "We're not going to let this thing beat us ... we're a family and were gonna lick this thing together!" There was a quiver in her voice but she looked at each of us in turn to get our assurance.

Freddie moved closer and took Terry's hand into his. I looked out the window into the bright sunny morning. If only we could start it over again. If only we could change a course of events by merely having only coffee. The newspaper, crumpled and forgotten, lay on the table, having lost all importance.

The Long Road

19

We were back in New York. We stood in the huge rehearsal hall, among the actors and actresses, some reading books with provocative titles and spooning down yogurt-much more sophisticated than our sodas and cigarettes. But being musicians and therefore entertainers as well, we felt a kinship with them nevertheless.

A tall intellectual-looking type walked to the center of the hall and began to speak. His voice was huge and magnificent, his English, formal and proper. "Could I get your attention ... please!" The murmurs turned into silence. "I would like to welcome you to 'Bacchus In Black'. This is the name of this off-Broadway production and trust that all of you are here to work hard. My name is Art Crumley and I am the director. If you are not sure that you are supposed to be here then please come forward!" No one in the room moved.

He turned his attention to us, "You are the musicians I suppose." Mike nodded. "Splendid! Just sit tight and I will get to you shortly. The rest of you can now come forward so that I can check you off the list and so that we can get acquainted." The others assembled around him as he called the roll.

"Man. This guy's really a trip," said Fast Freddie, quietly, aside.

"Very artsy ... I must say," said the Polack, and joked, "His name i-s-s 'Art'!"

"Hey, I think it's kind'a neat. Different," I added.

"You would," quipped the Polack.

"All right, cool it you guys. Here he comes!" Mike whispered.

Art approached us, I watched him, his demeanor. He was all business. "Well ... let me see. So... we are the band aren't we?" he said in a dramatic, formal style.

"Yes ... we are the band. Aren't we?" said the Polack mockingly.

Art looked at him in disgust but then continued. "And comedians too I see!"

"No ... musicians," said Fast Freddie.

"Yes ... musicians ... Steve Hientz spoke highly of you. I trust you can do the job?"

"It should be an interesting project," I replied.

"Interesting? ... yes ... Here's the music for the show," he said as he handed me a pile of sheet music.

I studied the sheet on top with a puzzled look. "Well ... we don't exactly read music. I mean ... we play by ear."

"I see ... are you sure you can handle this ... 'interesting project'?"

"Look we can handle it. Just give us a place to practice," said the Polack.

"Very well! Rehearsal starts tomorrow at nine. He abruptly turned and walked away.

"He's a pompous ass!" said the Polack.

"Yeah ... he's weird," Freddie said, joking.

"Hey, come on guys!" I said, "Let's go back to our hotel room and work on this stuff. We've got a lot to do."

"Well you start back to the room, we'll get some beer," said Freddie.

"Get some beer?" I exclaimed, "I just said, we have a lot of work to do. This isn't a party!"

"Look 'Lawrence Welk'," he teased, "you do the musical arrangements and we'll meet you later." Everyone laughed.

Outside, I left the others and turned the corner. The city was essentially walls of concrete and steel buildings. The afternoon sun made a luminescent glow in the alleys, through smoke and dust that filled the air. I stepped carefully over the trash-strewn sidewalk. In the boarded entrance-way of an abandoned building, there was an old lady sitting on the stoop. She was drinking a beer; beside her-a tattered bag of rags. She raised her eyes to mine. She looked tired. Then she looked away with cold indifference.

Our hotel was old and run-down, but it was cheap and affordable. The lobby had drab ratty furniture and worn out carpeting. I pushed the button for the elevator. When elevator door opened, a woman appeared behind me. I could feel her eyes watching me. We both stepped in. The doors closed.

"Hey fella," she said.

"... Hi ..." I said meekly.

She leaned closer. I could smell her strong perfume. "I ... ah .. I'm what you might call a 'workin' girl'," she said, "you think you might wanna come up for a drink?"

"Ah ... No. No thanks," I said sheepishly.

She smiled at me and straightened my hair with her hand, softly, gently, almost as in a motherly way. "New in town ... aren't 'cha fella?"

"Well ... yeah ... sort'a ..."

"Sort'a?"

"Yeah ..."

She smiled and winked at me. "Four-twenty-seven ... if ya change your mind."

"Yeah ... sure ... okay ..."

She leaned over and kissed me on the cheek. I felt embarrassed and even more, angry, angry at my own innocence-obviously a small town boy in the big city. I was relieved when the elevator stopped and she got off on her floor. The door closed. Suddenly, I felt sad, disappointed in myself. Here I was in New York city with a New York city hooker, and I blew it! How cavalier I had imagined myself at times. Why was I so nervous? After all, I was a musician, an entertainer and in my own mind's eye I was a man of the world. I closed my eyes and exhaled deeply.

When I got off on my floor, the hallway smelled like insecticide. Our room was a 'suite' as we were told by the hotel clerk, but I opened the door to look upon two double beds without sheets and a broken window that remained open. The air conditioner had ceased to work long ago and remained in the other window as a reminder of some glorious past. The room was hot. I walked into the kitchen and roaches scurried into the hidden recesses.

The truth was, this was cheap, flophouse hotel room in Bowery district. I threw the sheet music on the bed and fell down beside them. I was tired, hot and sticky, but decided to forego the bathroom. I closed my eyes and thought of Jackie. Poor Terry. I was falling into a deep sleep when a loud rap came from the door. I jumped up to open it.

"Hey man. We got the brew!" Fast Freddie said. He pulled a gallon jug of cheap wine from the brown paper bag as the others filed into the room. They had a stranger with them.

"Who is this?" I asked, alluding to the stranger.

"Oh, this is Leon," said Mike. "We met him down at the liquor store."

Leon was a sight with his mirror shades. He was thin and haggard with long greasy hair. What was remarkable was the monkey on a chain that rested on his shoulder.

"Hey Leon, how's it goin?" I said, trying to be sociable.

"Great man. Great man," he replied. He appeared to be stoned.

"What ah ... who is the monkey?"

"Oh, this is 'Shithead'," he said. "That's his name, 'Shithead'." He laughed. The monkey grabbed a lock of his greasy hair.

Freddie poured the cheap wine into paper cups and passed them out.

"Christ! What is this shit?" exclaimed the Polack, spitting the wine to the floor.

"Hey, what do ya want for two-fifty?" Freddie replied.

"Give me some wine ... Fruit of the vine ... When ya gonna let me get sober?" sang Mike.

"Hey, Leon here says he can get some drugs," said Freddie.

"How about cocaine?" I asked.

"Hey, man. Anything you want man. Anything man!" said Leon.

"Wait 'til payday. We'll get high on some New York City coke man!" Mike exclaimed.

"Anytime man. Anytime my man! Gib me five!" replied Leon. He laughed a silly laugh and held out his hand for the reciprocating hand slap.

"Any one got papers? Let's smoke some weed," said the Polack.

"Here man," said Leon. He reached into his pocket and pulled out a pack of Zigzags. "Anything you want man! I can get it for ya!"

"I think we should go over some of these tunes for the show," I said.

"I got a better idea. Let's jam!" shouted Freddie.

"Yeah ... let's jam! I've heard the show tunes. They'll be a breeze to learn," added the Polack. "Here take a hit." He passed the joint.

Freddie pulled out his guitar and ripped off some licks. The Polack pulled out some drum sticks and beat out a rhythm on the empty guitar case.

Maybe they were putting on a show for Leon, but Leon turned his attention to me.

"Hey man," he said, offering me the joint. "Good shit man!"

I took a hit. "It's ok ..." I started to cough. Each time I hacked I could feel myself getting higher.

"Take it slow man," he said. I could see my reflection in his mirror shades, distorted and unreal. The monkey chattered wildly.

"I'm ok. Really," I insisted.

But, the others seemed distant now as I could feel the drug taking me away. I was stoned. Again my face grew flush and I found it hard to breath. The anxiety was coming back. I was about to panic.

"Hey man. This pot feels good. Hey man?" asked Leon. The monkey jumped from shoulder to shoulder and then defecated. The excrement rolled off Leon's dingy shirt to the floor! Leon went on smiling.

"Hey ... that's weird," I said from the drug induced stupor.

Leon only smiled. With the mirror-sunglasses, I couldn't see his eyes. It made me feel uncomfortable and I started to hyperventilate, sure that I would not take another breath. My heart started to pound.

I walked over to the broken window and stuck my head out into the evening air. Down on the street, there was the relentless flow of traffic and thick film of dust and smoke, but I took a deep breath and felt relieved. Somewhere out there, among the trash, the litter, the prostitutes and the losers was the glittering prize of success. This was the showbiz capital of the world. This was the place where dreams came true, where it all happened for the lucky few. I wondered if it would offer us an avenue to success, the same passage-way to the heights of stardom that always seemed to elude us.

20

"Once again from the top!" Art urged the cast. "Band ... whenever you are ready!" Groaning could be heard as the actors took their places for the umpteenth time. The air in the room was stagnant, hot under the spotlights. Freddie took one last drag of his cigarette and then counted into the song. A member of the cast started to sing.

"Stop! Stop!" screamed Art again. "Would you please at least try to sing on key?"

The actor, young and handsome, looked over at the us in condemnation. "The band's playing out of tune. It's not me," he complained.

"Right!" Freddie contested. "Look the key of 'A' is the key of 'A'."

"How would you know what key it is? You can't even read music!" he said sarcastically.

"Let's not argue!" Art said calmly, "Let's take five," trying to prevent a senseless argument.

We put down our instruments and went outside for some fresh air. Sitting on the stoop, Freddie lit another cigarette as the rest of us gathered around.

"Man ... I don't know if I can take this shit much longer," said Mike.

"... Only a few days left to opening night. The way things are going, I can't see how this thing is going to get off the ground," said the Polack.

"This was all your idea Freddie," Mike continued.

"Well shit! Let's just pack up and go home. Fuck it!" said Freddie.

"Look!" I said, intervening, "We can't fight among ourselves!"

"Fuck you! You're always so goddamned self-righteous!" screamed Mike.

"No, he's right ... anyway ... it'll be over soon enough," said the Polack.

We sat in a blue fog as we watched the parade of cars go by.

"Whoever said this was the 'Big Apple' was full of it," Mike complained. "Shit. I haven't had a good meal in two weeks."

"Yeah ... really," added the Polack.

"And we're gonna get our big break in New York City?," Mike continued, "I'd rather be back in D.C. at the Pilgrimage."

"Hey, all you do is complain," I said, "You ought to listen to yourself."

But I remembered the terrible audition at Gotham Studios a year ago. Maybe New York City was not our path to success?

Suddenly, Freddie jumped to his feet and ran across the street. We all followed and gathered around the old Chevy. The tires had been slit. All four. "Goddamn it! Somebody trashed my car!" He exclaimed as he checked the doors and found the front passenger side jimmied.

"Did they take anything?" I asked.

"Nah ... there's nothing to take," he said as he inspected the glove box.

"What are ya gonna do?" asked the Polack. "We're all broke!"

"Well ... don't worry ... I'll take care of it," Freddie said, "I've got a deal going with Leon."

"What kind of deal?" I asked.

"A deal ... that's all."

"A drug deal?"

Over across the street we could see Art peeping out the door looking for us.

"It's the director extraordinaire beckoning," said the Polack. "Coming Arthur d-a-h-l-i-n-g!" he quipped.

We ran back across the street and entered the intense atmosphere of the rehearsal hall. "Now ... let us rehearse the chorus scene. Would all of you please form a group over here," said Art, pointing to the corner of the room.

Once again we started a song. The exhausted bunch in front of us sang out in disarray. And, once again, "Cut! Stop please!" Art shouted. Then, he pointed his finger at someone in the crowd. "You there ... yes you. Would you be so kind as to ... go get a soda or something? We won't need you for this scene." A young girl stepped away from the others. Tearful, she left the others and walked off to the wings. A tough break. We started again.

After the rehearsal, the band met out on the street corner. "I'm going down to the 'Village' with our tape. Anyone wanna come along?" I asked.

"What are you gonna do?" quipped the Polack.

"I'm gonna try to get us a real band job ... that's what! How about it?" I said to Freddie.

"I've got to meet up with Leon," he said.

"I'm going with Freddie," Mike said.

"Me too," added the Polack.

"Drugs huh?" I asked.

"What if it is?" said Freddie.

"Are we musicians or drug-dealers?"

"Look, you go on and sell the band, leave my personal life out of it. Okay?" He poked his finger in my chest to stress his point.

"So that's the way it is huh?" I said with resignation.

"Yeah ... I guess it is ..." Then, he laughed a good-natured laugh. Mike and Polack laughed too.

Then I laughed with them. "Sure, see you guys in awhile." I watched them as they turned the corner before I crossed the street and headed for Greenwich Village, 'the Village'.

I wasn't sure of my way but I knew the general direction and just kept walking until I came to Washington Square. There was a street musician playing the fiddle. On the ground, in front of him, was his opened violin case filled with loose change. There were others throwing Frisbees, and those in small congregations, talking and drinking beer. The smell of pot smoke was thick in the air. I crossed the street and what a scene. There were people walking everywhere, sidewalk stands selling hot sausage sandwiches and hotdogs.

And nightclubs! Behind every other door you could hear the faint sounds of music or laughter. This was indeed the showbiz world. I so much wanted to be a part of it. This was my place. This was what it was all about. But, I felt lost. Where would I start? I passed door after door but did not dare enter. I walked around the block several times before getting the courage to stop in front of one club.

I looked up to read the sign 'Cafe Wha?'. I walked inside. It was dark but I could see a folksinger on the stage. Carefully, I walked to the bar and took a seat.

"What'll it be?" the bartender asked. I thought about the two dollars that I had crumpled in my jeans. "Look ... if you want to stay, you'll have to drink," he said sternly.

"How much is a draft?"

"Seventy-five cents."

I knew that getting that beer would mean little or no dinner that night, but I wanted to stay. I had to stay.

"Yes ... I mean I'll have one."

He grabbed an empty mug and started to pour. I handed over one of my dollars and crammed the other back into my soiled pocket. With courage I spoke up. "I was wondering ... could I speak to the manager?"

He looked at the tape box I had in my hands. "What do you want with him?"

"I'm in a band ..."

He grinned as if he had seen my kind before. "You see that man at the end of the bar? Go talk to him."

The man at the end of the bar was slightly balding and overweight. Next to him was a black man with dark sunglasses. I moved down to the stool next to them as they conversed. Feeling more aggressive now, I tapped the black man on the shoulder. "Excuse me," I said.

They stopped talking and the black man turned to me. He didn't say anything. Perhaps it was rude, my interruption, but I was determined. "I was wondering if I could speak with the manager?"

The black man grinned at me. I couldn't see his eyes through the dark sunglasses. He said nothing.

The big, bald-headed man spoke, "You w-o-u-l-d would you? Well, I am the manager."

"I'm in a band and-"

"And you want an audition? Right?" The two of them chuckled, as I put the tape on the bar in front of them.

"You know how many guys come in here wanting an audition? Who sent you?"

"Well ... no one."

"I'm sorry son ... go someplace else. I'm busy," the manager said. He pushed the tape back in my direction.

"No ... you see I'm in the band that's playing the music for 'Bacchus in Black' on Astor Place. The off-Broadway production."

"Oh yeah! Art something ..."

"Art Crumley," I said.

"That's right ... Art Crumley ... that Shakespearian director, producer," the black man said.

"Do you know who this is?" the manager asked, pointing to the black man. "This is Jackson Miller the 'Ice Man'!"

"You mean t-h-e 'Ice Man'?" I said "... the famous jazz trumpet player?"

The Ice Man flicked an ash from his cigarette and looked on. "I've heard some of your records ... I'm pleased to meet you," I said as I offered my hand in friendship. He refused to notice my gesture and I pulled my hand back slowly.

"Do you really think you're good enough to play in the same club with the 'Ice Man'?" asked the manager.

"I played with 'Big House' Johnson!" I said, defensively.

The Ice Man smiled. "So you know all about the blues huh?"

"Well ... I've played some."

He took a long drag off his cigarette and crushed it out on my tape box. He leaned close and I could see my image in his dark sunglasses. "Look here Mr. 'Bluesman'. Why don't you stop kiddin' ya'self!"

"Hey kid," said the big man, "the Ice Man is right .... really I can't use you ... you're wasting my time."

"Can't you even just listen to the tape?" I pleaded.

The big man picked up the tape casually and wiped the ashes from it. "... Ok ... I'll give it a listen, but I'm not promising you a job. Understand?"

The Ice Man leaned over to face me. "Watch out for 'dem blues white boy ... 'dey gonna kill you," he whispered with a smile.

From within the dressing room downstairs, you could hear the sounds of an audience, talking, rustling, noisy sounds that only a large audience of anxious people can make. Meanwhile, the actors and actresses were busy getting ready, some rehearsing their lines, others lost in their own world. This was the last chance to make final adjustments because tonight was opening night for 'Bacchus in Black'.

My throat was dry. I reached down for a drink of soda on the dressing room table. "Christ! What's this?" I said, spitting the drink to the floor. Someone had put out a cigarette in it. I could hear laughter from a distant stall. "Shit! Who did this?" I demanded.

"You really think they're gonna tell ya?" said the Polack. "It's probably that faggot actor who can't sing."

"Here's the costumes," said Freddie, as he entered the stall and hung them on a nearby hook.

"What costumes?" asked Mike.

"I didn't know that we had to wear costumes," I said. I pulled the plastic away. "Man you have got to be kidding! Tacky sequined robes!?!?"

"'Fraid so," said Freddie. "Just put them on ... no one will see you ... you'll be in the darkness."

"Right! We'll all be weirdoes before this thing is over," teased the Polack.

Upstairs, the rehearsal room was transformed into a theater-in-the-round. Except for the props and several curtain backdrops, the audience was free to sit anywhere. We were setup off to the side and, although we were part of the cast, from our vantage point, we felt like an audience too.

Quickly, we took our places and Act One was under way ... "Hail Bacchus! ... How long it has been?"

"Not long enough!" whispered the Polack sarcastically.

"There are troubled times ... they have forgotten how to revel ..."

"No shit!" he whispered again.

"Look ... be quiet and be ready to play," I whispered.

Being behind the audience, luckily our remarks went unnoticed. Freddie counted us into the first song.

"... Bring out the wine my fellow brothers ... folks ...
Let's drink a toast to one another ...
... to the great Bacchus!"

The actor sang. He was still slightly out of tune. My stomach turned as he strained to make the notes. When he finished the audience applauded moderately.

"Great Dionysus! ... Bacchus! ... Son of Zeus and the mortal Semele! ... We knew you would return!"

"Not even the fire of Hades could impede my journey ..."

"Tell me of the troubles ... where are the Pan pipes ... the Bacchantes?"

"Bacchus ... There is all work and no play ... the merriment you had brought us has soured like a bad wine ..."

"This can be remedied. Bring out the drink! ... the dancing Bacchantes!"

Several girls, barely dressed, came out dancing as we played the music.

So it went, Bacchus spent the next hour and a half weaving his spell of lust and folly until his mother, Simile herself, to end his useless revelry, puts her son to death ...

"Bacchus ... my son ... you have turned the farmer against his plow ... the carpenter, his tools with your folly ..."

"Mother ... see how they revel and dance. They love my ways!"

"There is frivolity in their celebration and their song holds a hollow tone ... forgive me Great Dionysus!"

Someone in the audience shouted "Bacchus sucks!". The audience laughed, but the cast and crew tried to ignore the remark.

She stabs him. He falls to the floor bleeding and the audience grows silent ...

"Dear Mother ... I accuse you not for it was fate that guided your dagger ..." he said, gasping.

"In your revelry you have brought false meaning to the harvest!"

"Yes ... what a fine line is drawn that separates work from play, the muse and his lyre ..."

"But the line must be drawn ... so it goes for you Bacchus ... your pleasure knows no boundaries and the youth no end to the festival!"

"Very well Semele ... but as the Spring follows Winter, my spirit shall return like a cool breeze on the bough ... to quiver the muse's string and awaken the fire in a lovers heart ..."

Bacchus dies and the lights grow dim and then ... darkness ... The play was over.

The audience gave a luke-warm round of applause. The lights were raised as the audience filed out of the room and the players headed for the dressing room stalls. Art Crumley walked over and looked dejected.

"What's wrong Art?" I asked, "You should be pleased. I mean ... we did ok ... right?"

"Walter Harrison left after the First Act."

"Who is William Harrison?"

"That's Walter Harrison. T-h-e Walter Harrison ... the top theater critic ... that's all!" he exclaimed.

"Is that bad?"

"Of course that's bad!" he screamed at me. "Do you think he would walk out after the First Act if he liked it you ass!?!?"

Everything stopped and he had the attention of the entire room. No one said a word. We had never seen him totally lose it. He tried to regain his composure. He settled down, "There will be a reception at the Four Aces restaurant. All of you can of course attend. I thought you did a good job, but or course, tomorrow night must be better!" He watched us quietly for a few brief seconds, and then walked back upstairs.

The dressing room started to once again buzz with conversation. "Let's go down to the 'Cafe Wha?'," I said. "Maybe they listened to our tape. Maybe we got that gig!"

"Ya really think we got'a chance huh?" asked Mike.

"Man, how many times have I told ya, ya got'a believe in yourself," I replied.

"Ok ... let's go check it out," said Freddie. "But first we got something else to do."

"What's that?"

"Don't worry about it."

Outside, Leon was waiting for us. 'Shithead' was with him.

"Hey Leon my man! Is everything together?" asked Freddie.

"Sure man. It's totally together man!"

"Good. let's go."

"Hey wait ... are all these guys coming with us?" he said, alluding to the band.

"They're cool. Anyway they can wait outside," Freddie said.

We descended the stairs to the subway, into the bowels of the city, where the walls were covered with graffiti and the air was damp and heavy, We waited for the next train. When it arrived, we boarded and took a seat. Like the subway walls, the interior of the train was also scrawled with graffiti. Trash littered the floor. Into the dark tunnels we rode, station to station.

Klikity-klak-klikity-klak. I felt hypnotized from the steady motion. Suddenly, Leon realized our mistake and came alive. "Oh no man! We missed our stop!"

"Can't we just get out at the next one and walk back? It's only a few blocks," said Freddie.

"No man! We can't get out here. It's a bad neighborhood. Bad dudes man! Bad!"

"What do we do?"

Leon looked worried. "I tell ya what. When the train stops, follow me. We gotta run to the other side to catch the other train back. Don't ya stop to talk to no one man. No one!"

"Aren't you over-doing this whole thing?" asked the Polack.

"Hey man ... you wanna get cut? Beaten up? These are rough dudes man. Believe me! " He poked his finger into the Polack's chest to stress the point.

When the train stopped, we ran and jumped over the turnstile. Shithead chattered wildly. We were like fugitives, the way we ran. We got to the other side of the tracks and stopped on the loading platform, totally out of breath. Meanwhile, Leon watched carefully for gangs that patrolled the area. We were outsiders on their turf, and would be considered enemies. I had never seen Leon this serious about anything, and I knew, at least for these brief moments, we were in danger. Finally, a train arrived. We boarded and fell into the vacant seats relieved.

We rode back two stops and got off. This time, we walked slowly up to the street above, and then several blocks farther on. Leon constantly watched everyone and everything. We finally stopped at a corner.

"Now you guys wait here ... Leon and I will be back soon," said Freddie.

"How long will you be gone?" I asked.

"Half hour ... maybe less."

We waited on the street corner as Leon and Freddie walked several doors up the street to an old brownstone and entered. Suddenly, coming up the street was a dark figure emerging from the shadows. My heart was in my throat. I stared over in the direction of the park, trying to ignore him, but all the time, aware of his presence. I heard his footsteps as he came closer. They slowed down and then stopped. I didn't turn around.

"Hey you!" I heard the stranger say. I turned slowly. He was a dark figure and wore a stocking cap. His face was hidden by the shadows.

"Hey ... " I mumbled.

"Ya got'a smoke?" he asked.

I reached into my pocket and pulled out a crumpled cigarette and handed it to him. He put it to his lips and lit a match. In the flashing light, I could see his eyes. He threw the match down to the ground and puffed the cigarette. I watched in relief as he walked off into the shadows. I heard Freddie's voice and I turned around to see him and Leon walking back toward us. Freddie had a guitar case.

"Back already?" said the Polack.

"What's in the guitar case?" I asked.

"What's this? Twenty questions?" said Freddie. "Let's just get out of here."

We walked back toward the subway and entered the stairwell. The Mike bumped into, of all people, a policeman! He fell down and the policeman backed up a few steps. "Sorry officer," said Mike.

"You should watch where you are going!" he said. He eyed the guitar case in Freddie's hand. "Do you boys have some identification?"

Freddie looked at Leon, not knowing what to do.

"Well ... officer ... you see ... we are musicians ... we're headed to the Village ..." I said calmly.

"Musicians huh?" He looked at the guitar case again. "Let me see what's in that guitar case."

Leon backed up a few steps as if he was going to make a run for it.

"Really officer ... we are musicians and we have a gig in the Village. We have to be going or we'll be late," I insisted.

"Where are you working in the Village?"

"At the 'Cafe Wha?'," I said.

Freddie shook his head in agreement. I was sure the cop could hear the pounding of our hearts. See the fear in our faces. He looked us over again and then said with reservation, "All right. But you punks watch out where you're going next time!"

Quickly, we descended the subway stairs. "Man that was close!" said Leon. "That was good thinking man!" he said to me.

"Just what is in the case anyway?" I asked.

"Only four pounds of pot ... that's all," said Freddie.

"Christ! You almost got us all busted!"

"Not so loud!" Freddie whispered as he looked around to see if anyone was nearby.

"I can't believe that you would put us all in jeopardy like this," I continued.

"Look 'Lilly White', if it was cocaine you'd be all for it."

"But not like this. Walking around the streets of New York City with four pounds of pot. We could be killed."

"Hey, next time I'll remember to leave the women and the kids home ... okay?" Fast Freddie said jokingly.

The train arrived and we boarded. This time Leon and Freddie sat across from the rest of us. I looked at the guitar case on Freddie's lap and wondered if Freddie, in spite of his good natured charm and charisma, was our own 'Bacchus in Black'. Our own Dionysus, leading us to a life of festive chaos.

Back on the street, we gathered around to plan our next move. "Look ... I think maybe we should go back to the room," said Freddie.

"Really," said the Polack. "We've had enough excitement already."

"What about the club? Don't you guys want to find out about the gig?" I asked.

"No. Not now. There are more important things to do," said Freddie.

With anger, I took the guitar case out of his hands and threw it to the ground. "Hey! We're not drug dealers!" He looked at me sternly.

We had never come to blows before over anything. But things were changing. Maybe it was the last three weeks we had spent in this hell-hole of a city. Our tempers flared as we eyed each other wearily from under the dim street lamp above.

Then, he smiled. It was that old charm again. "Hey ... what's the big deal anyway? You go. You're the manager of the band anyway, at least in spirit."

"Yeah ... you go. You can bring us the good news!" said Mike.

I looked away disgusted, knowing it was futile to argue. I left them on the street corner and made my way back to the Village. As I approached the entrance to the Cafe Wha?, I saw the bartender standing outside. "Hey you!" I heard him say as I started to enter.

"What's the matter?"

"Don't go in there."

"You remember me? The musician with the tape from the other night?"

"Yeah I remember you ... but don't go in."

"Well ... I came to ..."

"He don't want t' see you." He interrupted me.

"What about my tape ... didn't he listen to the tape?"

He reached behind the door. "Oh yeah ... here's the tape ... he told me to give it to you," he said, as he handed me the box.

"Did he say anything about ..."

"Look kid ... he told me to give you back the tape. He said it was the wrong kind of tape ... it wouldn't play on his machine."

"But ..."

"Just go away kid ... believe me ... he don't want to see you ... he's busy." He stood there looking at me. He took a long drag off his cigarette and threw it into the street. I watched it as it rolled in the gutter and came to a stop.

I knew it wasn't the tape. He had probably not listened to it, or our music was not appropriate, or he didn't like my looks. So much for the 'Cafe Wha?'.

22

The swanky hotel was mountain of glass, just another Tower of Babel that dotted the New York City skyline. We, including Leon wandered into the luxurious lobby like fugitives from another time, another place. The clerk behind the desk looked at us with a great deal of concern and I realized what a sight we were with our long hair and dirty jeans.

"Can I help you?" the clerk asked.

"Yes ... we're here to see Mr. Bill Wilder."

"Let's see ... Wilder ... yes ... that would be room eleven twenty-two. Do you have business with him?"

"Yes ... he's expecting us."

He look at me with disbelief. "Well ... let me see." He dialed a number on the phone. "Mr. Wilder, there are several gentlemen here to see you ... I see ... right." He hung up. "Yes, I suppose you are okay. The elevator is straight ahead."

We walked to the elevator door, drawing disconcerting stares from the people walking by. The doors opened and we entered. Freddie pushed the button and we settled back for the long ride up. "Man ... this is how the other half lives!" he said.

"Class man ... this is class ..." said Leon. The monkey jumped out from under his black leather jacket.

"You're lucky the clerk didn't see Shithead," the Polack said with a laugh.

On the eleventh floor, we found eleven twenty-two and knocked on the door. Wild Bill greeted us.

"Hell! You guys look like shit!" he exclaimed.

"Hey Bill ... how's it goin'?" said Fast Freddie.

"Better than you ... obviously!"

The room was luxurious. Very large and well furnished. It had been a while since I had been in a clean room. Over on the sofa was a man stylishly dressed. Wild Bill introduced us, "Oh by the way ... this is Pinky Thompson from 'Revolution records'. Pinky ... this the band ... Who in the fuck is this?" he said looking at the stranger with the monkey on his shoulder.

"Oh ... this is Leon," said Freddie. The monkey chattered mindlessly.

"Which one? ... The monkey?" quipped Wild Bill.

Pinky laughed.

"Hey man!" said Leon.

"It's ok Leon. Don't take offense ... I like monkeys," said Wild Bill.

On the table in front of Pinky was a large pile of cocaine and a few bottles of booze.

"Is that coke?" I asked.

"Yes," said Wild bill.

"How about a line?"

"In time ... in time ..."

The bathroom door opened and a tall blond walked out. She was wearing a tight dress and platform shoes. "This is Crystal ... say hello Crystal," said Wild Bill.

"Hi fellas," she said politely, but in a uninterested way.

"I like that used pussy," teased Wild Bill.

"Oh Bill! Watch your mouth!" she replied.

We gathered around the pile of coke. Wild Bill pulled out his knife and started to cut out lines on the table top. We watched hungrily.

"Come on Bill ... give me a line," Crystal pleaded.

"Just for that ... you'll be last," he said.

She fell back into the sofa and looked away with disgust.

"Pinky here is thinking of releasing your song 'It's a Long Road' ... isn't that right Pinky?"

"Yeah sure Bill," he replied. His eyes were on the lines of coke.

Wild Bill handed him a rolled up bill and he snorted two lines. "I like your song ... Long Road ... " he said, "Ooo that is good coke!"

"I'm glad you like it ... the song I mean," I said.

Pinky laughed. "It doesn't matter whether I like it or even if it's good ... being good doesn't have anything to do with it!"

"What do you mean?"

"Look ... money is what it's all about. ... Will it sell? ... that's what's important! Don't be so naive ..."

I was surprised and embarrassed.

Wild Bill offered us the rolled up bill one at a time. Freddie, the Polack, Mike, Leon and then me and finally Crystal. Wild Bill appeared to enjoy tormenting us with our addiction, and he would take his time in choosing who would be the next to snort the delicious drug, the cocaine. It was almost sadistic, the way he made us wait. Each of us did a line and settled into the glorious high. I soon felt the warmth in my head as my heart started to pump wildly.

"Are you trying to tell me that a good song can't be sold?" I continued to talk to Pinky.

"Well ... what does 'good' mean?" he asked. "I'm not in this business to be a patron of the arts ... really. There are thousands of bands like you ... what makes you any different from the rest? You may be the best in the world ... but who cares ... money my friend. Money! Making money, that's what it's all about. Bill?" He motioned for Bill to lay him out another line.

"Yes ... but ... When I look at album covers, the lyrics neatly printed on the sleeve ... this is art! Doesn't this have anything to do with it?"

"Look kid, you be the artist ... I'm a business man ... I'd sell that monkey over there if I thought I could make a buck! I like your song okay? Consider yourself lucky."

It was getting hard to breath. I started to loose feeling in my hands and I was hyperventilating badly. I thought I was going to pass out. Perhaps it was the lack of food and sleep. I walked to the bathroom on shaky legs and closed the door behind me. I rubbed my hands together to try to regain the feeling in them and strained for another breath. I turned on the water from the tap and let it run over my hands. I drew a breath. I looked into the mirror and saw my tortured face among the elegant fixtures in the room. What a strange person I had become. Drugs were destroying me and I couldn't stop.

23

There was the sound of a glass bottle rolling on the pavement, down in the alley. I opened my eyes and saw the morning light coming through the window. It was summer-time in Atlanta and the air was heavy and humid. Upstairs, I could hear the hacking of sick men from another hellish night. I was in a flophouse-a ten dollar a night room. Cheap yes, but that cost couldn't be measured in dollars and cents. For me it was just a room, a place to sleep. But for others, the end of the line, the end of a long list of failures and broken dreams, lost loves, lost friends. Perhaps in a way, this place was a sanctuary, a place to hide from the past, a place to hide from the eyes of the world.

As I got up and sat on the edge of the bed, several roaches scurried away at my feet. I put on my jeans and a tee shirt. It was already getting hot outside and it was useless to take a bath. Over on the other bed, Andy was still asleep. On the table was the paper and pencil where I had been writing the night before. It was a sad song. I picked up the paper and read the lyrics ...

"Late August ... passing through ...
I guess you thought I wouldn't recognize you ...
Late August ... seems you're gone ...
And then you're back again ...

Late August ... lazy day ...
You break my heart and then you slip away ...
Late August ... summer skies ...
The deepest shade of blue ...

Melancholy is your nature ...
Memories are all you know ...
How can anybody think of their future ...
When you've got them feeling so low ...

A sudden breeze is your warning ...
Of turning leaves and skies of gray ...
When I felt you coming this morning ...
I felt my troubles comin' ... right away ...

Late August ... passing through ...
I bet you thought I wouldn't recognize you ...
Late August ... summer's end ...
Ain't ya got a friend? ......"

"What's that?"

I turned around. Andy, becoming awake, was leaning up on one elbow.

"It's a song idea."

"Another song! How many of those things have you written?" he chuckled.

"Oh ... I dunno ... a lot I guess."

"Shit! If you had a dollar for everyone of 'em ... you'd be rich!" he teased.

"How 'bout some breakfast?"

"Sounds good ... give me a minute."

When Andy had dressed we left the room. I locked the door behind me. Outside on the front porch was a man lying passed out in front of the door. We stepped carefully over him. Other men were sitting on makeshift stools of fruit crates.

"He's sick ... don't pay him no mind," said one of the men. He took a drink from his soda can. I knew it was booze. These men would fill their soda cans with booze and lie to each other about drinking it. Perhaps it was their last vestige of pride.

"Hey friend ... you got'a quarter? ... a dime you could 'gib me?" asked another.

"Here," I said. I handed him two quarters.

"Thank you ... God bless you sir," he said solemnly.

Andy and I walked on for a few blocks to The Majestic diner. Inside, we took a booth. Across from us were two taxi hacks drinking coffee after the night shift. One of them had a huge pistol hanging from a holster on his belt.

"Hungry?" I asked Andy.

"Nah ... just coffee," he said. "We ain't rich ya know."

"Yeah, you're right."

"I mean ... you give that bum back there fifty cents ..."

"I know what it's like to be broke," I said solemnly.

"Hey look, I don't feel sorry for him ... he ought'a go out and find a job."

"It's hard to work a job ... well ... when there's nothing to work for. I guess that guy really needs to find himself."

"Well he's not gonna find himself climbing into a bottle."

"I suppose you're right but I wonder ... if he ever had dreams of a bright future?" I said, thinking deeply.

Andy looked at me strangely. "How's that record doing? ... 'It's A Long Road'," he asked, changing the subject.

"I dunno ... I haven't heard from Pinky. I'll call Wild Bill later. Maybe he's heard something."

The waitress brought the coffee. Mike and the Polack popped in the door and sat down in the next booth.

"Hey," Andy said.

"How's it goin'?" asked Mike. "Did you hear the hacking this morning?"

"Yeah ... it's sad isn't it?" I said.

"Doesn't do much for your appetite," said the Polack.

"Anybody seen Freddie and Jackie this morning?" Freddie and Jackie were staying with friends.

"Not yet," said Mike.

"What's on for today?" asked the Polack.

"I'm going to an agent. Anything would be better than the 'End Zone'," I replied. Everyone agreed. The End Zone was the club we were currently playing and it wasn't the classy type of hotspot we were used to. Sort of a college hang-out. "How about you guys?"

"I'm gonna get stoned and cruise the record shops," said the Polack.

"Right on!" said Mike.

I looked at Andy. "I guess that leaves you and me."

"Yeah ... what the hell ... I'll go along with you."

Andy and I got into his old VW bug. We pulled out and drove downtown. "Are you sure you have the right address?" he asked me.

"Yeah ... I think this is the right street."

The directions that I had scrawled on a match book cover had taken us to a shabby part of town. There were only old store fronts and topless clubs.

I saw the address that matched the one I held in my hand. Andy pulled over and parked. The sign above the entrance read 'Play Pen Escort Service'.

"Geez, this is a whore house!" said Andy, "Are you sure this is the right place?"

"That's what this says," I said looking down at the old match cover.

We entered, and were greeted by a shapely brunette in a slinky black gown. She stood up as we entered. "Well fellas ... what can I do for ya?" She said with a sexy voice.

"Is there a Lucky-"

"Lucky Starz?" she responded quickly.

"That's right," I replied.

"Follow me." She led us through the hall. I looked into a room and saw a single bed freshly made. There was a sickly smell of air freshener, a bottle of cheap cologne on the night stand. At the end of the hall she pointed to a stairway.

We ascended the stairs and found at the top, a small office. The door was ajar so we entered. The walls were covered with faded posters and old band pictures. A small bearded man sat at the desk. "Hey fellas ... how are we today?" he said.

He wiped his nose with the back of his hand and then wiped his hand on his shirt.

"Hi ... I called yesterday."

"Yeah yeah. Don't tell me ... the band from DC." He lit a cigarette and a threw the match into the ashtray which was overflowing with old butts.

"We're playing at the End Zone on Peachtree."

"The 'Zone'. How's it goin' there?"

"Well ... okay ... business is slow ... we were interested in getting into another club."

"Aren't we all ... aren't we all. Got'a tape ... a glossy?"

I handed him a tape and he turned around to fidget with a tape machine. I looked up at the promotion pictures of the bands on the wall and studied them closely. They were all the same-four or five guys or four guys with a girl-each with saccharin smiles, wearing tuxedos and gowns. He turned on the tape and then swiveled on his chair to face us. The ash from his cigarette was getting precariously longer. I wondered when it would fall of onto the desktop.

Our song started to fill the room. It sounded muffled on the old sound system.

"What song is this?" he asked annoyed.

"It's one of our songs" I replied, "It's an original song."

He turned off the tape player. The ash from his cigarette which had been hanging from his lip, fell onto his lap. He didn't seem to notice. "Look, do you do any current pop tunes?"

"Well ... we do some blues."

He leaned back in his chair and looked at Andy. "Hey ... what can I say? I can't book a band without a good club repertoire, good dance music."

I shifted in my chair. It was as if the eyes of the people in the pictures on the wall were looking down on us. Judging us. I cleared my throat. "We have a single out on Revolution Records ...'It's a Long Road' ... maybe you have heard it on the radio?"

"It's a long what?"

"It's a Long Road," said Andy.

He paused and then smiled. "Hey boys! It's just the name of the game ... good tunes ... and bouncy chick up front ... that's what does it in this town. Look, nobody's heard of you guys let alone your record." He pulled the tape off the tape player and placed it on the desk in front of me. "Have you got a glossy?"

"Here's a picture of the band taken recently."

I handed him the picture that Jackie had taken of us recently. He glanced at it and handed it back quickly. "I'm sorry but I can't use you guys. You're just not what I'm looking for."

"We're-" I was about to say.

"No!" Interrupted Andy angrily. "Let's not take up anymore of Mr. Starz's very valuable time. I'm sure he's a very busy man!" Andy pulled me by the arm and I stood up, grabbing the tape.

"Come back and see me when you've got something ... some new tunes maybe a professional picture with tuxedos ... a good lookin' chick, okay?"

"Don't bet on it," said Andy. "You'll be sorry when these guys make the big-time."

"Sure! That's what they all say!" I heard him say, laughing to himself as we walked back down the stairway.

Out in the car, it was quiet. Andy spoke first, "What a jerk."

"I don't know what to do," I said. "Everywhere I turn it's always the same-a brick wall."

"Hey you guys are good. Remember the first club job ... the one I found for you guys at Sal's Place? You believed in yourself then. Don't give up just because of jerks like that. You guys are a concert band not a club band ... you're beyond that."

I knew what he said was true. I had been over and over this in my mind many times like a tired old story. Sometimes I felt like I was trying to convince myself. How long could I keep the faith?

24

I brushed my long hair back, looking into the mirror. It was cracked and made me look like two halves of a person, a distorted picture of myself.

There was a knock at the door. It was Fast Freddie. He was standing in the hallway dressed in a white suit, a style of suit from the nineteen forties, the style of suit that Humphrey Bogart or Clark Gable would wear in a romantic, foreign setting. His long hair was neatly combed. I could see what Jackie saw in him. The charismatic 'Fast Freddie', always the life of the party, made also a handsome man. "Hey ... Ya ready to go?" he asked, grinning in a good natured way. No ... he reminded me of Robert Redford.

"Yeah sure Robert my boy!"

"What?"

"Nothing ... forget it." I threw on a jacket and turned off the light. Outside in Andy's car, was Jackie. I sat up front with Andy. Freddie and Jackie sat in the backseat. Jackie, not to be out-dressed, had on a red silk dress and high heels. It hurt to look at her she looked so good. "And how are you tonight?" she asked me.

"Oh fine. A little out of my league though ... you two look really good."

"It's fun to dress up. I love nice clothes. Do I look good?"

"Well ... yeah ... you both do."

Jackie's dress rode up well above her knee and I tried not to notice her legs. She had great legs.

"Hey let's burn one!" said Freddie. He pulled out a ready-made joint and lit it up. The pungent pot smoke filled the small car. I took a toke but then coughed violently. "You never could handle your pot," said Freddie jokingly.

When we arrived, we walked to the entrance of the 'Underground'. It was much like a city below a city. There, literally underground, were streets and sidewalks. There was a boutique, a pizza shop, even a nightclub. People were milling about, eating, talking and laughing. Tourists with their families took pictures of the sights and of each other. The atmosphere was carnival-like.

"Let's go dance!" said Jackie.

"First I wanna drink," said Freddie.

"I could use a beer," Andy added.

We stopped at the first door that had music and went in. There was a band on stage playing and the dance floor was full. We took a table and ordered our beers.

Jackie was visibly excited. "Freddie I want to dance ... you promised!" she begged.

"In a minute ... I need a few drinks first."

"Oh you're no fun!" She looked up at me. "How about you ... you can dance with me."

"Uh ... I dunno," I said unsure.

"Oh come on!" she insisted.

She pulled me up from the table and we got lost on the dance floor. We swirled and twirled through the crowd, and all the time, I couldn't take my eyes off her. Suddenly the music ended and we stood there trying to catch our breath. The next song started and it was a slow song. I started to walk away. "No ... it's ok," she said softly. I held her in my arms as we started swaying slowly to the music. I was becoming aroused.

"I've got to have you," I whispered into her ear.

"I know ..."

"When?"

"I don't know ... don't rush me," she said as she kissed my ear.

When the song was over I tried to gain composure as we joined the others. Freddie and Andy were doing shooters of whisky and were starting to get drunk.

"Hey let's get another round!" said Andy.

"Really!" said Freddie. "You guys looked good on the dance floor."

"Oh yeah ... like I can really dance," I laughed.

"Better than me. That's for sure," said Freddie.

"Freddie, I thought you were going to take me sightseeing ... I wanted to see some shops," said Jackie.

"Hey relax sweetie ... have a drink."

"I don't want a drink ... you promised!" she said pouting.

Freddie looked over at me and winked. "Why don't you take this lady off my hands for awhile," he said.

"Well ... I ..."

"Really it's ok ... I'd rather stay here and party."

"Well you heard the man ... let's go ... it'll be fun," she said.

"Okay ... we'll be back soon," I said.

"Take your time ... hey Andy ... order another round of shooters," said Freddie drunkenly.

Jackie and I left the club and walked down the street. We walked hand in hand as we looked in the boutique windows. She would stop and pick out her favorite things and I would nod in agreement.

When we turned the corner I could not stop myself. I pushed her against the wall and held her in my arms. I kissed her passionately. She responded to my kisses hungrily. "Yes I want you ... I want you more than anything," she whispered.

"What about Freddie?"

"I don't care ... I want you!"

We went back up outside, not knowing where to go but knowing that we had to have each other. That was all that mattered. Without thinking, I hailed a cab and gave the driver directions back to my flophouse room. In the backseat of the cab, with the street lights passing by in the darkness, I pulled her close to me. She writhed, moaning with pleasure. I kissed her uncontrollably.

When we arrived, we got out of the cab and I handed the driver the fare. We walked up to the front door and went in. Neither one of us cared what would happen, only that we would have each other. Nothing would stop us. I fidgeted with the key knowing that we would finally be alone. I opened the door and Jackie entered. She threw her purse on the table as I locked the door behind us.

I reached for her wantonly but she pushed me playfully onto the bed. "Not so fast ..." she teased. She stood before me and smiled devilishly. "This what you've wanted all this time ... so have I," she said lustfully. She unbuttoned her dress and it fell to the floor.

"You are so beautiful," I whispered.

"I'm all yours ... tonight all yours ..."

There was nothing else. No band, no music ... no Fast Freddie. Just she and I. We made love violently, our hearts beating wildly!

Afterwards, I rolled over and looked up at the ceiling. Quietly we realized what we had done. What we had anticipated all this time had finally culminated here, on the old rickety bed in that flophouse. I felt her squeeze my hand.

Suddenly the door flew open breaking away part of the frame! Freddie looked down at us with rage. "You fucking whore!" he screamed. He threw a beer bottle against the wall and it splintered onto the floor.

Jackie covered her eyes with her hands. "You don't understand!" she exclaimed.

"I can't believe you would do this!" he yelled.

"I love you too!" she said sobbing.

"You love me too huh? You love him more than you do me!" He was standing there with our clothes at his feet, his chest heaving with anger and his eyes on fire.

"Look Freddie it was my fault," I said.

"You!... you self-righteous bastard!"

As I stood up he reached back to swing. He hit me square in the face, and I knocked over the table behind me as I fell. Jackie quickly got up and ran out into the hall clutching her dress.

"Look Freddie you don't understand," I said holding my face.

"No you understand this ... stay away from her ... okay?" He turned and walked out slamming the broken door behind him. My head was exploding with pain as I laid on the floor with the beer and the broken glass, wondering what this would ultimately mean.

25

The next night, I went to the End Zone to play. I hadn't seen Freddie or Jackie since the night before and I didn't know what to expect from them.

As soon as I entered the door, I headed for the bar. The barmaid approached. "How are you tonight?" she inquired.

"Oh ... okay I guess." My head was throbbing with pain.

"A rough night last night huh?"

"You might say that ... could I have a vodka tonic please?"

My nose was still sore where Freddie had punched me, not to mention the headache I felt from the stress. Perhaps the vodka would take the edge off.

I lit a cigarette and looked down at the floor. I was tired and no matter how much sleep I had, I was starting to feel weak and dissipated. Andy appeared and sat down on the barstool beside me. "Hey dude. How's it goin'?" he asked, patting me on the back.

"Well ... I guess you know the story."

"No, not really ... only that Freddie and Jackie are having problems and you got a bloody nose ... I figured you wouldn't want to talk about it."

"You really wouldn't want to know ... really."

The phone rang behind the bar. The barmaid answered it and turned around. "It's a Mr. Bill Wilder from Washington DC. ..."

I took the phone. "Hey Bill ... how ya doin'?"

"Pretty good you wimpy white boy!" he joked.

"It's good to hear from you ... things aren't really so great here."

"That's too bad 'cause they really stink here," he said.

"What do you mean?" There was a silence on the line. "Hello ... Bill are you there?" I said into the mouthpiece.

"... Look I hate to tell you this ... but I have a review of your record that ran in the Old Mystic Review ... It isn't good ..."

"Well ... What does it say?"

"Shit! It goes on to say that ah ... 'the song 'It's a Long Road', though cleverly written, lacks excitement and has poor arranging throughout. Notably there is no hook line ...' and so on and so forth ..."

"Great! Who wrote it?"

"Bryan ..."

Yes fate. Firing Bryan as our manager years ago, was coming back to haunt us. "... Is it really that bad?"

"Let's put it this way ... Pinky called today ..."

"Well?"

"... He's not happy with the way it's working out ... he's going to stop promoting the record ..."

There was a void in my mind for a moment and I wanted to be someplace else, if only to pretend this wasn't really happening. "Hey! Are you there?" I heard Wild Bill in the earpiece..

"Yeah ... I'm here ..." I said sadly.

"Look ... No guts no glory ... Fuck it! We gave it a good run for the money ... it's not the first deal I've seen go sour ..."

"Sure ... If first you don't succeed and all that bullshit! ... I've heard all that crap before!" I said bitterly.

"Hey look man, what can I say ... it's your show. I've done what I can ..."

"Yeah ... that's right ..."

"I got'a go ..."

"Yeah ..."

"Later."

"Well ... what happened?" Andy asked.

"Our record is bombing ... that's all ..."

There was a brief moment for pity. It was sickening and ugly and I hated that moment. No one was meant to share that kind of moment.

"Can I buy you a drink?"

"Yeah ... maybe you can buy me a drink ... yeah ..."

Freddie and Jackie came in the front door of the club. Freddie passed me on his way to the stage without uttering a word. I looked at Jackie who took a seat at a table near the back of the club. Both of them were avoiding me. There was only one other customer, and he was sitting at the other end of the bar talking to the barmaid.

I walked up the steps to the stage wearily and put on my bass. The Polack was tuning his drums, while Freddie and Mike were looking down at their feet. I could see the manager looking at his watch. He didn't look happy. We threw out a small plastic football with 'End Zone' written on it to the lone customer as was a silly club gimmick of sorts.

"What are we gonna do?" asked Mike.

"... Doesn't much matter ..." said the Polack.

"Let's play 'Long Road'," I said. "Let's just play."

"Oh fuck you!" replied the Polack.

"Well look ... got a better idea?"

"Let's jam!" said Freddie. As before, He ripped off some mean guitar licks. Only this time, there was no one there to hear them. The sound reverberated off the walls and died away to silence. The magic just wasn't there. He played again, urging and pleading a response from the drums or the bass. This time, the Polack answered with a snare drum and then another. The band propelled itself into a blues rendition. We gave it our best as we trudged through the song. After endless nights in the same empty club, we had lost the cutting edge. Our music sounded dull and our movements were mechanical. Our song ended in a cluttered crash.

Then the silence ... The man at the bar didn't turn around. He was still talking to the barmaid.

"Do we have to play? ... I mean there's no one here," said the Polack.

"Maybe someone will come in. We have to play ... it's our job to play," I said.

"You play you asshole!" said Mike.

"Look ... we should play ... let's just go down the list of songs and play 'em ... it doesn't matter really," said Freddie.

I called out one of my songs and I start to sing ...

"Saving your heart from a sure misery
Was the first thing I had on my mind ...
But all my intentions were lost in the dust
When I knew that I needed your love ...

Lovers they are such fools ...
Lovers breaking the rules ...

Fly with the wings of a bird on your back
And you'll know what it means to be free ....
To remember the night that I spent in your arms
And you'll know what it means to be loved ...."

The words, though heart-felt by me, now seemed lifeless as I sang them into the microphone. When that song ended, Jackie and Andy clapped. That sound of just a few hands clapping was sad and almost comical as it too died away to silence.

So it went. We played one song after another as if we were in a paid rehearsal. On the next to the last song, Jackie and Andy got up and danced and it almost made us want to play.

Suddenly, a stranger walked in. He was tall and dressed in faded jeans and a black tee shirt with a leather vest. He had on a hat on with the brim turned down and sun glasses. He looked at us briefly and then sat down at the bar. I had a feeling that I had seen him before. We started our last song of the set. A Chuck Berry song ...

"... Well the joint was a'rockin' ...
Goin' round and round ...
Yeah reelin' and rockin' ...
What a crazy sound ..."

The song, which was usually played to the scene of wild dancers and merriment, sounded precarious as it projected out from the bandstand into the rows of empty tables and chairs. The stranger turned to watch us, but then turned back around to the solitude of his drink.

Suddenly I knew who he was. It was 'CC' of the 'CC riders', perhaps one of the new and greatest rock bands in the country! He was the singer-songwriter and the leader of the band. I winced as I thought of how ridiculous we looked playing to this empty room.

When we went on break, I put walked off the stage and over to the bar. He looked at me as I approached and then I knew it was him. "How ya doin'?" I asked nervously as I sat down beside him.

"Ok ..." he said reluctantly, and then looked away.

The barmaid came up and I ordered a drink.

"Did I say that you could sit there?" he asked without looking over at me. He just looked straight ahead, at the row of bottles behind the bar.

"Well ... no you didn't ... I didn't think that you would mind."

Still, he looked straight ahead as he took a sip of his drink.

"Hey, I hate to bother you, but aren't you 'CC' of the 'CC Riders'?" I asked. My voice cracked. I winced.

"Maybe ... What of it?"

There was an awkward silence.

"You see ... I'm a songwriter too ..."

"That's real good," he said as he finally turned to face me. He seemed unimpressed. "... With a little work you might go someplace," he said as he looked at the silly football jersey I was wearing.

The barmaid came by and he ordered another drink. I continued. "I guess it's pretty exciting writing songs and getting all the acclaim ... It must be a real trip!"

"Yeah ... it's a real trip ..." he replied unemotionally, still looking ahead.

"I mean ... doesn't it mean something to be able to express your ideas through you music and share it with the world?"

He turned to face me. "You really think it's great huh? There's a big difference in writing your songs ... the songs you feel you just have to write, to share, and having to write songs because some bastard owns your soul. Not everyone can be the Beatles ..."

"What do you mean?" I was surprised and confused.

He continued, "I mean having to write a dozen songs in six months because there's a hundred thousand dollars on the line ... You have to have a hit man! Do you know what I mean? A big hit or it's your ass! I don't think you really understand."

"I guess I don't ..."

"Just play your songs man ... play 'em in your bedroom ... tell the world about your feelin's at the local coffee house man ... you might be better off ..." He spoke almost with regret and took another long drink and put the glass carefully on the bar.

"Your songs are great! Most of them have a message."

"I've been lucky ..." He looked at his watch and then put a twenty on the bar. "Hey look ... I gotta go ... I'm going out side for a jolt ... you want some?"

"Yeah sure."

"Is there a backdoor?" he asked quietly, looking around to see if anyone had noticed him.

"Yeah ... follow me."

We made our way past the bandstand and then out the rear exit into the alley. We walked over to the far wall, into the shadows, as he brought out a baggie. It was a lot of cocaine. My eyes watched hungrily as he put a straw into the bag and snorted. He handed me the straw and I took a big hit.

"Hey ... take it slow," he said, as he put the baggie into his pocket and patted me on the shoulder. "This is primo stuff."

Then he simply left. He started walking down the alley and watched him as he turned the corner and went out of sight. I couldn't believe it! I had just done coke with 'CC' of the 'CC Riders'! No one would believe me, but it was true.

My head was getting numb and my heart began to pound. I knew I had done too much cocaine. Walking back into the club, I stopped by the stage railing. My legs had lost their feeling and I was starting to hyperventilate. It was worse than ever. I took a step for the bar but then fell to the floor. Andy came running over. "Are you ok?"

"I can't breath ... I can't breath," I whispered.

Jackie and Freddie came running over and stood over me. "What's wrong with him," asked Jackie.

"I don't know ... he say's he can't breath!" Andy exclaimed.

I was starting to lose the feeling in my hands and arms and began to panic. "Hospital ... take me to a hospital," I gasped.

"Well let's go!" Jackie screamed. "You heard him!"

Andy picked me up as Freddie ran out to start the car. With help, I walked outside, and then fell into the backseat as the car sped off. "Hurry ... hurry Freddie ... " I whispered, trying to catch my breath.

Freddie ran several red lights as Jackie was looking for a hospital, when suddenly, as luck would have it, there was one on the right.

"Thank god!" Jackie said almost in tears. "Hurry Freddie!

"I'm trying damn it! I'm trying!" he yelled.

He pulled into the parking lot and screeched to halt at the door to the emergency room. There was a pain in my chest as Andy helped me out of the car. We entered the emergency room with Jackie running wildly ahead of us. "You have to help him!" Jackie pleaded.

The nurse behind the desk looked at us calmly.

"Hold on ... now what is the problem?"

"Look ... our friend here ... we think it's a drug overdose!" said Freddie.

"I need some information," she said, as she sat down to her typewriter. "What is the name, address and insurance company?"

"Can't you see he may be dying?!" Jackie screamed. The people in the waiting room looked up from their coffee and magazines.

"Get him some help now!" yelled Freddie, as he pounded his fist down on the desk.

The nurse looked at me again and then reached for the intercom. "Send an orderly up to the desk please!" Resounded in my ears.

The doors across the room flew open and two men in white came rushing in. Andy helped me into the wheelchair. My arms and legs were totally numb and the pain in my chest was worse. I was wheeled into a large room where I was laid on the table and then left alone.

It seemed like an eternity, the time I laid there. I turned my head and looked at the bottles and equipment surrounding me. I was starting to black out when I felt a hand grab my wrist. I opened my eyes. It was a young man and his hands seemed steady and gentle. "What did you take?" he asked quickly.

"It was cocaine ..." I said, my voice shaking badly. I closed my eyes as I gasped for breath. I don't want to die! I don't want to die I kept thinking to myself over and over.

"Roll over," he told me. I felt him pull my pants down and then poke a needle into my buttocks.

I rolled back over and opened my eyes. I was alone again. I thought about Terry dying of cancer and the fear and misery that she was going through.

Soon, the pain subsided in my chest. I heard someone come near. I opened my eyes to see an elderly doctor standing over me. His eyes were clear and wise. He looked into mine inquisitively.

"Did I have a heart attack?" I asked.

"No ... no heart attack."

"Will I be all right?"

"It depends on what you mean by all right," he said sternly.

"I guess it was pretty foolish ... taking drugs ...."

"Yes it was foolish ... but it wasn't just the cocaine that almost did you in ... you are suffering from anxiety, you're on the verge of a nervous breakdown!"

He sat down in a chair next to me and folded his hands on his lap.

I was shocked, "A nervous breakdown? ... It can't be."

"Look at you ... you're a nervous wreck! I imagine that you have been under some mental strain ... not eating and sleeping well."

"Well ... yes in a way I guess ... but really I feel fine now ..."

"You need rest." He looked at me in earnest.

"My friends are waiting for me ... I feel ok now ..."

"You can go but let me give you something." He scribbled on a clip board and then handed me a small packet. "These are valium ... five milligrams. Take one every four hours or whenever you feel anxious."

"Thank you."

"I don't want to tell you what to do but ... also you need to talk to someone ... maybe a psychologist."

"Hey ... really ... I'm not crazy! I'm ok ... really!"

"Of course you're not crazy but you do have emotional problems, a drug problem and maybe other problems. It wouldn't hurt to talk to someone ... would it?" the doctor said in earnest.

26

When the End Zone gig was finished, I decided to fly back to DC. I wanted to patch things up with Steve Hientz. Maybe I could persuade Pinky to release another record. Maybe Wild Bill would have some dates for us to appear at the Pilgrimage. It was urgent. I felt like our careers were at stake. Maybe it was all over.

"Can I get you something?"

I looked up and saw the pretty face of the stewardess. "Yes ... a vodka tonic would be fine." I really didn't need the drink. The valium had me feeling more relaxed than ever. The drink was a habit, a prop, maybe a crutch, but it felt soothing as I drank. My mind was wrecked with the problems that the band was having. What could I do to turn the tide?

I met Howie at the airport, and it was good to see a familiar face. "How was Atlanta?" he asked.

"Sucked," I replied, as I tossed my bag into the back seat of his car and climbed in.

"It doesn't sound like things went too well."

"Not too well ..." I said sadly.

"That's too bad. Where's the rest of the crew?" he asked.

"Oh, Andy, Mike and the Polack are driving back ... by the way, have you heard our record on the radio lately?" I asked in earnest.

"'Fraid not ..."

"How's Terry?"

"Not good ... in fact it's a good thing Jackie flew back last week 'cause Terry is ... well she's close to death. I don't know if Cathy and I could handle it without Jackie's help. She's really something."

"Yeah ...," I said thinking about her. I wondered if it was over for us.

We entered the old neighborhood and when we pulled into the driveway at Pine Avenue, I knew that I was home. Finally, really home. I walked into the kitchen to see Jackie wiping off the table.

She broke a slight smile, but somehow, it was different, not the kind she always had for me. "Hi," she said, as she looked down to avoid any eye contact.

"How have things been ... I mean with Terry?"

"Maybe you should see for yourself." Wearily, she put the hand towel across the back of the chair and straightened her hair. She was visibly tired and over-wrought. "In there ... in the living room," she said as she pointed in the general direction.

I walked through the hallway and there on the couch was a person whose face was thin and pale. It was hard to believe it was Terry. I came near and noticed that she was asleep. Gone was her long flowing hair and rosy cheeks. I was sickened and turned away.

Cathy, sitting in a chair by the fireplace, looked at me and then at the floor. Jackie came in and leaned against the door frame.

"How long has she been like this?" I asked quietly.

"For about a month ... the last week has been the worst," said Cathy.

I knelt down beside the couch and ran my hand across Terry's forehead. She opened her eyes and looked at me. She tried to smile and I could tell that she was in pain. I tried to fix her blanket when I heard her whisper something. I put my ear to her lips. "Are you okay?" she asked me.

"Yes ... I'm fine ... it's you I'm worried about," I said softly.

"Don't worry about me ... soon I'll be where dreams reside ... a wonderful place ... a place you and I know well ..."

"Yes ... in our dreams ..." I said quietly.

She raised her finger towards Jackie. Jackie came over and took Terry's hand into hers and they talked in sweet low tones. Suddenly, Jackie dropped her head onto Terry's chest and started to cry.

"What's wrong?" I asked.

Jackie stood up and wiped her tears. "She's gone ... she's dead ... I can't believe it ..."

I took her into my arms to comfort her as Cathy came over and put the blanket over Terry's face.

"She once had so much life in her ... so much to live for," Jackie sobbed.

"She can rest now," I said.

Cathy reached over for Terry's pain pills that were on the table next to the couch.

"What on earth are you doing with those?" asked Jackie.

"She doesn't need them anymore."

"Terry is lying here like this and now you're gonna get high on her medicine?"

Cathy backed away and then started to run up the stairs. Jackie chased and caught her by the leg and the two of them fell to the floor. The bottle of pills flew across the room and spilled the contents over the floor, the pills rolling everywhere. "How could you do this?" Jackie exclaimed.

"Do you think it's been easy for me ... and Howie?" Cathy said, as she put her hands over her face in shame.

"It's hard for all of us but we can't turn into animals because of it," Jackie protested.

"I didn't mean any harm. I just wanted to take the edge off ... ya know?"

"Just go away Cathy ... just go up stairs ... I don't want to see you right now."

Cathy looked out the window for a minute and then went up stairs.

Jackie and I went back to the kitchen. "Can I get you some coffee?" she asked.

It all seemed so unreal, so sudden.

"Yeah ... I suppose we should call someone for Terry," I said.

"Who do we call? I never really thought about her dying. We're really unprepared for this. I mean she's gone ... I can't believe it."

She turned on the stove and then sat across the table from me. I looked at the head of the table, where Terry used to sit. It was sad not to see her there.

I reached for Jackie's hand but she quickly pulled it away. "No ... not now," she said shaking her head.

"Okay ... I know it's not the time or place but we need to talk about us sometime ... maybe tomorrow."

"Try never! Not now! ... I don't know .... That's the trouble with you. You think life is all there just for you to mold to your liking. You can't write a song about you and me ... make it rhyme ... give it a pretty ending. You can't bring Terry back with your verses ... this is real! You can't paint a pretty picture of the world with your songs! Can't you see?"

"I know that."

"No you don't know that! You and me and Freddie ... and Mike... we can't go on this way."

"What are you saying?"

"I don't know ... I don't know what I'm saying ... I love you ... but I loved Mike first. Then Freddie ... what a mess I have made of everything ..." She said sadly. And I knew there was really nothing I could say to make it better.

She got up and made the coffee. "Now Terry's gone. She was really the only thing that held us all together ... We have to find our own way now."

"But I need you Jackie," I said, as I got up to reach for her.

"No! No ... I can't!" she said, as she pushed me back. "Terry's lying dead out there and this is all you can think about? Talk about selfish."

"Yeah you're right ... ", I was ashamed to admit it, she was right.

"Just go away! We need to be apart and besides ... you've got your music ... your dreams of stardom!" Her words hurt.

A car pulled up the driveway. Freddie appeared at the door. "Well I knew you'd be here!" he sneered angrily when he saw me.

"It's not what you think Freddie," said Jackie.

He clinched his fists as he started towards me. Jackie tried to hold him back. "Freddie wait! It's Terry! ... Freddie ... she died just a few minutes ago!" she said, hugging him, holding him back.

Freddie stopped and looked on in disbelief. "Oh God," he said. He closed his eyes and shook his head slowly.

"Let's try to have some dignity ... at least for Terry's sake." said Jackie.

It was quiet in the room, and I could feel Terry's presence there with us, as though she was still sitting at the head of the table. How quickly things had changed. Terry's passing. And Jackie, Freddie and I, our lives would never be the same again.

In fact, it was evident that Mike, Fast Freddie, the Polack had all lost the faith of hitting the 'big-time'. The magic of the music wasn't there anymore. All our contacts, our songs, our records, the nightclubs, our curious adventures ... it was all dissolving away. It seemed that our quest was over.

The Crossing

27

The road stretched out ahead, across the rolling countryside, past old farms and store fronts, winding its way in into the heartland. Like the yellowed pages of an old book, this highway was an untold adventure yet to be discovered by us. Andy and I were heading for California ... Los Angeles. Perhaps that is where my future awaited me.

We had been driving since dawn in Andy's old red VW bug. The back seat was heavily laden with our clothes and my guitar, leaving only the front seats for our comfort.

As Andy drove I studied the road map. "I thought maybe we could stop for the night in Nashville," I said.

"Sounds good to me," he said. "Boy could I use a cold beer!"

It was late October but the hot sun above made it feel more like August. The Blue Ridge mountains stood tall in the east as we made our way down route eighty-one on our way through southern Virginia to Tennessee.

"Are you sorry we came?" I asked, "I know it was all my idea."

Andy looked over at me and grinned. "Nah ... not really."

"You know ... being out in the country reminds me ..."

"Reminds you of what?"

"My childhood."

"How's that?"

"I remember when we were kids ... back home we would swing on the swings at the playground. I would go high in the air and from that vantage point, I could see the rolling hills that surrounded our neighborhood, the neat row houses with white fences."

"Yeah, I remember that playground ... we used to play ball there."

"... Back then nothing seemed to matter ... everyday was ours to do what ever we wanted with it ..."

"All play and no work huh?"

"Not that ... more like no boundaries ..."

"You mean no pressures ... we were just kids then."

"And there were no limits to the imagination ... a few boxes and we built a house, a pile of sand and we built a castle."

"We were just playing games."

"Yes ... but we didn't know the word 'impossible', the phrase 'it can't be done'. Where and when did we ever lose that spirit?"

"Nobody said that growing up was going to be easy."

Andy watched as I popped a valium in my mouth. My dependence on them reminded me vaguely of the winos in Atlanta with their soda cans filled with booze.

"It does sound childish ... doesn't it? Making outlandish goals for ourselves?" I went on to say.

"Well I guess there's nothing wrong with having goals ... you have to be realistic ... that's all," he said soberly.

"Realistic ... that's the hard part ..." I said, weighing the word in my mind.

Up ahead I saw someone hitching a ride. He stood up as we passed by. I saw a guitar case at his feet. "Andy stop!" I exclaimed.

"You can't be serious? There's no room!"

"Hey ... we can make room somehow. I really think we should offer him a ride. He may not be going far."

"Man, I don't know about you sometimes," he said as he jerked the wheel and brought us to the side of the road. I turned around and saw the stranger running toward us. He was wearing cowboy boots and he ran with a strange awkward gait.

As the stranger approached, "Where ya headed?" asked Andy.

"Nashville," he drawled.

Andy looked at me disapprovingly.

"We're going to Nashville," I said.

"All right ... if you insist ..."

It took some doing, but I managed to make room for our guest in the back seat. Then we pulled back onto the highway. The stranger eyed the guitar case I had on my lap. "You a picker too?" he asked.

"Yeah."

"Is that so? Well, I'm a songwriter headed for 'Music City USA'," he said.

"Are you from Nashville? I asked.

"No ... Lynchburg."

"You been there before?

"Jus' visitin'", he said, "but I reckon to stay there tho' if things work out right."

"That's funny ... I'm a songwriter too and I'm headed for Los Angeles."

"That's good! That's good ... don't like that hard rock stuff tho' ... no offense taken o'course."

Andy looked over and gave me a look. I shrugged. "I like country music," I said.

"You do? Whose your favorite singers?" The stranger asked.

"Well ... I don't know ... I don't have anyone in particular. I mean in general ... I like it in general."

I looked up to see the state line. We were in Tennessee. "Perhaps we may make it to Nashville before sundown," said Andy.

"Sounds mighty nice t'me," said the stranger.

"Do you have friends in Nashville?" I asked.

"I got an uncle there. He'll take me in. He tol' me to come on down. Ya see my wife threw me out ... there was nothin' in Lynchburg holdin' me. No sir!"

"Yeah ... I know what you mean," I agreed.

Then we were quiet. It was a long ride. I was thinking of my own situation. The valium had made me tired. Andy mentioned something about Knoxville as I fell asleep.

Andy's old car lurched as it drove over the uneven places in the road. We were in the older section of Nashville where small shops lined the street. We turned the corner and pulled over to the curb.

There before us was the old Ryman Auditorium, known to millions of country music fans as the home of the 'Grand 'Ol Opry'. We staggered out of the car and stood gazing at the old building with wide-eyed stares. The sun was setting and the orange sky gave the old edifice an aura and a dream-like appearance.

I walked over to the side door and found it locked. The parking lot surrounding me was empty. To me, this was a sacred place, not long past it's heyday. I tried to envision the parking lot filled with cars where perhaps Hank Williams drank with his pals before going on to a packed house. Maybe George Jones passed through this door. Patsy Cline walked here around midnight. I could almost hear the audience inside, cheering the stars of country music. If only I could be a part of it. I could play the guitar, or put on grease paint as a comic and make 'em kick up their heels with laughter, or perhaps sing the lilting love song, touching tender hearts of young girls.

"Let's get a room," said Andy, tugging my shirt sleeve.

"Yeah ... let's go," I said, taking another look at the old walls. We walked back to the car.

The stranger was sitting on the hood. "By the way, I never did get your name," I said to him.

"Jimmy ... Jimmy's m'name," he replied.

"Where can we take you?"

"I can go along with y'all to a motel. I can use the phone there to call my uncle."

"I've got a better idea," said Andy. "... let's hit a bar first! I'm dying for a cold one."

"Well hell ... we just passed a bar around the corner when we were a'comin' in!" said Jimmy.

"Great. Let's leave the car here and walk. We can get a room later."

We locked the car and walked down the sidewalk. Turning the corner, we entered 'Tootsie's', one of Nashville's landmarks. On the wall were old autographed pictures of the stars of the Grand 'Ol Opry. I strained to read the signatures as we made our way to the bar.

"What'll it be?" Andy asked me.

"The usual..."

"What about you?" he asked Jimmy.

"A draft would be fine if you're a' buyin'," he replied.

The barmaid brought our beers and Andy peeled off a ten from his wad of bills. Jimmy looked at the money with interest. "You boys gotta good grub stake I see!"

"It's quite enough to get us through 'til we get to California," said Andy. He stuffed the wad back into his jeans.

The jukebox started playing a song. The syrupy steel guitar melted over us.

"Ya know I just got t'thinkin' ... I'm gonna call my uncle and tell 'em to meet us here. He's a nice feller and you guys might like to meet him."

"Sure! Tell him to come on down! We can have a regular party!" Andy reveled, suddenly feeling the effects of his beer.

Jimmy walked back to the restrooms where the pay phone hung on the wall.

"He seems like a harmless kind of guy," I said.

"He's all right," Andy replied, uninterested.

Jimmy came back and pulled up a stool beside me. "I called him up and he said he'd be right on over. Hey thanks for the beer."

"No problem," said Andy, waving it off.

My stomach growled a little and I knew I had to eat. I remembered the famous Roy Buchman at my first recording session ... 'I'll eat later' he would say. Roy Buchman. He was one of my idols. Perhaps now, only now, I could really understand just who Roy Buchman really was; maybe a jaded musician like myself with little or no money but a pocketful of dreams? And hungry.

"Well here they are! Tol' ya they'd be right on over," said Jimmy. A older man approached us. His hair was combed neatly unlike Jimmy's shaggy locks. I noticed his western style suit and boots, but most of all, I noticed the beautiful blond bombshell that hung on his arm.

"Well how ya doin' Jimmy? It's sure good to see ya," the man said, shaking Jimmy's hand vigorously.

"Hey Johnny, I want ya t'meet some friends of mine ... what's your names?" Jimmy exclaimed.

Andy stood up to shake his hand. "My name is Andy and-"

"Pleased to meet both of you!" he said, interrupting my introduction. "Why any friends of Jimmy's is a friend of mine," he said, "Just call me 'Big John' ... 'Big Bad John'!" He joked.

The young girl stood by quietly. Our attention turned to her. "Oh ... I plum forgot! Boys this here is Melinda!"

"Hi," said Andy. "You're the best thing I've seen all day."

"Why how nice ... thank you! You're sweet!" she replied.

"Pleased to meet you," I said shaking her hand.

"I'm charmed!" She replied.

Jimmy brought over two more barstools and we made a huddle by the bar. Big John immediately turned to me. "Jimmy here was telling me that you are a songwriter headed for California," he said.

"Oh that does sound excitin'!" said Melinda.

"That's the plan," I said.

"You know ... I think songwriter's are very romantic people," she said, squeezing my hand. It was an intimate gesture and I looked at 'Big John' to get his reaction. He noticed but didn't seem to care.

"I know some 'big-wigs' in this here music business," he said. "I might be able to pull some strings for you too ... that is if you're interested." He lit a cigarette.

"I told ya!" Jimmy exclaimed. "Big John here ... he knows what he's talkin' about!"

"Oh well ... it's really nothin'," said Big John modestly.

"Well I don't know ..." I said.

"Oh you should stay for a few days. I want you to!" said Melinda, holding my hand in hers.

"I won't take no for an answer!" said Big John. "Have you boys got a room?"

"Not yet," said Andy.

"Yeah, maybe we should," I said. I was tired.

Andy pulled the wad of bills out and paid the bill as we got up to leave.

"Hey I've got a good idea!" said Big John,

"Let's get a bottle and have a party."

"Oh yes!" said Melinda.

"Sure! Hey what the hell!" said Andy.

We went outside and turned the corner. Behind Andy's VW was a fancy late model Buick. It was Big John's car.

"What about a motel?" Andy asked.

"There's a place right up the street ... You'd like it ... reasonable rates," said Big John.

"Okay," said Andy.

We started to get in the car when Melinda grabbed my hand. "You can ride with me and Big John."

"Yeah ... come on ... ride with us! Jimmy can go with Andy," said Big John.

"Well ... okay," I said with reluctance.

"Come on!" insisted Melinda.

I got into the Buick. Melinda sat between us. He pulled out and waved for Andy to follow. As we drove off, Melinda loosened her shoe and rubbed my leg with her bare foot. I wondered if Big John was aware of her playfulness but he did not seem to notice. A few blocks up we pulled into the driveway of a motel, and Andy jumped out of his car and into the office.

"Yeah ... like I said. I could do a lot for you boys. I really could," Big John continued.

"Well I ..."

"Hey son. There's no need t' thank me. Any friend of Jimmy's is a friend of mine!"

Melinda squeezed my hand again. Andy came out with the key and came over to the car. "It's the room down on the end," he said.

"I tell ya what," said Big John, "You boys go on in and get comfortable and I'll go out and get a bottle ... be back in a jiffy!"

"Oh I'm tired of bein' in this here ol' car!" said Melinda. "I'll stay here with them."

"Ok sugar ... you do that! Jimmy can come with me. We'll be right back. Then we can talk about the music business!"

They left as Melinda and I followed Andy to the end of the complex. We entered an ordinary looking motel room-two double beds and a TV.

"Man ... I'm beat," said Andy as he threw his bag on the bed.

"I bet you are after such a long drive!" said Melinda.

"I'm a little tired too," I added.

"Oh not you! We got a lot to talk about!" she teased me.

"Well ... I don't know about you guys," said Andy, "but I'm gonna take a hot shower. My back is aching."

"You just go ahead and do that. We won't mind ...will we?" she said, looking at me, smiling.

Andy went to shower and closed the door slightly, throwing his clothes outside the doorway onto the floor. Melinda watched and then turned her attention back to me. "Well ... here we are just you and me," she said playfully. She leaned over to give me a kiss. I pulled her closer. But then she pulled away and fell back across the bed. "Oh it is hot in here," she said, brushing her long blond hair off of her face. "You know, I wonder if there's any ice out there in that ol' ice maker?" she wondered. "I need a cold drink of water ... then we can talk!"

"All right ... first the ice." I got up and found the ice bucket. I noticed that there weren't any glasses. "I'll have to go to the night clerk and get some glasses too ... there aren't any here. Be back in a minute. Don't you go away!"

"I'll be right here," she cooed playfully.

Outside, I hurriedly walked up to the ice machine and filled the bucket, and then waited impatiently for the night clerk to bring out some cups. I was anxious to get back to the room and Melinda. But when I got back, I found Andy brushing his hair. Melinda wasn't there. "Where did you go?" he asked.

"I went for some ice ... where's Melinda?"

"She said she was going to find you."

I looked out the door into the parking lot expecting to see Big John's car, but there was no one.

"Oh no!" Andy shouted. I turned around. He had his jeans in his hands.

"What's wrong?"

"You stupid asshole! We've been ripped off!" he screamed. He held out his jeans with the pocket turned out for me to see. "It was her ... she took it! She took all the money! Christ! All of 'em must have been in on it. The whole thing was a scam!"

I examined the pocket where the wad of money had been. It was empty. I looked at Andy with a heavy heart.

"It's all gone! Almost three hundred dollars!" he exclaimed, "We've just started the trip and now we're broke!" he said sadly, sitting down on the edge of the bed. "What the hell are we gonna do now?"

This bad luck was so sudden and unexpected. We had a serious problem now, being miles away from home with little money. "I've got about a seventy dollars ... we're not totally broke," I said, trying to make a bad situation better. "... We could go to the police," I said, knowing it was probably out of the question.

"We don't have much to go on ... and we can't afford to stay here for several days while they hunt for 'em," he replied. I agreed. "We can't go to California on seventy dollars!" he scoffed. "Maybe we should go back to DC."

"We could go on to Denver. Maybe we could get jobs there for a while ... we can't turn back now," I insisted.

"I dunno," said Andy. "It's a long way to Denver."

29

The next morning, against Andy's wishes, we headed back onto route forty west, headed for Arkansas, and then Denver. I felt awful having fallen in with 'Big John' and his gang and losing Andy's money. If only we hadn't picked up Jimmy, which was all my idea. And now, as if that wasn't bad enough, I had succeeded in convincing him to continue in this, perhaps foolish adventure.

As we rode along, I felt compelled to take out my guitar, to run my thumb down the strings to hear the tones. I looked out the window as we crossed the Mississippi River. In the distance, I could see a barge heading south on it's long journey to Louisiana and then the Gulf of Mexico. I started to play Old Suwannee but couldn't remember the melody. The song reminded me of my Dad. He was from Mississippi. He gave me my first guitar and taught me my first song.

... I remember being allowed into the living room to get my birthday present. It was my twelfth birthday and my eyes lit up as I saw the guitar propped up on the couch. It was an inexpensive beginner guitar, but to me, it was the greatest gift ever. I marveled at the wood finish and reached out to pluck a string. Its sound was all I could hear.

"Pick it up son," my Dad said.

"Don't rush him dear," my mother said to him.

I sat down on the couch and took the guitar in my hands. It felt awkward. I put my finger on one of the strings behind a fret and picked the note with my thumb. It made a muted, dull sound. "I can't play," I cried. "I can't play it!"

"You'll learn ... it takes time honey," said Mom. "Go ahead dear ... show him how to play!" she told my Dad.

He took the guitar and picked some of the strings to get it in tune. Then he started to play. He sang...

"Down in the valley ...
Valley so low ...

Hang your head over ...
Hear the wind blow! ..."

My ears heard him singing the words but my eyes never left the guitar. I watched his big hands make the chords. The sounds were smooth and warm. It was magic.

"... Hang your head low dear ...
Hang your head low ...
Hang your head over ...
Hear the wind blow! ..."

In my mind, I pictured him playing at the town dances, the ones he had told me about, when he was young, back in Mississippi. Someday, I will play the guitar I thought. Someday, I will make music, make the magic...

"He could play the guitar!" I said, thinking out loud.

"What?" asked Andy.

"Oh ... I was just thinking about my Dad. He taught me how to play the guitar you know."

"I remember ... I remember the Saturday nights at your Grandmother's house! You would make us sit on one side of the room. You and Mickey would come out and play for us. You were little show-offs!"

"Yeah ... when we finished, my Grandmother would give us ice cream and cookies."

But it wasn't always like that. I remember my old house. I would push my dresser up against my bedroom door to make sure no one could come in. I would put on the old Elvis records, Roy Orbison. I would sing along with my weak straining voice. I couldn't sing in front of anyone at first. I was shy, very shy at first.

Then came the Beatles. Like the other countless millions of teenagers, I too sat there that Sunday night, waiting anxiously for them to come on the Ed Sullivan Show. Suddenly they appeared-the excitement, the screaming girls. Paul sang 'All my Loving', and time stood still. And, that night, that moment belonged to us kids. I don't think I ever stopped living, and reliving that moment. I was hopelessly hooked. This music was all that mattered. I went up to my room and closed the door. On my guitar, I struggled to play the song, play it just like Paul. I had to capture that moment for myself. I fell back on the clean bedspread, to relive it, and to dream ...

We drove on for hours. I napped. Suddenly, There was a rapping sound. Was that my Dad knocking on the door? ...

"Shit! That's all we need!" Andy exclaimed.

"What's wrong?" I said.

"Can't you hear that rapping sound? It's the wheel, the axle maybe!" He pulled the car over to the shoulder of the road. We got out to survey the damage. He touched the wheel, but then pulled his hand away.

"Man it's hot!" he said waving the heat off his hand.

"What's wrong with it?"

"I dunno ... maybe it's the bearings ... I dunno ..."

"How far can we go with it like this?"

"Maybe just a few miles ... maybe a while ... it's hard to tell," he said, shaking his head.

"Great! Where in the hell are we?" I asked.

"... somewhere in Arkansas."

I looked out across the rolling hills. There was nothing but lonesome highway in sight. "Let's go on ... there's nothing else to do," I said.

"Right!" He looked disgusted and I knew he was at the end of his rope. There we were, with a broken car and little money. "Look ... I don't know ... Maybe this wasn't such a great idea!"

"Like I said, let's just go on," I insisted.

"Right!" Andy was nearing the end of his rope.

I went on a rant, "Okay! Then fuck it! Tell me I told you so! Go ahead! Little good that's going to do. Go ahead. Tell me I'm a fuck up!"

We just stood there on the side of the road, thinking of our alternatives. We both knew that we had to go on. There was really nothing else we could do.

"Let's go," he said. We got back into the car and continued on.

30

We drove on for several hours. It was nighttime and we were somewhere in Oklahoma. Undaunted, as if there was nothing else to do but drive on, drive on until the axle gave out, or we ran out of gas. I felt a sadness, being so far from home in this strange land. We were very tired, and we could drive no farther. The next exit was Oklahoma City and we pulled into a truck stop. The sound of the axle was worse than ever.

"I can't believe we made it," said Andy, too tired to move. It had been a long day's drive. "Come on ... I've got to get out of this car."

We opened the door and stood up to stretch. My leg gave way and I fell down on one knee in the dust. Andy came over to help me up. "I'm getting weak."

"You need some rest ... you know that," he told me.

"Let's go in and eat. I need food first."

Inside, there were several rough looking men who looked at us with displeasure. We were 'hippies' and not welcome in some places. I felt conspicuous as we sat down in a booth. An old man in the booth next to ours looked into my eyes. I looked away.

"I'm so hungry," I said.

"We don't have much money so you better eat light," Andy reminded me.

The old man in the adjacent booth, still continued to study us carefully.

The cook from behind the counter came over. "I'm sorry boys but this place is for truckers. I seen that old 'hippie wagon' you pulled up in!" he exclaimed.

"We just want some food and then we'll leave," said Andy.

"Well you can't eat here!" He exclaimed.

The old man, who had be staring at us, interrupted him. "Let 'em eat! They look like they been through hell!" The cook looked at the old man. They appeared to be friends. "'Pops' you know how I feel about these kind. Hippies! I don't want 'em in here."

"They look all right t'me ... I been watching 'em," replied the old man.

The cook took out his pad and pencil. "Well ... what'cha want?" he asked us.

I looked up at the prices on the wall behind the grill. "Just give us two ham and cheese sandwiches and ... two cups of coffee."

He scribbled down the order and walked away.

The old man got up and came over to our table. "I noticed the tag on your car says Maryland ... you boys are kind'a far from home ain't 'cha?"

"We're on our way to Denver," I replied.

"Goin' t'Denver heh?" The old man smiled. "Can I have a seat? I don't meet people from the east much ... m'name's 'Pops'!"

"Yeah sure."

The old man pulled up a seat and sat down. He looked at Andy. "You must be the silent partner?"

"When I've got something to say I'll talk," Andy replied.

"Yeah, that's what I say ... speak m'mind sometimes ... nothin' more. You boys are a little light on money ain't 'cha?"

I looked at Andy remembering Nashville the night before. "Well ... sort of ...."

"I can tell. I can tell," said Pops, "Two young men like yourselves bein' on the road s'long would order more than just two ham and cheese sandwiches!" I looked at Andy again. "Don't worry! I ain't gonna try to rob ya if that's what you're thinkin'!" Pops continued.

"Well ... you see ... we had trouble in Nashville," said Andy.

"And there was a good lookin' gal right?" added Pops.

"Yeah ... Melinda. Sweet Melinda!" I said with sadness.

Pops laughed, "Ya got'a watch out for them high flyin' women when you got that pocket full o'money and a gut full o'booze!"

The cook brought the sandwiches and we ate them eagerly. Meanwhile, Pops continued. "Well I heard that car a'chirpin' when ya drove up. It ain't gonna make it t'Denver with them bearin's burnin' up like that!"

"Yeah well ... we don't have much money," said Andy.

"... I reckon I could get Junior to fix it for ya."

"Whose Junior?"

"Junior's my nephew ... m'sister's boy. He's good with a car."

We finished the sandwiches and Pops took us out back of the restaurant. There were two men there sitting on crates around an oil drum, where a fire was burning. As we approached, I could see their faces in the firelight. One was young man and the other appeared to be an old Indian. They had a bottle which one passed to the other. The two of them peered at us as we came near. Pops introduced us.

"This here is 'Junior' and this is 'Cousin Dan'. His Indian name is 'Red Wing' ... he's Cherokee ... but we call him 'Cousin Dan'." The two of them nodded. "Pull up a crate or a log ... this here is m'parlor ya might say ..."

I got an empty crate and sat down. Andy bent down on his haunches. The fire snapped and cracked in the night air. Up above, the stars twinkled in the wide open sky.

"Junior ... 'gib me that bottle!" said Pops.

"Sure Pops," said Junior as he handed it over.

Pops took a long drink and put the cap back on. He handed it to me and I took a sip. It was whiskey. I passed it to Andy.

Pops looked at my hands and grinned. "You ain't worked much have ya? Them ain't a workin' man's hands."

"I'm a musician," I said. "I write songs."

"'A musician ... and I write songs'," said Pops mimicking me. Junior and Cousin Dan laughed.

"Didn't mean nothin' by it! It was a joke son ... a joke!" said Pops.

My stomach burned from the whiskey.

Pops was talkative. "I guess you don't take no shit from no one ... playin' that music. Sort'a come as ya like ... do as ya may," he said, taking the bottle back into his hands.

"It's a hard life sometimes," I replied.

"Yeah ... but it ain't like workin' for the boss man! Ten'r'fifteen years o' that can eat at a man's soul. That is ... what the 'licker and the hate don't kill!"

Across the fire, I could see the old Indian staring into my face, never flinching for an instant. Suddenly he spoke in what I assumed was Cherokee. Although I couldn't understand what he was saying, I knew he was talking about me. "What is he talking about?" I asked.

Pops started to laugh and then coughed and wheezed. "Don't worry ... he was talking about the 'God of the Singin' Winds'!"

The old Indian starting talking again, and I could only imagine what he was saying as he made hand gestures. Pops interpreted. "He says that the 'God of the Singin' Winds' can be heard only by a select few ... only they can use these gifts to make music."

The fire flared and in the distance I could hear the sound of an owl hooting. I felt a shiver from the late autumn chill. The Indian continued. "You may have the power yourself ... you may be able to hear the 'God of the Singin' Winds'! When you do you will know it and your music will tell of many things ... things which will be revealed to you!"

I looked around at the others and then at the old Indian. I was sure he was just kidding, but he never broke a smile. He was dead serious. "I play rock music. I'm sure it's not quite the same thing," I said nervously.

Pops turned to the Indian and told him what I had said. He answered immediately. "The sound from the rock music is the same. This God is truly powerful and he lives in all songs in all tongues. It is all one and the same. It is the language of the chosen!"

"I'm sorry but I can't really believe this ... it's too ... weird."

The Indian spoke again and threw his hands around in the air. When he stopped he folded his arms and looked on with a dead-pan expression. Pops interpreted, "He says don't be afraid. You have been on a long journey ... longer in time ... one that seems long but has just begun. If you are a chosen one, your song will guide you to your own destiny. These things have been foreseen ..."

Pops took another hit from the bottle and spit into the fire. "Look, I wouldn't pay him no mind boy ... these Indians are half crazed most of the time anyway. Why he's been'a jabberin' all week .. somethin' about a 'long road'! I think the sun's gotten to 'em, the poor devil!"

31

It was an old wooden door, an old door in an old apartment building. But I welcomed the heat that emanated from the rusty radiator in the hallway. My hand shook slightly as I put the key into the slot. The door opened. I picked up my things, trudged inside and fell onto the couch in an exhausted heap.

"Where's the light switch?" asked Andy, groping in the darkness.

"At least we made it to Denver! All I need is a bed and sleep!"

Andy found the lamp and illuminated the room. The place was truly a furnished apartment. There was a couch and chair, with a coffee table up against one wall. I got up to look at the rest of the apartment. At one end was a small sun room with a single bed. It afforded some privacy with a curtain that hung across the entranceway. In the kitchen, there was a table and two chairs. I opened the drawer next to the stove and found silverware.

"This place isn't bad," I said.

"Beat's the hell out of that run down hotel in New York, that flophouse in Atlanta!" shouted Andy from the living room.

Turning around, I felt a tight pain in my chest. I leaned against the table trying not to let Andy see my condition. I shook my head trying to get rid of the feeling but the room swayed in front of me.

"All we need is a TV," said Andy, as he entered the room.

"I ... yes ... a TV ... maybe we could rent one," I said gasping for breath.

Andy looked at me with concern. "Look ... I know there's something wrong with you."

"No really ... I'm tired that's all," I replied. But it was happening again. This time without drugs. I started to hyperventilate and my hands tingled and felt numb. I pulled up a chair and sat down.

"You really need to see a doctor ... maybe a shrink."

"Goddamn it! You think I'm crazy don't you!" I said agitated.

"I'm not saying that. It's just that you've been under a lot of strain."

"Just get me my bag. I need a valium ... just get me a valium."

"Fuck you man! You get your own valium!" he said bitterly.

"Okay ... I'll get my own valium, thank you!" I went into the living room and picked up my bag. He charged over, took it out of my hands, and threw it into the corner.

"Fuck you!" I screamed.

"No! Fuck you! I can't just stand by and watch you do this to yourself!"

I went for the bag but he pushed me back. I fell onto the floor clutching my arm where I fell. He stood over me.

"Look ... I just need a pill ... I'll be fine ... really."

"And what will you do when you run out of pills? You've got a drug problem and you might as well face it!"

"Who the hell are you to tell me what to do?"

"Look! It was your idea to go to California! Then we get ripped off in Nashville! Then the wheel bearings go. We end up in this ... this cow-town with about twenty dollars to our name. All this so you can write your stupid songs! The big rock star! Sitting on the floor begging me for a valium ... look at yourself!"

He leaned against the wall and exhaled heavily. I rolled over on my back and closed my eyes. The nervous seizure had started to subside.

"I'm sorry ..." I said weakly.

He looked down at the floor and shook his head in shame. "No ... I'm sorry ... I guess the last three days ... the last three months have been pretty heavy. I shouldn't have said what I said ... I'm sorry ..."

It was quiet for a few brief moments as we were both deep in thought.

Finally I said, "... Maybe you're right ... I need some rest ..."

"You need to get your life together ... that's what you need!"

I opened my eyes and looked at the room around me. I needed time I thought ... I need healing time. Perhaps I really needed help.

Sessions

32

I made an appointment with a local drug rehabilitation clinic. It was located in a run down part of the city and looked more like an old convenience store as I entered the office. There was an older woman behind the desk. She looked up. Her eyes were warm. "Can I help you?"

"I'm here to see Elizabeth Schwartz."

"Yes ... have a seat, she'll be with you shortly."

There were several plastic chairs and a table with old magazines in the corner. I sat down next to the table. Across from me was a ragged, elderly man. He looked at me and nodded. I nodded back. Oh God! I thought. What was I doing here?

On the table was a pencil and an old envelope. I took them and started to doodle, sitting in the bright sunlight that was streaming through the window. I leaned my head back and thought about Jackie back home. What she was doing just now? I missed her. A love song, a love song for Jackie. I would write a love song for Jackie. Not the regular love song with 'I love you' and 'I need you' in the verses, a special kind of song! We were two of a kind we were, carefree at times, restless, like leaves blowing in the wind. I wrote ...

"... Dead leaves that rustle ..."

I stared at the words on the yellowed envelope. What do leaves do? I thought. They cover the ground. Color ... that's it! Color! Browns and yellows....

"... And color the white snow ...
Are like you and me and no one ..."

I could hear a possible melody in my mind. I looked up at the old man but then down at the lyrics, my mind deep in thought....

"... Rain drops that glisten ...
and linger on nothing ...
Are like you and me and no one ..."

I smiled. I ran the words over in my mind tapping the pencil on the piece of paper. I needed a bridge. Something different! Something striking against the idea of the verses. Leaves ... rain drops ... sea shells ... 'She sells her sea shells...' No! That's silly! Then it came to me and I wrote ...

"I hear oceans ... in your sea shells ..."

I liked that. There was more ...

"... Windy sea breeze take me with you ..."

That's kind of dreamy. I wanted to hear it with the melody. I would have to wait. The next verse came easily...

"Flowers that mellow ... to dried ..."

No! Colors ... remember the colors! I erased and then wrote ...

"... to pungent gold rust hues ...
Are like you and me and no one..."

That was it. This could be a song! I raised the old envelope and read the words from the top...

"... Dead leaves that rustle ...
And color the white snow ...
Are like you, and me, and no one ...

Rain drops that glisten ...
And linger ... on nothing ...
Are like you, and me, and no one ...

I hear oceans in your sea shells ..
Windy sea breeze take me with you!

Flowers that mellow ...
To pungent gold rust hues ...
Are like you, and me, and no one ..."

I couldn't wait to get a guitar to try the melody. It was a love song but different, different from other love songs. It was for Jackie. In a way, we were like each other, and not like anyone else.

"Excuse me ... Ms. Schwartz will see you now," said the receptionist.

I folded the envelope and put it in my back pocket. A young woman about my age stood by the desk. She was wearing jeans and a grey sweat shirt. We shook hands. I followed her into a room and she closed the door. The room was empty except for several chairs and a table. There was an ashtray on the table. She sat down on one of the chairs and I on the other. She lit a cigarette and leaned back.

"How are you feeling today?" she asked.

"Okay I guess ..."

"When you first called for an appointment, you complained about nervous seizures or attacks I believe."

"Well ... Ms. Schwartz ..."

"Call me 'Liz'." Her long dark hair flowed down past the rim of her glasses. Though she seemed 'cerebral', I found her moderately attractive.

"Well ... Liz ... I've been ... under a strain." Already, I could feel the muscles tightening in my chest.

"Why don't you start at the beginning."

"My childhood?"

"Any place you like ... this session is for you,"

"Well ... I guess it all started in New York ..."

"What were you doing in New York?"

"I'm a musician ... we .. I mean my band was playing there in an off-Broadway play."

"That sounds exciting!"

"Well ... it wasn't what you would think."

I was getting nervous and found it hard to breath.

"You're feeling anxious now aren't you?"

"Yes ... it's really crazy!"

"Not at all ... you're mind and your body are trying to fight back ... that's all ... Let me show you something."

She laid down on the floor. "Lay down here along side me ... just like I am."

I got down on the floor beside her. I had no idea what was going on.

"Now tighten all your muscles ... now release ... tighten ... release ... take a deep breath!"

I did as she said. It seemed to help a little.

"Now lay still ... try to feel your toes ..."

"Try to feel my toes?" I asked. We both laughed.

"Really! Just try to concentrate on your toes ... and then your legs ... just concentrate ..."

I tried to feel my toes. We were both silent as we lay there on the floor.

"Now concentrate on your body ... your chest ... lay still and take a breath ... try to imagine that you are at the beach in the hot sun ... you can hear the waves ... rolling ... gently ... on ... the ... beach ... now, take a breath ..."

I felt completely relaxed. It was amazing. I hadn't felt so relaxed in months. I laid there for several minutes. Then I opened my eyes and looked up. She was sitting back in the chair smiling.

"Feel better?"

"Yes ... I do feel better."

"See? You c-a-n gain control of your mind and your body if you try."

I was impressed.

She laughed. Then, became serious. "Do you do drugs?"

"Yes ... I do pot and cocaine ... LSD ... actually we used to do all kinds of drugs."

"We?" she asked.

"The band."

"Funny how drugs and music seem to go together ..."

"... I'm not sure why but it does seem that way."

"Do you think the drugs help you play your music?" she asked.

"I dunno ... sometimes when I'm stoned I get lots of ideas."

"Don't you think you might get the ideas on your own, without drugs?"

I thought about the song that I had just written, folded in my pocket. "Perhaps yes ... yeah. I guess it is kind of stupid ... doing drugs ..."

"I'm not here to make judgments ... I'm just saying that if you can control you body as you just did a moment ago, don't you think that your mind could be more creative if you were straight ... more aware?"

"Then why do musicians and artists do drugs?" I asked her.

"Everybody does drugs and they do them because they think that it feels good ... actually they may be trying to escape from problems ... tensions."

"I've heard the whole escape thing before."

"Well ... do the drugs make you feel good?"

I thought about my experiences, " .... Well ... no ... not really. Look, I just want to know what is wrong with me ... am I going crazy?"

"No, you're suffering from acute anxiety ... the drugs only make it worse."

"What causes the anxiety?"

"That's what we're doing here ... trying to find out the cause of the anxiety and then find a way to relieve it."

Silence. She was quiet. It was if she wanted me to make the first move.

"A lot has happened," I said.

"What has happened?"

"Well ... my band broke up a while back ... I had put five years of my life into that band."

"It meant a lot to you ... it's good to have something that's important to you. ... How did you parent's feel about it ... the band?"

"They were really behind me in the beginning, but ... after a while ... they tried to talk me out of it. I think they thought that it was going to ruin my life."

"As if you couldn't take care of yourself?"

"Something like that."

"How did that make you feel?"

"I dunno ..."

"Scared? ... Maybe a little angry?" she asked.

"A little angry I think."

She lit another cigarette. "I hate to go there, but did you have a happy childhood?"

"Psychologists always ask that don't they?"

"It's a good place to start."

"Yes ... I had a good childhood ... they were happy days."

"You got along well with the other children?"

"Sure ... I had a few scuffles like most kids but we generally got along well."

"Why did you have scuffles with other kids?"

"I don't know ... I used to make up many of the games we would play ... I guess I was sort of the leader sometimes."

"The other kids didn't like you being the leader?"

"I wasn't really a leader ... I just had ideas all the time."

"Sounds like you were creative at an early age."

"I dunno ..."

She puffed her cigarette, a pause, and then she continued.

"When did you start to play music?"

"I was about twelve. That's when I got my first guitar, on my twelfth birthday."

"Did you play with the other children or did you spend most of your time alone with the guitar?"

"I played with the other children ... but I did practice a lot on the guitar. Sometimes I would get in front of the mirror and pretend that I was Elvis Presley or Paul of the Beatles ... it was silly really."

She smiled. She was calm and healthy. Meanwhile, I was troubled, nervous and awkward. But still, we seemed to be on the same page, or maybe, better yet, looking at my life from two different perspectives. Somehow I knew she had been here before, here in this frightening place, between sanity and insanity, digging into the dirt and the secret places, exploring the quick phrases, the explanations, the odd things that I said without thinking. Together, we ventured into the hidden recesses of my mind, my life. I continued freely.

"You know my dad played guitar a little when he was young. He used to play for town square dances back in Mississippi. My cousins used to play too. I think that's where I get my musical talents."

"Did you used to think about making it in music when you were a child?"

"All through High School I spent the weekends hanging around the nightclubs, even though I was a little under-age ... I guess I didn't have a lot of friends at school ..."

"I see ... did you feel like a loner?"

"Yeah ... I guess so ... I remember one day in the locker room in the gym after class, I found chewing gum in my shoe. It was a prank. You see, I had this pair of shoes with high heals. They were the style for rock musicians at the time. The other kids made fun of me when I wore them. I was a 'long hair' and they were ... they were 'preps'."

"Did that make you feel bad?"

"Sure ... but in a way I didn't care ... I was different from them."

"Different? ... How?"

"I had my music."

"In other words ... you had musical talent and they didn't ... and this made up for them not liking you?"

I thought about that. "That's a strange way to put it."

"Maybe they thought you were stuck up?"

"... I never thought about it like that ... maybe ... I wasn't trying to be."

"How about college?"

"I didn't want to go to college."

"The band?"

"Yeah ... things started happening for us ... I just wasn't into school. I started college but was a terrible student, so I dropped out."

"What do you mean things started happening?"

"Well ... we won a contest at a local radio station and we got a chance to record in a studio."

"That sounds like fun."

"It was exciting ... to hear the music in your mind. Then put it on tape and then be able to hear it played back ... I love recording."

"You guys must have been popular."

"Not at first ... we used to play at the teen clubs. Sometimes we would play at civic centers and there would be five or six bands. We would be one of the first to play and we were usually ignored. Everyone would be waiting for the top band to play. Sometimes we were booed."

"That's tough ... being booed!"

"Well ... it's all part of the game. I got used to it."

Andy was working hard at a warehouse and I felt guilty seeing him come home at night exhausted. I knew that I had to get a job. After searching in the employment section of the newspapers, I resigned myself to the only job that seemed open to me, a dishwasher.

I felt desperate as I stood at the counter of the restaurant, as the manager looked over my job application. "It seems that you have been self employed ever since high school," he said, as he put the application down on the counter top.

"Well ... I am a musician but I'm out of work and I need the job."

He looked down at the application. "I'm not sure ... there are long hours and the pay is minimum wage."

"That's ok ... really I could use the job," I said, trying seem energized. I really didn't want the job but I was totally broke, I needed the money.

He looked back at my application and thought for a moment. "... All right, follow me." He led me through the double swinging doors into the kitchen. There was a long counter, loaded with racks of dirty dishes. Inspecting the layout, it seemed simple. There was a housing where you could press a button and hot water would spray to actually wash the dishes. At the end of the room was an old black man. He had an old, non-filtered cigarette on his lip which seemed a permanent feature of his face. "This is Reggie ... he can show you the ropes," said the manager, who then disappeared through the swinging doors, leaving us alone.

"Well ... you ready t'wash some dishes son?" the old man asked me.

"Yeah I guess so ..."

"You broke huh?"

"Sort of."

"Nobody would work here unless 'dey was broke!" he joked. He lit another cigarette to replace the one that had burned down on his lip.

"How long have you been working here?" I asked him.

"A long time ... ol' Reggie been here a long time!" He started to hum a tune, a cheerful tune. He seemed like he was always happy, just humming a tune with that cigarette on his lip.

I started to clean off a dish. I scraped it off carefully, not to dirty my hands. Reggie just watched and then chuckled. "Don't worry! You won't be here long ... none of 'em last long. Here's an apron and there are hats on that ledge over there."

I put on the apron and a paper hat. Within minutes I was filling the racks with dishes, as Reggie ran the spray machine. He was robot-like in his movements and soon I too got into a rhythm. It helped to pass the time, just working on and on. I thought of home. What were Magic Mike, Fast Freddie and the Polack doing now? How was Jackie? Joanne and my child? I started to feel a sadness as I scraped the food from the plates, the garbage running down my arms and onto my apron. I tried to get my mind off the mess and I thought about my new song. It was a good song. I new that it could be a hit! I could be a rock star living in Hollywood. To win a Grammy. As usual, my mind wandered and I conjured up a visions of what could be ...

"Hey! Hey you! What's wrong with you?" I looked over. It was the manager! He was saying something. "Hey you! I need you to mop up a mess out on the floor ... the mops over there," he said pointing next to the door.

I grabbed the bucket with the mop and followed him out into the restaurant. He pointed to a booth where two young couples were sitting. There was a mess all over the floor where one of them had knocked over a glass of water.

The Juke box played and the volume was up just loud enough for me to hear the song that was playing. 'I love you ... I always will ...' sang a voice. It was a girl's voice and the music was clean and slick. I had heard that voice before but I couldn't remember where.

"You missed a spot," said one of the girls as she giggled. I reached the mop under the table to try to get at it. The song on the juke box continued to play. '... How can you say goodbye when I'm feelin' so blue!'

Then I realized who the singer was, "That's Beth Williams!" I exclaimed, thinking out loud, "That's Beth Williams!"

"Hey! He can talk!" said one the guys laughing.

"No ... I mean that's Beth Williams on the radio!" I stammered.

"No shit Sherlock! Where you been? ... Beth Williams is one of the hottest new singers out there."

"Don't you listen to the radio?" one of the girls teased. All four laughed.

"Really ... I used to know Beth Williams! I used to play at the same nightclub she used to play!", I said in earnest, remembering The Pilgrimage and 'Wild Bill'.

"What kind of drugs are you on?" One of the girls teased. Again, they laughed at me.

How could I let them know that I wasn't just a dishwasher? I was a musician too.

Meanwhile, I could see the manager looking over in our direction. Quickly, I put the mop into the bucket and started walking back to the kitchen. In the back, I took the mop and twisted it several times to ring the messy water out. I was so upset, I could have twisted it until it came apart!

Jealousy raged inside my heart. I couldn't believe it, Beth Williams on the radio! What had happened to her protest songs for gay rights? With a frustrated mind, I tried to rationalize the meaning of it all. Perhaps she had sold out. Instead of an acoustic guitar, she had the polished sound of a rock band behind her! Before, she had been one of us, struggling to pay the rent, just another musician like me. But now, like a butterfly from a cocoon, she had cast off the shroud of anonymity. Her prayers had been answered. She had started her ascent into the unattainable heights of stardom. She was living the dream, and, meanwhile, I was racking more dirty dishes!

34

This time, Liz sat on the floor and I on a chair. It had been a week since our last session. "Are you feeling any better these days? A little less tension?" she asked.

"I've been a lot better. Those exercises really help."

"Good ..." She thumbed through some notes that she had written on a yellow legal-sized pad. "Last time you mentioned that your band used to get booed a lot ... at least in the beginning ... and you said something like 'it's all part of the game'. Could you explain that to me 'it's all part of the game'?

"Well ... being in front of people, an audience ... you are ... vulnerable. You have to get used to being booed, or ignored I guess."

"You mean in other words you have to get used to being rejected?"

"When you start out ... people don't think you're good. You have to prove it ... you have to fight for it."

"That seems very demanding on your ego, don't you think ... to have to prove yourself all the time?"

"... Like I said, you get used to it."

"Don't you think that this makes you a callous person, or at least a weary person?"

"... Yes some I suppose ... but it's not all bad either. I mean when you spend years playing night after night in front of crowds ... especially small crowds, the ones you can reach out and touch both physically and emotionally ... you learn the worth of it."

"I'm sorry. I'm afraid I don't understand."

"... Sure you get hard ... But you get soft too. You learn how to touch people, how to let go of yourself and perform! Sometimes I think that's what people get off on the most, the feeling that they can see themselves performing in your place ... of course ... there are bad nights. You have to get used to the criticism as well as the acclaim."

"This seems tough. It probably gives you a different perspective ... especially with relationships."

"I dunno ... There have been many people in and out of my life." I said, suddenly feeling sad.

"Do you want to talk about it?" she asked.

We were heading into more of the deep recesses of my life.

"... Sure ... why not?" I said, with hesitation.

".... talk about what you want to talk about."

I put my head down, thought for a brief time. "... I was married once ... we had a child ..."

"You say that as If you were sorry."

"No ... not that ... I still don't know how I feel about it."

"About what? The marriage or the breakup?"

"About everything ... you see ... it was my fault."

"How was it your fault?"

"The music ... and the drugs took me away from her and baby too much. I was out chasing my career ... and other women."

"This music career of yours seems to have had a heavy price ... careers can demand a lot ...", she said, as if she herself understood. As if she was exposing a part of herself.

"You had problems over your career?" I asked.

She ignored my question and continued on about me. "... In other words you think that music ruined your marriage?"

"In a way ... yes ..."

"How so?"

"It was hard ... not so much the music but the life that went along with it."

"Can you be more particular?"

"Being in and out of work ... then being on the road, away from home?"

"Financially hard?"

"At times ... emotionally hard too, especially on her."

"The drugs?"

"Yeah ... I guess that didn't help."

She lit a cigarette.

"... You miss her don't you? Your wife?"

"Yes ... sometimes I regret that we broke up."

"What was her name?"

"Well ... her name was Joanne but I always called her 'Ol' Green Eyes'."

"That's cute ... Green Eyes ..."

"She had beautiful green eyes."

"Do you feel guilty about the outcome of the relationship?"

"... In a way ... yes ... I wish ... I dunno ..." I was beginning to feel choked up inside. Tears came to my eyes.

She slowed down. "I think this is a touchy subject right?" she said.

I couldn't speak. This was an unresolved part of my life. Liz took charge. "Here I have an idea ... let's talk to Joanne."

I was confused. "What? What do you mean? ... She's not here."

"Let me show you." She got up and put the other chair in front of mine." Here ... this is Joanne ... sitting here in this chair."

"Come on ... you can't mean that I'm going to talk to an empty chair?"

"Why not? Just imagine Joanne is sitting there."

I looked at the chair. This was ridiculous.

"Come on ... talk to Joanne," she insisted.

"Joanne ... I'm sorry for ... everything ... I really loved you really," I said, choked with tears.

"Now sit in the other chair. You will be Joanne," said Liz.

I was confused. This was crazy. I got up and sat in the other chair.

I thought about Joanne and tried to envision what she would say. "What happened between us? ... What ... Could your music mean this much to you ... to loose me?" You couldn't get a 'real' job?" I said, thinking what she might say.

"Now sit in the other chair and answer her!" said Liz.

I changed chairs. Words were burning in my mind. It was a secret place where I had dared to venture until now.

"Answer her!" Liz insisted.

I stammered. More tears welled up in my eyes. "I ... I don't know ... I ... Why make me decide between you? Why couldn't I have you both? You and my music. Music was my life! You know that!"

"Don't change chairs ... just answer ... answer the way she would if you were she ... Do it!" Liz continued.

"Is this all that matters? ... The band? ...You were my husband!" I screamed. "What about me?! You selfish bastard!!!"

I was crying now, uncontrollably.

"Now be yourself. Aren't you her husband? ... Answer her!" Liz demanded.

"Yes I was your husband but ... I ... I'm lost without the music ... That's all I am ... The music is me! It's not your fault! It's not my fault ... That's just the way it is! Oh God I'm sorry!!!" I put my head in my hands, my tears falling through my fingers.

"Okay, take it easy," said Liz softly. She put her hand on my shoulder. "That's enough ... calm down. It's okay ..."

I wiped my tears away. "I'm really embarrassed!"

"Don't be. I'm sorry to put you through this but it is something that you have to face. It will help you feel better to think about these things, to try to sort it all out."

"It wasn't her fault," I said.

"Maybe it wasn't your fault either. Maybe it was just the way it had to be ... things work out like that sometimes."

"I know I sound selfish but that's how much music means to me. Maybe I am crazy!"

"You're just a sane as I am ... really. But you seem to suffer from a lot of insecurity. The music gave you an identity crisis. You may want to look into that."

"I guess I really have to come to grips with it," I said sadly. Maybe the music was just a crutch for me? I would never make it in music. I trembled at the very thought of that. I would think about it later. Not now. Not now I thought.

Liz got up and sat in the empty chair. "It seems as though this music, this career of yours is a big factor in your relationship with other people ... Joanne ... maybe others."

"Yeah ... maybe it is."

"How about other women?"

"Sure ... there were others but sometimes there was a wall around me."

"What do you mean a wall?"

"Sometimes when women see you on stage, they get a generalized picture of what you are like in their minds."

"An example?"

"Well ... I would meet a girl who has seen me play and she thinks that I am ... well ... you know exciting. Actually I'm kind of quiet. They wouldn't really know me. Not the real me."

"It's hard to live up to being the life of the party?"

"Well ... sure."

"What about other relationships?"

"You can't always know what people want. In this business people use you and you use them."

"That sounds hideous!"

"Everybody wants something, something that you have ... they may have something that you need ... it's a mutual dependency."

"Political?"

"Yeah you could say that. It's who you know."

"An example?"

"Well ... let's say that you're at a party ... doing cocaine with the right people can be very prestigious. Turning on a rep can be to your advantage."

"Here we go again with the drugs."

"Well yes! But even hanging out with the right people can win you points. Everybody loves a winner."

"Is that how you feel?"

"No. It's bullshit!"

"Why do you think it's bullshit?"

"Because it has nothing to do with music. Art ..."

"This must be hell on your mental health."

"Maybe that's why I'm here."

"True ..."

We became quiet and we reflected on what I had said.

Liz then continued, "What about close friends?"

"Well sure ... there's Andy. He's probably my best friend. I've known him since childhood. Perhaps if it wasn't for him, I wouldn't be talking to you right now. He talked me into having therapy."

"Women friends?"

"Well ... there was Jackie ..."

"Is this relationship sexual or platonic?"

"I'm not sure ...."

"Did she have anything to do with your break up with Joanne?"

"No but our relationship may have had something to do with the break up of the band."

"A love triangle?"

"She was Fast Freddie's girl ... 'Fast Freddie' was our lead guitar player."

"Let me guess ... Jackie stayed with him and you rode off into the sunset in search of fame and fortune."

"That's close enough."

"And again, its the music that fills the void?"

"I never thought about it like that but maybe it's true. The music is always there. I can count on it no matter what. My music is all I have."

Fortunately, I was able to quit washing dishes and got a job playing music in a restaurant. I strolled from table to table, as I sang to the dinner guests. They would pleasantly nod as I finished each tune. They wouldn't applaud, just nod. At one table were two young women; one with light brown hair neatly braided. Her brown eyes watched me intently as I strummed the guitar. I sang to her...

"... Time, time, time ...
Set me free ...
From my memories...

Cause I've been waiting oh so long
I've been singin' all my songs
Of my sorrows ... my gone tomorrows ...

You know I've been told you can't help a friend
If they can't even help themselves ...
I guess that it's true that I worry too much
I guess I should be somewhere else ...

People they'll tell you they know about life
And you will be talking to dawn ...
When I get through well, I'm still at a loss
I guess we are each on our own ...

Time, time, time ...
Turn me on ...
To tomorrow ...

Cause I know I'm gonna make it!
I'm gonna reach out, I'm gonna take it!
My tomorrows ... forget my sorrows ..."

The guitar sounded it's last note. The girl with the brown eyes was impressed. "That' great! Is that one of your songs?" she asked.

"Yeah."

"You're talented."

"Thanks."

"Would you care to join us?"

"Well ... I would but-"

"Please!" She interjected, and looked to her friend who nodded approval.

"Yes ... do join us," her friend replied.

"I guess it would be ok. I'm about due for a break," I said, sitting down and resting the guitar beside me.

"My name is Julie," she said, "and this is Janet. What's yours?"

I moved one hand onto the table and carelessly knocked over the salt shaker. "Oh! I'm such a klutz sometimes!"

"You're more at home with a guitar in your hands I see!" She laughed.

"Maybe you're right."

"Are you from Colorado?"

"No ... I'm from Washington DC. ... and you?"

"Well Janet is from Denver, but I'm from California."

"Really? What part?"

"Near Los Angeles."

"Really!. I'm planning on going to Los Angeles soon."

"The music business?" asked Janet.

"Yeah ... I guess lots of musicians end up there sooner or later."

"Going to be a rock star huh?" asked Julie, teasing.

"Well ... I dunno ... I figure I would give it a try."

I glanced up from the table at the surroundings. It was peaceful, there in the dinning room. I studied Julie and Janet. They were the first people I had really met in a while. Being with them felt good. Julie continued the conversation. "How long have you been playing here?"

"I just started last week."

"There are so many singers ... there must be plenty of competition."

"Well ... actually on the day I auditioned, there was someone else."

... I remembered the audition. I had just come in from the cold. It was early in the morning and the waiters were just getting their morning coffee and sorting their silverware.

Someone else, another musician, had gotten there first and already had his guitar out of its case. He sat down on a chair and started tuning. Then, he started to play. It was a song I had never heard before and I assumed that it was one of his own. It was good; catchy, and his voice; soulful. Half of me liked what he was doing. And the other half? I wanted him to fail-perhaps his voice would falter, or he would play a sour note on his guitar. I conjured up the scenario from the depths of a black heart and there was a sadness as I realized how ugly the situation was. But, he was my competition and there was only one job. One of us would be the winner, and the other, the loser.

He finished his song. It was great. He was great. As good as me. Maybe better. A lady from the back of the room walked over to him and talked in low tones. I couldn't hear what she was saying, but then he put his guitar away and she came walking toward me. "I'm the manager in charge of entertainment," she said, shaking my hand. "I suppose you are here in response to the ad in the paper?"

"Yes ... should I go ahead and play?" I asked, hoping that the job was still available.

"Yes, set up over there by the piano ... that will be fine."

I passed the other singer as he walked by. We didn't look at each other. I sat down, ran my fingers over the strings and started to sing. I sang one of my songs. I projected my voice into the quiet stillness of the room. Carefully, I wove my words into the music, trying to capture the feeling, to let the song take me where it wanted to go, where it had to go.

"... Friends that I have known ...
Have left me here ... I am alone ...
Faces I have seen ...
I only see them in my dreams ...

I don't know why I even care ...
The world has people scattered here ...
and scattered there ...
But do you think it's really fair?...
To have so much and lose it all ...
I don't know how ...
I don't know where ...."

The sun ... you know there's only one ...

And I will wait to see it come ...
Warm ... you know it always comes ...
I think I'll wait to see the dawn ...

I finished. I opened my eyes. The lady approached. She looked puzzled. "Well ... I don't know what to say." There was indecision in her voice.

"I also do cover tunes," I replied, trying to impress her.

"Well, like I told the other singer, I really would like to have someone who can also play piano."

"Well ... I play piano too!" I said quickly, without thinking. I didn't really play piano. Sure, I knew the major and minor chords and a few songs that I had taught myself, but I was not a piano player. This was crazy!

"Really? That's great! Can you play me a song?" she asked.

"Sure ... this piano?" I asked, pointing to the only piano in the room.

"Yes, that's the piano."

Behind the keyboard, I tried to remember the songs that I had taught myself years before, when I was much younger. One song came to mind. It was 'Yesterday' by the Beatles. I played a C chord. The harmonious sound rumbled through the old upright. I started singing the first verse. The words came easily.

Suddenly, to my horror, I realized that I couldn't remember the middle part, the bridge! What was the chord that started the bridge? My mind reeled, trying to remember that part of the song as I entered the second verse. I only had a few measures to go! What was that chord? What would happen if I got to the bridge and I didn't remember? Would I stop the song looking like a fool? Why did I consent to do this? Maybe I could fake it? I closed my eyes. I would remember the part when I got to it I thought. Just relax I told myself! I came to the bridge. Somehow, I remembered. A B-Minor chord! That was it! A B-Minor chord! I played the first measure to the bridge. I smiled. I sang and I smiled. The rest came naturally as I finished the bridge and started the last verse. I was almost through the song. I was going to make it! Perhaps I would get the job! I looked up. The other singer had left ...

Julie touched my hand. "Didn't you even hear a word I said?" she asked.

I realized that she had been talking to me while I was daydreaming.

"Oh I'm sorry ... I was thinking ..."

"What a day dreamer you are!"

"Yeah ... I guess I get spaced-out sometimes."

"Like the absent minded professor," she giggled.

I looked down at my watch. "Oh! I have to start playing again."

"Good. Play another one of your songs."

"That's the only kind I know!" I teased.

I went to the next table where a family was seated, the husband, wife and small child who was busy dropping food on the floor. As I started singing, I looked over at Julie. She was my audience...

"Looking back ... at the things I've done ...
Good and bad ... they have brought me here ...
All the years ... that have lingered by ...
They have stolen ... each precious day ...

Looking back ... is the world!
She neither laughs ... nor does she cry ...
She just looks on ...

Looking back ... all those dreams abandoned ...
Some were foolish ... yes I know that now ...
And though my life ... is not yet half over ...
Still I think I know ... what the rest will be ...

Looking back ... is the world!
She neither laughs ... nor does she cry ...
She just looks on ..."

A mother was wiping the child's face clean as the father smiled at me nervously. They were done eating and were ready to pay the check and leave.

I continued on to another table and then another. At one point, I would go to the piano and play a song. My piano playing was choppy and inconsistent, not as flowing and natural as when I played the guitar, but I knew I had to keep up the facade. I wanted to keep the job and dreaded the thought of going back to the restaurant to wash dishes.

When the night was over, I looked up to see Julie still sitting there. Janet was gone. I put my guitar in the case and walked over to her. "Still here I see".

"Yes ... I'm still here. Won't you have a seat?" she asked in a sweat voice.

"I could use one for the road." I ordered a snifter of brandy. She wasn't drinking.

"Where is Janet?"

"Oh ... she had to go home."

"How 'bout you? I mean ... how will you get home?"

"Well ... I kind'a thought ... you might take me." She said, looking down at her folded hands on the table.

"Well ... actually I don't have a car."

"Really? How do you get home?" she asked, looking up, surprised.

"My friend Andy should be here soon ... Andy's my roommate."

"I'm sorry. I have been presumptuous. I hope I won't put you out of your way."

"Oh no ... really! I ... he wouldn't mind ... really!"

There was an awkward silence.

"... Where do you work?" I asked.

"In Evergreen, sort of an antique store ... for the tourists."

"I like antiques. I always wonder where the things came from ... who the original owners were ..."

"Really? I do too! It's kind of fascinating when you stop to think of it ... What do you do? I mean, besides the music?" she asked.

"Well ... this is all I do."

"You don't have a day job?"

"Well, I was washing dishes for a while ... just to tide me over until I got another gig."

"So, you are a dedicated musician!"

"Yeah, not the first nor the last of 'em I'm afraid."

Another awkward silence before Julie spoke, "You know, I have noticed something ... why are all your songs so sad?"

For a moment I was speechless, "... I ... I don't know ... I never stopped to think about it." What she said was remarkable. Most of my songs w-e-r-e sad! She was right. Wow. I thought about it for a brief moment.

Then Andy came in the door. He saw us and came over. As he approached, his eyes were fixed on Julie. "Well hello there!" he said.

"Julie, I want you to meet Andy ... Andy ... Julie."

"Where in the hell did you pick up this loser?" he asked her jokingly.

"Actually ... I picked him up!" she said, smiling at me.

"I guess by now he's been boring you to death with his songs and music talk."

"No ... I like his songs and he can talk about anything he wants. I'm all ears!" She replied as she reached over to hold my hand. I squeezed her hand gently and all attention turned to our hands. It was a sudden and odd, intimate gesture for two strangers to share. But it was different. More friendly and caring than sexual.

More silence.

"... Well," said Andy, "shall we go? Your chariot awaits you sire!" he teased.

"I told Julie we'd run her home ... didn't think you'd mind."

"Of course I don't mind!"

Outside, up above, stars twinkled in the cold, black sky. Julie and I rode in the back seat, and held each other close in order to keep warm.

"Where do you live?" Andy asked her.

"Oh ... I'll show you," she replied, as we started to enter the Denver city limits.

"You know ... the night is still young," I said softly.

"Yes ... it isn't that late really ..." she replied.

"Why don't you come over to our place for a little while. I can drive you home later."

"I know you musician types ... you just want me to spend the night with you ... don't you?" she teased.

"Well..."

"That's all right, I accept."

"Really ... I didn't mean ..."

"Don't worry ... you worry too much."

I took her hand and raised it to my lips. I kissed it gently. "Andy, just drive us home!" I yelled up to the front seat.

When we got to the apartment, I fumbled with the keys to the door. "You'll have to excuse the place ... we don't always keep it clean," I said, apologetically.

"I would be surprised if you did!" she teased.

I opened the door expecting to see a messing room, but Andy had put the couch back in order where he slept.

"Well I don't know about you guys but I'm tired," said Andy.

"Is this where you sleep? On the couch?" asked Julie.

"'Fraid so. I'm sure you two love birds would want to be left alone!"

"Well ... where do you sleep?" she asked me.

"That's my little cubby hole over there," I said, pointing to the sun room.

"Well ... take me to your cubby hole!"

In the tiny room and I reached up and pulled the curtain across. She took off her coat and sat down on the bed. "What's this?" she asked, picking up a book I had left there. "'The Meaning of Happiness' ... by Alan Watts," she read from the cover.

"An old friend once turned me on to it," I told her. I remembered Terry.

"I like Watts. Are you a Zen Buddhist?"

"No ... but I like the ideas."

"You know what?" she asked.

"What?"

"I like you!" she teased.

I took her into my arms and kissed her. Her breath was warm and sweet. "I'm a little tired too," she whispered. "You get in bed. I have to go freshen up," she said and then disappeared through the curtain.

I turned off the light, took off my jeans, and slipped beneath the covers. The sheets were cold and I tried to warm up. Suddenly, I thought of Jackie. Julie was different somehow. But I hardly knew her! We had just met. A one night stand? But was she? She would be back any minute and for some reason, I felt hesitant. Was I ready for another entanglement, even if it was just for one night? How cavalier! I would put on my best macho moves and make love to her in the darkness. An escape? Yes maybe. Maybe we would or could simply lose ourselves to our emotions. There in the little sunroom in the midst of a Winter night, the girl with the warm brown eyes and I would pull the curtain on the world around us, and forget ... just forget ...

"Well don't you look warm and cozy!" said Julie from the darkness. In the dim light of the moon, coming in the window, I watched as she removed her flannel shirt and then her jeans. Like a goddess she looked, tender and beautiful. She pulled back the covers and climbed into the bed with me. Warm was her body.

We kissed. I was aroused but I remained limp. I rolled back over away from her. "What's wrong?" she asked.

"I ... I don't know ... I just can't ... well ... you know."

"That's ok ... maybe you're just tired ... that's all."

"I'm sorry."

"Why do you have to feel sorry?"

"I dunno ..."

"Just being here with you is good enough for me."

"... I know what you were expecting."

"No. You tell me what I was expecting." She raised up on one elbow.

"Well ... you meet a guy ... a musician and we go home and then ... well ... I can't perform ... I can't do it."

"First of all, what difference does it make if you're a musician or not? As for a performance;, your performance was over back at the club, when you put your guitar away."

"I'm embarrassed ..."

"Don't be. I still like you."

"You like my songs."

"It's not just the music."

"You don't know me", I protested.

"You don't know me either really."

"It's different."

"How different? ... You're a musician and I'm not?"

"No. You're right ... that is silly isn't it?"

She leaned over and kissed me. We held the embrace until sleep overtook us.

"You told me last time, that music was your life. I remember you saying that ... "Music was your Life," said Liz. I was back in another therapy session.

"I probably said something like that ... sure."

"That's a heavy statement, if you take it literally."

"Maybe ... it depends on who you are ..."

"You consider yourself an artist, don't you?"

"Yeah ... in a way ... yeah."

"What is that you have there?" she asked, looking at the spiral notebook in my hands.

"Oh ... this is a collection of some songs, my original songs."

"May I see them?"

"Sure."

She sat back and turned a few pages, silently reading the lyrics to herself. I watched her lips move as she read. She looked up and grinned at me. "Well some of these are interesting! You have the music too I suppose?"

"For most of them. Some could takes months to finish though."

"They all seem so sad," she said. I thought about what Julie had sad. It was true. There was a sadness to most of my songs.

Liz continued, "Do you really think that rock music is an art form?"

"Yeah, why not?"

"I think of art as ... well, as an expression that has a timeless quality to it, more of a classical nature. Isn't rock music more of a craft?"

"I've heard that said before ... I dunno ..." I remembered Howie and our first conversation at Pine Avenue. Now, looking back, it seemed like such a long time ago.

"I mean, rock music is here today and gone tomorrow ... isn't it?"

"Some of it. But that doesn't mean it isn't art."

"What is an artist? I mean, to you, what does being an artist mean?"

I momentarily stopped to think. "Well ... sometimes ... I think it's like standing on the sidelines and taking notes."

"Like a spectator on the outside looking in?"

"In a way ... yes ... maybe it's like having a sixth sense ... an intuition ... an insight. Perhaps you can see things that others miss."

"Can you give me an example?"

"Well ... what about the sixties? Many writers saw the hypocrisy around them."

"You haven't given me an example."

"How about 'A day in the Life' by the Beatles? Didn't John Lennon see the apathy in society? Someone dies in a car crash and it's really no big deal, just another news piece on the TV."

"And artists are the only ones that can see this?"

"No, certainly not, but they write about it ... they can make other people more aware."

"Yes, but aren't you just caught up in the sixties? What about the great classical composers? How do they fit in to this scheme?"

"Well ... there's Handel's 'Messiah. Could he have been inspired by some divine providence? But that was popular music back then. They just danced to a different beat."

"You make it sound exciting, romantic ... being an artist."

"It's a curse!" I exclaimed.

"A curse?"

"Sure! The ability to see a reality. It had caused many to burn the midnight oil. It nagged and gnawed at the consciousness, that moment of insight. And the fruits of this madness? What has entertained millions of people throughout the centuries has been the product of these few lost souls. And that force that drove them to create may have ruined many of their lives. Why do you suppose so many talented, famous people take their own lives?"

"I'm sorry but I can't see how you can compare rock music with the greatest minds of all time. This is ridiculous!" she said. She was being surprisingly subjective.

"Hey! I can only hope that there is much more to be said, more ideas to be shared. I can't imagine that we could spend the rest of our lives looking back at the Classics. I think that some rock music will have an impact on history. Some tunes may become classics themselves."

She countered, "I don't know ... rock music seems to be merely a commercial form of entertainment."

"That makes me sad."

"Perhaps you are being unrealistic."

"Maybe I am ..." I said, thinking.

Liz continued her train of thought, "I mean, this rock music is just a business. I don't think that any of these people really think that they are really creating art, they are being artistic yes, but it's just top 40 music on the radio, here today and gone tomorrow."

"I still believe that I can say something with my music."

"There are probably others, like yourself, that feel that way."

"I guess we are a bunch of freaks, living on our dreams ... in a way maybe were the last comic book heroes left."

She continued, "I don't know ... to me it seems a cruel trap, trying to work in a medium you consider an art form and then sell the results with such Madison Avenue flair."

"A cruel trap ..." I whispered to myself.

"Did you say something?"

"Ah ... no ... it's nothing ..."

There was something in my mind but I couldn't find it. It was a flashing thought that had come and then gone. Perhaps I wanted to keep that thought hidden in my mind.

"So this is your life, this business of music ... writing music."

"I feel compelled to do it."

"Compelled? That sounds rather drastic! " she exclaimed, "It really is an obsession for you isn't it ... writing songs?"

"What else is there in life? It's all that matters to me."

"Do you think you're any good?"

"You tell me, you read some of my lyrics. What do you mean by good?"

"Well ... good at music, art ... What does being good mean to you?" she asked.

I thought for a moment before I spoke. "... Maybe good means being more clever than your audience."

"I like that."

"I dunno ... it probably means many things."

Liz paused, and then finished her thoughts. "Well ... anyway ... I wish you luck! ... Let me give you some advice ... don't place so much importance on your music. You may have to face the fact that you will not be a successful musician, a successful songwriter. That may be difficult for you to accept. I think it might be just a way of avoiding any insecurity you may be feeling. Remember, there may be other options in your life. Something that never occurred to you. Something else that can give you strength. Just think about that."

37

High atop Mt. Evans I stood, cold and knee-deep in snow, looking down into a valley. It was high up, up among the clouds. Down below, Denver was lost in the distance. I turned and gazed at the majestic, peaked horizon, feeling humbled by the sheer magnitude of this expanse.

The sun, waning in the western sky, made multi-colored streaks in the heavens. A lone eagle soared above. Below, you could see the frost rising like a white cotton pillow. There was a clearing just below the timberline and I pulled a pine branch away to find a doe and her fawn. They peered at me for only an instant, and then scampered away to safety. I walked farther past the pines. Over a rocky ledge, again I could see the doe as she watched me wearily. Then, finally, she sped away, totally from sight.

A cold wind blew into my face. It sang to me as it whipped through the towering tree limbs. Suddenly, I was aware that Julie was standing near me. But I didn't turn to face her. We simply stood there, frozen, silent in the peace that enveloped us.

"It's ... wonderful isn't it?" I remarked.

"One of the most wonderful places I could imagine," she said. She came nearer.

"Such a sight used to fill me with ... thoughts of power and of ambition ... dreams ... " I said, thinking out loud; thinking of my youth. My dreams of success.

"Anyone who is truly alive would be filled with some kind of emotion."

"Yes. But maybe some dreams are too big, some plans too farfetched ..." I said wearily.

"... You don't believe that ..." she said softly.

Silence.

"... I must go to California ... I must ..."

"... I know ..."

"Will you ... could you ... come with me?"

"Yes ... If you want me to ..."

"I do ... I want you to."

I took her into my arms. Again, the wind cut through the pines but we stood strong against the gusts.

City of Angels

38

Joshua sat across the table. His bearded face, lacking emotion, was like a stone mask; resolute, as though there was a wisdom, some robust knowledge that only he possessed, which was not easily dispensed, especially to a stranger like myself.

Intimidating? Not really, not in a personal way. Though I was younger in years, there was much I had seen and done. Perhaps I too had a knowledge, secrets to share.

Friendly? Yes, he was, but his eyes, those eyes! They watched me, probed, analyzed. There could be no doubt that I was under his scrutiny.

We were sitting in his backyard on a the hill which overlooked a small valley, not too far from downtown Los Angeles, a splendid view. The afternoon sun was setting low and left shadows everywhere, save the surrounding mountain tops. In the west, the sky was turning to dusk and below, the lights of LA were starting to twinkle. Nightfall was approaching.

"We really appreciate your hospitality," I said, reaching for a pear from the wooden bowl on the table.

"Think nothing of it," he responded.

"Julie said you were an artist ... a sculptor I believe," I said.

"Close ... actually I like to work with iron and steel. I work with a blow torch, not a chisel."

"I would like to see your work sometime."

"You're sitting on one of my pieces." He broke the slightest, perceptible trace of a smile.

I looked down at the chair I was sitting in. It was an odd assortment of metal pieces welded together. "It's ... nice ... I hadn't noticed."

"It is also functional."

"Yes ... it is ..."

His piercing eyes made me feel uncomfortable, awkward. It was as though he was waiting for me to speak. "Julie told me she used to live here ... sort of an artist colony."

"Artist colony?" This time, he grinned, as if I were a child making yet another foolish remark.

"Well ... I don't remember the exact words she used ... but it was something to that effect."

"We try to live a ... particular lifestyle."

The sound of footsteps. Becky and Julie came to the table with dinner. "Well ... it is a beautiful sunset isn't it?" said Becky. Becky was Joshua's wife. She too had quality about her, a lofty stature, as if being hip was an exclusive and irrevocable trait of being a Californian. No hamburgers or hotdogs on this dinner table, dinner was a platter of enchiladas, filled with red peppers and goat's cheese.

"And you! You will ruin your appetite, eating that pear!" Julie scolded me.

"Wine, anyone?" asked Becky.

"Sure," I said, trading my pear for the glass.

I looked around me. It was really an enjoyable setting. "Do you always eat dinner out here? This view!"

"Most of the time. The weather's always so nice," Becky replied.

Still, even as we ate, I could feel Joshua's eyes on me. "How do you like LA?" he asked me.

"Well, considering I've only been here a few weeks ... it's ok."

"Auditioned yet?"

"Yes. Yesterday in fact ... at the Record Factory."

"And?"

"Nothing happened."

... I remembered it. I had gotten the tip from a music store sales clerk in Culver City. He said that a producer named Mr. Gabriel was looking for talent at the Record Factory. Hurriedly, I jotted down the address and left immediately. With difficulty, I found the place. It was a modern building encased all in glass. Inside, it was air-conditioned, clean with suave-modern art and a leather couch. Curiously, there was no receptionist. I simply sat down. On the coffee table were the usual assortment of magazines and on the walls were several gold records. They glistened in the sunlight like beacons before my eyes.

Suddenly, a young girl appeared from a doorway. She walked behind the desk and sat down. "Hi. Do you have an appointment?"

"No, not really. I came to see Mr. Gabriel."

"Well I dunno ... he's busy! Perhaps you could come back tomorrow?"

"I can wait."

She looked distressed and picked up the phone.

"Mr. Gabriel ... I have someone here to see you ... I'm sorry. Hold on." She cupped her hand over the receiver. "What is your business?" she asked me.

"I would like to audition some songs."

She smiled and went back to the handset. "He wants to audition ... uh huh ... ok." She hung up the phone. "Mr. Gabriel said that he is busy at the moment but if you would be kind enough to wait for an hour, he might be able to see you."

My heart pounded. He was going to see me! I couldn't believe it! "That would be fine! I can just sit right here if it's all right." I said.

The anticipation! Just think! Here I was in Hollywood, sitting in the lobby of the Record Factory of all places! Waiting to see a producer. Surely, he was one of the gods, a patriarch of the music underworld!

But, my anticipation waned as timed passed. The receptionist had disappeared again. The hour went by and there was nothing. Maybe he had forgotten about me? Then, the phone rang. It rang again. I waited for it to ring. It remained silent. I stood up to stretch. Another half hour had passed. I looked into the hallway, tempted to see what was there. I moved cautiously to the door and stuck my head into the hall. There was another doorway at the far end next to a soda machine. I decided to investigate.

I ventured to the door and I looked inside. It was a recording studio. Microphones, stands, plush chairs and miles of cable! There was the mixing board room. The console was an ocean of knobs. This was the place, the place where the magic happened! The machinery of the industry! I could only imagine the stars who had made their careers here, who had explored the depths of their talent here. Maybe this was my destiny, to make music here within these sacred walls!

"You shouldn't be here!" Stunned, I turned around. It was the receptionist.

"Oh ... I'm sorry ... I wanted to get a soda and just ... wandered in," I said, quickly fabricating a story.

"I'm sorry, but Mr. Gabriel had to leave for the day. He won't be able to see you." ... 'He won't be able to see you' ... 'He won't be able to see you' ... 'HE WON'T BE ABLE TO SEE YOU!!!' rang in my ears, tortured my mind like a bad dream ...

"Would you like more wine?" asked Becky, my mind returning to the dinner.

I shifted my weight in the chair. I had almost finished eating. "Yes ... please," I replied.

"That was delicious," said Julie.

"Did you get enough to eat?" Becky asked.

"Oh yes. I'm stuffed!" I replied.

The girls removed the dirty dishes and left Joshua and I alone. The sky was almost totally dark now, except for an orange glow that hovered over the heart of the city. Joshua spoke. "I think that you will find this town a harsh, cruel place for those like yourself ... trying to find success here."

"It's not just finding success ... it's just getting the c-h-a-n-c-e for success ... just getting the chance."

"Do you know how many there are like you?"

"Hundreds, maybe thousands, I would guess," I replied.

"This city is full of winners and losers, a Mecca for dreamers of every kind," he said. "Someone told me once ... making it in show business was ten percent talent and ninety percent luck."

I thought about that - perhaps he was right.

We looked out over the city. The twinkling lights were like stars that had fallen from the heavens.

39

Andy started the car as I climbed into the passenger seat. "Do you know where you are going?" he asked me.

"I was there just the other day. The Record Factory."

"The place where the guy wouldn't see you?"

"Yeah ... it's the same place."

"You must be a glutton for punishment!"

"Hey, the guy didn't exactly say that he wouldn't see me ... he had to leave."

Andy pulled into the traffic, heading downtown.

"How did your job hunting go?" I asked him.

"Nothing yet. I'm afraid the unemployment situation in this town is hell."

"Where did you look?"

"Shit! I couldn't even get a job bagging groceries!"

"Don't worry, something will break for me soon. I know it will. It just has to."

When we got to the Record Factory, Andy sat with me in the lobby. The reception came back to her desk. "Back again I see?" she commented, amused. "Well persistence has its virtues."

She picked up the phone. "Mr. Gabriel ... the gentleman who was here the other day is back ... the one with the songs for you to hear ... " My hand gripped the handle to my guitar case as I waited impatiently. "... Yes ... okay good!" She hung up. "Okay. He will see you. Follow me please."

I turned to Andy and he smiled. "I'll wait here ... you go on. I can't be of any use to you in there," he said. He grabbed my arm. "... Good luck."

I followed her into the hallway. We walked past the soda machine, past the studio. We came to a heavy oak door. She opened it and I entered. Mr.

Gabriel sat at the end of a large conference table. He was of medium build and was bronzed from the sun. He swayed back and forth on a leather swivel-chair. He was smiling. He was a remarkably handsome man. I couldn't imagine him ever not smiling. The girl shut the door, leaving us alone. I was nervous. This was it. The chance of a lifetime.

"Well ... I can see you can't take no for an answer," he said.

"I had to see you."

"I know. What can I do for you?"

"I have some great songs ..."

"Do you know how many people I have heard say that?"

My hands trembled slightly but I tried to conceal my nervousness. "I ... well ... a lot I guess ..."

Awkward silence.

"Would you like some papaya juice?" he asked. "I love it!" There was a bottle of juice on the table next to him with several glasses.

"Ah ... no ... I'm not thirsty ... but thanks."

"I see ... well ... so ... let's hear a great song. I can always use great songs!"

I bent over and fumbled with the latches on my guitar case. As I pulled out the guitar, I accidentally knocked it against the edge of the table. The sound from the guitar was jarring and ugly.

"Oh I'm so sorry! I hope I didn't damage the table."

"Forget it," he said as he looked at his watch.

I knew I had one chance, only this one chance to win him over. I strummed the strings of the guitar. The E string was flat. I turned the key to bring it up into tune. I was ready. I started to sing...

"... Hey you!
You say you're living in paradise ...
Yes I see you smilin' ...
I can see it in your eyes ...
Cause the music's playing
and the stars are in the sky ...
Everybody is laughing
and they're feelin' high ...
The nightlife is fun when spot lights
are shinin' bright ...

... Hey you!
I see you're livin' in paradise ...

Yes I hear you laughin' ...
I can see it in your eyes ...
But when the bar's let out
at the break of day ...
And your dreams are broken
and you loose you way ...
It's hard to be free when you're livin'
in such a disguise ...

Hey you!
I hear you're livin' in paradise ...
But I heard you cryin' ...
yes I could see it in your eyes ...
And your boyfriend's cheatin'
with a lover on the side ...
And your girlfriend's crazy
and you can't confide ...
All the things that you feel ...
deep down inside ...

... And when you really need a friend
and you pick up the phone ...
And you call somebody and ...
there not home ...
I'll come and see you ...
I'll come and see you ...
Yes ...I'll come and save you ...
from your paradise ...

Yeah ... Yeah ...
You say you're livin' in paradise ...
Dancin' in the moonlight
You've been livin' in paradise ...
Drawn by the firelight
Just livin' in paradise ...
Livin' in paradise ..."

I strummed the last chord as the song trailed off to an ending. Mr. Gabriel smiled. "I like it," he said.

"You do? ... I mean you like it?" I asked.

"You have more like this one?"

"Sure. I've got lots of songs ... lots!"

He got up walked over to me. I stood up. My head was swirling.

"I think we can work something out. We can always use good songwriter/singers. Let me see ... do you need money?" he asked..

"Well ... I have some money but ..."

He interjected, "Here let me write you a check for a few hundred dollars. Will that tide you over for a few days?"

"Sure! I mean you really liked the song?"

"Yes ... I liked the song ... really!" He exclaimed.

He looked at his watch. Then he pulled out a check and scribbled out the amount and handed it to me.

"Do you have a number where I can reach you?"

"No. I don't have a phone," I replied, somewhat embarrassed.

"That's ok. Just come back in a few days ... we'll talk more then." He got on the phone. "Patty ... look ... our friend will be back on Thursday. I'll need a song-writer's contract drawn up ... good ... also I gave him a check ... two hundred ... put it on the new account ... thanks."

He hung up and we moved toward the door. We shook hands. "Take care of that voice will you, I want to hear you sing more on Thursday ... okay?" Again, he looked at his watch and I stepped out into the hallway. "Don't worry about a thing. I'll see you on Thursday."

Out in the lobby, the receptionist Patty smiled. "Congratulations! I hear he liked you! That's marvelous!" she exclaimed. She shook my hand.

Outside, Andy was stunned not knowing what had happened. "Tell me what happened!" asked Andy excitedly.

"Andy, I got a break! He liked my song!"

"Really?"

I shook him eagerly. "'Livin' in Paradise' ... he really liked it!"

"Really? No shit?"

"Look! A check for two hundred dollars! Just to tide me over!" I gushed and unfolded the check and handed it to him.

"I ... I don't know what to say," he said dumbfounded.

"We're gonna celebrate ... that's what we're gonna do!"

"You're chariot awaits you sire," he teased, opening the car door.

"No. Let's walk. Let's just walk! I feel as light as air!" I looked down. On the side walk were bronze stars with famous names written on them. "Look, movie stars ... directors ... composers ... producers ... they're all here!"

"Yeah."

"This is where we belong ... we belong here!" I exclaimed.

"Hey! Don't let this thing go to your head!"

"No, but this is a start. Perhaps I have finally gotten a break!"

Andy joined my enthusiasm, "... Oh hell, Okay ... go on and be crazy ... you deserve it!" He laughed.

"Let's just walk on and on. Let's just walk until we can't walk any longer. This is the yellow brick road!" We walked on, drunk from the excitement. I couldn't come down. We looked into the store windows and I felt my jeans for the check to make sure that it was still there in my pocket.

"Let's cash the check and go to a restaurant. A bar! Anything you want!"

"This is a crazy day!" Andy rejoiced.

"It's a crazy, beautiful, wonderful day!" We turned a corner. "This is the famous Chinese Theater!" I exclaimed.

"The what?"

"Where all the premiers, opening nights of movies take place! You know ... the premier showings ... the limos ... the red carpet!"

There were cement blocks with the foot and hand prints of the stars. I walked to each one and examined them. "Look ... 'Bogie's' foot prints," I said.

"Really?" Andy was catching my giddiness.

"Yeah ... These are Humphrey Bogart's foot prints!" I carefully placed my feet into the places where he had stood. My feet didn't fit.

"You're feet are too big!" Andy teased.

His remark went unnoticed. My mind was far away. "I wonder what made these people different from any of us?"

"They were talented, famous people I suppose."

"I think they were people with dreams ... big, outlandish, unshakable and, beautiful dreams ... but people like you and me ... that's all ... people just like you and me!"

"Wait a minute! This is crazy." Andy teased.

"Why? To imagine that anyone of us could become famous?"

40

One of Joshua's friends had a beach house and was out of town. We decided to spend the day there. We would picnic, swim, bask in the sun. In Joshua's Mercedes, we drove south, past the huge glorious homes, ones of wealth and opulence. I could only imagine what richness and refinement lay hidden behind grand doorways, the palms and eucalyptus trees that hung lazily over the long driveways bathed in golden sunlight. These were the prizes of success, spoils for the victors to whom life had been kind. For myself, I could only look on them with wonder, like a child with his nose pressed against the glass, straining, trying to get a better view.

Heading down along the coast, along the steep cliffs as the waves pounded the sand and rocks below. When we reached the beach house, we piled out of the car with our blankets and baskets.

"Let's go swimmin'!" shouted Andy gleefully. He looked comical with his cutoffs and heavy work boots.

"Maybe you should take off those gun-boat shoes first!" said Julie, teasing him.

"Let's get in the sun!" said Becky.

"That sound's heavenly," said Julie. "How about you?" she asked me. "Well ... in a while ... first I want to work on a song."

"Of course ... but promise me you'll come out soon."

"Yes. I won't be long."

Andy and the girls headed around the side of the house, and I accompanied Joshua to the front door. Inside, it was gorgeous. There was a fireplace with cushions spread around and a wet bar. Through the sliding glass doors-a magnificent view of the ocean. Joshua went up stairs to check things. Meanwhile, I took out my guitar. I sat down on a cushion and put a pad and pencil down beside me. Sitting there with the warm sun on my face, I strummed the guitar and fashioned the song that was in my mind ...

"I wish I could write a song ...
Just like all the one's on the radio ...
On every old jukebox and TV show ...
Just to say I love you ....

And when I write my song ..."

"One of your creations I suppose?"

I stopped singing and turned around. It was Joshua. "It's just an idea right now," I said, a little disturbed.

"Another love song huh?" He pulled out a bar stool and sat down across from me.

"Yeah ... love songs sell don't they?"

"Oh ... it might sell." Again, he replied and smiled down at me. I found it a bit offensive.

"You know ... since we met, I get the impression that you don't approve of what I am doing."

He leaned back and raised his eyebrows. "Whoa!" he exclaimed. "Wait a minute! I'm sorry ... I didn't mean to give off those vibes."

"Well frankly ... you have!"

"... sorry ... I didn't mean to.

"Well ... That's cool," I said, looking down at the floor away from him.

He leaned down closer. "You see ... in a way ... you remind me of myself."

"Really? And how is that?"

"I was like you once, I had stars in my eyes ... but then I saw the reality of it all."

"The reality of it all? What on earth are you talking about?" I was perplexed.

"Oh I made the rounds, all the galleries ... the shows ... I was going to be a great artist. Yes, I too was going to be great!"

"I think you're jealous," I said.

"Oh no! Don't get me wrong. I'm happy for you. But don't get caught up in it ... that's all."

"I'm sorry, but I don't need your bullshit rap, your advice," I said bitterly.

"It's not bullshit. Believe me. I hear your songs ... I like them too. I really do, but you could be setting yourself up for a fall."

"I'll face that when it comes. For now I have to follow this thing wherever it leads me."

"Oh I was like you once ... my head in the clouds! My career meant everything to me ... everything."

"Well ... what happened?"

Joshua paused, shifted in his chair, thought for a moment before he spoke. "I truly became an artist."

"You were always an artist ... you're an artist now."

"Not before ... now maybe ... but not before."

"I don't understand." Now I was totally perlexed.

He got up and picked up a magazine from the table. He leafed through the pages and then handed it to me. I looked at the page. It read, 'Josh White's Heavy Metal'. On the same page were pictures of his work.

"This ... this is you ... Josh White!" I said looking up from the page.

"Yes. That's my work. But it's my work! My work, not somebody else's."

"... I still don't understand."

"Look ... these people out there ... the business types, they don't care about art ... they want to make money ... that's all ... money!"

"I know that ... I've heard that. I'm aware of that."

"I'm not sure ... your work ... it's not something that you can bend and mold for their purposes ... your work ... well ... it's you. Your work is you ... you are what you create."

"I know that ... I feel strongly about that."

"What about this song that you are writing?"

"Well ... what about it?"

"You're writing a love song ... why? Because in the back of your mind you know that's what they want to hear."

"That's only natural in this business ... anyway ... it's easy for you to say-you've already made it."

"Yes ... I have found some success ... but that's not really important to me now."

"Oh come on!" I said with disbelief.

"It's true. Can't you see? I've learned well ... believe that!"

"I'm sorry, but I still don't understand," I said.

"It's not the art itself that really counts ... it's creating the art that counts ... living the artistic lifestyle. If the outcome sells then so much for the better."

"The artistic lifestyle?" I was confused.

"Come here," he said to me. He was standing beside the sliding glass door. I walked over to him. "Look at them, playing in the surf," he said. Julie and Andy were running along the beach. "What about them he asked.

"What about them? I was still confused.

"Do you think that they can express themselves as you can with your music?"

"No .. not really."

"That's where you miss the point. Look at Julie ... look at her!" he commanded.

I watched her as she ran along the surf. Her hair was flowing in the breeze. Her smile was as refreshing as the water that was splashing at her feet. She was beautiful. "She is ... a work of art," I said softly, solemnly.

"The way she lives her life is a work of art. It may not be for sale, but it is art to me. The whole world is a work of art. You ... yes you are a work of art even before you pick up your guitar!"

I remained silent. He continued.

"Everyday when I get up out of bed, I make some coffee before I work. But it's not the work that is really important, it's living the life that is the real art. The way I measure the coffee, the way I pour the water, the way I feel about myself before I even think about creation, and the result? Perhaps it is art, but it is art that comes to life through me. This is the art my friend, the real art, the art of living, and the whole world is my gallery ..."

At the end of the day, when the sun had gone down over the ocean, Julie and I laid on the cushions in front of the fireplace, alone. The fire felt hot against the soles of our feet. The orange glow caressed our faces. Outside, there was the sound of the surf.

"It's been a fun day," Julie sighed.

I reached for a drink of wine. The bottle lay next to me. "It has been a long day, a good day." I pulled her close. We kissed and then rolled apart. We lay there both looking up at the ceiling. I could feel her breathing next to me.

"Tomorrow's a big day for you," she said quietly.

"Yes ... it will be a big day."

She rolled over and looked at me. "What if ... what if it doesn't work out? ... I mean ... what if things don't work out for you in the end? What if it all fell through? What would you do?"

"I dunno ... I guess I would just go somewhere else with my music. If he liked my songs, I'm sure someone else would."

"Sure ... but what if thing's don't ever work out for you and your music? What would you do? I'm just being hypothetical of course."

"I ... I never really thought about it ... I dunno."

The fire cracked and popped in the fireplace.

"You could always sing your songs to me," she said softly.

"I know ... but you're biased-you like me."

"No, that's not true ... I love you."

I closed my eyes and squeezed my her hand. I tried to speak but the words wouldn't come.

"That's all right," she whispered, "you don't have to tell me that you love me too. I wasn't trying to make you say that."

"I know."

"... I listen to your songs a lot. There have been other women in your life ... I can hear it in your songs ... I can see it in your eyes."

"Yes ... there were others," I confessed.

"You don't have to tell me about them ... I don't really want you to," she said. I remembered my talk with Joshua earlier. Julia was special. She continued, "No, really ... being with you here tonight ... this is all I could want ... just to be with you like this tonight,"

I tried to speak but she cupped my mouth with her hand and giggled. I rolled over and took her into my arms. The light from the fire danced on her face. I kissed her. We made love.

41

At the Record Factory, Patty was watering the plant on her desk when I entered the lobby. "Hi. How are you today?" she asked.

Fine," I replied. There was the sound of music coming from the hallway. "Is there someone in the studio?"

"Oh yes, there is a session ... they've been jammin' for a while now."

"Who is it?" I asked.

"I dunno ... some group, a girl singer ..." I started to sit down. "Oh don't sit down ... just go on in ... he's expecting you."

I passed her desk and went into the hallway. The doors to the studio were closed, but from within, there was the sound of bass and drums.

Suddenly, the door opened and a pretty young girl stepped out. I almost ran into her. "Excuse me," I said. She didn't acknowledge my apology. She stumbled and fell against the wall. She was wearing a pair of high heeled shoes and was having trouble walking. At first I thought she was sick but as I watched her, I realized that she was high on drugs.

"Can I help you?" I asked. Again, she didn't respond. She just kept walking down the hall, holding on to the wall for support. I watched her until she made it to the restroom, a few doors down.

At Mr. Gabriel's office door, I knocked gently. There was no answer. I knocked louder. A voice from within told me to enter. As before, he was sitting down at the end of the long conference table. But somehow, this time it was different. He rubbed his face with his hands, as though he was tired. "How's it goin'?" he asked.

"Oh just fine ... I spent the day at the beach yesterday ... it was great ."

"That's nice," he said, "Would you like a drink?"

I thought about the girl in the hall. "Ah ... no ... ah ... yeah ... sure."

He put an ice cube in a glass and poured some scotch over it. He handed it to me. "Look ... I'm not going to beat around the bush ... we had meeting yesterday and ... well ... I'm afraid I won't be able to use you. At least not in the near future."

"What?!?!" I replied, astonished.

"There was a meeting. We decided that our budget was only suitable for one project and we decided to back a female singer ... they are the 'coming thing' you know."

"But ... what about the song? What about the two hundred dollars?"

"Oh that ... forget it ... you keep it."

"I don't understand ... the other day-"

"That was the other day," he interjected, "... now it's today ... things change."

"Look if there's anything I can do to convince you-"

"No, I'm sorry ... maybe some other time ... you never know. Like I said, things change."

"So ... that's it?" I asked, still dazed.

"I'm afraid so ... sorry." I looked down at the glass in my hand. He looked at his watch.

"I've got business to attend to ... you can stay and finish your drink."

I couldn't look at him as he got up and passed me on his way out. I heard him open the door and then close it behind him. I looked up at the long empty table in front of me. Carefully, I placed the glass on the table. I got up and slid the chair up to the table, opened the door and walked down the hall, past the soda machine, past the studio doors. When I reached the lobby, I walked straight for the door, I couldn't face Patty. I felt tears welling up inside, but I couldn't cry. I wasn't going to cry.

Out on the street, I started walking. My mind was simply numb. I walked on. For a long way. For a long time. I came to the ocean and the Santa Monica pier. There was a merry-go-round and it twirled around and around. I sat down on a park bench and watched it for a long time. It was funny, I thought; the people on the merry-go-round were going around and around, but in fact, like me, they were really going no where at all.

I sat there in a daze for a great while, my mind wrecked with sadness, pity, and depression. My big break had come and gone in just three days. There would surely be other chances, other producers. Perhaps I would have to spend more time in this city, knock on more doors. There would be other chances. But to be so close, and now to fail again.

The sun had descended below the water and it was getting dark now. I noticed that on the other side of the street was a bar. I decided to go in.

"Give me a shot of Jack Black," I told the bartender. I drank it in one gulp. In the mirror behind the bar, there was the reflection of a face, my face. How strange I looked. I was the same person, I thought, but maybe not. So much had happened in my young life.

I remembered when we used to practice as kids after school, up on the hill overlooking the farm houses with the white fences. And the great highway, winding its way into the horizon, into my future. I was so confident then. It was all so different then, no disappointments, only dreams of glory. But I couldn't go back, not now. There was only the dull reality of failure over and over again; the great test that I faced again and again-me against the world, and the world always beating me down.

"Another!" I shouted to the bartender. I lit a cigarette. The smoke floated overhead as I took the drink in my hand. And my friends, those close to me, I thought. Where did they go? I had let them sift through my life like sand through my fingers. My wife Joanne, my daughter ... Mickey, Duane, Mike, Fast Freddie, the Polack, ... and Jackie. I wondered where they were and what they were doing.

Bryan, ... good ol' Bryan! If only things had been different. He was a good friend, maybe the best friend you could have in this business. I screwed him. I screwed him good!

I ordered more booze. I drank that one and ordered more. I was getting drunk. I just sat there thinking and drinking, and had no idea what time it was. Someone sat down next to me. It was a woman. I turned to look at her. "Good ol' Green Eyes!" I exclaimed. She looked at me fearfully. "Oh ... you're not 'Green Eyes' ... are you?" I said with slurred speech. She picked up her purse and moved to another seat. "Ol' Green Eyes ... I am so sorry" I stammered. The room swayed before me.

I thought about Jackie. She would understand. Like me, perhaps she was a dreamer too. Or perhaps she lived on my dreams and I had dreams enough for both of us!

Julie, now Julie was different. I dreamed on but Julie was always there to break the fall. Good ol' Julie! I took another drink.

What about the rest of the band? I wondered just what in the hell they were doing now? Playing the blues ... as if life wasn't 'blue' enough. Maybe they were jealous of my talent. Oh but Fast Freddie ... perhaps I was always jealous of him! I always loved him. He had the charisma. I bet he could just walk into the Record

Factory and Mr. Gabriel would sign him. He'd show 'em. Maybe together, we'd show all of 'em.

Mystic records, Karma records, Revolution records, the studios, the producers, the promoters, club owners, all the chances at success, but all eventually ending in failure. Maybe I was just fooling myself.

Perhaps the 'Mr. Gabriel's of the world' were all just using us. All of 'em. 'Wild Bill' and his cocaine. Everything was just a game to him. Steve Winter, Greg and James, Steve Hientz, and Pinky Thompson. They were all part of the story, this 'game' that was my life. And oh shit! ... and you lose! "Bastards! ... They're all bastards!" I shouted. Everyone near gazed at me, other customers, stopped talking. "They were all evil, using bastards!" I said drunkenly, loudly.

The bartender rushed over. "Look buddy ... one more out-burst and you're out of here ... understand?"

"No problem barkeep ... no problem," I said. My speech, slurred.

"Hey, are you ok?" he asked.

"Just fine ... here get me a drink and you a drink ... I've got plenty of money ... front money from the top man! Mr. Gabriel! I pushed the money toward him. He just looked at me.

The jukebox started playing another song and conversations resumed. Meanwhile, my mind continued to be a cauldron of bitterness. They were all using bastards. Just like Steve Hientz was using Big House Johnson. 'Fifty dollars and a steak dinner', that's what Big House said that Mr. Hientz promised him. The poor fool! The using bastards!

And that fat pig in Atlanta, 'Lucky' whatever his name was, ... that agent. Art, music meant absolutely nothing to him, him and his snot stained shirt!

Oh yes ... Mr. Gabriel! Mr. Gabriel and his girl singer! She would probably pay off her tab in the back seat of his limo.

I looked up. Someone had turned on a TV behind the bar. There was music. It was Beth Williams! "Oh shit! It's the bitch herself!" I said drunkenly. She looked better than ever. As she sang, the camera panned in on her face. She smiled. When the song was over, the crowd in the studio audience went wild. "Hurray, hurray!" I yelled. "After all, female singers are the coming thing!" She made it! She fucking made it! Hey there's your fucking dream up on the TV. Watch it! Watch where your dreams can take you! Watch it you unlucky bastard!" I pounded my fist on the bar. It's not fair I thought. "It's just not fair!" I shouted in a drunken stupor.

More time passed. I drank more and at one point I passed out for a brief spell. "Hey fella," said the bartender, shaking and waking me. "Are you okay? You can't sleep here, you will have to go."

"Sleep? Hell no! Bring me another drink!" I said, totally drunk.

Through blurred vision, I saw Julie and Andy come in the door. Julie saw me and came running. "Where have you been?" she asked. She was out of breath.

"I've been here ... right here. Let me buy you a drink," I said in a drunken stupor.

"You're drunk!" She exclaimed.

"Good for you ... I'm very drunk and I'm gonna get drunker!"

"We searched all over town for you," said Andy, "you had us scared out of our wits."

"What's wrong with you?" asked Julie, "What happened?"

"I'm just partying ... celebrating yet another of life's big disappointments."

"Oh no ... something happened?"

"Well ... you see ... Mr. Gabriel ... he said they needed a girl singer see?"

"And he couldn't use you?" She said.

"Oh ... you are brilliant tonight, aren't you?"

"Well fuck 'em," said Andy, "it's just one studio ... one producer."

"You think I'm gonna get another chance huh?" I said, "Not like that ... not like that. But us pros are used to hard knocks, aren't we? Just fuel for the fire. Try and try again ... shit! I need another drink. Let me buy you a drink!"

"You've had enough to drink and it's already in the wee hours of the morning," said Julie. "You should go home. It is very late."

"Where's home?" I shouted loudly. Again, those few left in the bar looked up in disgust. "This place is open all night and I'm gonna stay here and shut her down!" I shouted. "I'm loaded with money ... look at my money!" I shoved the pile of money toward Julie. She looked at Andy with a look of resignation. Both of them sat down next to me.

"Hey barkeep! Another round and some for my friends!" I shouted.

The bartender came over to us. "Another for me ... no ... make it a double and a beer for him and ... what will you have?" I asked Julie.

"A soda ... that's all ... just a soda for me," she replied. She looked down at the floor.

"Well ... what a lively party! It's not everyday you can party with a loser ... winner's yes! But losers?!?"

"I don't know how you can say that ... we love you, we believe in you," said Julia.

"I'll carry the torch for all of us," I said facetiously.

"That's bullshit!" said Andy bitterly. "You're doing this because you want to do it. It doesn't have anything to do with us."

"That's true ... I've brought you both into this nightmare. Haven't I?"

"It's not a nightmare. It's all in your mind," said Julie.

"Yes, it's all in my mind ... isn't it?!" I screamed.

I put my hands to my face. I was tired. It was very late. "I dunno ... it seems the farther I went with the band, the farther I got away from my plans, more people to please, more schemes, more crowds to overwhelm ... but where did my music fit in? My music? And now that I'm here ... here in glorious Hollywood, it's still a game! It's too bad I'm not a woman, girl singers are the coming thing don't you know ... maybe I should have been black ... who knows ..."

"You need to get some sleep ... it's very late ... you're tired," said Julie.

"Oh, I'm more tired than you'll ever know - sick and tired."

"Let's go," said Andy.

"No! This is my party and were gonna have fun whether you like it or not. Barkeep! Another round!"

"No!" Julie pleaded.

"It's ok," said Andy. "Just play along if he wants to make an ass out of himself."

The drinks appeared before us. I took my glass and raised it in the air. "To dreamers everywhere!" I exclaimed. Andy and Julie sat motionless. "Maybe I should just sit in my living room and sing my songs for the rest of my life. Maybe what I want can't be. Liz! ... you remember Liz? She was my therapist, my 'shrink', she said that I was being unrealistic ... here's to you Liz!" I raised my glass in a toast and drank alone.

"I don't have to stay here and listen to this bullshit!" said Andy. He got up to leave. "You're just feeling sorry for yourself! Look, what makes you so god-damned special, so different from the rest of us? Don't you think that I may have dreams of my own? ... hopes ... aspirations? ... What about Julie?"

"That's different." I said, spitting the words out drunkenly.

"How different? If you don't make it ... if the great lord of a songwriter doesn't make it big ... what then? It's not the end of the world. You might have to settle for just being a lowly, untalented person like us!" Andy exclaimed.

"You don't understand ... I've worked for this my whole life. You don't understand!" I stammered.

"No, you don't understand! What if you're just not good enough? ... what then?" Andy shouted.

"Not good enough!" I screamed. I became enraged. I stood up and threw my drink on the floor.

"You're an asshole!" Andy yelled.

"Fuck you!" I shouted.

He drew back to hit me, but Julie got between us. With unsteady legs, I climbed up on my barstool and then up on top of the bar! "Not good enough! You don't know what good is!"

"Please come down from there!" pleaded Julie.

I kicked a beer bottle onto the floor and it smashed into pieces. "I'm as good as anyone in this fucking bar! I'm as good as any of you!" I screamed. I ripped at my shirt and fell down on one knee.

The last of the late-night, hard-core customers were aghast. I was the center of attention. Julie started to cry.

"Come down from there!" shouted Andy.

"Fuck you! ... Fuck you Hollywood!" I screamed.

Nobody moved. There was a silence in the entire room. The bartender tried to grab my arm. "Look, get this guy out of here or I'm calling the police!" he yelled.

"He's drunk ... that's all, he's just drunk," Julie sobbed.

"Get him out of here!" he demanded.

Julie grabbed me by the leg. "Listen to me!" she screamed. "Stop feeling sorry for yourself! Fuck the music, fuck the songs, fuck Hollywood! ...

Can't you see what this is doing to you?"

Everyone was motionless. It was quiet as Julie pleaded, her voice choked with tears. "Why can't you see? You are a person ... that's all, a person just like the rest of us. Sure, you are talented. Yes. But that is a gift ... just a gift ... a God-given gift. It doesn't give you a special privilege. The privilege to have dreams. Sure, we all have dreams. And it's not a privilege to feel pain ... we all feel pain. We all get up in the morning. We all have to trudge our way through life. We are all warriors here ... Yes, perhaps you can see the shallowness in life, the greed, the pain ... perhaps better than the rest of us, but don't wallow in it! Sure you can use your gift to expose it, but better yet, make us forget about it. If you can't sing about it on a record, sing about it on the street corners ... just sing it out. That's all that matters. Sing it to me. I love you ... Oh yes ... I love you, you poor fool!!!"

She was crying. Her words were riveting. They lingered in my ears, mingled with her soft gentle sobs. I lowered my head onto my chest and suddenly, I realized what a pathetic person I had become. Tears came to my eyes. Quietly, I slid down from the bar and took Julie by the hand. Totally drunk, and with difficulty, I walked with them out of the bar.

Outside, the first hint of light was just beginning to come up over the horizon. It was just before dawn. Andy went to unlock the car door. "Your chariot awaits you sire ... where to?" he asked.

Julie threw her arms around me. We looked up to the sky. It was going to be a beautiful day. It deserved a song.

1987

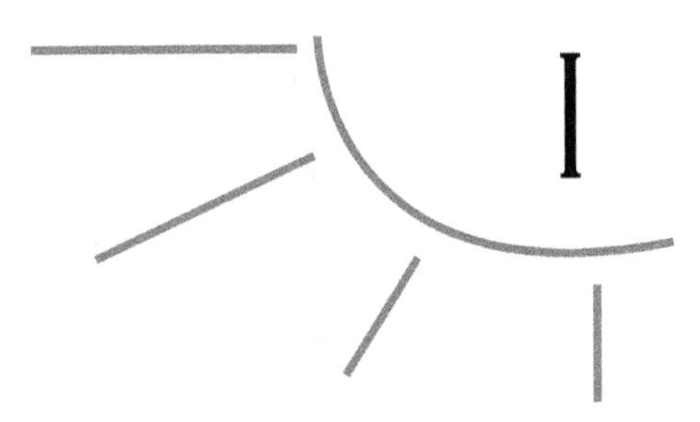

I

There was a tug on the line. Carefully, I placed it between my thumb and forefinger. Again, there was another tug. I knew the fish was nibbling the bait. I pulled back, hoping to snag it. I waited. The line remained limp. I looked down into the water as it trailed off into the aqua depths.

The sun poked out from a cloud and illuminated the ocean floor below, but it was too far to the bottom to see clearly. Patiently, I waited, but there was still nothing. I placed the butt of the rod into the cup and sat down next to the cooler. Inside I knew was the cool taste of an ice cold beer. I glanced at my watch. It wasn't quite eleven o'clock in the morning. Not yet. I wouldn't take a beer yet, I thought. It was still morning. I removed my old cap, and wiped the sweat from my forehead.

Raising my hand to my brow, I scanned the coastline. It was a clear day, and the clouds hung like wisps of cotton in the blue heavens. In spite of the cool breeze over the water, it was a hot day, another clear hot day, and the kind that was common in Southern Florida.

I thought about Maggie. I knew she would have dinner ready early, about three o'clock. Good ol' Maggie. How could she put up with me? I would go home, walk into the clean living room, throw my soiled sweaty cap on the couch, and, as always, she would quietly go behind me and get the cap and put it on the hat rack by the front door. I knew she would do this. She would never complain, she would just do it. The thing was, she knew that I would throw that cap down on her clean couch, and I knew she would pick it up. There was no problem with this. It was a part of our lives. I liked it and she liked it too.

Again, I wiped the sweat from my brow. Off the bow, I could see a large yacht, maybe a fifty footer. She was doing about ten knots and heading south. She was heading for Miami. Maybe Fort Lauderdale. The man at the helm waved as she made way. I waved back. My small cabin cruiser rocked gently in the wake, as I held firmly to the handrail and read the name on the transom -'PLAY MONEY MIAMI'. I smiled. It was a grand vessel.

My mind wandered ... It reminded me of a thirty footer my Dad had bought many years ago. I was only a child then. I think I must have been ... I guess I was about nine years old. We used to live in Maryland. My Dad, my Grand-dad and I, we took the boat all the way down the Potomac from Washington D.C. to the West River near Annapolis, all the way around Point Lookout, where the Potomac and the great Chesapeake meet. I never forgot that trip. There was rough weather. My Dad was at the helm. My Grand-dad and I clung to the rear railings. The wind blew hard. It was in April but the rain was cold and stung as it pelted my face. We were cruising into the wind and the hull swung high in the air. Then, it would crash violently down into the water. I gripped the railing. My knuckles were white as I held on. I looked over at my Dad. He seemed calm in spite of the turbulence around us. He was like a rock, as steady as a rock. After a few more heavy waves, he looked at my Grand-dad. They didn't speak, they just looked at each other.

He brought us around and headed for shore. The storm was too much for us and he knew it. We pulled into a cove where we found a dock and a restaurant. The wind was calmer but the rain fell heavily. We pulled into a slip and tied up.

Inside the restaurant, although small and dirty, at least it was warm and dry. After eating, I watched as they played pool. They drank beer. I remember the cigarette smoke, and the loud laughing and voices of the men as the night wore on. Later, my Dad took me out to the boat and I laid down in the cabin to go to sleep. He left me there alone and went back in. I was tired, very tired but I couldn't sleep, and I could hear the laughter and the music from the restaurant.

I closed my eyes. As I lay there, I thought about just how great it was that day, gassing up in Washington at the Wilson Bridge, near the old torpedo factory. As we shoved off, I collected the mooring lines from the bow as Dad pulled around to the open harbor. The old man back at the pumps waved to me and I to him. I was a useful hand on the docks. Though just a child, in this, I was one of them. I knew the ways of the water and of boating. Yes, I was proud, I was one of them.

I heard footsteps. Someone boarded. I could feel the boat rock as they stepped onto the deck. Their footsteps seemed unsteady. I heard the sound of a rushing stream of water. The person was urinating over the side. Somehow, I knew it was my Grand-dad. He was probably drunk. It was alright though, I thought. He was a man and men could get drunk if they wanted to ...

Suddenly, the line went spinning off the reel. I rushed over and took the rod into my hands. I switched on the drag to fight with the fish. It pulled the rod down hard to the water and I knew that it was quite a big fish. I started taking in the line when it slacked and then pulled back to make the line taught. The fish broke the surface of the water. Its skin glistened in the hot sun. Again, I took in the slack line and pulled the fish closer. It fought violently and made one more try for the open sea. I held firm, and reeled in more line. The fight was over. I pulled the fish from the water, brought it on deck, and removed the hook. I put it into the tub of ice. Its eyes stared blankly as I pulled the tarp over the tub.

For a while, I simply fished. I fished and I thought, lazily. It seemed that lately I thought too much. I found myself at times drifting off into dream-like states. I would lay the rod across my lap with the shaft hanging over the side railing, and I would doze off almost to sleep. Spittle would gather and hang from my mouth and flies would dance on my brow as I lay there in that dopey near-sleep state. And I would dream, at least it was like a dream. Everyone daydreams and I did not find this unusual, but still, these episodes came so frequently, that sometimes I feared for my own emotional well being. The visions that flashed through my head had such realism that I wondered if perhaps I could be losing my mind.

I looked at my watch. Now it was almost one o'clock. I reached into the cooler and pulled out a beer. As I pulled back the tab it sprayed a cold mist into my face. The sun was in the middle of the sky and the heat was intense. Drinking the beer in big gulps, I welcomed the coldness, the wetness. I reached in the cooler and opened another. This time I drank slower. My thirst had been quenched.

Soon, I brought in the fishing line, placed the rod on the deck, and started the engines. Opening the throttle, I made my way back along the coast. In the distance, I could see the light house and the inlet, where the inland waterway met the great Atlantic. Normally it was rough going in, but today, the water was calmer than usual. I pulled back the throttle, and made my way through the channel. I slowed down again. I would come back in slowly today, I thought. I would enjoy the ride back.

I looked down at the water rushing by. It was so clear you could see the bottom. As I scanned the shoreline, I couldn't help but admire the full, green palms moving slightly in the breeze. Above, the sky was as blue as the water beneath me.

As I pulled up to the dock, I saw Ol' Tom waiting for me. I wasn't surprised. He always came over in the afternoons. Ol' Tom was Thomas Finnley, but to me, he was just Ol' Tom. He was retired from a career in the Navy. He was overweight, balding and he was my friend. He threw me a mooring line as my boat came near.

"Hey Jack!" he exclaimed.

"Hey Tom ... what'cha know?"

He had a brown bag. I knew he had a bottle. I turned off the engines.

"Been out fishing again?"

"I thought I'd give her a try."

"What did you catch?"

"Well ... actually ... only one ... a big one."

I pulled back the tarp to show him the fish.

"Jack White! ... You mean you've been out all day and that is all you have to show for it?" I looked at the fish. It wasn't quite as big as I had remembered.

"Hey ... what's the big deal ... it's relaxation for me ... what the hell."

There were two lawn chairs on the grass. We both took a seat, the way we did every afternoon. It was our thing, sitting in those chairs.

"How 'bout a drink?" he asked.

I looked at the brown bag.

"No ... I've got beer."

"Right ... I know you want one ... but if you've got beer then you can have a beer."

I looked at the bag again.

"Yeah ... okay ... I'll have one."

"I knew you wanted one."

"Tom ... you'll be the death of me yet! Everyday you come over and ask me if I want a drink and everyday I say no ... but you know I will give in don't you you bastard!"

"Yeah Jack ... nag, nag, nag!"

He put some ice cubes into two cups and poured the scotch. He handed me one and I took a long drink. It felt good.

"It's hot as hell out here," I said.

"Well August in Florida is hell ... you know that."

We got up to move the chairs into the shade of the palm tree to get out of that hellish heat.

"You know ... you never go out fishing and bring back just one catch."

"Yeah ... well this time I did."

He poured more scotch into his cup.

"Old Jack White and his one fish ... let's drink to the one damned fish!" he said playfully. He was needling me. He knew me well. He wanted me to talk. He knew in time I would.

"Look Tom ... what the hell is the big deal with the one fish ... I mean who gives a damn anyway?"

"Hey I was just making an observation about the fishing today ... but you know as well as I ... something's on your mind ... you know it is ..."

"Shit Tom! You should have been somebody's mother-in-law!"

"Could it be that your birthday's coming up? You're going to hit the big six-oh."

My birthday was near. I was going to be sixty, but we both knew that wasn't it.

"No damn it! I don't give a damn about that." I held out my cup and he poured more scotch.

"Well ... I can tell you don't want to talk about it ... I can tell."

"Look ... you come over and get me drunk and then you tell me not to talk about it ... you know damn well what it is."

"It's Bill isn't it?" I knew he would get there.

"Yes Tom ... Bill is coming on my birthday." It had been quite a few years since he had come to visit.

"Hey maybe it'll be different this time ... who knows ..."

"How does Maggie feel about it?"

"Maggie's fine ... you know Maggie ... more than my better half."

"Yeah ... good Ol' Maggie ... you've got that right."

The sun was moving across the sky. Again, we moved our chairs into the available shade of the palm trees.

"Well ... what in the hell have you been up to?" I asked.

"This is it my friend ... this is it," he said brandishing his cup.

"You know you a-r-e an old wino!"

"We're all old winos Jack ... we're all winos at heart."

He poured some more scotch. He motioned for me to offer my cup. I refused. I didn't want any more.

"Well ... so Ol' Bill is coming for your birthday."

"Shit Tom! ... Do we have to stay on that subject!"

"Hey ... it might be therapeutic ... who knows ..."

"For who? Me or you?"

"Okay pal ... I can tell you're not up to it ... I just want to help," he replied.

"... Those were the days huh?"

"Yeah those were the days ... We were all young, dumb and full of cum," he said laughing.

Suddenly, "Well Tom ... I can see you're getting my husband drunk again," said Maggie.

She had walked up behind us. Her hair was neatly pulled back. As always, although she may have been tired, although she may have worked in the house all day, she was just as beautiful as ever. There was always a radiance that surrounded her and every time I looked upon her, I knew why I loved her even to this day.

"No. I've had three drinks to his one ... he's been a good boy ... take my word for it," Tom replied.

"See ... Ol' Tom has spoken," I said.

We all laughed.

"I suppose you will be staying for dinner?" she asked him.

"Well ... if there's enough and the lady of the house will have me ..."

"Let's eat ... I've already laid a place for you."

We got up to enter the house. I turned around to check the mooring lines to make sure the boat was sound. I looked across the water. In the distance, I could see the flashing red light of the lighthouse. Its presence gave me a sense of security. I knew all was well.

Inside, the table was set. I was hungry. We sat down to eat.

"Steak! Did you do this for me?!" Tom exclaimed.

"No ... I just decided to have steak ... that's all," Maggie replied.

"Sounds good to me," I added.

We started eating. Our attention centered on the meal until Tom started talking.

"Well ... I understand Bill's coming ..."

Maggie stopped momentarily and looked down at her plate, but then resumed, "... Yes ... Bill is coming to visit ..." she said plainly.

"It will be a good visit this time ... I have a feeling about it. It will be fine. I just know it," he continued.

"Look Tom," I said, "... yes Bill i-s-s coming ... but we'll just take it as it comes. There's no need to make anything of it ... he's my brother for God's sake!"

"Well I just hope that it works out this time ... that's all."

I changed the subject.

"Haven't you been doing anything this week worth talking about?" I asked him.

"Well ... I am going hunting tomorrow."

"Really? That sounds halfway constructive."

"In fact, I was wondering if you wanted to come along ... that is if the old lady will let you."

"Where are you planning to go?" I asked.

"Well actually I was going with Sonny Jacobsen out to Pratt Whitney."

"Shit Tom! That's off limits for hunting ... it's trespassing ... you know that!"

"Well ... if you don't want to go ..."

"I don't know."

I looked over at Maggie. She shook her head. "Look Jack White! If you go with them, I won't come and bail you out of jail!"

"Just who is this Sonny Jacobsen anyway?" I asked.

"Oh ... just a redneck. He's quite a character."

"Oh?"

"Seems he's got quite a reputation. They say he knows the woods better than anyone."

"Sounds interesting ... Pratt Whitney huh?"

"It's got plenty of game ... more than is in the surrounding areas, and besides ... it really isn't hunting season yet."

"Well ... maybe ... let me sleep on it," I said.

"Okay ... but we're leaving at three o'clock in the morning ... so don't sleep on it too long."

We finished eating and Maggie took the dishes away. Tom and I went back outside. The sun was setting in the sky.

"How about one for the road?"

"One more for the road? I'm not going anywhere."

"Well I am ... I've got to be up early. How about tomorrow? Are you in?"

I looked back at the house. The kitchen light went out.

"Yeah ... what the hell. Three o'clock huh?"

"Three o'clock. I'll come and get you early."

"Tomorrow?"

"Tomorrow ... good night."

I watched him walk away, and sat back. The evening brought the cool breeze off of the ocean. How good it felt. I took a last drink of the scotch and reveled in it's soothing effects.

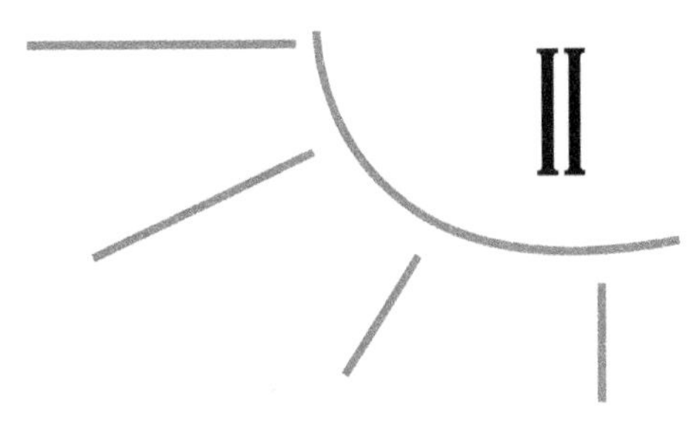

II

We parked off the road in the darkness, in the bushes where no one could see the truck. Ol' Tom and I got out of the cab of the pickup, and Sonny got out from behind the wheel. He was a young man in his early thirties and he had a strong physique. He was a man of the woods, the backwoods, rough and crude.

He opened the tailgate and let the dogs, two pit bulls, out on a leash. One was white with black spots. The other was all dark brown.

Standing there in the darkness, we checked our rifles, Tom with a thirty-thirty, and Sonny and I with shotguns. I opened the breach to make sure that it wasn't loaded. It was hard to see in the darkness, so I lit a flashlight to see.

"Put that out!" shouted Sonny.

I turned off the light.

"You're gonna go and get us in trouble," said Ol' Tom.

But out on the road, there were no cars to be seen in either direction. We crossed to the other side and hopped the fence. There was a steep drop, and we descended until we came to a canal. With our rifles high above our heads, we crossed the water. The bottom was muddy and then dropped off. We swam to the other side, and climbed up an embankment. I loaded two shells into the shotgun and shivered in the cool night air.

The dogs shook vigorously to dry off, as Sonny gave us instructions. "Look ... now I'm gonna let the dogs go loose. I want you guys to follow behind me ... okay?"

"Sure ... anything you say," Ol' Tom replied.

"Now the security people will be a'lookin' round for poachers ... we gotta be careful."

I felt foolish. What we were doing was against the law. We were on private company property with a wildlife preserve nearby. But I was already there. It was too late to turn back now.

Sonny let the dogs loose and they immediately walked on ahead. Sonny and Tom walked behind them. I brought up the rear. Up at the black sky, it was ablaze with a multitude stars. I felt the sting of a mosquito, as I walked through the brush. We walked on for what seemed like a few miles until we came upon another fence. We climbed it and continued on. My shoes squeaked as I walked. They were still wet from the water in the canal.

Suddenly, the dogs took flight, and we quickened our pace to keep up with them. They veered off the trail and we followed into the thick bushes. I could hear them barking from somewhere up ahead. I wondered if others would hear them as well. The foliage became even more dense, and it was harder to make way. Soon I knew we would be confronted with our prey. My heart pounded with anticipation.

I pulled back the brush and came upon Sonny and Tom. They motioned for me to be still. Sonny pointed ahead to a clump of bushes. Inside, there was the sound of the dogs barking. The bushes moved. Out jumped a wild boar! It froze as it saw us. Then, it ran for another clump of bushes where it was too thick to enter. It turned around to confront us. It was vicious.

Dawn was breaking, and there was now enough light to see the boar's eyes. They were bestial and menacing. It was going to make a stand and fight for it's life. It stood at bay with the pit bulls barking.

Then in a flash, the boar swung it's head and cut the brown dog's chest with it's sharp tusk. The blood splat onto Tom's pants. Still, the dog barked and made for the cornered beast. As Sonny pulled the dog back in an attempt to save it's life, I lifted my gun to shoot. He waved me off. He pulled out his knife and walked cautiously behind the boar whose attention was still directed on the dogs that tormented him. Quickly, he stabbed the boar in the neck! He stabbed again. The boar fell to it's side with it's legs still moving. Blood poured from the gaping wound. Slowly, as the sun came up on the horizon, upon this world in the wild, the boar drifted off to the quiet finality of death.

"Why didn't you just shoot him?" I asked.

"Because I don't want anyone to hear the shots this early in the morning ... that's why you asshole!"

"Oh ... right."

Sonny took the dead boar and rolled it over on it's back. He took the knife and cut along the stomach. Then he cut around the anus to remove the guts. They oozed out into a steamy mass on the ground. With our help, he pulled the carcass over beside a tree.

"We'll leave it here and pick it up on the way out," he said.

In the distance we heard the sound of a helicopter. The sound was getting louder and we knew it was approaching.

"Quick! Get out of sight!" Sonny shouted.

We headed for the underbrush to hide. The chopper came upon us. It hovered above momentarily, then continued on. I wondered if it had seen one of us hiding or maybe one of the dogs that walked nervously around us. Slowly, we came back out from hiding.

"Do you think they saw us?" asked Tom.

"No ... I dunno ... probably not."

"This is crazy!" I said, "Maybe we should have never come!"

"Look," said Tom, "You made your own decision to come ... don't look at me."

"Hey you pussies!" said Sonny, "... let's get on with it!... We only gotta few more hours before we should head back for the truck."

"Who are you calling pussies?" Ol' Tom shouted.

Sonny held his knife at eye level, but then put it back into his sheath. He looked at Tom fiercely.

"Look old man ... I never should'a brought ya out here if ya didn't think ya could cut it!"

"Hey! Let's cool it!" I said.

Sonny looked away, but we knew he was riled. Perhaps we would have more words later. He looked out into the woods around us. He was thinking about what the next move would be.

"I think we should break up and hunt alone ... Tom, you go east. Jack you go west and I'll head south. We can meet back here in a couple of hours."

"Sounds okay to me," said Tom.

"Sure ... okay," I said.

I left the others and walked west into the heavy underbrush. On the other side, it opened up into a vast, wide open space of sparse trees and everglades. I walked on for some time along line of trees, trying to keep out of sight. The mosquitoes were biting now, but I tried to ignore them as I made my way cautiously through the swamp. With shotgun in hand, I watched for movement in the bushes, any movement. Maybe at any moment I might be attacked by a wild boar. I remembered the sharp tusks and the wounded dog.

I removed my cap, and wiped the sweat from my forehead. The morning sun was rising in the sky and the air was getting hot. Farther ahead, I saw a clump of trees and decided to move into the shade. There was a dry spot there, and I sat down and put the shotgun down beside me. I laid my head back onto the tree trunk and closed my eyes. I was tired.

I thought about Bill, Bill and I. I remembered being out on the porch, the back porch of my Dad's house. Bill and I were sitting on lawn chairs. We were both young men. Dad had gone inside to make a drink ...

"How's school?" Bill asked.

"Okay ... the same as always ... okay," I replied. "How's your job? ... I mean ... aren't you doing well at your job?"

Bill had a job in Dad's used car lot. Dad was going to send me to college. Bill decided to work for Dad for a while. Sometimes I thought maybe he held it against me that I was destined for college and he wasn't. But it was his decision not to go. It wasn't my fault, but in a way, it seemed as though he held it against me. He never said it, but I felt it.

Dad came back out. He sat down between us. He took a drink and placed the glass on the small table and lit a cigarette. "Now, it's good to have you both together," he said.

Bill and I shifted in our seats. It would be another lecture we thought, another lesson in life. That was okay though, we loved and respected my father. It was just that we were young, young and restless, and, impatient. After all, we had our whole lives in which to learn and be wise. And my father's words were often ill-spent on us.

"Someday ... this will all be yours," he said, waving his arm out over the yard.

"We don't care about that," I said.

"Yeah Dad ... but we don't want to talk about when you're gone and all that," said Bill.

"Yes I know that, but someday I won't be here ... I won't live forever."

He took a drink and then a drag off his cigarette, his drink in one hand and his cigarette in the other. That was the way I remembered him.

"You have to think about the future, both of you do."

"Maybe I should go to college," said Bill.

I shifted nervously in my seat.

"Well ... I dunno ... maybe school is not the thing for everyone. I know ... I know what they say ... you've got to go to college, well maybe not. I didn't go to college and look at me. I did okay. Maybe someday you can take over the business for yourself ... hey Bill?"

"Yeah ... that would be okay I guess." He was looking off into space, thinking of himself and his future. The prospects of our futures seemed so wonderful and magnificent back then. It was that unknown expanse in front us of.

"Now Jack here ... what in the hell are you going to do anyway? You are graduating high school soon."

I cleared my throat. "Well sir ... I just haven't given it much thought ... I just don't know yet ... I just don't know ..."

I looked down at the ground as I spoke, but my father put his hand on my shoulder. "That's okay son ... that's okay. I'm sure someday you'll find out what it is you're looking for ..."

I looked into his eyes. I loved him. Bill looked away. Sometimes it seemed as though we were rivals for his affection.

"Just remember boys ... the greatest wealth you can have is your honor. A man is only as good as his word. It's the kind of respect that one man can have for another. Without it, you will never really have anything." Honor was everything. 'Honor' I thought ...

A mosquito bit me on the forehead and I awoke from my memories of the past, my sleep-like state. I swatted at it and looked out across the swampland in front of me. I had been resting there for quite a while. I stood up, grabbed my shotgun, and walked out into the sun which was nearly in the middle of sky. I surveyed the horizon and started to walk on.

Carefully, I watched each movement from the brush. I came upon a large clearing and decided to walk out in the open air away from the bushes in spite of the fact that I could be easily be spotted from the air. The breeze felt refreshing. Suddenly, in front of me, maybe one hundred yards away, I saw a buck. I stopped in my tracks, hoping that maybe it hadn't seen me. But it looked at me wearily. It did not move. Then, it took off running. Strangely, it ran somewhat towards me. I stood still in the ankle deep water and slowly raised my shotgun. I put the buck into my sights.

It veered to my left and then to the right. Don't aim for the head, I thought ... aim for the body. I would want the magnificent head and antlers as my prize. It veered again to the left and then away from me. He would soon be out of range and I knew I had to take my shot. To the right or the left? I thought quickly, my mind racing. I shot to the left. The sound rang in the air and echoed in the woods. My aim was true. The buck fell to it's knees and then to the ground.

I ran. When I reached the spot, I could see the animal taking it's last few gasps of breath.

Suddenly, as if in a dream, I saw not the buck laying there, but Bill. Bill was laying there bleeding, wounded in the sun, there in a field of tall grass. I shook my head to erase the vision from my imagination.

"What in the hell are you doin'?" said a harsh voice from behind. I was startled and turned around. It was Sonny. Ol' Tom stood behind him.

"Shit! Why did ya shoot out here in the open? Are you crazy?" screamed Sonny.

"Look ... I wanted to take him ... that's all."

"It's a fine buck," said Tom, looking down at the dead animal.

"Yeah ... real fine," said Sonny looking around for the helicopter. "They might be looking for us now ... we have to get out'a here!"

I handed Tom my shotgun and bent down to take the buck. I raised it up onto my shoulders.

"Are ya sure ya can carry that out 'o here old man?" asked Sonny.

I looked at him with a air of defiance. "Tom ... you carry my gun and I'll make it," I said. I was tired, but I would carry the buck out of the woods.

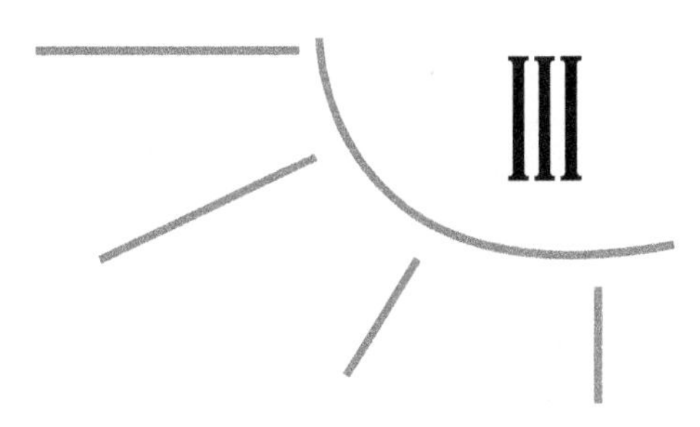

III

It was very early in the morning. Sonny opened one eye enough to see the dimly lit alarm clock on the nightstand. It was 5:29. Only about ten minutes had passed since he last looked at it.

He rolled over and closed his eyes, but it was useless to try to sleep. He had barely slept all night. Wearily, he pulled himself up to a sitting position on the side of the bed. A roach scurried underneath. Looking out the window, he could see the coming of the morning light and the vacant driveway where Candy's car was supposed to be parked.

He dragged himself to his feet and walked out into the small living room of the trailer. The air was cool, but soon he knew that the sun would heat the metal walls until it would be like an oven. He opened the refrigerator door and pulled out a beer. It was the last one. Sitting down at the kitchen table he pulled the ashtray near and lit a cigarette. It glowed orange dimly.

There was the sound of a car coming up to the driveway. Through the screen door, he could see that it was Candy's car. She was home. When she entered the trailer, she stumbled slightly. She was very pretty, but with her long hair, stringy, and in her face, she was an ugly sight. She was surprised as she saw Sonny at the table. She glared at him defiantly.

Sonny erupted. "Just where in the hell have ya been Goddamn it!"

"It's none of your business where I been you son-of-a-bitch!" She said drunkenly.

Sonny stood up and threw his beer can into the wall beside her. The beer spewed onto the carpet. He approached her but stopped at arm's reach.

"Go ahead! Hit me fucker!" She cried and pulled her disheveled hair away from her eyes.

"Damn it Candy! What in the hell is wrong with ya?"

"There ain't anything wrong with me ... we ain't exactly married ya know!"

"I've been up all night worryin' bout ya bitch! ... Don't ya ever think 'bout that?"

"You're not worried about me ... you just want to know if I screwed somebody ... right?"

"Well that might'a crossed m'mind."

"Don't worry ... if I had, it would have beat the hell out of your love makin'!"

Sonny pulled back to hit her but resisted.

"Yeah ... you don't have the guts," She said whimsically.

His eyes became enraged and he backhanded her across the face. She fell backwards and to the floor.

"You bastard!" she screamed. She tried to get on her feet, crying.

Sonny walked back to the table. When he turned around he saw her near the sink. She had a kitchen knife in her hand. She held it out viciously, waving it in front of her.

"Now try somethin' you bastard!"

"Come on ... gimme that knife ... you're drunk," he said carefully.

"No ... you come on and get it."

She stabbed the air near him. He backed up.

"It's all those damned people you call friends ... those crazy damned friends of yours ..."

"I told ya ... it's none of your business who I hang out with ... we're just 'shack ups', that's all we are ... just shack ups. Can't ya see that?"

"Look honey ... I'm sorry ... I just love ya that's all ..."

"Love ... huh! What do you know about love?"

She sniffed and wiped her tears away with her free hand, all the time coming toward him with the knife. Then, she reached out and tried to cut him but only caught his tee shirt. Quickly, he grabbed her arm and wrestled the knife out of her hands. She fell down to her knees and started sobbing uncontrollably. Sonny threw the knife onto the table and raised his hands to his face. "Oh God! What in the hell is wrong with us?" he pleaded as if someone would answer.

She crawled off to the couch and started to fall asleep. Sonny came near and carefully brushed her hair away. She smelled of booze. She would forget this, he thought. Just like all the other times ... she would just forget. They had to forget.

He went over to the screen door and leaned against the frame. The sun was up full and clear. The dew was drying on the grass. Across the trailer park, he could see Kristen in her front yard.

Kristen was Candy's friend. Unlike Candy, she was older, and care-worn. Her two children played nearby in a mud puddle. She saw him and started walking over.

"I see you two are at it again," she said as she stood in front of his door.

"Yeah ..."

"You can hear ya'll fighting all through the park."

"... I guess ya could at that."

"Well are ya gonna invite me in, or are ya just gonna let me stand out here?"

He brushed his sweaty hair back and exhaled wearily. "Yeah ... come on in. There ain't much t' see." He held the door open for her as she entered the battered trailer.

"Passed out again huh?" she said, looking down at Candy sleeping on the couch. "I really don't know what's wrong with that girl anyway."

"It's the damned bars an' rowdy friends of hers. Seems like all they want to do is party."

"Sonny! Why, you sound like a saint or somethin'!"

"Well ... I been thinkin' lately ..."

"'Bout what?"

"... I dunno ... changin' m'life ... I dunno ..."

"Yeah ... I think about that too sometimes ..."

She pulled a paper towel from the roll and bent over to clean up the spilt beer. Sonny sat down at the table. He was tired.

"Where's Butch?" he asked. Butch was Karen's boyfriend and father to her two kids. "I ain't seen him around lately. Y'all having problems too these days?"

"Well ... you know how it is. He's been in the woods huntin'. Ain't nothing gonna stop Butch from huntin'... you know that. I wish he's come home soon and get a job. I'm just about out 'a food stamps and the kids are hungry."

"Yeah ... I been laid off at the site last week ... I guess I should get back out and look for a job too."

She sopped up the last of the beer from the old carpet and put the soaked paper towel in the trashcan.

"I guess times are tough for everyone," she said. "... Been out in the woods?"

"Yeah ... couple of days ago ... took two old farts, Tom Finnley and his pal, into Pratt Whitney ... got a boar and a buck. Hell ... the ol' brown dog nearly got killed!"

"Sounds like you guys had a good ol' time, but one o'these days you boys are gonna get caught poachin' out there," she said shaking her head. She put a pot of water on the stove and turned on the burner to make coffee. "Where in the world did you meet this guy Tom anyway? Sounds like he's a little old for you to know him?" she asked, sitting down at the table.

"Yeah well, he's been datin' Candy's mom. I don't think she likes him though ..."

"Dating Candy's mom? ... Candy's mom, the rich lady? What in the hell would she want with him? Does he have money too?"

"I dunno ... more money than us that's for sure."

"That wouldn't be hard," she said laughing.

"Just how did Candy's mom get her money anyway?"

"Land ... jus' land. She, like a whole lot'a people, bought land dirt cheap back in the fifties, sixties. When the land prices went up, they cleaned up. That's all...investin' in land."

"It all sounds so simple don't it? Making money... I wish me and Butch could make us some."

"Me too ... I wish I was around back then. I'd have me some money too. I know I would," said Sonny, looking down at the floor and then at Candy sleeping peacefully on the couch.

Kristen noticed him looking at Candy. "Love her don't 'cha?"

He looked away from Candy, and then at Kristen. He looked for a trace of sincerity. "Yeah ... I do. I love her, but I don't think she loves me."

"She loves you too. I know she does. She's just a rich girl ... that's all. I think it's hard for rich people t' love somebody ... they always got a way out. They got s'many choices. They don't have to make it work. Know what I mean?"

"Well ... she might love me, but her mama ... I know she don't."

"Hey, this is between you and Candy, not you and her mom. Right?"

Again, he looked at her in earnest and nodded his head. "Ya know Kristen, for being just plain crazy, you're alright. Yeah, you're just ok," he chuckled.

Kristen smiled and looked over at Candy, but then remembered the stove. "Oh damn it! I forgot about the coffee! The water's nearly boiled away. Can I make you some?"

"No ... I don't really want none ... might as well try to get some sleep."

"Well the day's gettin' on and I'd better see what my kids are gettin' into. See you later ... ok?"

As Kristen left and walked across the yard to her trailer, Sonny watched her from the doorway. He saw her kids playing in the dirt road. Their clothes were old and torn. He saw the old rusted cars and trash that littered the neighborhood. He wiped the sweat from his face.

IV

The water behind my house shimmered in the afternoon sun. It wasn't quite still. Every now and then a fish would jump and stir the water. I looked over at Ol' Tom and then at the cooler at his feet. There was beer in the cooler.

"Want one?" he asked. He was smiling, as if he could read my mind.

"I might ..." I had already had a few and knew that one might be one too many.

"Hey ... I've got a few left ..."

It was funny how no one liked to drink alone.

"Sure ... hand me one of those bad boys." I took the can and pulled the tab. From it came the sound of rushing air and a cool mist. I took a sip. It felt good. It helped take the heat from my head.

"Let's move these damned chairs back, nearer the shade," I said, wiping my forehead with the cold can.

We moved the chairs into the shade of the palm tree. Tom moved the cooler closer, within easy reach.

"Ah ... that's better," I said. "I wonder ... it seems the older you get the hotter that sun seems to be."

"... Hey, it's August ... what do you want?" Ol' Tom commented.

"Huh?" I was lost in thought again.

Tom looked at me with interest. "Huh what?"

"I was just thinking ... to be young again ... just to be young again."

"You think too much maybe."

"Yeah ... yeah ..." I took another drink of the beer. It was already getting warm.

"It's life's regrets ... how we live with them" I said.

"Maybe turning sixty w-i-l-l be traumatic for you?"

"It's not that ... really ... it's not that."

"Maybe it's Bill's coming to visit?"

"Maybe it is ... maybe it's a lot of things ... I don't know ..."

"Not only do you think too much ... you worry too much too!" added Tom.

Silence.

"Hey look ... maybe your right ... we shouldn't talk about it," he said.

"Hell ... you're the one who keeps talking!"

Once again, he opened the cooler.

"Only two left ... how about it?"

"What the hell!"

We opened the last of the beers.

"I mean ... how in the hell can you tell any kid what the hell he should be doing with his life," I said.

"You learn by experience. When you're older you're wiser ... hopefully."

"Wiser why? Because the path you took turned out to be the wrong path? There are a lot of wrong paths." I said.

"Okay ... that's one way of looking at it I suppose," he said, resigned as if he was tired of talking. I was.

The backdoor opened. It was Maggie. She looked at us with disgust as she came near.

"Well ... I see you guys are at it again!"

"He's a big boy ... quite a big boy wouldn't you say?" Tom replied.

"Yes he's quite a big boy," she said as she bent down to kiss my forehead. "What on earth d-o-o you two talk about out here?"

"Well Ol' Jack here is in one of his philosophical moods again."

"I see ..." she said, amused.

"What's wrong with being philosophical?" I protested.

"You haven't been talking about Bill by any chance?" She asked.

Tom looked at me without speaking.

"Not really ..." I said, sheepishly.

She shook her head. Tom sensed her concern. He tried to change the subject. "What's that delicious smell coming from your kitchen dear lady?" he asked cheerfully.

"Yes ... there's plenty. I've already set a plate for you."

"Thank you dear lady. Would it be alright to use your facilities to tidy up?"

"And yes Tom, you can use the bathroom ... you know where it is ..."

Tom stood up and started walking to the backdoor. When it closed, we were alone. She turned away from me and folded her arms.

"Look ... I ..."

"No ... that's alright," she said, cutting me off.

"Look ... you're right ... I have to find a way to forget the past."

"You have spent your whole life immersed in this sorrow ... when will it end? Just when will it end?" She pleaded.

I rubbed her shoulders. "You're right Maggie ... you're right. Let's just get ready to eat. You go in, I'll be there in a moment. You go ahead."

She turned around and held me close for a moment. Then she turned and entered the house. I sat down. I took my head in my hands. I looked down at my tennis shoes. They were getting old and shabby. Old tennis shoes ... I used to wear old tennis shoes like these many years ago. In high school, like at the basketball games. My mind wandered back in time. The basketball games at my old high school ...

... The buzzer sounded. I looked up. It was halftime. Nervously, I looked straight ahead, knowing that she, 'Mickey' was sitting beside me. I had to speak to her. Before I could turn and open my mouth, she spoke.

"Good game huh?"

I looked into her eyes and smiled, "Yeah ... great ... maybe we'll win this one," I said half heartedly, my mind not really on the game. Carefully, I reached for her hand. She quickly withdrew it and looked around, into the crowd around us to see if someone had noticed. "I'm sorry," I said, looking off in the other direction.

"You shouldn't do that in public ... we agreed on that ..."

"Yeah..."

Again, we looked at each other cautiously.

"He could come back anytime ... he just went to get a soda."

"I know ... but shouldn't we tell him? He's going to find out sooner or later."

"I don't know ... I just can't think about it right now."

"Alright Mickey ... " I said sadly.

"I need time ... I just need time." She said with worry.

I knew she was right, but I couldn't stand being near her like this. So near and not be able to hold her hand, to kiss her. Passion burned in my young heart. Our love had to be a secret. At least for now.

"What a-r-e you going to do after graduation?" she asked, trying to change the subject.

"Oh I don't know ... everyone asks that."

"It's hard to believe that graduation day is so near. I am excited for you!"

"I'm excited about us," I said softly.

"I told you ... I don't want to talk about us ... not right now. Can't you understand?"

She got up and walked down the aisle toward the refreshment stand. She was probably going to find him. Once again, my impatience had chased her away. Exasperated, I looked back down at my old tennis shoes. Those old shoes ...

"Jack! ... Dinner's ready!" I heard Maggie yell from the house I came back to my senses. I was sitting there, drunk in the lawn chair in my backyard. I was an old man trying to cling to the past, to conjure up the places, the people ... all lost in the ancient dust of time. I closed my eyes and tried in vain to go back again, but that time was lost, out of reach. I looked up at the backdoor. Dinner was probably getting cold.

V

Ol' Tom turned the corner and headed down the boulevard in his faded green station wagon. As he ascended the bridge to Palm Beach, he could see the bobbing masts of the luxurious yachts and beyond. With it's ritzy restaurants and small, plush boutiques, it was a scene of opulence and a thriving hotbed of activity for the rich.

He pulled into a parking space and looked into the rear view mirror. He pulled out a comb and tried to straighten what hair he still possessed. Getting out of the car, he proceeded to walk toward the cluster of shops near the ocean. He marveled at the bikini clad girls that walked down the sidewalk, and entered 'Christine's', an Italian restaurant.

Inside, it was dark compared to the bright sun outside. The pretty girl behind the counter saw him and smiled. "Good afternoon ... here by yourself?"

"Ah ... no ... I mean ... I am here to meet someone," he said nervously.

"Fine. Is there a reservation?"

"No ... can I just poke my head inside and see if they are here?"

"Oh yes ... sure."

He went into the dining room trying to adjust his eyes to the soft candlelight. He felt awkward, not that he had never been to an expensive restaurant, it was just not his style.

Over in the corner, he saw her. It was Lois, Lois Cartier. She was older but attractive and well preserved, her auburn hair pulled back slightly. As he approached she looked up to see him. Her eyes were of blue, light, clear, heavenly blue.

"There you are!" she exclaimed.

"Hi!"

"I thought you weren't never gonna make it. You wouldn't stand me up would ya?" She teased.

"No! Not in a million years!"

As he pulled up a chair to sit down, he saw his image in the mirror behind the table. He winced as he saw his paunchy figure and his balding scalp. He had envisioned himself much handsomer in his mind's eye. Did she see him as such, he wondered?

"I'm glad you finally made it. I'm so hungry I could eat a horse!" She exclaimed.

"I see you haven't a drink. Can I order you one. I'm thirsty myself."

"Oh yes!"

A young man came to the table. He was dark and handsome. "Hi ... I am 'Franz', and I will be your waiter". He placed a large menu in front of them and then stood by patiently for a moment.

Opening the menu, Tom tried to hide his surprise. Sixteen ninety five ... eighteen ninety five, the prices were high. He reached down and felt his pants where his wallet hung snug in his pocket. There were three crisp twenties there. Sixty dollars. Only sixty dollars. He felt the perspiration on his brow.

"Would you care for a cocktail? An appetizer maybe?" Franz asked.

"Yes ... I would like a pina colada ... yes ... a pina colada! I l-o-v-e pina coladas!" Lois exclaimed, getting the attention of a few nearby tables with her enthusiasm.

Tom looked at the menu nervously. The waiter grew restless.

"Ah ... Sir ... would you care for something?" he asked.

"Yeah ... I'd like a beer. How much are your beers?"

Lois stirred slightly and the waiter broke an embarrassed smile.

"Well ... a draft is three twenty five ... and ..."

"Yes ... a draft ... a draft would be fine," said Tom quickly. A bead of sweat reached his shirt collar.

Lois wiped her forehead with her napkin and took a drink of water.

"Fine ... a pina colada and a draft," said Franz. He walked away.

Tom gazed around the room. There were numerous couples seated here and there, quite a romantic setting. "This is quite a place," he remarked.

"Yes ... it i-s-s! One of my favorites! You mean that you've never been here?"

"No ... I've seen it before. You know, whenever I'm about town, but I've never come inside. Never did. Wanted to though ..."

The drinks appeared before them. Tom grabbed the cold beer and took a long gulp, ignoring Franz who stood by, now, a little impatient.

"Would you like to order now?" he asked.

Tom took another drink of beer, while Lois looked over the menu.

"Let me see ... it all looks so good! ... I'll take the lobster tail with the fillet mignon ... Surf 'n' Turf!"

"Good ... and you?" he asked Tom.

Tom looked at the price of the Surf 'n' Turf. It was twenty five-ninety five. His mind reeled as he made quick calculations in his head. Let's see ... the beer, the pina colada ... the Surf 'n' Turf ... about thirty five dollars. That left about twenty five dollars. He felt relieved.

"Yes ... I'll take the Club Steak," he said quickly. It was the cheapest item on the menu.

"Are you sure? Is that all you want to eat?

You're gonna make me look like a pig Tom!" she said loudly. Her comment drew stares from the surrounding tables.

"Why yes ... I'm really not that hungry ... really ... I ate a big breakfast this morning ... really." He felt another bead of sweat roll down the back of his neck.

"Very well ... will there be anything else?" Franz asked, seeing that Tom's beer glass was almost empty.

"Ah ... no," said Tom.

Again, Franz nodded politely, and left them.

"Is there somethin' wrong with you Tom? It's not like you not to have another beer. Not like you at all."

"I'm just not thirsty right now."

She looked away, sighed, and then took another drink of her pina colada which was ornamented with pieces of fruit hanging over the tall glass.

"Well ... what have you been up to lately?" she asked.

"I went hunting with Jack and Sonny the other day."

"Oh God! Sonny!... that redneck son-of-a-bitch!"

"You don't like him? I thought he was going with Candy, your daughter Candy?"

"Damn right and I don't like him! What she sees in him is a beyond me."

"I didn't know ..."

"And, her name is Candice! Not Candy! ... I can't stand that name 'Candy'! And as for them being together ... no ... I don't like it! He's just white trash!!"

"Sorry ... I didn't know how you felt about him."

Tom drank the last of his beer. He was thirsty, but he knew he couldn't afford another one. Or could he? He went over the menu items in his head. Lois kept the conversation rolling.

"And as for you! Sonny? I don't know why you even hang out with him for Christ's sake!"

"I don't think he's such a bad guy."

"Look honey 'chile... there ain't nothin' sorrier than a man that ain't got no job. No money!"

Tom thought again about the three twenties in his wallet. He felt the perspiration on his forehead again, and now craved a beer more than ever. He looked up, with relief, to see Franz coming to their table with the food. But he wasn't really hungry.

"Hey ... could you bring me another beer please," he said, trying to hide his impatience. He wanted another beer more than ever.

"Yes and I'll have another drink too," added Lois.

Oh God! He hadn't counted on her getting another drink, another pina colada! That was it. He might not have enough money to pay the tab, let alone the tip! What if she wanted desert? Why didn't he bring more money? He didn't have a credit card. He looked down at his cube steak with disinterest.

"Doesn't this look delicious!" Lois said, starting to eat.

"Yeah ... boy what a spread," he said, trying to seem enthusiastic.

He took the knife and fork into his hands and started to cut the meat. His head was pounding. Thoughts were racing in his mind. What would happen when the check came? He tried not to think about it. He would worry about it later.

"What d-o-o you do with yourself all day anyway?" she asked, with her mouth full of food.

"Well ... I go see my friend Jack White. He's a very good friend of mine."

"I suppose he's a redneck too?"

"Who? Jack? Of course not. He's quite a gentleman."

"Really? Maybe I should meet him," she said playfully.

"Sorry ... he's married."

"All the good ones are taken," she teased.

Tom looked up to see Franz coming with the drinks. He looked at the glass of beer with welcomed relief. He immediately took the glass in his hand and took a big gulp. He looked to see if she noticed his preoccupation with the beer. She was too busy eating her lobster.

"Has he got money? This Jack?"

"Yeah ... I mean he's got money, but he's not 'rich-rich' if that's what you mean."

"Oh ..."

He found her attitude annoying, slightly insulting. "Money isn't the most important thing in the world."

"Oh ... yes ... I've heard it all before ... 'money's not the most important thing in the world'. If it ain't ... what in the hell is?"

"Health, happiness ... love ..."

She took a drink to wash down her food. "Look honey ... I've heard all that shit before ... love. Huh! Just like Sonny and my Candice! Do you think they could make it? Let me tell you one thing ... you can love a rich man just as easy as a poor man. Easier actually! And brother there is a big, b-i-g difference! Have you ever heard that one?"

"I'm sorry Lois but I can't quite agree with that."

"Oh you can't huh?" she said laughing. "What do you think really attracts a woman to a man?"

"Probably a lot of things ..."

"I'm not talking about some dumb poor bitch out on the street, I'm talking about a real woman, a woman who knows what it's all about. Power. That's what she looks for ... power. A powerful man. And in this day and age that means money ... pure, simple, beautiful money. You can learn to love anyone ... if he's got enough money!"

She stuffed another forkful of food into her mouth and glared at him over the soft candlelight. He placed the knife and fork down on his plate, took a drink of beer, and looked off into the distance.

"What? Not hungry?"

Tom looked back at her. He knitted his brow and took a long look at the woman. "You know I haven't a lot of money ... Why do you go out with me?"

She took another drink, settled back into her seat and smiled.

"Just to have a good time. Aren't you having a good time?"

"... Well ..."

"You're not being a good sport Tom ... not at all."

Franz appeared from nowhere. "How is everything?" he asked.

"Just fine ... just fine. Really ... they couldn't be better," said Lois cheerfully.

"Look Franz! Could I have the check please!" Tom interjected.

"The check! I'm not finished eating yet! I might want desert ... did you think of that?"

"I'm finished eating and I want the check!" Tom said firmly.

"Really!?" She scoffed. The other people in the room looked up at her loud remark.

"Look ... could you please keep your voices down," said Franz.

"Look 'Frenchie'! Just give me the check please!" Ol' Tom was riled.

Franz took the check out from behind his black tuxedo jacket and scribbled on it quickly. Then he placed it in front of Tom. Lois looked away, as he took the check and turned it over to see the amount. With taxes, it was sixty one dollars and thirty seven cents. Forget about the tip. If only he hadn't gotten that last beer!

Tom hesitated, but then leaned over close to Lois, "Look ... Lois ... can you lend me ten bucks?"

"Ten bucks!" she screamed. She was absolutely horrified. "You mean I have to put up with your insults and then turn around and lend you ten bucks?"

"Look ... I'll pay you back ... I'm just a little short."

"We accept Visa and Master Charge ... American Express," said Franz quietly.

"I ... I don't carry credit cards," said Tom, smiling at him nervously.

Lois glared at him for a moment. Then she opened her purse and took out a ten. She threw it on the table in front of him.

"Thanks ... this is quite embarrassing ... really ... this never happens to me," he said as he fumbled with his wallet.

He handed Franz the seventy dollars. Franz took the money and swiftly walked away with Lois not far behind. Tom followed her out of the restaurant and out the front door. She stormed out into the parking lot and got into her car, slamming the door as he came near.

"Look ... Lois ... I'm sorry ... I ..." He stammered.

She started the engine and sped away.

There, in the middle of the parking lot, he stood. Dazed. He looked over at the sidewalk. Three of the bikini-clad girls were standing there. They were giggling.

VI

Sonny's old pickup pulled into the parking lot of the 'Wagon Wheel Bar and Grill'. He drove slowly, looking for Candy's car. It was out in back, parked in the grass. He pulled up along side and turned off the engine. It was two in the morning and he had hit every bar in town looking for her. He was tired. He drank the last of his beer, threw the empty can into the passenger seat floor amid the other empties, and got out of the truck. He walked around the side of the building. Inside, he could hear the sound of country band jammin' and loud voices. A burly man stood beside the door.

"That'll be three dollars buddy," he said, shifting his weight as he leaned against the wall.

"Hey, it's after two."

"I said three dollars ... we're open 'til four."

"Look ... I just want to see somebody."

The big man pushed off the wall and straightened himself. "I said ... it'll be three dollars!"

The muscles tightened in Sonny's face and he clinched his fists behind him. He looked at the wall, thinking for a moment of what he wanted to do. Then, he pulled out three crumpled dollars from his jeans and handed it over. He was drunk and tired and in no shape for a fight.

"Great! You have yourself a real good time okay?"

Sonny opened the door and walked into the smoke filled room. Over in the corner, a band was blaring out a song and the dance floor in front of it was full. He scanned the bar in search of Candy and saw her at the other end, talking to a group of people. One of them was a guy. Sonny walked over and stood behind them. Amid the loud music and the cluttered scene, they didn't notice him standing there.

"Hey!" he yelled above the noise. Still, they didn't notice him. "Hey!" he shouted again.

This time one of the girls in the crowd turned around and saw him. "Oh! Well if it ain't good ol' Sonny," she said so that the others could hear. Candy didn't look around, but she knew it was her Sonny standing there. Another girl turned around.

"Hey Sonny ... how's it goin'?" she asked.

"Ok Sharon ... how's it goin' for you?"

"Aren't ya gonna say hi t' me?" asked the first girl.

"Hi Gloria ..."

Candy and her friend still didn't turn around. The guy was big and strong. Slowly, he raised his beer bottle to his lips, perhaps thinking about Sonny, thinking about what was going to happen.

"Wanna beer?" asked Sharon.

"Yeah ... that sounds good," said Sonny looking straight at the back of the guy's head.

A stranger came up to Gloria and put his arms around her. She raised the cap from his sweaty brow and gave him a kiss.

"What's wrong with you?" asked Sharon, amused.

"What in the hell do ya think is wrong with me?" Sonny replied.

The guy at the bar with Candy, slowly drank his beer as Candy lit a cigarette. They didn't turn around. It was as if they were pretending he wasn't there.

Gloria pulled away from the stranger to speak to him. "Look ... Candy don't want any shit from you!"

"You ain't got no room to talk ... what about you're husband? I bet he don't know what you're doin'!"

"That ain't none of your business!"

The stranger turned and glared at him. "Look buddy, there ain't no use in gettin' uptight ... there's plenty of pussy t'go around! My wife don't know I'm here either!" he said laughing.

All of them started laughing, all but Candy and her friend. Sonny grabbed a beer from the bar and took a long drink. The band started a new song and Gloria and the stranger swaggered onto the dance floor. Sharon turned to face Sonny, but Sonny couldn't take his eyes off of Candy and her friend.

"Sonny ... maybe you ought'a go on home," she said.

"Oh, I'm goin' home alright ... but I'm goin' home with Candy."

Candy's friend slowly placed his beer bottle on the bar. Sonny's arms were tense. He was like a time-bomb that could go off at any minute.

"You don't want to start any trouble," said Sharon.

"I'm not gonna start any trouble ... Candy and I are gettin' ready to go home, that's all ..."

Candy lit another cigarette. Her hand was shaking slightly. Her friend held his beer bottle tightly in his hand.

"Sonny ... what in the hell is wrong with you? You and Candy aren't married ya know."

"Being married don't seem to make a whole hell of a lot of difference 'round here," said Sonny, as he looked over at Gloria and her drunken friend on the dance floor.

"Sonny ..."

"No!" he shouted. "I'm tired of this shit!"

He grabbed Candy by the arm and turned her around. She looked at him fearfully.

"Sonny! What gives you the right t'come in here like a knight in shinin' armor? I don't want to go home with you! Can't you understand that?" she pleaded.

"Shit! This ain't no way for people to act. You ... Gloria and Sharon ... just like a bunch of two bit whores! Come on, we're goin' home!"

He pulled her up off of the bar stool. Her friend turned around and stood up. He was taller than Sonny.

"Look buddy! She said she ain't goin' home with you," he said gruffly.

"Fuck you! This is my girl and we're goin' home!"

Sharon backed away. Everyone in the bar knew that a fight was about to start. Candy picked up her purse and stood up. "Alright Sonny ... I'll go," she said.

"No you ain't!" said her friend, putting up his arm to block her way. "If you don't want to go ... you don't have to go."

"No ... it's okay ... I'll go."

"Wait a minute! ... you ain't goin' no where!" he insisted.

Suddenly, everything exploded. Sonny could hold back no longer. He took a swing. The punch landed on the big guy's face and forced him back onto the bar. But he regained his balance and took the beer bottle in his hand. He broke it on the bar and held the jagged weapon in his hand. Again, with lightning speed, Sonny punched him in the belly, but he swung back and caught Sonny on the arm with the broken bottle. Sonny fell backwards onto the table behind him. His arm was starting to bleed from the wound.

The bouncer, hearing the commotion, came running over but someone put their foot out to trip him and he too fell to the floor.

Sonny threw a punch and missed, as he took a punch in the face. Then another and then another. He fell backwards into yet another table, but as the big guy came at him, he countered with a blinding left and then a right, leaving his assailant crumbling to his knees amidst the blood, beer and broken glass. Suddenly, Sonny caught a punch in the side of head from somewhere. The punch took him by surprise and he too fell to the floor.

When Sonny regained consciousness, he was looking at the side of a car. He was lying outside in the parking lot. At first, he couldn't remember how he had gotten there, but as he raised himself and saw the blood on his shirt sleeve, it came to him. He could only have been there for just a few minutes.

He put his head back down onto the cool concrete and closed his eyes. His arm stung with pain, but there was a stronger pain in his heart. He wondered where Candy was. Perhaps she was with that other guy, still inside, drinking and laughing. What had happened to their love? They used to be so happy together. Maybe there was no such thing as real love, love that endured.

He winced as the pain in his arm raged. He opened his eyes and looked skyward. The stars glowed dimly in the black heavens. He reached inside for strength, for something to believe in. It seemed futile. He felt broken both physically and mentally. His dreams, as dim and as distant as the stars above. He never thought he would be like this. It was so much easier when there was nothing to care about, when love meant nothing to him. Yes, he had cheated on past loves. He had lied. It was only now that he longed for some meaning to it all. He noticed the shallowness and the aimlessness in others and felt compelled to make his own life right. Perhaps it was Candy who instilled this feeling in him. She was his love, his quest. With her, he would make the jagged pieces of his life fit smoothly together. But how could he do this without being a hypocrite? 'Sonny' - The wild one! How could anyone, especially Candy, take him seriously? Maybe he was just fooling himself.

He felt his arm and looked at his hand. The bleeding had stopped. Inside the bar, he could hear music playing, sounds of people laughing. He looked at the cars beside him. He wondered if he should get up and try to drive home. He got up on one elbow but fell back to the ground. Not yet he thought, not yet. He would wait a bit longer.

Then, he heard the sound of someone sobbing quietly, gently in the shadows. It was the sound of a woman softly weeping. He turned his head slowly. He had no idea how long the person had been there. A soft profile of a face could be seen in the shadows. He knew the face. It was Candy's face.

"Hey...," he said softly.

She didn't speak as she wiped her tears away.

"Are you ok?" he asked.

"Am I ok? How about you? How is your arm?" she asked, as she came near, out of the darkness.

"I dunno ... I guess it's ok ... I'll live ..."

She knelt down beside him and took his head into her lap. She softly stroked his forehead. "I'm sorry ...", she said quietly.

"No ... no ... darlin' ... that's ok. Maybe we gotta take some hurt. Lovin' ain't always gonna be good ... not all the time."

He reached up and softly caressed her soft cheek with his coarse, callused hand.

"What are we gonna do?" she asked.

"We'll just love each other ... that's all ... love can keep us together."

"Love ... huh ... love ..." she scoffed.

"You love me ... I know you do. I just know it."

"I don't know ... " she said, shaking her head. "I don't believe in love. It didn't work for my parents and it didn't work for yours ... or anybody else I know. Love is just a word, like in fairy tales."

"No Candy. Love is here ... and here," he said, as he placed his hand on his heart and then on hers.

She shook her head, "I mean ... just how are we gonna forget these things we do to each other ... the things I've done to you?"

Sonny reached around to hold her with his good arm as she cried. He consoled her. "... Don't cry. Someday ... why someday we'll have everythin' ... Things will be great then. I know they will ... they'll be fine."

"Will there be a real home ... We'll be happy?" she wondered, sobbing.

"Oh honey ... Why don't we get out of this damned town, this hell-hole of a place? Maybe we could go somewhere and start all over again. We could ... we could ..."

"Oh Sonny you are a dreamer."

He smiled a boyish smile.

Candy went on, "Anyway ... we don't have any money. You don't even have a job right now."

"I'll get a job, I can get a job!"

"... We'll see ..." She bent down and kissed him tenderly. It was late. Others were leaving the bar and they gazed at her and Sonny.

"Let's go home ... it's getting late," she said.

"Yeah ..."

"Can you walk?"

"I think so."

She helped him to get up on his feet, and he leaned on her as they made their way to the car. Once inside, he grimaced with pain, holding his arm, as she turned on the engine and pulled out of the parking lot. The neon lights of the bar flashed on and off in the near dawn's early light.

As she pulled out onto the road and headed for home, Sonny looked out over the quiet neighborhoods whose people would soon be up to start another day. Unlike them, Candy and he would sleep all day and into the late afternoon.

VII

I watched curiously, as the creature bobbed it's head near the water's edge. It was a manatee. It resembled a dinosaur. Perhaps it was a dinosaur, one of the last of a dying species left to live in the chaos of this modern world. Again it surfaced, but then vanished back into the murky depths. I watched to see if it would resurface, but it was gone.

I hadn't seen Ol' Tom for a few days. It was unlike him to stay away so long. I hoped that nothing had happened to him.

I laid back into my chair and let my mind wander, to relax, just to relax. If only I could. It was now only a few weeks until my birthday. Soon, Bill would arrive. There would be tension. The innuendos would linger throughout his visit. And the guilt. Like the manatee, it would vanish into the depths, only to resurface now and then to haunt me.

Could I remember the days, oh ... way back when? The long and happy days. The ones that came one after the other with no stipulation, no obligation; before fate was cast. I remembered my graduation from high school. Perhaps it was then that it all started, really started ...

... "Alexis R. Wantling!" said the loud voice over the loudspeaker. I looked up to see the girl approaching the stage to get her diploma. They were in the 'W's' and soon it would be my turn. I adjusted my cap. I should be proud. I knew there were others proud of me. But more than a celebration of achievement, it was a day of leaving one world and entering another, one step towards becoming an adult, and casting off the cloak of innocence.

The Principal read another name, but it seemed distant and monotone. I thought about Mickey. Only Mickey.

"John C. White!"

Why that was my name! I got up and walked to the stage. As I ascended, I looked out. There she was, Mickey. She and Bill, and ... Mom ... and Dad. They were smiling. The Principal handed me my diploma and shook my hand. Camera bulbs flashed. Then suddenly, that moment was over.

After the ceremonies, we threw our graduating caps high in the air. It was a moment of jubilation. Some of us would end our quest for knowledge that very day, but nevertheless, life's journey would begin. Decisions would count. I made my way through the crowd and found Bill, and then my parents. Mickey stood by, quietly.

"Well little brother! ... I guess you're not just my little brother anymore!" said Bill, mussing my hair.

"Yeah ... sure ... you'll always be my big brother and I'll always be your little brother."

Dad interjected, "We are very proud of you son."

"Thanks Dad," I said, shaking his hand. His was always a strong, firm handshake. He pulled Mom in close with his other arm. Ours was a happy family.

All the time, I couldn't take my eyes off of Mickey. She was beautiful. "Now can I get my hug?" she asked.

"Sure." As she came into my arms, I could feel her body against mine. I wanted her more than ever. It didn't matter that she was my brother's girl. We broke off the embrace.

"Well Bill," said my father, "Would you go get the car? Your mother and I can wait here."

"Sure Dad," Bill replied.

"I guess I should turn in the cap and gown," I said.

"Bill ... I'll walk with Jack. Ok?" asked Mickey. "I want to make sure those girls don't make mincemeat out of our handsome graduate!"

"Sure ... see ya in a jiffy," Bill said as he gave her a peck on the cheek.

While Bill went for the car, and my parents waited, Mickey and I left and walked through the double doors of the auditorium into that warm May night. The air was sweet and fragrant.

"I'm so proud of you! We're all proud of you!" she said, as we walked along. Bill and she were both older than I, and I felt intimidated at times. She was trying her best to play along with our innocent facade, until we turned the corner. There with the ivy covered wall, out of sight of the auditorium, of the parking lot, I took her into my arms.

"So ... I can finally kiss you!"

"Our own little celebration," she whispered.

In the sky, the stars were coming out. The smell of her hair was intoxicating. The feeling was back, that feeling that only being with her could bring. I took her face into my hands and tenderly, ever so tenderly, we kissed. Suddenly, she pulled away. "We have to be careful!"

I looked around cautiously. "Look ... the longer we drag this out, the harder it's going to be to tell him," I said.

"I know. I know."

"Well ... when?" I asked.

"I don't know ... I told you not to rush me!", she cautioned.

"I know but ..."

"No! I just can't ... not right now!"

She pulled farther away. As I pulled her closer, someone turned the corner. My heart almost stopped as I realized that it was Bill! He looked at us with surprise and curiosity. "What ... what is wrong?" he asked, a bit confused.

Mickey was quick thinking, "Oh ... I almost fell ... I caught the heel of my shoe on the sidewalk and ... well ... if it wasn't for Jack ... well ... I might of had a nasty fall."

"Well ... well thank God!" He took her into his arms and they hugged each other. He smiled at me. "Way to go Jack! You are getting to be quite a man now aren't you?" ...

... "Jack! ... Hey Jack for Christ's sake! Wake up!" I looked up. Ol' Tom was shaking me.

"Hey Bill ... I mean Tom ...", I stammered.

"Are you okay? You looked like you were in a trance."

I wiped sweat from my face, a cold sweat.

"Yeah ... yeah ... I was just daydreaming."

"You just called me 'Bill'."

"I did?"

"Yes, you just called me Bill."

"Oh ... well ... like I said I was just daydreaming that's all," I said, rubbing my face with my hands.

Tom pulled up his chair, his usual chair.

"Where in the hell have you been? I haven't seen you in days," I said.

"I had to patch things up with Lois."

"Lois?"

"Yeah ... you know Lois Cartier. I know I told you about her. Lois Cartier."

"I'm sorry ... I don't remember any Lois Cartier."

"I told you about her ... I know I told Maggie about her."

The sun was hot and I moved my chair into the shade of the palms. I could feel the breeze from the ocean and breathed easier.

"Well?" I asked.

"Well what?"

"So why did you have to patch things up with Lois ... Lois ..."

"Cartier." he said.

"Yeah ... with Lois Cartier?"

"Oh ... I had to go and lose my temper over dinner ..."

I heard the back door open. Maggie was coming out to join us. She had a pitcher of iced tea and glasses.

"Boy ... could you read my mind," said Ol' Tom, wiping the sweat from his forehead.

"Is that like 'Thank you'?" she asked, teasing.

"Yes ... my own particular way of saying 'Thank you' ... Thank you dear lady."

I got up and opened another lawn chair. Maggie joined us. We sipped the iced tea.

"Now what was this about ... losing your temper over dinner?" she asked Tom.

"Oh ... you overheard our conversation?"

"I don't usually listen to the two of you carry on, but I did catch something about losing your temper."

"Ol' Tom here is having girl troubles," I said, shrugging my shoulders.

"Oh no!" she said laughing. "I'm sorry Tom ... I don't mean to make light of your ... your lady problems."

"Tell us Tom, you playboy you ... tell us all," I said.

"Well Lois ... I told you about Lois didn't I?"

"Yes ... Lois Cartier, the rich lady from Palm Beach I believe you said."

"See?" said Tom, taunting me. "I know I told you about her."

"Okay. So I forgot ... now tell us what happened."

"Well I took her out to dinner, or I should say she met me at a restaurant. Well ... I should have taken more money."

Maggie looked at me and put her hand over her mouth, trying to hide her amusement.

"Life in the fast lane?" I remarked.

"Let him finish!" Maggie urged him on.

"Well ... she got to talking about money and guys that have money ... and ... well ... what made it even worse was that I didn't even have enough money to pay the check!"

"Oh Tom! That must have been embarrassing!" Maggie exclaimed.

"Yeah."

"I think she should have understood," I said.

"Well you don't know Lois ... she believes that men should be powerful, and money is power ... so on and so on ..."

"It sounds as though she is not the girl for you," said Maggie.

"Just how much money d-o-e-s she have anyway?" I asked.

"I don't know ... lots!"

Maggie poured the iced tea.

"... Well ... in a way I agree with her," I said after a pause. "I think in general ... in general mind you ... women look for powerful men ... and money I suppose means power."

"Oh Jack! ... and love has nothing to do with it?" asked Maggie.

"Well ... it was good enough for us obviously ..."

Ol' Tom smiled. "I hate to say it ... but maybe Jack has a point there."

"I think it makes women sound like horrible beasts!" said Maggie.

"Not like beasts ... but women do have a choice," said Tom.

"What do you mean ... choice?"

"They have a choice ... they can marry rich men."

"And men can't marry rich women?" Maggie countered.

"It's not the same."

Maggie was becoming aggravated, "I don't like this at all. You make it sound like women spend their whole lives looking for rich men to marry. That's not true. Women can have careers of their own too!"

"Yes ... they can have careers ... but they can always marry a rich man and live happily ever after."

"That sounds ridiculous!" she scoffed.

"No ... not at all. After all ... who will take care of a man? No one... he will have to make his own way in the world," said Tom.

"You a-r-e a chauvinist!" She looked away from Tom and at me. "Well? ... What do you think? You have been quiet all through this conversation."

I smiled. "Do I really have to say? Maybe I don't have an opinion."

"You have an opinion ... of course you do!"

After a pause to think about it, I went on, "I think ... I think that women don't realize the power they possess."

"Oh boy! I can see that I'm out numbered!"

"No ... I mean ... men are men and women are women."

"Really?! Could you elaborate?"

"Well ... I think that men can marry rich women too ... but ... there is a difference."

"What do you mean? ... difference?"

"Boy ... I'm sorry we got into this," said Tom, joking.

"No ... it's okay" said Maggie, "I'd just like Jack to tell us about the differences between women and men."

I twirled the ice in my glass before I continued. Thinking. "... Men have to work. That's all ... they h-a-v-e to work. They work their whole lives, sometimes not even liking what they do. But they do it because they have to do it. Sometimes they have dreams, dreams of doing big things, but as the years drag on, the dreams fade. But ... the mortgage is paid, the kids are sent through college ... somehow it all comes about. And in the end ... perhaps ... he wonders about it all. Maybe there is a feeling of pride, accomplishment. But it was hard, a hard life. If a woman goes through that ... then I can tip my hat to her."

"Well lots of women do that! Lots of women have hard lives too!" said Maggie.

I looked over at Tom's old, tired frame of a body. "Yes ... but they can always marry a rich man."

VIII

The chicken was frying in the pan on the stove. The girls sat around the dimly lit kitchen table, the kitchen table of Sonny's old trailer. Candy got up to check the stove, as Sharon and Gloria drank from their cans of beer. She looked out the window to see Sonny changing the oil in his old pickup. He was dirty, his arms covered with black oil, but he was handsome. It was times like this that she realized that perhaps there was some love between them. Perhaps there was something there after all.

"Hey Candy," said Sharon from the table. "Ya got anymore beer?"

Candy turned her attention back to her friends. "Yeah ... there should be a few more in the fridge."

Gloria reached over and opened the refrigerator door in the small kitchen and grabbed the last two cans.

"Well tell us 'Glorie' ... did ya make it with that guy from the Wagon Wheel the other night or ain't you gonna 'kiss and tell'?" Sharon teased.

"Shit! What kind of road dog do ya think I am anyway? If Phil ever found out about that ... well he'd beat the shit out of me!"

"Hell, he's been out around town a few times I've heard."

"Yeah. That's what I've heard too. Anyway ... that guy from the bar was plum better than average, let me tell ya!"

The two girls laughed. Candy looked away. Gloria noticed her disinterest. "What's the matter Candy? You can't tell me that you been true blue yourself. We have no secrets here girl!"

"... Well ... I want to be true to Sonny ... sometimes I want to be," said Candy. She thought about Sonny outside.

"Don't kid yourself darlin' ... if ol' Sonny out there could knock off a piece 'a strange, believe me he would," said Sharon.

"No ... no I'm not sure of that. He's been acting mighty good for a change, and that's really somethin' for Sonny, believe me."

"There ain't a good man in all of Palm Beach County as far as I'm concerned!"

Candy turned the pieces of chicken over in the pan. She glanced out the window again only to notice Kristen and her two kids coming out of their trailer. "It's Kristen. She's comin' over again the poor thing."

"Now there's what I'm talkin' about. Her and them two kids. It's a cryin' shame what Butch puts them through," said Gloria.

Kristen appeared at the front door. "Candy ... could I come in?" she asked.

"Sure."

As she walked in she could see the others at the table. "Hi Sharon ... 'Glorie'. I hope I'm not disturbin' ya'll."

"Not at all," said Sharon.

Candy came closer. She could see the apprehension in Kristen's eyes. "What's wrong?"

"Well ... it's Butch ... he's ... well he's been out on a drinkin' binge and ... well ... could I borrow five dollars? I promise I'll pay it back. I'm out'a food and these kids just gotta eat."

Candy looked at the two children with dirty faces peering in from the rusted screen door. "Sure Kristen ... just wait a minute." She went to her purse on the counter and pulled out a crumpled ten dollar bill. She came back and handed it to her.

"Oh ... you don't have to give me ten. I only need five."

"No. You take it and feed them poor young 'uns."

Kristen unraveled the bill and looked at it. "I promise I'll pay it back. Just as soon as Butch gets back on his feet."

"Don't worry about it. You don't have to pay me back. Don't worry." Candy put her hand on Kristen's shoulder.

"Thanks Candy ... you're an angel."

Kristen walked back to the front door, but then turned around and looked at all of them. She bit her lip with grief. Then she went out the door and walked away with her children.

"Now that there's what I'm talkin' about. That poor, poor woman," said Gloria.

"That no good son-of-a-bitch Butch! He's just got to be the sorriest man God put on this earth!" added Sharon.

The screen door opened again. This time it was Sonny.

"Well if it ain't Sonny ... the 'stud-stallion' of West Palm Beach!" teased Sharon.

"Christ! You smell like you been out rollin' in a pig pen," said Gloria.

Sonny looked at her with disgust. "Well Gloria ... it takes one t' know one."

"Sonny!" said Candy. "It's not all the time I have my friends over. You could show them some respect!"

Her remark went unnoticed as he went to the refrigerator and opened the door. "Shit! You drank up all of the beers!" He slammed the door loudly, and went to the sink and ran the tap for a glass of cold water. He drank two glasses and then turned around to face all of them.

"I'm sorry Sonny!" said Sharon. "We'll go out and buy you some more lousy beers!"

"Well that might be a good idea," he said.

"Sonny!" said Candy, with a look of disgust in her eyes.

He looked at her angrily. "Okay ... sorry ... but a cold beer sure would be nice."

Outside, a car pulled up. Sonny turned around to look out the window and see who it was. It was Candy's mother and Ol' Tom.

"Damn! Great! It's your Mama!" Sonny exclaimed.

"Oh shit!" said Gloria.

"Maybe we should head out the back door!" said Sharon, forgetting there was no back door.

"You might as well stay and join in the fun," said Candy.

There was a loud rapping at the screen door. "Coming mother," said Candy as she went to let them in.

Lois stood on the door stoop as Tom stood dutifully behind her. "Well? Ain't ya gonna invite me in?" she asked angrily.

"Yes Mama! ... Yes of course! Do come in! ... by all means come in!"

"Oh shit," Sonny said under his breath. Turning around, so that no one would hear.

Lois entered the room. She observed the ratty furniture and surroundings with displeasure. Carefully, she sat down on the edge of the couch. Tom remained standing.

"Hey Sonny," said Tom.

"Hey Tom," said Sonny.

Lois looked at the girls at the table who had remained motionless and quiet, not knowing just how to act.

"Well? Ain't ya gonna introduce me to your friends?"

"Oh yes ... Mama ... this here is Gloria and Sharon ... girls ... this is my Mama ... Lois Cartier."

"Pleased to meet ya'," both girls said meekly in tandem.

Lois's attention turned to Sonny who leaned against the kitchen sink with an air of indifference. "Ain't you gonna say hello Sonny?" she asked.

Sonny pulled himself away from the sink but remained casual. "Hi Ms. Cartier ...", he replied.

She smiled a grimaced smile. Both her and Sonny's gestures were painfully token and void of sincerity. She reached into her purse and pulled out a Kleenex and wiped her forehead. "It does get hot in these old trailers don't it?" she remarked.

"Yes Mama ... it does get hot in trailers in the summertime," said Candy in a trying manner.

It was quiet.

"I ..."

"You ..."

Both Candy and her mother spoke at the same time, caught up in the tension that filled the room.

"What?"

"No you go on," said Lois.

"I was just going to say ... we're havin' fried chicken for dinner and ... oh! I plum forgot about the chicken!"

Sharon jumped up and raised the frying pan lid. The steam billowed into the tiny corner of the room. "It's okay ... a bit done ... but it'll be okay," she said.

"Good!" exclaimed Candy. "Anyway ... would you and Tom like to stay for dinner?"

"Yes ... I think that would be alright," said Lois, quickly. She didn't ask Tom if it was alright with him.

Sharon and Gloria stood up and grabbed their purses. Well ..." said Sharon, "I guess we should be runnin' along. Ms. Cartier ... It sure was good t' meet ya."

"Same here," added Gloria.

Lois looked at them and smiled that same grimaced smile. "Yes ... I hope we can meet again sometime. When we could ... spend more time together."

As the girls quickly made their exit, Sonny came over to where Tom was standing. "Hey Tom ... let's you and me take a ride and get some beer."

"Well ...", Tom looked at Lois nervously.

"Yes Tom ... why don't you do that. I would like to spend some time alone with Candice."

The two men left. Candy went to the kitchen sink and busied herself. Lois threw her purse down on the couch.

"Damn! I thought they would never leave! I wanted to talk to you Candice!"

"I know that Mama," she said, looking up to the ceiling.

"Why do you insist on livin' in this ... this shack with that no good bastard is totally beyond me!"

Candy looked down and put her head on her chest. She didn't say anything.

"And those girls! ... they're nothin' but two-bit, uneducated whores!"

"Mama ... you're not educated and neither am I!"

"Well you can still try t' better yourself!"

"Mama please don't raise your voice."

"I'm not raisin' my voice 'chile!"

Candy walked over to the table with a dish towel and nervously wiped the clean table clean.

"Sonny's got no money! He never will! Can't you understand that?"

"Mama ... a long time ago you had no money. You were poor once. Can't you remember that?"

"That's different ... I made my money and now it can be yours ... if only you would leave that ... you know what!"

Candy pulled out a chair and sat down, putting her head in her hands. Her mother came over and put her hand tenderly on her head. "You can't tell me that you really love him?"

"I don't know ... I just don't know anymore. I want to do what I-I-I want to do ... not what you want me to do ... not what Sonny wants me to do ..."

"Look ... if you would leave him ... I could send you to college ... help you buy a house or a condo ... there's so much that I could do for you."

"Why can't you do that for us ... Sonny and me?"

"Him? Huh! That no good redneck son-of-a-bitch! That'll be the day I die!"

Candy buried her head deeper into her hands. She was on the verge of tears. "I just don't know what to do," she said.

"... I don't either ... I don't know what to do with you!"

Lois sat back down on the couch.

"Mama ..."

"Yes Candice ..."

"... I'm ... I'm pregnant ..."

"Oh my God 'chile!" Lois quickly stood up and went to her. "What are you gonna do?"

"I don't know ... I don't know!" She started crying.

Sonny's pickup pulled up out front and Candy raised the dish towel to dry her eyes. When Sonny and Tom came in, Candy was putting the plates on the table. Lois was looking out the kitchen window.

"Well ... we're back!" said Sonny.

"We got a bottle of rum from the store ... can I make you a drink?" Tom asked Lois.

Candy tended to the fried chicken and Lois was still gazing out the window, as though her mind were far, far away. Both the women were quiet and the men knew something had happened in their absence.

We were in Sonny's pickup heading down state road eighty, out into the flat expanse of the mainland, on our way to 'twenty mile bend'. We were going 'gator huntin' - hunting for alligators.

It was early in the morning, about six thirty, and the sun was just coming up on the horizon. Shades of purple, pink and orange shown majestically against the endless fields behind us. There, among the sand, mud and swamp water, laid the very heart and soul of this land known as Florida. A country side that, except for the miles of sugar cane and swamp land, seemed virtually a wasteland.

Two headlights approached in the distance. As they came near, I could see a flatbed truck loaded with a ragged group of people.

"Who are they?" I asked.

"Migrant workers ... mostly Haitians I guess ... the poor devils," Sonny replied.

"They're headed for the cane fields I would think," added Ol' Tom.

"Hey ... one of you guys pour me some more coffee," said Sonny.

I looked over to see Ol' Tom almost dozing off to sleep. So, I reached under the seat and pulled out the thermos. When I removed the lid, the smell of the hot coffee was comforting. It cut the stench of canal water that was all around us. I poured some for Sonny and then a cup for myself.

"How far is it to twenty mile bend?" I asked him.

He looked over at me for an instant. "Jus' like it says ... twenty miles."

I looked back out the window, feeling stupid for asking the question. "Isn't hunting alligators illegal?" I continued.

He looked at me again, but smiled this time. "Yeah ... it's poachin'."

"Seems like every time we go out on these trips we're doing something illegal."

"Well ya know ... 'there ain't no rest for the wicked and the righteous don't need none'!" he said laughing.

"No rest for the wicked ..." I mumbled to myself.

"Like I told ya before ... ya didn't have to come if ya didn't want to."

I looked over at Tom. He was now asleep. His head rested on his chest and rolled with the swaying of the old truck on the road.

"You go with Lois Cartier's daughter don't you?" I asked.

"Yeah ... that's right. It's a free country ain't it?"

"I didn't mean anything in asking. It's just that Ol' Tom here is going with her mother, Lois."

"No shit! I knew that."

"It seems that he and Lois haven't been gettin' along too well lately."

"Hell! There ain't nobody in the world that could get along with that bitch!"

"I take it you don't like her?"

"Not really ... she don't like me ..."

"Sorry to hear that."

He leaned and spit out the window. "Ain't no big deal. That whole family is just plain nuts. Maybe that's what money does to ya."

"You and Candy getting along? Her name is Candy isn't it?"

He wrinkled his brow. Perhaps I had gone too far. "You're kind'a nosey. Did anybody ever tell you that?" he said.

"Forget it. I was just making conversation."

"Well shit! People in these parts don't like strangers gettin' too friendly ... too familiar."

Up ahead, I could see the road turn off to the south. After countless miles of the straight highway, I knew that this must be twenty mile bend. There were picnic tables and boat ramps. A few people had already arrived with their airboats. Instead of stopping, we went on down the road.

"Aren't we going to pull over?"

"You sure are a city slicker ain't ya? We can't stop here for gator. We gotta go onto one o' the side roads."

We drove on for a few miles and then turned off onto a dirt road which continued on for miles into the thick underbrush and the vast cane fields beyond. Finally, we pulled over into a grove of trees beside a canal. Tom woke up as the truck came to a lurching halt. "Where are we?" he asked, yawning.

"In heaven boy ... redneck heaven!" Sonny replied.

He opened the door and got out, as Tom and I got out the other side on shaky legs.

"Boy we must be out in the middle of nowhere. I bet nobody could find you out here," said Tom.

"That's the idea ... I don't want the game warden breathin' down m' neck!"

Tom and I stood by watching as he went about setting up the trap. First, he pulled out a large metal hook and fastened it securely with a heavy rope to a nearby tree. Then, he reached into the back of the pickup and pulled out a sack, and emptied the contents onto the ground. It was a large piece of meat, an animal organ of some kind.

"What in the hell is that?" Tom asked.

"Calf heart," he said nonchalantly, "Bait."

He took the meat and rubbed it into the grass, carefully, turning it over several times.

"Why are you doing that?" I asked.

"A gator ain't as dumb as ya think ... he can sense the smell of men. I'm tryin' to get our scent off the meat."

"Oh ..."

"You a-r-e a city slicker ain't ya?" he said jokingly, as he then ran the hook deep into the meat and tossed it into the shallows of the canal.

"That's it?" I asked.

"That's it."

"Well ... what do we do now?"

"We get drunk and wait. We can go over to that clump of trees across the road and wait ... just wait. Tom, get them groceries out'a the truck."

We proceeded to cross the dirt road and lay down in the cool shade of the palms. Tom pulled out a loaf of white bread and a pack of bologna, and made some simple sandwiches. I was hungry and couldn't imagine that they could taste so good. A slight breeze blew over the saw-grass and after a while, time seemed to stand still there in the marsh.

We sat there for some time, and it was about noon when Ol' Tom, again, fell asleep and left Sonny and I alone. I found Sonny to be very interesting. Trying not to provoke him, I yearned for another conversation.

"I'm sorry if I got a little nosey back there in the truck this morning."

Sonny looked over, but this time seemed more at ease. Perhaps the boredom had overtaken him too.

"Well ... that's okay. I just ain't use t' talkin' about my problems."

"Yeah ... well I didn't mean to pry."

"I guess an older guy like yourself knows a whole lot about life ... women."

"No ... those are subjects you never really figure out."

He unscrewed the cap from a bottle of bourbon and took a long drink. He motioned to me to take the bottle. Although it was way too early, I accepted. As I drank, it burned going down.

"You know ... that really does take an edge off nicely," I said.

"That's one way of puttin' it."

Suddenly, there seemed to be a feeling of closeness that had been lacking. He started talking freely. Maybe it was the bourbon.

"You know ... some men spend a lot o' time jus' runnin' round. Ya know what I mean?" I was surprised at his sudden openness. I didn't reply, I just nodded. He went on. "Yeah ... but then something clicks inside 'em and they want more, like settln' down. That ever happen to you?"

"I think that happens to all men."

"But then ... then ya gotta start carin' and everything counts ..."

He looked at me in earnest. I didn't know just how to react.

"... I guess I'm not making any sense," he said shaking his head.

"No ... no I ... I think I know what you mean."

"... Have you ever been afraid to love somebody? I mean really love someone?"

"Sure ...", I thought about the past and Mickey.

"Sometimes I'm afraid of it, just how much to give ... who to give it to ... seems as though it ought'a be easy ... but it ain't. It really ain't an easy thing."

"Perhaps ... perhaps a person, man or woman, shouldn't ever give a certain part of themselves away. That special part, that private part that only they can know deep in their soul."

"Yeah ... I think I know just what ya mean ... sort'a like that part of a man that makes him a man ... his pride."

He took the bottle back and took another swig. I looked up to see the sun well overhead. We were both getting drunk from the drink.

Sonny spoke to me. "Ya know Jack ... my Daddy told me once ... go out and get yourself a woman and learn to like her, cause if you ever fall in love with her ... you'll be a goner."

"Maybe he was trying to say the same thing ... about giving away that secret part," I said.

"Maybe ... love can be a wonderful thing but it can make a man do strange things too."

"Yes ... love can change your life ..." I said thinking very deeply, touching that scar in my past, that memory that haunted me, that regret.

He handed me the bottle with his free hand but his eyes never left mine.

"Ya know ... you're alright Jack!"

"I think you're alright too."

"For a city slicker that is!" he laughed.

"Yeah ... for a city slicker."

Ol' Tom stirred slightly as a fly danced on his face.

"Maybe we should wake him up," I said.

"Quiet!" Sonny whispered loudly.

We stood up quietly, peering across the road into the canal. Something had happened. There was the sound of splashing in the water. Sonny headed across the road. "Shit! We done hooked one!" he exclaimed as he ran.

I reached over to wake up Tom. He sat up with a start. "What?" he asked in amazement.

"I think we've caught an alligator!"

Hurriedly, we crossed the road to where Sonny stood, staring down. It was an alligator, all ten feet of him! He had swallowed the bait and was now caught with the hook in it's mouth, at the end of the tightly stretched rope. It was frightening to be so close to the dangerous animal. It's sluggish movements were suddenly enhanced by a quick slashing of it's tail, a hint of the deadly power was in our midst. I was filled with terror!

"What do we do now?" asked Tom.

Sonny said nothing. His movements were quick and precise. With blinding speed, he took a hunting knife and while placing his foot on the alligator's snout, he ran it deep into the beast's head, right between the eyes! The wounded animal stirred with fury as Sonny held steadfast.

After a few fleeting seconds, it quivered and then died. I was beside myself with horror and astonishment. Sonny removed the knife and wiped off the blood on the grass where we stood. Tom and I were speechless, still in awe.

"Well ... that's how ya take a gator," he said, grinning.

"Wow, the most damned thing I ever saw," said Tom.

"Really," I said in disbelief.

"Help me get him up on the road. I'll take the good meat and the hide. We'll be eatin' gator meat boys ... yessiree!" Sonny exclaimed gleefully.

With our help, he drug the carcass up onto the side of the road. Skillfully, he made the necessary incisions and removed the skin. The large portions of meat he placed in a cooler which he had brought for such a purpose. He took the rope and tied stones to the remains. We threw it into the canal.

Then, we simply got into the truck and pulled away, down the road and back toward the main highway. The sun was hanging lower in the sky as we pulled back onto state road eighty. Though we had done literally nothing, we were tired. It was probably the booze and then the excitement.

Driving back into town, the cane fields turned to backwoods with shacks dotting the landscape, and finally, trailer parks and neighborhoods. We were entering Palm Beach County.

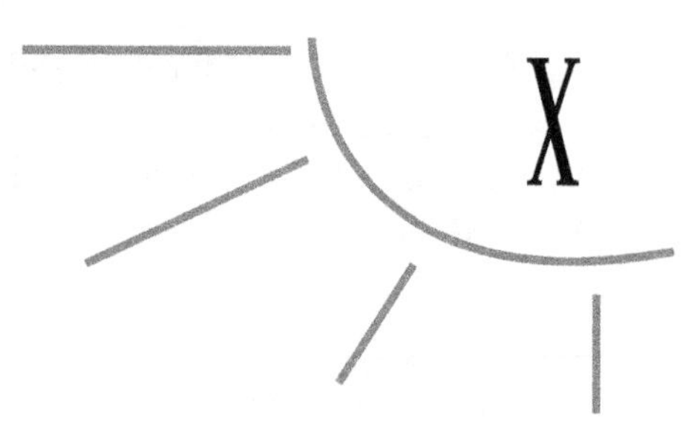

X

... I remembered the distant past ... the sound of thunder rumbling in the distance, and it made me feel especially comfortable lying there in my bed. The rains were coming. The heavens would open up and quench the thirst of the land and the trees and the hot summer sky. In the same way, Mickey satisfied a thirst, my yearning for her. I was in love. She was my first love. I longed to be with her and every moment that we were together was joyous. It was my first step into the mature world. Perhaps love is always a youth's first look into adult life. And if this was so, mine was ever so normal.

I turned and looked upon her as she laid there beside me. The storm outside made it dark inside the room, and her face was but a silhouette against the faded light. But even in the darkness, her beauty surrounded me, not the shadow that filled my eyes, but the essence of her, the intimacy that was ours.

"When I was young ... I was afraid of the thunder," she said simply, softly.

"And you hid under the bed?"

"No ... but it made me sad ..."

"And now? ..."

"Now I'm with you ... and I'm not afraid anymore."

She laughed and the sweet sound filled my heart. I consumed it. I bathed in it.

"And now you're a big girl," I said. We both laughed.

I rolled over into her arms and felt the tender warmth of her body, the beating of her heart. We were as one, there in the darkness. The sky cracked and groaned in the far off heavens. I held her ever closer.

"Mmmm ... you're good," she cooed.

"And I love you ..."

The words came easy. It all seemed so natural-being there. I kissed her tenderly. Then, suddenly, she released our embrace.

"Doesn't it bother you?"

"What?"

"Doesn't it bother you to be with your own brother's girlfriend? Like this? ... Like we are together right now?"

I rolled back, away and looked off into the dark corner of the room. The somber colors now made all of this seem dim and ugly; what we were doing was wrong. We were sneaking around, in my bedroom with the lights off, behind my brother's back.

"Is that how you feel?" I asked.

"I ... I don't know how I feel."

I closed my eyes hoping that this guilt would all go away.

She spoke again in soft, even tones. "I love you and Bill ... but I love you more ... Perhaps I never loved Bill. I don't know ..."

I turned to face her again.

"Can loving someone be so wrong?" I asked.

"I couldn't imagine that loving someone could be wrong ... It's just the way everything has worked out ..."

"How could the feelings that we share be wrong? This thing ... this thing between us ... Can this really be wrong?"

A flash of lightning lit the sky and I could see the small of her back, the soft curve of her body. She was looking the other way. "You're right ... I love you! It's you ... not Bill. That can't be so wrong!" she said, almost weeping.

She flung around and we came together in an embrace as the rain pelted the window.

"We have to tell Bill ... we just have to," she said in earnest.

"When?"

"I don't know."

"Should you tell him or should I?"

"Maybe we both should tell him." she said.

Again the thunder struck out as the two of us huddled together in that loving embrace.

"Oh yes Bill ... by the way ... your little brother and I are in love," she said whimsically.

"I know it won't be that easy."

"Oh but of course ... we'll just take a nice long drive in the car out to the country and then lay it on him."

"Mickey ... I know it won't be that easy ... but we can do it! We have to do it for you and me and Bill!"

It was quiet. We were lost in thought. This was a sad situation.

"... I can't! I just can't!" she cried.

"I'll do it!"

"No! No! Maybe I should just go away ... away from you ... away from Bill ... away from everyone!"

She got up and walked out into the middle of the room. I got up to console her. Again a sudden flash of lightning lit the room and I could see our shadows cast against the wall. Desperate, like two fugitives we were. But we were young and strong and at that moment, this love we shared was a powerful and curious thing.

"You can't go away! I won't let you!"

"Oh Jack! What are we going do?"

"I love you Mick."

"I love you too!"

There in the darkness, holding each other, I could feel her warm tears roll down my shoulder.

"I can't let you go ... not now!" I told her.

"I know ... I couldn't go anyway ... not away from you!"

We kissed as we tumbled to the bed and I could feel her body gliding gently over mine. As the rains fell outside in torrents, we made love in my bed, the bed I had had from childhood. The walls, covered with the old pendants and toys of my youth, swirled around and around and around ...

... My head was still swirling as I opened my eyes and saw the dim light of dawn approaching out my window. As I looked at the sobering world outside, I realized that it had only been a dream, another dream of youth.

Maggie was still asleep. I turned, carefully, as not to wake her, and laid there. I thought about the past, Mickey ... and Bill. I closed my eyes and tried to sleep, to get back to the dream, to the young man I had once been. But it was useless. It was but a fleeting instant in a lifetime. I was but an old man looking back over the years, the number of which were much greater than those left in front of me. If only I could have it to do over. Would I have done differently?

Outside, I could hear the sound of birds chirping. The sound had always made me feel sad. I didn't know why really. There was a black cloud looming in my mind. It nagged at me, gnawed at me.

Oh yes ... would I have done differently? Would I have let sex rule my life? But isn't that the way it was for young men, for young women too? No one could tell me. No one could know the yearning in my heart, the nights I laid awake, the undying love that harbored deep within. My parents? My friends and least of all Bill? Poor Bill. Perhaps he had felt what I felt for Mickey. How cruel was this love triangle, how tragically classic. Little brother and big brother pitted against each other with the girl suffering hellish torment in the middle, feeling something between helpless devotion and that of being a cheap whore out of a drug store novel. I closed my eyes and exhaled deeply. Oh God the guilt! The regret.

But alas! Time had passed. Lot's of time and they say that time heals all wounds. But does it? Could it? I looked down at the floor from my bed, and as I studied the nothingness there I knew only too well that time hadn't cured all. I was about to celebrate sixty years of living and I had carried this shame and guilt around like a dark cloak for more than half of those years. Perhaps like a badge, a purple heart, I wore it. It was there in my face, in my gestures, in my mind whenever it was free to wander, like it was now, simply peering down at the plain simple floor beneath me.

Bill, I know I had hurt him deeply. How I wish I could just forget it, that you could forget it, that I could just place a rug on that floor and sweep everything and all underneath. Tuck it neatly and completely away forever!

I pulled myself up and sat there for a moment trying to regain composure, to face the day, to push the demon back into the bottle until next time. I had to go on living.

I got up and walked into the bathroom and turned on the light. In the mirror was my reflection. I looked to see the lines and creases that time had eroded into my face. Then I looked into the eyes, searching for the strength that I knew was hiding somewhere within. After all, I had to believe in my own salvation.

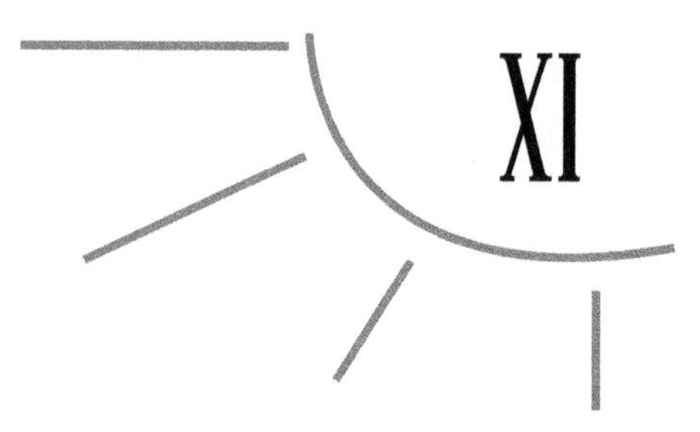

XI

We sat there well pampered. The waiter had just brought our drinks. He placed them neatly on the small square napkins which had the letters 'PBKC' printed in royal blue on their faces. The letters stood for Palm Beach Kennel Club. We were at the track and we were sitting in the club house high above the mob below.

Occasionally, we would peer down at them, those in the bleachers. Somehow I felt out of place. Down there was where I belonged, with my racing forms and paper cup of lukewarm beer.

Maggie and I sat across the table from Ol' Tom and Lois Cartier, the lady of whom I had heard so much about. Frequently, I watched her from the edge of my highball glass, studying, trying to piece together a picture of the person of whom I had, up until that evening, only imagined from various accounts. She was of average height, had light brown hair, and was attractive for her age. Her flashing blue eyes took everything in with such great enthusiasm, as a child would. From her speech, I could tell she was uneducated, but she was obviously street smart and had a taste for the good life. Although she never once looked at me, I knew she could sense my utter fascination. Suddenly, her eyes caught mine.

"Is this you're first time at the track?"

"Well ... no ... but I don't go often," I replied.

"Well I love it. It i-s-s very excitin' isn't it?" she asked, turning to Tom.

"Yeah ... sure," he said, trying to share her enthusiasm. He too was no regular at the track. Actually, it was Lois's idea to come tonight.

"Oh ... I do love the thrill of it all!" she exclaimed. "Don't you find the idea of bettin' on the races just thrillin'?" she asked Maggie.

"... Actually ... I don't bet ..." Maggie replied, as if she was apologizing. She looked at everyone and then at me with a nervous smile. I squeezed her hand under the table in reassurance.

"Well how about you Tom? I know there's some sportin' blood in you. There's just got to be!" she said, goading him.

"Oh yeah ... sure ..." he replied awkwardly.

I covered my smirk with the rim of my glass. Lois cocked her head and peered over my shoulder, as if she were trying to see something or someone behind me. I started a new conversation.

"Lois ... I know your daughter's boyfriend, Sonny. We have gone hunting several times together out in the everglades," I said, starting a new conversation. She glared at me momentarily. Obviously, I had said something wrong.

"Uh ... Jack ... Maybe we shouldn't talk about Sonny and Candy tonight," said Tom.

"Candice! Not Candy!" Lois scolded. "How many times do I have to tell you that!" She said chastising him.

"Yes ... Candice ... sorry ..."

"I hate that name Candy! And as for that Goddamned red neck Sonny!"

"Ah ... let's just drop it. Not tonight ... " said Ol' Tom.

"I'm sorry if I said something wrong," I added.

Lois stood up and looked over my shoulder, totally ignoring my apology. Something else had caught her attention. "Jack! Oh ... Jack!" she yelled.

I thought she was talking to me, but then I realized that she was motioning to someone behind me. I turned around to see who it was. He was a large gentlemen, not fat, just very tall. He had heard her loud voice and turned around and smiled. He started walking over from the far end of the room. I studied him as he came closer. He was a very impressive figure of a man with a ruddy complexion, sandy hair graying at the temples and steel grey eyes that seemed to smile at you. He stopped and stood in front of our table.

"Oh Jack ... how nice to see you!" said Lois, smiling. "Hey y'all ... I want you t' meet a very v-e-r-y good friend of mine ... everyone ... Mr. Jack Doogan!"

"The one and the same doll!" he replied.

Tom and I stood to make his acquaintance. I couldn't help but to notice his large diamond pinky ring as he offered me his hand.

"Jack ... my name is Jack White and this is my wife Maggie," I said courteously.

'Ol Tom just stood there quietly.

"Oh ... this is Tom," said Lois.

"Pleased to meet you," said Tom, shaking Mr. Doogan's hand.

There was a brief moment of confusion as to where our new found friend would sit, but Lois wasted no time. "Pull up a chair Jack ... please!"

"Ol' Tom spoke up, "Yes ... do join us," he added, being courteous.

"Oh I couldn't ... really," replied Mr. Doogan.

"Oh no ... really ... we would love to have you at our table," said Lois, speaking for all of us, presumptuously.

"Well ... sure! Fine!"

He pulled up a chair next to Lois, who pulled hers ever closer to his, leaving Tom a slight distance away. Lois all but turned her back to him to face her friend Mr. Doogan. "Now here's a sportin' man ... Jack Doogan! How much are ya good for?"

"Hey ... Jack Doogan will never say die!" he exclaimed in a good-natured way. With that, he pulled out a large stack of bills and placed them on the table in full view.

"Oh look at all that money!" said Lois excitedly. "Now here's a r-e-a-l bettin' man!"

He pulled out a cigar, lit it, and exhaled the smoke. It was all we could not to cough. His pinky ring twinkled as did his is gleeful eyes. Our guest was now the life of the party and Lois was alive with excitement.

"Over here!" said Mr. Doogan loudly, motioning to the waiter to come over to our table. "Give us fresh drinks all 'round," he instructed.

"That's not necessary," said Tom.

"Hey ... there's never an empty glass at this table now that Jack Doogan is here," he said merrily.

"Ain't he somethin'? You're always such a darlin'," said Lois, giving him a peck on the cheek.

The interaction between Lois and her friend was entertaining, but I could tell that Tom was becoming slightly jealous. I decided to start a conversation again.

"Well Mr. Doogan ... what business are you in?"

I realized what a sudden and very personal question it was to ask a stranger, but he didn't seem to mind. He put his cigar down into the ashtray and looked at me with a grin. "You might say I'm in the bill collecting business ... collecting on bad debts if you will ..."

The ambiguity of his answer left me wondering just what the nature of his business was, but I decided that it was best not to pursue it. Maggie sensed my predicament and came to the rescue.

"I wonder just w-h-e-n the first race begins? We've been sitting here an awful long time!" she interjected.

"I think they're ready now!" Lois chimed in.

Down below, we could see the magnificent greyhounds lining up for the first race.

"Who do you like?" Lois asked Mr. Doogan, putting her arm on his shoulder.

"'Midnight Ride' ... I think I might lay a wager on him ... on number four," he replied.

He looked at me, for what reason I was not sure. I felt embarrassed and obligated to make a remark, to say something. "Well ... like I said ... I don't come to the track much ..."

"Yes ... I'm sure Mr. Doogan knows all the 'good dogs'," added Tom with a whimsical tone.

Maggie put her napkin to her mouth to cover a smile, but with Lois, it went unnoticed.

"Well if you good people will excuse me ... I think I will go and make a bet," said Mr. Doogan. "Aren't you gonna let me make a bet too?" he asked Lois.

"Why sure sugar!" She put her hand on his pile of money as if she was going to take some of it.

"Oh I see! ... you want to bet some of m-y-y money," he joked.

Lois acted very coy. "Well you know what I always say? What's mine is mine and what's yours is mine!"

"Why sure sugar ... you just tell me what you want to wager and Jack Doogan will back you all the way!"

Lois laughed. They both laughed, as a black fog hung in Ol' Tom's eyes. Maggie and I remained silent, appalled by Lois' chicanery.

"Would anyone else like to get in on this race?" Lois asked.

"Ah ... no ... maybe later," I replied.

"Well ... I guess that leaves you and me!" she said to Mr. Doogan.

"That's right sugar!"

Lois and her Mr. Doogan left the table. Tom looked down at the dogs below. Somehow, I knew he was not really looking intently at anything at all.

"Do you think we should bet on 'Midnight Ride'?" Maggie asked me. I knew she knew the answer. Her question was only raised to break the silence and the obvious gloom that surrounded Tom's 'date' with Lois.

"No ... maybe later ... maybe later. I'm content to just watch the races really," I answered.

Tom looked over across the table at me. "You think I'm a fool don't you?"

"Well no ... for what? I mean ..."

"You know what I mean ... Lois and me ... that's what!"

I looked at Maggie. We both loved Tom and knew that it took courage for him to even mention it.

"Tom ... I think that Lois is a very charming lady ... a little outgoing and vivacious maybe," said Maggie.

"Outgoing ... vivacious ... she's a Goddamned gold digger ... why don't you come out and say it ... I know what you're thinking!"

I looked at Maggie again, trying to figure what to say, how to respond. "Look Tom," I said, " ... you're a full grown man ... I don't want to tell you how to run your life."

Tom took a long drink from his beer and wiped his mouth with the napkin in front of him.

"'Palm Beach Kennel Club!' ... Do you think I can afford this kind of thing? All this ... just to try to win her affection. And to make matters worse ... any guy like this ... this Doogan guy that comes along and Lois is onto him like flies on shit! It's humiliating! ... Why am I doing this to myself?"

"I suppose Lois i-s-s a very attractive lady ... I suppose that is what attracts you to her ..." Maggie replied.

Tom threw his napkin on the table. "I am being a fool ..." he said in resignation.

"Hey Tom ... don't be so hard on yourself. I'm sure in time you will figure out what's best for yourself."

Over my shoulder, I could hear Lois' voice as she and Mr. Doogan came back to the table. Again, Ol' Tom gazed out onto the track, trying to seem composed and unaffected.

"Well ... how's everyone on drinks?" asked Lois as she sat down.

"Just fine ... fine for now," said Maggie.

I nodded in agreement.

"You sure?" asked Mr. Doogan. "How 'bout you Tom?"

Tom looked over at him coolly. "No ... none for me ... I'm fine," he said. His beer was almost empty.

Suddenly, the race was on. The entire clubhouse came alive as the dogs rounded the near turn. They were gorgeous animals, long, sleek ... agile. Their motion was sheer beauty. As they came into the final turn, everyone rose to their feet with drinks and programs in hand to see the finish. The excitement swelled to an intoxicating high, and then, it subsided quickly and everyone sat down. Number four, 'Midnight Ride', came in next to last.

"Oh well ... so it goes," said Lois.

"No guts ... no glory. It was only two hundred dollars," said Mr. Doogan. "Now ... how about more drinks!"

And so it went.

Lois and her friend Mr. Doogan getting drunker and more chummy with each successive race. All the while, Tom sat there, stewing with contempt. Maggie and I looked on, wondering when it would all be over. Finally, the last race ended. I looked at the others over the empty glasses, bottles and cigarette trash that littered the table. It was time to go home. At least that's what I thought.

"Ah ... well ... that was fun," said Maggie, yawning. I knew she was just being polite. I knew she was as tired as I was.

"Hey wait a minute honey," said Lois. "The night is still young!"

"Yeah ... it's barely past midnight," added Mr. Doogan.

I looked at Ol' Tom who looked more weary than the rest of us.

"I really think we should call it a night," I said in earnest.

"Oh ... you are a bore bag aren't you!" teased Lois. "I've got an idea ... let's go to the Breakers!"

I looked at poor Tom. "It really is getting late," he said, knowing that it was futile to resist. He knew Lois was wound up and still ready to party.

"Oh ... come on y'all!" Lois pleaded. She swayed slightly. She was already a little drunk.

"Lois ... it is late," said Tom.

"Well Tom, if you don't want to go, I'm sure Mr. Doogan would be more than anxious to take me!"

Tom looked at her with a perplexed look. "... Sure ... sure Lois ... let's go," he said begrudgingly. He looked away. I knew he couldn't look any of us in the eye.

"Well as for us ..." As I spoke, I could feel a quick nudge from Maggie. I knew she wanted us to go. Tom was our friend and someone had to go along to keep him company. Things would probably get rougher as the night wore on. "... Yeah ... what the hell! Let's go!" I said with all the effort that my tired mind could muster.

We left the clubhouse rather disjointedly, that is, Lois and Mr. Doogan, Tom following slightly behind them, and Maggie and myself walking out last. I couldn't help but feel sorry for Tom, but after all, in a way he was bringing this all upon himself. It was obvious that Lois didn't really care for him. I wondered how long he would endure the agony of their relationship. Lois rode with her Mr. Doogan and Tom came with us.

As we rode along, there was a sadness among us. "Are you sure you want to go?" asked Maggie, turning around to face Tom.

"... I don't know ..." he said wearily.

"I mean ... we could call from a pay phone and tell them that we decided not to come."

Tom put his head down into his hands, but then righted himself. "Hell no! I'm not going to let that bitch get the better of me!" he said drunkenly.

I looked out at the road ahead thinking of how ugly this whole scenario was. I could feel Maggie's eyes upon me.

"Can we afford this? The 'Breakers' of all places?"

"I have the VISA card," I said glumly.

She looked out the window as we drove along in the darkness. I knew she too could sense the impending doom that probably was ahead. It was ridiculous to go. In the back seat I could hear Tom quietly snoring. He had passed out.

"Maybe we shouldn't go," she said.

"We are his friends ... if he wants to go let's go ... I mean ... we said we'd go. It was your idea to go in the first place."

I looked out over the road ahead of us. We were in the older part of town, old West Palm Beach. I couldn't help but notice the old buildings that stood on either side of the street. Old store fronts, tattered, some even boarded up. We neared the bridge and I could see the faint lights of Palm Beach across the inland waterway. That bridge was the dividing line between West Palm Beach and Palm Beach, between the rich and the poor. Waiting for us on the other side was another world, that of wealth and opulence without equal, that of grace and of inheritance.

We crossed the bridge and on the other side, were greeted by royal palms which lined both sides of the street. Expensive cars, shops and boutiques were abundant. This was indeed a world apart from that on the mainland.

As we pulled into the rather long driveway that led to the Breakers, it was really a magnificent sight, one of the few five star hotels on the east coast. I cringed as I thought of how ridiculous it was for Tom to meet Lois here, of all places. Pitted against the likes of Mr. Doogan, he would surely be an impotent foe.

I parked the car. Maggie shook Tom to wake him from his drunken sleep. "Tom ... Tom ... we are here," she said.

He stirred, then sat up. He was a mess.

"Hey Tom ... maybe we should forget this. Maybe another time," I said.

"Oh hell! Let's go!" he stammered drunkenly.

I looked at Maggie again and shook my head in resignation.

"All right Tom ... let's go, but let's not stay too long okay? It's really getting to be quite late."

Maggie and I got out of the car. I opened the door for Tom and he stumbled. In fact, even as we entered the front door of the grand lobby, he seemed not too steady on his feet. Walking through a great hallway that led to the restaurant, he nearly knocked over a large vase and if Maggie hadn't caught it, it would have been in pieces on the floor. I was relieved when we finally made it to the Alcazar Lounge entrance. The maitre d'hotel greeted us.

"A table for three?" he asked, seemingly unaware of Tom's condition.

"We are here to meet some friends ... a Ms. Cartier and a Mr. Doogan," I said.

"Ah yes ... " he said scanning the room. "Would you please follow me."

We followed him into the dinning room. There was a band playing a rather lifeless rendition of some forgotten song. I found it slightly annoying. Maybe it was because I was tired and there was a pain in my back. When we got to the table I could see that Lois and Mr. Doogan already had drinks.

"Well ... you finally made it I see?" said Lois cheerfully.

"Let me buy the drinks," Mr. Doogan added.

"Like I said before ... Mr. Degan ... that won't be necessary," said Tom, his speech slurred.

"That's Mr. Doogan," said Mr. Doogan.

"Oh ... I'm sorry ... Mr. D-o-o-gan," Tom replied with slurred speech.

The table was quiet after Tom's remark until our drinks arrived, quiet until Lois started her mindless chatter again. "Well ... I didn't know it was so late. They ain't serving food anymore."

"I'm not really hungry," said Maggie.

"Oh honey 'chile I'm so damned hungry!" she replied.

The band struck up an upbeat version of 'Mack the Knife' and we all turned our heads to face the bandstand.

"Oh!... I want to dance! Come on Jack ... dance with me!" Lois said to Mr. Doogan excitedly, pulling on his arm.

Tom grabbed Lois. "Lois ... you're my date! I think you should dance with me!"

"Get your hands off me you drunkin' fool!" she screamed at him. "You can't hardly walk!"

Her loud voice drew stares. Maggie and I looked down at the floor.

"Look Tom ol' buddy ... don't start anything. Okay sport?" said Mr. Doogan.

"No you look Mr. high and mighty! She came to the track with me and she's my date!"

Tom reached over to pull Lois' chair closer to his, but she reached back and slapped him in the face, the force of which, knocked him clear to the floor. I jumped up and went over to help him back to his feet as the waiter arrived. "Please ... you will have to control yourself or I will have to ask you to leave," he said to us.

"Yes sir ... sorry," Tom replied, straightening his clothes and trying to regain composure.

I picked up the chair and helped him sit back down.

"Come on Jack ... let's dance," Lois said to Mr. Doogan, pulling him up off his seat. As they made their way to the dance floor, Tom glared at them.

"Tom ... Don't you think you should go home and forget this whole thing? I mean really." I said.

"I think Jack's right," added Maggie.

"Hell no! Lois is m-y-y date and she's coming home with me!"

Tom turned his head and watched them as they danced, mumbling under his breath. I was dismayed. When the waiter came, he ordered another round for all of us, two just for himself. He was getting very drunk and I knew he soon would be totally out of control.

The band stopped playing and Lois and Mr. Doogan came back to the table. I braced myself for the worst.

"Oh that was fun!" said Lois. "Now you are going to behave yourself ... aren't you?" she asked Tom. It was a humiliating remark.

"Bitch!" Tom scowled.

Lois ignored his remark and turned her attention back to Mr. Doogan.

"Mr. Doogan and I are thinkin' of goin' into a business together ... ain't we?"

"Why yes ..." said Mr. Doogan.

"What type of venture ... if I may ask?" I inquired.

"Land development o' course ... is there any other?" said Lois. She hiccupped. "Why, Florida is growin' by leaps an' bounds ... you don't think we should just sit back an' let someone else make all that money do ya?"

"Yeah ... yeah," mumbled Tom.

"There's a piece of land out near the Corbet area I've had my eye on," said Mr. Doogan.

I thought about our hunting escapade there several weeks before. "Isn't that state owned?" I asked.

"Yeah sure ... but there are ways around these things," he said. "It's a trivial matter really."

"It sounds like quite an undertaking," said Maggie.

Lois hiccupped.

"It would require draining the swamp ... getting certain zoning privileges ... that sort of thing," said Mr. Doogan.

"I thought that the Corbet area was used as a game preserve ... for wildlife," I said.

"Who the hell cares!" said Lois. "If it means makin' money than I say the hell with it!" She hiccupped again.

"Fuck you!" mumbled Tom from his stupor.

He laid his head back onto his chest as if he were going to go to sleep. Everyone tried their best to ignore him.

"It is getting late ... maybe we should be leaving," said Maggie looking at me with earnest.

I looked over at Ol' Tom who stirred slightly. "Yes ... we should be going," I said. I reached around for my wallet.

"No ... I will take care of it," said Mr. Doogan.

He pulled out some bills and threw them onto the center of the table. suddenly,

Tom awoke and teetered on his chair. "No! I said I'm gonna pay for the check!" He picked up the money and threw it back at Mr. Doogan.

"You drunken fool! You can't afford to pay that tab!" teased Lois. She picked up one of the bills and threw it at him. She laughed. Mr. Doogan took the other bill and threw it up into the air as if it were a mere table napkin. He too laughed heartily.

Tom blew up. "You scum! I bet you're gonna take her home and fuck her aren't you? ... you son-of-a-bitch!"

"Watch your mouth you little asshole!" Mr. Doogan replied.

Tom stood up but then fell back to his seat, too drunk to stand on his own two feet.

"Oh ... leave him alone ... the poor fool has had too much to drink," said Lois. "You a-r-e a poor sport," she said to him.

Tom just glared at her.

"Look ... we had better be going," I interjected.

"Yes ... I think you should," said Mr. Doogan.

He motioned to the waiter for the check. I was very tired and my back was killing me. My head was starting to throb. I looked at Tom. How pitiful he was. Maggie looked at me and took my hand into hers. I peered out the window near our table and could see the dim lights among the palms, the surf rolling on the beach. It was a shame to have this drama among us. The night turned out to be a nightmare.

XII

The water sprinkler went pitter-pat against the window of Tom's trailer. Though the sound was ever so quiet, it resounded in Tom's poor aching head. He was hung-over. He lifted himself gently to listen to another sound, not the water drops, something else. No he thought, it was the sprinkler. He heard it again. Someone was knocking on the front door. He got up to the answer it. Every footstep brought pain, every move he made. The door opened. It was Sonny. He was holding a brown paper bag.

"Sonny!" he said surprised. "How in the hell did you find this place?"

Sonny shifted his big frame from one foot to the other. "Hey ... I just drove 'round 'til I saw your car."

"Well ... good. Come on in ... come on in ... I was just resting," said Tom, as he shuffled across the floor and slid back into his reclining chair. Sonny stood in the middle of the room.

"What's in the bag?"

"Oh ... I brought some beer. Want one?"

"Oh yes!"

"A little hair of the dog huh?"

"Boy you know it," Ol' Tom said with glee.

Sonny sat down on the corner of the couch and leaned over to pull the beer from the bag. He handed one to Tom and then pulled the tab on another. They drank.

"Shit that's good!" said Tom.

"Yeah ... ain't nothin' like a cold 'un."

"Yeah ..."

The sprinkler splattered water on the window.

"Sure tastes good ..." Tom felt somehow relieved.

"Yeah ..."

"Well ... what brings you here? I mean ... I'm glad you came over. I'm just ... surprised."

Yeah ... well ... I got problems." Sonny looked down. He didn't want eye contact.

"Well son ... what can I do for you?"

Sonny continued to look down. Tom was curious but didn't want to be pushy. The two of them just sat there for a minute, Tom waiting for Sonny to say what he had to say.

"Well ..." Sonny paused ...

"Hey Sonny ... if it's too personal ... but if you want some advice I'll try to help."

Sonny kicked the bag of beer gently with his foot and looked off to the side. "Look Tom ... I ain't one to go an' tell people my problems, but I need ya to help me."

"It's Candy right? You and Candy?"

"Yeah ... ya see ... she's pregnant ... she's pregnant with my kid."

It was quiet for a few moments. Finally, Tom inquired, "Well ... what can I do?"

"You and Lois ... you guys are gettin' along pretty good these days ain't ya?" Obviously Sonny was unaware of the circumstances.

"Oh Yeah. We're gettin' along fine ... okay ..." Tom told him, lying.

"Well maybe you could talk to her for me. Me and Candy want t' get married."

"I don't know Sonny ... you know how Lois is."

"Yeah ... but she's your woman. You can talk some sense into her. Can't ya?"

A bead of sweat rolled down Tom's cheek. "I'd like to help ... but ..."

"There ain't no 'buts' about it ... Candy and I love each other. We belong together."

"I can see that. But with Lois it's a different story. She doesn't see it that way."

"Ain't there anything you can say to her? I want it to be with Candy, jus' like it is with you an' Lois."

Tom's eyes became glossed over as he looked off into the corner of the room.

"You're older ... you would know what to say ... how to handle it," Sonny continued.

But Tom said nothing. He just kept looking at the opposite wall, as if he could see through it.

Sonny went on ... "That's how it is when a man loves a woman. He would do anything for her ... anything ... ya know what I mean? Do ya know what I mean Tom?"

"Yeah ... I know what you mean," he replied, his voice breaking slightly. He broke off his stare and turned toward Sonny. There was a tear welling up in his eyes. "Yes ... what a man would do for a woman? I could tell you what a man would do for a woman ..." His voice quivered as if he were going to cry.

"Shit Tom! I'm sorry if I said somethin' to get ya riled."

"Oh how I could tell you what love can do to a man!" He wiped the tears away as he started to cry.

"Shit! I know you an' Lois ain't always got along but ..."

"Got along! Shit! She doesn't love me Sonny! She doesn't love me!" Tom now started to cry with tears rolling down his cheeks.

"Gee Tom! Get a hold of yourself man!"

Tom fell off his chair in front of him. He was on his knees!

"Do you really think Lois loves me?" he screamed.

"Oh shit!" Sonny was now taken back.

Tom grabbed onto the cuff of Sonny's pant leg. He was choking on his tears. "She doesn't love me Sonny! Is that what you think? That she loves me? She doesn't love me Sonny! And I'm gonna help y-o-u?"

"Shit! ... Tom! ..." Sonny was in shock.

Tom was groveling on the floor, weeping pitifully.

"Goddamn it man! Get away from me you panty-waisted motherfucker!" Sonny kicked Tom off of his pant leg and stood up to get away from him.

"Sonny, you came to me for help! I'm-m the one who needs help with Lois!"

As Tom laid there crying, Sonny walked in circles totally at a loss for words.

"I love her Sonny ... Oh I love her. Oh God! She treats me like shit! I just want her love! I just want her love!" He put his hands together and looked up at the ceiling as if he were praying, praying to God Almighty to help him!

"'Geez' Tom! Ain't you gotta lick o' pride?"

"P-r-i-d-e?!? I love her Sonny!"

"Get a hold yourself Tom!"

"Oh God ... make her love m-e-e! I can't stop it! You wanna see what love can do to a man? Look at me Sonny! Look at me! ... Poor Ol' Tom!"

Sonny slapped him in the face, trying to bring him to his senses. He fell off to one side and his mouth started to bleed.

Still, he went on. "Hit me Sonny! Hit me again! Knock some sense into me! Make me stop loving her! Make me stop!" Tom fell to the floor in a pitiful heap, as Sonny circled the room nervously.

He was at a loss for words. "Shit! ... Oh God! ... I ... a man ... a man ain't suppose 'ta act like that... a man ... a man's got to do ... like ... Candy and me ... I mean ... I don't know ... Goddamn it Tom! Stop it ... Stop it Goddamn it!"

Sonny walked over to the doorway and leaned against the wall. Tom, still laying on the floor with the bag of beer, gently sobbed. He knew Tom would be of no use to anyone, let alone himself.

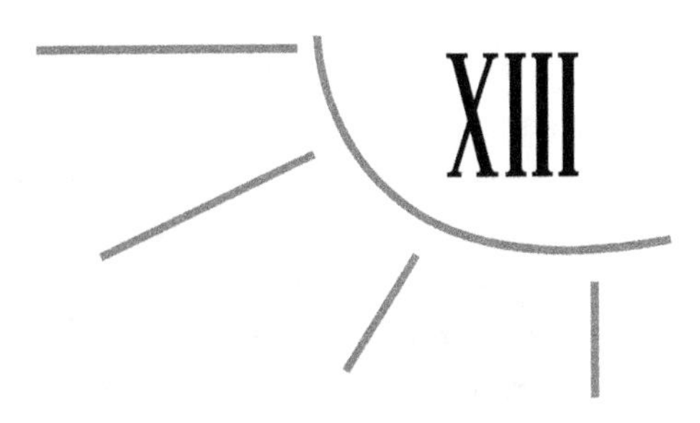

XIII

... It was a different day in a different time, long ago. They say that one can mark time in one's life by events. A song on the radio, a picture in the attic, a face of an old friend. They are reminders. Like book markers, they hold a place in the pages of our memories. Mine was a fall day. A simple fall day. A day that would change my life and fill me with regret.

It was fall sky in a fall field of ripe pumpkins and dried corn left from the harvest. And the tall grasses waved in the wind like an ocean all around us, Mickey and I. It was the fall of the year but the spring of our lives. We laid in the tall grass, Mickey and I.

"Can you see the geese?" I asked her. We were both looking up to the heavens.

"Where?"

"Up there ..." I said pointing skyward.

"Yes ... yes ... I can see them ..."

Up among the clouds they were, seemingly forever ascending.

"I wonder where they are going?" she asked.

"South I guess. Don't geese fly south?"

She rolled over on one elbow. Her eyes were opened wide, and in them I could see the world.

She said, "Don't you wish ... I mean ... just for a moment ... don't you wish we could fly like those geese? Just fly away ... higher and higher ... just you and I ..."

"You sound like a dreamer ... what a beautiful dreamer you are ..."

"Yes ... but just think. Then we wouldn't have problems. Not like we have."

"Problems like you and me and Bill?"

"Yes ... oh yes ..." she said softly.

I looked back at the sky. The geese were almost gone from view. "I don't know ... geese have problems too you know."

She put her arms around me and I kissed her. It was a warm kiss given and taken freely. Then we fell away from our embrace.

"What kind of problems do geese have?" she asked me playfully.

"I suppose they have no problems. They can only fly south for the winter and I can only go on loving you ..."

"Oh silly! No ... tell me in ten words or less ... what it's like to be a goose?" she asked, teasing me.

"Well ... they have to find food ... and a place to live ... and ..."

She put her hand over my mouth, " ... and I love you ..." she teased.

How those words lingered in my ears! " ... I love you too ..."

The sun beat down on our bodies as I pulled her near. The blanket twisted beneath us. The wine bottle fell over and spilled into that good earth.

We made love. Gently, we shared our passion. And then laid quietly in the aftermath. In the tall grass.

Suddenly, in the corner of my eye, a shadow appeared. It loomed over our naked bodies. It was Bill!

I pulled away as Mickey grabbed the blanket to hide her shame. I flinched. Surely he would beat me I thought! Surely he was enraged! My mind reeled! But, to my surprise, he didn't raise his hand, nor his voice. He simply stood there. Gently, ever so gently, he cried.

"Oh my God! I ... I'm sorry Bill," Mickey said. She looked at me. I was speechless. "Bill ..." she said, trying to find words.

Bill shook violently. Then he took a few jagged steps and turned away. Mickey took my arm. "Jack! Say something! Anything!"

"I ... Bill ..." I said, my mind lost for the moment.

Bill walked away as we fumbled with our clothes. We had to catch him. We had to stop him. We had to talk. We ran and saw him standing there alone in the tall grass. He was like a wounded animal, and my heart was sick and saddened.

"Bill ... don't go away ... I want to talk to you!" Mickey yelled as she ran. She was choking on her tears.

She reached him first. Perhaps I wanted her to reach him first. Coming upon them, I could see her put her hand on his shoulder. He shrugged it off.

"Please Billy! Please listen to me! ... We didn't want to hurt you!" she pleaded.

"Get away from me!" he screamed.

He turned to look at me. "And you! My own brother!"

"I'm sorry Bill ... What can I say? We never meant to hurt you."

"Well just how in the hell am I am supposed to feel? My own brother and my own girl? Oh shit!" He started to cry again. "Just get away from me! I never want to see the two of you again! Really ... I mean it!"

"Bill ... listen to me," said Mickey. "We were going to tell you ... really we were!"

"Sure you were ... all this time you were going around behind my back!"

"Bill ... we ... we love each other," I said.

"Oh fuck you!" he screamed. "It is all sex! I know that!" He flung out at me with his fist but missed. "I don't want to hear it! Oh please spare me ... please!"

The wind blew through the grasses and carried his words everywhere. I would never forget those words.

"And to think I was going to find you guys ... I was going to find you to tell you that I had been admitted to college ... I wanted to celebrate with you! With you cheating liars!"

His words reverberated in my ears. I was ashamed. Oh god! The shame of it all!

Mickey, trying to placate him,"Well ... congratulations! ... that's good Bill. I think you should go to college."

"Well the hell with school! The hell with you and the hell with everything!"

He fell to his knees like a broken, tragic figure, and Mickey fell down with him to hold him, to console him. I went to put my hand on his shoulder. He slapped it away bitterly. "Just go away! Just go away you bastard!"

"Maybe you should just go away!" Mickey said to me.

"I was just trying to help."

"Can't you see what we've done to him? You've done enough already!" she said.

"I-I-I've done enough?" I protested.

"You ... me ... I don't know ... just go away and leave us alone!" she said.

"But what about you and me? I thought it was m-e-e that you loved?"

"I don't know who I love! Can't you see? This is just impossible. Can't you see that?"

I stood there horrified. "Well ... fine. You just stay with Bill then ... fine!" I said.

With the two of them huddled there on the ground, she with her arms around him, I walked out farther into the field, away from them, to lick my own wounds. I looked skyward through teary eyes. Where were the geese? Where were they? Had our love flown away with them? Did she still love him? Did she love me? Maybe she would stay with him and not me. What a cruel turn of events! Over the tall grass I could see the tops of their heads as they walked away. leaving me there alone. Did I loose Bill's love forever? Would I ever see her again? I wondered ...

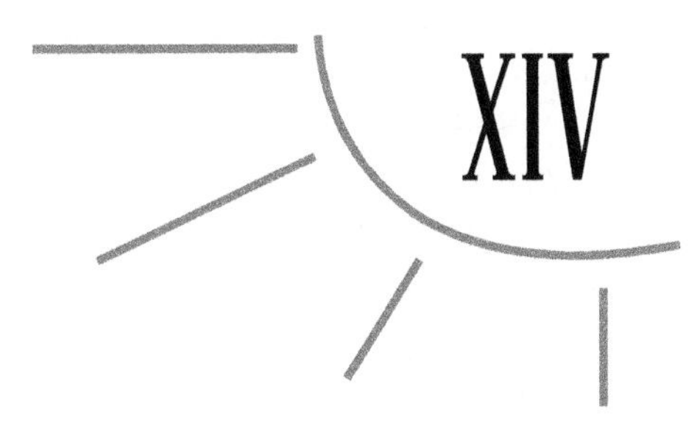

XIV

Ol' Tom was talking but it was hard for me to concentrate. I was looking out over the water watching the fish jump. It was not our usual afternoon chat though, Sonny was there as well. Tom continued. "The way I see it ... you're the best one to do it."

"I agree," Sonny added.

I put my paper cup of warm beer down and wiped my tired face with my hands. "Let me get this straight ... you want me to go to Lois and plead your case?"

"That's right Jack ... somehow I think you're the only one that she would listen to," said Sonny.

I looked up at the hot sun, and then back at the two them. "You love her Sonny?"

"Oh God Jack! She's carryin' my baby for Christ's sake!"

"... I don't know. I mean ... it's really none of my business. What could I say that would convince her otherwise? For some reason, she doesn't like you. It seems clear to me that she is dead against you and Candy."

"Yeah ... but you ... maybe you could make her understand ..."

Another fish jumped. I looked over only to see the concentric circles dancing in the water. Tom poured another scotch.

"How about you Tom? Can't you try to help?" I asked, realizing just how ridiculous a suggestion it was. Sonny jumped in.

"Shit! Tom? He's 'bout as pussy-whipped as they come!"

Tom said nothing. He just sipped the scotch.

"Anyway Jack ... you got a way with words and you know women," Sonny continued.

I thought about Mickey ... the past ... "Christ! Nobody knows women," I mumbled.

"Ain't that true!" said Tom, laughing. Sonny glared at him. He stopped laughing.

"I don't know ... I guess I could try," I said wearily. "But you could try yourself. At least try."

"I told ya Jack. She don't like me ... you know that ... You told me that yourself," Sonny insisted.

I tried to reason with him, "All you have to do is go to her ... not like that ... in bare feet and a beer in your hand. Get a good job. Get dressed up, tell her how you really feel. Tell her that you really love Candy. I'm sure if she could see that you were really in earnest, she might understand."

"Jack ... she don't care 'bout love ... can't you see that? Some people are like that ... they just don't care 'bout love."

I paused to think. Lois was not like any woman I had ever known. "Perhaps you're right," I said.

"Shit Tom! ... she don't care 'bout you," said Sonny.

"Damn it Sonny! Leave me and Lois out of this!"

"Well it's true! ... Everyone knows it's true. 'Cept maybe you!"

Tom looked down and kicked the dirt with his foot.

"Leave Ol' Tom alone. He isn't the first man to get smitten with a woman," I said in his defense.

"Anyway," said Tom, "I know you and Candy haven't had it so good all the time either!"

"At least I wasn't rollin' around on the floor like you ... like a wounded dog!" Sonny exclaimed.

"Goddamn it Sonny! A man's got to have his pride!" said Tom.

"Tell me 'bout pride you goddamned pussy!"

"Sonny! Lighten up!" I said.

They were talking about something of which I had no knowledge. I tried to protect him from Sonny's vicious remarks, but Sonny continued anyway.

"Jack! You should 'a seen him rollin' 'round cryin'... prayin' to God Almighty to make Lois love him!"

Tom had had enough. "Alright you stupid redneck!" He jumped to his feet, but he had had too many drinks and he was unsteady. That with his advanced age made the gesture seem ludicrous. "Come here! Hit me Sonny! Just try to hit me!"

"Oh shit! Not that again. I don't want to hurt you old man. Just sit down!"

"When I was in the Navy ... when I was in Korea ..."

I got up and put my hands on Tom's shoulders to hold him back. "Tom ... Tom ... please ... sit down!" I said.

"I ... I ... why I ... I ..."Tom stuttered. He was lost in time. He was big. In another day long past, he was tough. But now, he just old man stuttering.

"Sit down ... just sit down!" I commanded.

He looked at me strangely. He was bewildered.

"No one's blaming you," I said, "A man's got a right to cry sometimes. Not all the time, but sometimes. He's got to. He's just got to."

"Jack. You never cried. Not you," said Sonny.

"Sure I've cried. I've cried. I've cried hard."

Sonny looked puzzled.

"You've never cried? Never?" I asked him.

"Sure when I was a young'un."

"How could you love and not cry? At least on the inside?" I said.

He picked up a stone and threw it across the water. It skipped several times and then plopped into the deep. "Well yeah ... I've cried on the inside. Sure ... on the inside I have ..."

"Okay ... it is nothing to be ashamed about," I said.

"That's what I mean ... you got a way with words Jack. There ain't no way in hell I would ever admit to any man that I cried ... ever, but you made me." Sonny looked at me and smiled. Another fish jumped, but we didn't turn to look. "So you'll do it?" he asked..

I looked at him. "Okay ... I'll do it. For you ... I'll try."

I knew it would be awkward, going to see Lois, but in a way I wanted to. Perhaps I could do some good, something good for Sonny and Candy. Maybe even help 'Ol Tom. After all ... I knew what love could do and what it couldn't. I knew the strength of love, the depth of love.

But who was I to be so presumptuous? None of this was any of my business. This I knew. But I had loved and knew the cost of love, I had made that journey before. This I could understand. I could be of some help to someone else, lost in that tangled web.

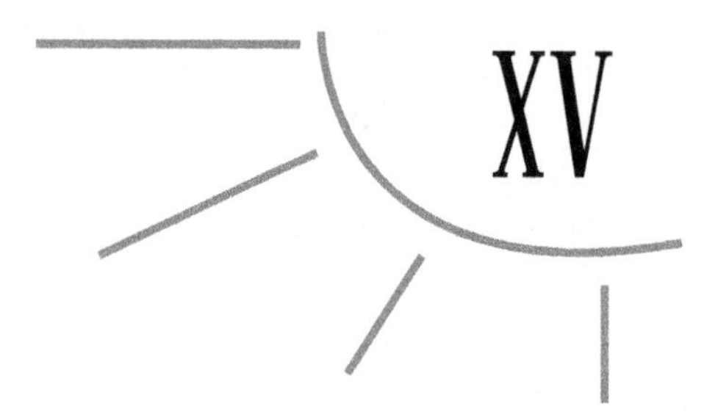

XV

La-de-dah-dah-dah ....

La-de-dah-dah-dah went the low tones of the saxophone. The man with the horn was playing a song. The sounds danced in my head and mixed easily with the drink I held in my hand as I sat in the lounge of the Palm Beach Hotel. I was waiting for Lois and she was late. I looked at my watch again.

"Waiting for someone?"

I looked up. A pretty face was looking into mine, a young face, carefree, the face of the girl behind the bar.

"Yes I am."

"Late?"

"Yes ... you are right again ... they're late."

She was wiping the bar off with a wet towel. The bar wasn't dirty and I was the only one sitting there. She stopped and looked up to smile at me again.

"You aren't very busy, are you?" I asked.

"No!" she said, laughing, "it's still the off season ... it's the pits!"

She turned around to tidy the bottles behind the bar. I couldn't help but notice her shapely figure in her little tuxedo uniform. I could imagine myself as the dirty old man, making small talk with the pretty young thing. She knew I was watching her. She didn't seem to mind. I was just another one of the countless leg watchers in as many countless nights.

"I bet you get a lot of people in here, waiting for someone or something."

She turned around and placed the folded towel on the bar between us.

"All the time. Would you care for another drink?"

It was business as usual. I looked down at the ice in my near empty glass, but then noticed Lois entering the lounge. "No ... that won't be necessary. My friend has arrived."

I could see her in the mirror. I turned around on my barstool as Lois approached. She looked especially lovely. The nightclubs were her habitat and she was dressed for a kill.

"Well hello Jack!" she exclaimed. "Have ya been here long?"

"... Well ... not really."

"I'm sorry if I kept you waitin'. I tried to hurry ... really I did."

"Should we have a seat?"

"Why sure!"

I looked around for a waiter.

"Should we just pick a seat?" I asked, unsure of what to do.

"Oh sure ... let's just sit any ol' where."

We picked the table closest the bar. It was quiet between us, until a waiter took our order and brought us drinks.

... Dah-dah-la-de-dah ... played the man with the horn.

"You're not eating?" I asked.

"No ... I'm not really hungry tonight."

"Me neither ..."

She took a long drink but kept her eyes, those childlike blue eyes, on mine. "So. Why tonight?" she asked.

"I asked you here because I wanted to talk to you."

"Well ... you could a' talked to me on the phone."

"I wanted to talk to you in person."

The band went on break and it became very quiet as we were essentially the only customers there.

"So talk." She was anxious.

"I'm not sure just where to start..."

"You just start any ol' place you like ... we got all night," she said as she leaned back. She crossed her legs and pulled her skirt up past her knee. She was attractive.

My mind was calculating, not knowing how or where to start. "... Have you ever been in love?"

"Oh God, have I ever!" she exclaimed.

"I'm serious. Have you ever r-e-a-l-l-y been in love?"

"Listen honey, I've been in love many times ... perhaps too many times!"

I wanted to start in about Sonny, but I knew I should work up to it. She would never listen to me if I came right out with it.

"Then you know how it feels ... to be in love I mean?"

"Oh yes. It's a wonderful feelin'."

"When two people are in love nothing else really matters, just the love, that's all there is ... Can you remember being young and in love?"

"My ... you a-r-e a romantic aren't you?" she teased. "Hey ... you aren't here to talk about me and Tom are ya?"

"Well no ... I didn't come to talk about Tom."

She swung her chair around and I could see her swing her shoe playfully from her bare foot. I realized just how dangerously sexy she could be.

"Oh good! I didn't really want to talk about Tom. He really is a great guy ... but I didn't want to talk about him tonight, not tonight. I don't love him."

The waiter came and we ordered more drinks.

"So ... go on," she said. She was getting curious, "You were talkin' about love and feelin' good."

"Yes ... well ... I wasn't sure that I should come here tonight."

"Oh no. I'm glad you did. I just had to get out tonight. I just had to!"

La-de-dah ... dah-dah ... The band had started up again, and the man with the horn was making love with his music. The song, Lois, the drink, I found it all slightly intoxicating.

"I want you to try to remember what it was like when you were in love, the way it made you feel."

"I can assure you ... I can remember very well."

"Well then maybe you can understand what I am about to tell you."

Dah-Dah-la-de-dah ...

Suddenly, I could feel her bare foot rubbing my leg under the table. To my horror, I realized what was going on. She was flirting with me! "Has anyone ever tol' you just how sexy you are for an older man?"

"I'm afraid I ..."

"Don't be nervous honey. I knew ya wanted me the first time I laid eyes on ya," she cooed.

Her dress slid down to her lap and exposed more of her shapely thighs.

"What about Tom?" I asked.

"Honey 'chile ... he don't mean a thing to me ... not a Goddamned thing!"

"He i-s-s my best friend you know ..."

Lois chuckled, "... it'll be our secret. Just you and me."

I moved back to fend off her advances. I knew my plan had backfired.

"Look ... Lois. I came here to talk about Sonny ... Sonny and Candy," I finally came out with it.

There was a look of horror in her face. Her whole demeanor changed. "Oh God! Sonny! That redneck asshole!"

"Well ... yes. I know Sonny and Candy love each other. I know about the baby. I really think that they should be together."

She reached over and took my hand in hers. It was if everything I said was meaningless.

"Honey ... let's not worry about them. Tonight it can be just you and me darlin'." Her voice was sexy and venomous.

"I'm serious. I asked you here tonight to get you to accept Sonny and to let them get married."

She released my hand and fell back in her chair with a look of disbelief. "You mean that's all you asked me up here for ... to plead a case for Sonny?"

"Yes. I believe in Sonny and Candy."

She pulled her dress down and righted herself in her seat.

I continued, "I really think Sonny is a good guy deep down inside."

"You do do ya?"

"Yes ... he's really trying to make something out of his life. I know he has a bad past, but I know he loves Candy and he wants to do right by her. I think I can safely say that."

"He's just out for a piece o' ass like all the other no good rednecks! No! Not with my Candice! Never!"

I paused but tried to stay on track.

"Can't you try to understand how they feel? They love each other."

"Love? You no good son-of-a-bitch! You come in here talkin' 'bout love and feelin' good, ... oh you're good you are!"

"Lois ... I ..."

"No you listen t' me! I don't need Tom and I sure don't need Sonny, and furthermore ... I don't need you either!"

"If you would only try to understand ... I wouldn't come here tonight unless I thought Sonny was good for her."

"Oh I understand alright. I understand about love ... it's just a word and feelin' good's just a' rollin' in the sheets ... that's all ... just a' rollin' in the sheets and some bastard's lyin' words in the dark. I know only too well!"

"Lois I'm sorry, perhaps it was a bad idea to come tonight."

"You bet your sweet ass it was! ... I can have any man I want! I can get any man I want!"

She threw her arm out knocking everything down. The drinks spilled from the edge of the table. Even the band stopped playing as she made a scene and stormed out of the room. I sat there stunned, as the girl behind the bar came rushing over.

"Is everything okay?" she asked me.

"Yes ..."

"What about her?"

"She's running away ..." I said deep in thought, watching her exit.

"Running away from what?"

"... away from herself I would imagine ... perhaps she is running away from herself ..."

The girl looked at me curiously.

XVI

Maggie was busy in the kitchen as I sat out in the living room. Today's newspaper was on my lap. I had picked it up several times but it remained unread.

"Well birthday boy! ... how does it feel to be sixty years young?" asked Maggie as she came into the room.

"You know, now that it's here, I don't really feel any different. I thought it would be much more traumatic."

She came up behind my chair and put her arms around my neck. "I think it's different."

"Oh and how is that?"

"I believe I love you even more."

I turned my head and gave her a kiss. "I love you too," I said, meaning every word of it.

The clock on the wall sounded one chime. It was one o'clock. We both knew that dinner would be ready soon. It was to be an early dinner. But that chime had an ominous ring. It reminded us that our dinner guest would be arriving soon.

Maggie went back into the kitchen as I laid my head back. There was just too short a time left to relax. I could feel a slight aching in my head. I closed my eyes in an attempt to relieve the tension. Maybe it would be different this time, I thought. It had been well over ten years since Bill and I had last seen each other. We never wrote and seldom called except on holidays, and then it was short and sweet, trite, and courteous. But there was always that impregnable wall between us.

Then, the door bell rang.

Maggie came and stood by the kitchen door. Pensively, we looked at each other. We knew who it was. No words were needed. I got up as Maggie quickly straightened her hair in the mirror that hung in the dining room. Together, we readied ourselves. I looked at her once more and smiled wearily. I opened the door.

Bill stood there quietly, motionless. He looked tired, his hair grayed slightly. He didn't smile. He just stood there. With sullen and heavy lidded eyes, he looked at Maggie.

"Hello Mickey ..."

In the awkward silence, his words, like a knife, tore at the tender flesh of our souls.

"... No one calls me 'Mickey' anymore, not in years," said Maggie softly.

Silence.

"... We're glad you came," I said.

"Yes. It has been a long time."

"Well, come in ... please," said Maggie.

She went to embrace him and he took her into his arms hesitantly. As he entered the living room, I took his suitcase and placed it by the door. Like a stranger, he stood in the middle of the room.

"Ah ... dinner will be ready soon. I'm sure you two have lots to talk about. Lots ..." said Maggie. She went back into the kitchen.

"Have a seat Bill. Please ... sit here. This is my favorite chair."

We sat down.

"How was your plane ride?"

"Oh ... a little bumpy but okay."

"I bet you're tired."

"Not really."

He looked out the back door at the water's edge.

"You know this is quite a place you have here ... nice boat."

"We like it."

"You've done alright for yourself. You've always done alright Jack ... haven't you?"

"We've all done alright I suppose."

Silence.

"Can I get you a drink?"

"Sure ...."

I got up and went to the liquor cabinet. In the kitchen, I could hear Maggie singing to herself in low tones. She could always handle tension better than I. Perhaps she was the strength between us.

I filled two glasses with ice, poured the scotch and then the water. It was just what I needed. This drink would help I thought. Maybe then we could talk. I handed one to Bill and then sat down. I sipped the scotch.

"So Bill ... how's business?"

"Okay I suppose. I've thought about selling though. It hasn't been the same since Dad died ... not really."

"Dear Dad. I think of him a lot." I said.

"Yes. I suppose we do think about Dad ... the past ..." Bill responded.

The past! Oh God! I didn't want to talk about the past. Not the past. Let's talk about anything, but not the past!

He looked around the house again. "This really i-s-s nice. Dad always did say that someday you would do well."

"Hey ... you've done well too. I'd say you've done quite well yourself," I said trying to show my caring for him.

"Yes ... but not like this ... not like this ..."

We could hear Maggie singing in the kitchen.

"Yeah Jack. You've got a lot to show for sixty years of living. College, this house, ... Mickey."

"Bill, her name is Maggie, Margaret. We haven't used that name 'Mickey' for years. Not since we were very young."

"I will always remember her as Mickey. Good Ol' Mickey," Bill said solemnly. I could see that nothing had changed. His mind was consumed with a preoccupation of the past.

Silence.

"I never married ..." he said.

"I know ..."

"Never did find the right one ... never did ..."

His remark was like a dagger in my heart. We looked down at our drinks. They had a bitter taste.

"Look Bill ..."

"No ... don't say it. For God's sake ... don't say it! I know what you're going to say and I don't need to hear it. Okay?"

Bill had raised his voice slightly and Maggie came into the room. Bill looked at her sadly.

"Bill ..." she started to say.

"No Mickey," he said.

"P-l-e-a-s-e stop calling me Mickey! ... Mickey! Mickey! Mickey!" she said, shaking her head with grief.

But Bill continued, "I've heard that name in my dreams ... in my thoughts for so long!" He was on the verge of tears. "To me you will always be Mickey ... you will always be Mickey to me," he went on.

In a rage, she picked up the folded newspaper, tore it in half and threw the pieces at our feet. She trembled as she spoke. "Can't you see? 'Mickey' died along time ago! A long, long time ago! Can't you get that through your head?"

"I loved you! You know I loved you! I've never stopped loving you!" Bill exclaimed.

Suddenly, we were transported back in time, in that field again. You could almost feel the autumn winds blowing through the tall grass and the sting of tears in our eyes.

"Bill ... that was a long time ago. An awful long time ago," I said.

"Oh it's so easy for you to say! Oh how easy it is for you!"

"We were just kids Bill. Just kids and we loved each other. We never wanted to hurt you!"

"But what about me?" He pleaded.

There were tears in Maggie's eyes. "There's no other way to say it Bill! I know it hurts but I loved Jack! I love him now and I will always love him! Can't you ever forgive us? Can't you ever find it in your heart to forgive? We've lived with this ... this guilt and shame and ... regret, all our lives. Please Bill! Oh Please I beg of you! We can't go on like this!" She fell to her knees at his feet, crying and shaking her head.

Bill sipped his drink and carefully placed the glass back on the table. There was nothing but the sound of her pitiful weeping. My heart was sick. I picked her up off the floor and she wiped her tears away.

"Forgive and forget ... it's the only way ... the only way we can live the rest of our lives ..." she said quietly.

"Maybe ... I don't know," he said, reluctantly.

"I can't believe you've been here less than a half an hour and we're fighting ..." she said sadly.

"Let's stop. Okay?" I asked.

Silence.

Disheveled and broken, Maggie walked slowly back to the kitchen. There would be no singing. Not now.

I looked at Bill grimly. "Bill ... this isn't right. You know that."

"What you two did to me wasn't right."

"We loved each other. What can I say? What can we do? If there was only something we could do or say ..."

"Say you're sorry. Just say your sorry again. Oh how I can hear those words! I have tried, but it doesn't work for me ..."

I looked at the torn paper scattered on the floor. They were like the shattered pieces of our lives.

"I love you Bill," I said softly.

Silence. He said nothing.

I looked at him in earnest. "You're never going to forgive me are you?"

With his eyes glued to mine, I saw his lips move and I heard his words. "No. I don't believe I ever will."

I looked back down at the torn papers.

Suddenly, outside, I heard the sound of a car enter the driveway. I wondered who it could be. I got up to see. It was Sonny in his old pickup truck.

"Bill, excuse me for a minute. I've got unexpected company."

I walked outside and greeted Sonny. I couldn't help but notice that his truck was loaded with all his things. "Happy birthday Jack," he said.

He shook my hand. "Hey ... are you okay? You look pale," he said.

I realized that I was still shaken by the drama we had had inside. "Oh ... it's nothing. Nothing really. Won't you come in. We're about to have a dinner celebration for this old warrior. I suspect Ol' Tom will be by."

"No. I'd like to but I ... well ... I just came to say goodbye."

I looked again at the truck.

"Goodbye? Where are you going?"

"I'm leavin' Jack ... I'm leavin'."

"Why? I mean it's all so sudden."

He looked skyward and then back at me. I could see the tiredness in his eyes. "You might say I'm going to go find myself. It ain't gonna work out with Candy and me. I know that now. I'm gonna have to start over and ... and forget I guess. This town just ain't a good place for me anymore. I guess in a way you could say I'm runnin' away."

I looked at him not knowing what to say.

"It ain't so bad to run away and try t' forget is it Jack?"

Looking back at the house, I said solemnly, "No Sonny. Sometimes there's nothing left to do but go away and try to forget."

"Where are you headed?"

"I hear there's a heap a work in Alaska. I thought I'd try m' luck."

"Alaska ..."

"I guess I owe you a lot," he said.

"Sonny ... you don't owe me a thing. You really don't."

Sonny looked through the opened door into the house where Bill was sitting inside.

"That's your brother Bill ain't it?"

"Yeah. That's him ..."

"... Well have a good time ..."

"I don't know ... Perhaps we all need an Alaska to go to," I said, realizing Sonny had no idea what I was talking about.

"Well ... goodbye Jack."

"... Goodbye Sonny ..."

"You know Jack. For an old man ... you're okay. You'll always be my horse even if you don't win." He laughed.

He got into the truck and I watched as he rolled out of the driveway. In that old battered pickup, he was rolling out of my life. Oh how I wished we could all just drive away. Forget.

XVII

Time had passed. It was near Christmas. Christmas in Florida was a strange time. I kept looking out the window to see snow. Even now, after many years the child in me wanted to see snow.

I could hear Maggie singing in the kitchen. She was singing again. She was singing a Christmas Carol. I couldn't for the life of me recall the name of the tune. I guess I w-a-s getting old. I laughed to myself.

I decided to go outside, out by the dock. I went out the back door and took my place there by the water's edge. I looked up at the sun beating down on my head. How hot it was, relentless, even in December. I had to get up once more and move the chair farther back, back into the shade of the palms.

Ol' Tom would be here soon I thought. Good Ol' Tom. He would bring his bag of beer or scotch and he would ask me if I wanted some. I would of course decline. Then he would goad me and, of course, I would give in. We would probably get a little drunk and waste the entire afternoon talking about nothing and everything, just two old men rambling on.

I thought about Candy. She was about to have Sonny's baby. I suppose she would have it and raise it alone. I wondered if she was still going to the bars. I could only hope that the baby would be alright.

I hadn't heard anything about Lois. Tom wasn't seeing her anymore and he rarely mentioned her in conversation. Maybe she was with that Doogan fellow. Oh well.

Lazily, I looked down at the stack of Christmas Cards that were on the small table beside me. One of them was Bill's. 'Hope you have a nice Holiday Season' it read. I wished him well. I sincerely did. Losing his love would be one of the great regrets of my life.

Near the top of the stack was a snapshot. I picked it up again, for I had looked at it many times and it's edges were getting torn and frayed. It was a picture of Sonny's truck. Behind it was a large sign that read 'Welcome to Alaska!'. I turned it over and read the words he had written-'Dear Jack, Just a line to let you know that I made it ok. Wish you were here. Ha. Ha!'. I could hear him talking in his nasal twang. I smiled.

The sun had drifted higher in the sky and the sunlight was hot on my face. I turned the picture over and studied the scenery. Alaska. In the picture, further in the distance, I could see the pines on the snow covered mountains. I knew the air was cool there, clean, and easy to breathe. Sonny made it alright. Perhaps he was the only one who had a chance. It was a new start for him. Maybe, just maybe he would find happiness.

I was thinking ... in a way, life could be like Hell, each of us trapped in a barren land of scorched and dry clay baking in the sun. Perhaps Hell wasn't below us. Maybe it was here, right here on earth, and we lived in private Hells that we made for ourselves. All our lives we would search for that oasis, that salvation locked away, hiding, hopelessly beyond reach, striving to do better in the face of adversity, and learning to accept the unacceptable.

Yes, perhaps Sonny had really done it, perhaps he had found the way out, a beginning, a path to end of the suffering - that cool, cool shade.

I heard footsteps behind me.

CPSIA information can be obtained
at www.ICGtesting.com
Printed in the USA
LVHW111353111118
596718LV00005B/33/P